Megan Morrison

Grounded

The Adventures of Rapunzel

Arthur A. Levine Books

An Imprint of Scholastic Inc.

Text and map copyright © 2015 by Megan Morrison
Map by Kristin Brown
The world of Tyme is co-created by Megan Morrison and Ruth Virkus.

ISBN: 978-0-545-89007-6

10 9 8 7 6 5 4 3 2 1   15 16 17 18 19
Printed in the U.S.A.   40
First printing 2015

For Ruth, who lives here too,
and for Cheryl, who kept the door open

CHAPTER ONE

ONCE UPON A TIME, *at the top of a shining tower,
high above the howling beasts and swallowing darkness of the
Redlands, there lived a perfect girl. Her hair was the most glorious in all of Tyme, for it was one hundred feet long, and it shone
like a river of gold.*

Her name, of course, was Rapunzel.

RAPUNZEL tossed the book out of the bathtub. It
thudded to the carpet, and her head lolled back onto the
marble bathtub rim. She stared up at her ceiling garden, where hundreds of fat, fragrant roses pushed against one another in a ring
around the skylight, blooming from the soil between the stones.

"Fall down," she said.

A breeze licked through the tower and shook the loose petals
from their flowers. Soft slips of bright color showered into Rapunzel's
bath, and she sank with a sigh into the glittering bubbles. She was
done with her book for tonight. The story always frightened her after
sunset, even though it was all about her.

But then, all books were about her. For one thing, she was beautiful, which made the stories interesting. It also helped to be beloved,
which Rapunzel was; Witch loved her so much that she gave her

whatever she asked for. Finally — and most importantly — Rapunzel was innocent. She wasn't sure what innocent meant, but she knew that she *was*, and Witch said it made her perfect.

Rapunzel wrung out the few feet of wet braid that had fallen into the bathtub and threw it out over the side. Her hair had been given its own bath yesterday and was already shining clean. It ran in a golden cord as thick as her wrist across the wide, round tower room and ended at the window, where most of it always remained, a hundred feet of braided rope wound tightly on a wheel. Whenever Witch arrived and wanted to climb up, Rapunzel turned the wooden crank and lowered her braid to the ground, nearly a hundred feet below. Witch was the only creature who had ever climbed Rapunzel's braid, and Rapunzel had no intention of ever allowing a stranger to touch it.

Especially not a prince. In one storybook after another, the relentless princes clamored for Rapunzel. They stood below and shouted up dreadful lies — about how beautiful the ground was or how fantastic their royal palaces were. They swore that Witch was evil, and they begged Rapunzel to abandon her home, but their attempts were usually in vain. In most of her books, she stayed safely atop her tower.

But sometimes she was foolish. Sometimes, her storybook self became curious enough to lower her braid and let a prince climb up or, worse, to follow a prince out of the tower and down to the ground. Those were the scariest stories. In Rapunzel's favorite book, a particularly persuasive prince lured her into a bleak wasteland that crawled with repulsive, ground-dwelling people. *Peasants*, the book called them, and they were nasty things. But in every book, no matter how terrible the danger, Rapunzel had only to call out for Witch, who rescued her and swept her straight back home.

Rapunzel sat up in her bath and gazed around the darkening tower, content. She would never be like the Rapunzel in those stories. What would be the point of leaving? She had books to read, a sea of hair to brush and braid, a balcony on which to run, and pretty gowns, jewels, and toys to entertain her. If she ever felt restless, she could play jacks for hours on end, or have Witch come up to adore and feed and play with her. Stories were all well and good in books, but she was much too clever to end up in one herself.

There was a distant thumping sound. Footsteps. Witch must be down on the ground, getting ready to climb up. Perhaps she had come to stroke Rapunzel's hair as she fell asleep. She often did that, and it was very nice. Or perhaps — Rapunzel felt a surge of real interest — Witch had brought something delicious, like a chocolate pie, or a box of sugar roses, or a bowl of biscuit pudding so thick that a spoon could stand up in it. After all, tomorrow was Rapunzel's birthday.

A loud, metallic clang made her heart jump. She looked at the glass balcony door, which stood closed. Of course it did; no one could get to the balcony except from inside the tower. The balcony circled almost all the way around, stopping on either side of the arched window where Witch always climbed through. Rapunzel looked at this window, which stood opposite the balcony door. Nothing was there.

"Witch?" she called.

There was no answer.

Quickly, Rapunzel got out of the bath. She pulled on her fluffiest robe and ran to the window. She squinted down at the ground in the falling twilight, but she did not see Witch.

Still, she had heard something. She was certain of it.

"Light!" she called.

The blue flames in her massive fireplace roared to life, casting watery shadows along the stone walls. Rapunzel shivered. It all felt very mysterious — especially the shadow shifting beyond the translucent curtains over the balcony door. The shadow was shaped like a person, and Rapunzel watched it move, amazed by its precision. It even had a gray hand, with long, distorted fingers that were reaching for the doorknob.

The silver doorknob twisted.

Rapunzel went still. It was impossible. A trick of the light.

The door opened a crack.

"Rapunzel?"

The voice was low. It did not belong to Witch. Icy fear shocked her bones and snatched the breath from her lungs.

"You in there?"

The door opened wider. With speed she didn't know she had, Rapunzel scrambled behind an armchair by the fireplace and huddled there, motionless. She couldn't hide her braid, but there was nothing to be done about it. She peeked through the narrow opening between the back of the chair and its seat.

A figure slipped into the tower.

Rapunzel bit her lips shut to keep from gasping. No one but Witch had ever come to this tower. No one. She was with a stranger.

She was with — Rapunzel realized, her terror mounting — a *prince.*

The prince stood still in the doorway, scanning the room with bright, black, slanting eyes that looked almost lidless. Black hair hung straight as a sheet to the line of his jaw. He looked tense, as though prepared to run, and his eyes moved quickly around the fire-lit room.

Rapunzel was overcome by an intoxicating mixture of fear and excitement. A prince had come — a *real* one. Witch had always warned her that it would happen, but none of the stories had prepared her for how it would feel. She glanced accusingly at her damp and abandoned book.

The prince narrowed calculating eyes, first at the lifelike constellations that glimmered from the indigo canopy above Rapunzel's bed and then up at her ceiling garden, where the roses rustled in the breeze that blew through the open balcony door. He peered at the mantel next, and, when Rapunzel realized what he was looking at, she remembered that there was nothing to fear. There stood her silver bell, reflected in the glass that hung above the fireplace. One ring of the bell would summon Witch.

The prince's gaze fell on a small table that sat next to the chair behind which Rapunzel hid. On the table sat a goblet, which he eyed with suspicion. Fingers twitching at his sides, he walked toward it until he stood inches from Rapunzel's hiding spot. He reached toward the gleaming goblet.

Rapunzel shot up from behind the armchair.

"Don't touch my things!" she yelped.

The prince screamed and jumped, flailing. His hand struck Rapunzel's nose, and she shouted in pain and covered it with her hands. When he finally caught his balance, he stood with his fists clenched and up in front of him.

They stared at each other for a moment, and Rapunzel was shocked to realize that the prince was short. He only came up to her nose, and he was in his boots. All the princes in her books were tall and strong and broad and dashing. She wondered what was wrong with this one.

The prince let out a heavy breath and dropped his fists to his sides. His posture relaxed, even as his expression grew sour. "Why'd you jump out at me like that?" he asked.

Rapunzel gazed at him, speechless, still holding her stinging nose.

"Well?" said the prince. "You trying to scare me to death or what?"

Rapunzel had no idea what he was talking about. In her books, princes fell to their knees, blinded by her radiance. They called her "sweetheart" and "darling" and "my love," and they refused to leave the tower without her, claiming that they would rather die than be separated from her. Didn't he know how he was supposed to behave? Why wasn't he doing his part?

Rapunzel looked down at herself. She was still in her bathrobe — perhaps that was the problem. In her books, she was always beautifully dressed whenever princes came to visit. She went past the prince toward her great wardrobe, which she flung open. Was a glittery red dress appropriate for rejecting a prince? Or the shiny blue satin with the pretty white sash? Or maybe the green one with all the gossamer layers. Yes, that one was nice. Rapunzel pulled the frock from its wooden hanger and considered the effect of the vibrant green gown against her pale skin.

"What are you doing?" asked the prince.

"I'm getting ready," she said. "Wait."

"Wait for what?"

"For the next part," said Rapunzel. "Where you tell me how much you love me."

"I don't —"

"I said *wait*," she said. "You're not a very good prince, you know. You don't even have a crown, or a cloak."

"Are you serious? I told you yesterday —"

"And your clothes are dirty," Rapunzel pointed out, noticing his shabby outfit for the first time. "That vest looks like it hasn't been washed for a month."

"I've been traveling."

"Yes, you've traveled far and wide to reach me," said Rapunzel, nodding. "Now, don't say anything else yet. Let me put on a gown, and then we'll do the rest of it."

"The rest of what?"

Rapunzel laid the green gown out on her bed and started to untie the knot of her bathrobe.

"What are you doing?" cried the prince. "Tie that back up!"

Rapunzel turned to frown at him. "But I have to take my robe off," she said. "I can't put my gown on over it."

"But you can't . . . I mean . . . I'm standing *right here*." The prince pushed his straight black hair out of his eyes. It fell back down again at once, but it could not entirely obscure his look of panic.

Rapunzel watched him, nonplussed. "Have you gone mad?" she suggested. She had never seen anyone do that.

"No!"

"Are you dying?" She had never seen anyone do that either.

"Just get dressed," begged the prince, and he covered his eyes with his hands. "I want to get out of here, but I need to get what I came for."

"What, me?" Rapunzel laughed at him. "You'll never get *me*. I've read all about the filthy, horrible ground and the nasty things that princes do."

"Are you dressed yet?" he shouted.

"Yes!" cried Rapunzel, tying up her robe. "There! I don't know why it matters so much!"

The prince uncovered his eyes and blinked. "Because it's what people *do*," he said.

Rapunzel bristled at his tone. "*What* people?" she retorted. "Short people with dirty clothes who climb into other people's towers without asking?"

The prince fixed Rapunzel with eyes so black and cold that she was unable to think of further insults. "I'm not *short*," he hissed. "You're *enormous*. And you're one to talk about looks when you've got a hundred feet of useless hair."

Rapunzel opened her mouth so wide that the corners of it ached, but no sound came out. She didn't care that he'd called her enormous — he was so short that he probably thought everyone was enormous.

He would *pay* for insulting her hair.

"My hair," said Rapunzel, rage roughening her voice, "is not useless, Prince."

"Stop calling me a —"

"It's *glorious*, for your information, idiot."

The prince clenched his jaw. "I'm not an —"

"Witch *needs* my hair so that she can climb up here. How else would she visit?"

"Let's see," said the prince. "Maybe you could throw down a rope ladder? Or get yourself some stairs? Or, if the witch is that into climbing, she could use a rope and grappling hook."

Rapunzel didn't know what he meant, but she wasn't about to admit it. "Who do you think you are, telling me what to do? I can ring my bell right now and tell Witch to throw you off this tower — and she'll do it."

The prince snorted. "Do it yourself," he said. "You're big enough."

"Anyone would be bigger than you, *peasant*." She spat the last word at him.

But the prince only grinned — a sharp, white grin that split his face. "You're learning," he said. "I am a peasant."

"It's an insult, peasant."

"Not if you know the right peasants." The prince crossed his arms. "You probably don't even know what a peasant *is*."

Rapunzel wanted nothing more than to shut him up. Since she didn't know how, she snatched up the book she had thrown earlier and marched over to find its place on the shelves that were built into the long, curving wall beside her bed.

"Why haven't you asked about the fairy?" said the prince, coming up behind her. "Or don't you care what happened to her after I took her away?"

"What should I care about a fairy?" she asked, tucking the book away. She saw fairies flutter by every so often, ruby red and tiny, but whenever they came within a few feet of the balcony railing, they were whisked away by the wind. Witch said they were useless.

"What should you *care*?" said the prince, and he grabbed her by the shoulders when she turned. "You practically killed one," he said. "She would've died if I hadn't shown up and carried her out of here. What do you have to say about that?"

"I don't know what you're talking about," said Rapunzel, trying to pull away. "I've never touched a fairy."

"Don't pretend you don't remember. It was yesterday."

Rapunzel grabbed his wrists, but his grip on her shoulders only tightened. "Get *off*, you mad peasant," she said. "Stop touching me!"

"Stop playing innocent."

"I *am* innocent!" She gave him a sharp push that finally sent him flying. The prince yelped, reached out for support, and smacked his head against the stone windowsill. "Ha!" she cried.

The prince stared up at her, rubbing his head. "What did you do to the fairy?"

"Nothing!" said Rapunzel. "You're remembering the wrong place and the wrong person, but since nothing else about you is very prince-ish, I would hardly expect —"

"I'm not the one who doesn't remember," snapped the prince. "And my name is Jack — and I *don't have time*." He pushed himself to his feet. "You *have* to tell me what you did, and you have to tell me *now*, understand? Did you feed her something? I need a piece of whatever it is so I can bring it to the fairies and they can make a cure."

Rapunzel was beginning to think she had been right in the first place. He was mad. "You're tiresome," she told him. "It's time for you to leave."

"But if I leave without the cure, then the fairies won't . . ." The prince exhaled. "Look. I don't want to be here, all right? But I don't have a choice. So *help* me, would you? What happened yesterday with the fairy?"

"Stop talking about yesterday and acting like we've already met!" Rapunzel clenched her fists so hard that her fingernails dug into her palms. "You're my very first prince, so behave the way you're sup-posed to!"

His black eyes flashed. "For the last time, my name is *Jack*. I come from the Violet Peaks." He tilted his head. "Do you really not remem-ber yesterday?"

Tears of frustration welled in Rapunzel's eyes.

Jack looked uncomfortable. "Look, don't cry," he snapped. "I'll just get what I need and get out." He began to study the room, moving from object to object. He marched toward her bathtub and climbed the three marble steps that led to the rim.

Rapunzel rubbed her runny nose and watched him. No prince — or peasant — would journey to the top of her tower if he didn't want to woo her. And there was no chance that she could forget things that had happened yesterday. There was only one explanation for all that Jack had said.

"You're a liar," she said, giving her nose a decisive wipe.

Jack had braced one heavy, dirty boot on the rim of the tub and was stretching a hand toward her ceiling garden, which he was too short to reach. He gave a disgusted sigh and glanced back at Rapunzel. "Give me one of those roses," he said.

"This story is over," Rapunzel replied. She walked to the fireplace, where the blue flames roared higher, beckoning. She reached toward the mantel.

"Over?" Jack asked, turning. "Wait a minute —"

Rapunzel curled her fingers around the stem of her silver bell.

"No, not again!" Jack jumped down from the bathtub rim and hurried toward her. He came near enough to grab the bell, but then hovered there, shifting from one foot to the other, his eyes darting from her fingers to her face. "Don't," he said. "Come on. Let me leave first, and then call your witch."

Rapunzel smiled. In the stories, it was always very satisfying when she cried out for Witch. The princes then showed how cowardly they were, and this one was no different.

"It's not funny!" Jack snapped.

"Did I say it was?" She gave him one last, long, disdainful look.

"You're the worst prince who ever lived, and I'll never go anywhere with you. Good-bye."

She rang the bell. Jack made a noise like he had run out of air. A strong wind raced around the room. The ceiling garden whispered in a fit, showering petals as it rustled.

"Rapunzel!" a voice called outside her tower.

Rapunzel grinned.

"Rapunzel! Let down your hair to me!"

It was Witch.

Pleased with her performance, Rapunzel pranced to the window wheel and began to turn the crank. For her first time thwarting a prince, she had done beautifully.

"I can't believe you!" Jack hissed. "She's going to kill me — is that what you want?" He dropped to the floor to crawl toward the balcony. "Just don't tell her I was here," he whispered.

Satisfied, Rapunzel turned the crank faster and faster. Jack was frightened, and she was winning. "I tell Witch *every*thing," she said.

"I *know*," Jack hissed. "That's why she almost caught me last time." He pried the door open with his fingers, and his voice grew muffled as he snaked out. "She caught the prince, did you know that? She probably even killed him, and all because he cut your stupid hair."

Rapunzel tensed. "Because he what?" She put both hands to her sleek, golden head. "My *hair*? What do you mean, he cut it? *What* prince?"

But Jack didn't answer. Rapunzel grabbed the wheel handle and gave it two final, furious cranks. When she saw her braid go taut and knew that Witch must be climbing, she raced out onto the balcony after Jack. He crouched at the railing, digging shaking fingers into the pockets of his shabby vest.

"Who dared to touch my hair? Tell me right now, you disgusting little peasant."

"Go to Geguul," Jack spat, yanking a small round object from one of his pockets.

Rapunzel didn't know where Geguul was, but it sounded like another insult. "You're not getting away, you know," she told him. "Witch is climbing my braid. She'll be halfway up by now. She's very fast."

"So am I," said Jack as he slammed the object against the balcony stones. There was a mighty *crack*. Rapunzel shrieked and jumped back.

"Rapunzel!" It was Witch's voice, quite close to the top of the tower. "Rapunzel, what was that? Are you hurt?"

But Rapunzel couldn't muster her voice. She stared, rapt, at the snake-like thing that was erupting from Jack's fist. It was the color of her hair and just as long, but slimmer and denser. Jack tossed one end over the balcony rail, and it tumbled to the dirt below. The end still in Jack's hand shimmered. To Rapunzel's amazement, it burst into a tripod of metal claws.

"Rapunzel!" Witch would be climbing through the window at any second. "Rapunzel, answer me!"

Jack hooked the claws onto the balcony railing, gripped the snake-like thing in both hands, vaulted over the rail, and vanished.

Rapunzel flung herself toward him. She was bewildered to see that he was already halfway down the side of the tower, dropping ten times faster than Witch ever had. He looked as though he had done this sort of thing before.

"Rapunzel!"

She heard Witch's quick footsteps crossing the tower behind her, but her eyes were still fixed on Jack.

"Rapunzel — my darling —"

Witch pulled her away from the railing just as Jack touched the ground.

"What's wrong?" Witch begged. "What happened? Can you speak? Are you hurt?"

Rapunzel gazed out across the moonlit clearing as Jack streaked like a shot toward the dark, forbidding forest.

Behind her, Witch jerked. Her arms closed around Rapunzel. "Who is that? Rapunzel, who is that?"

Rapunzel reached out to touch the metal claw that still hung from the balcony rail. He was dirty and short, a thief and a liar; he had spoken of dying fairies and hair-cutting princes, of peasants, and Geguul. He had insulted her hair, and climbed her tower, and he could make fantastic things grow from his fist.

"Jack," she said.

CHAPTER TWO

"AND then he called me stupid."

"What a fool."

"*And* he said my hair is useless."

"How little he knows."

"He even told me that another prince *cut* my hair yesterday. He was terrible, Witch. Worse than all my books."

Tight-lipped, Witch cradled Rapunzel. It had been an hour since Jack had bolted into the dark forests of the Redlands, and Rapunzel lay in her nice, clean nightdress in the downy comfort of her bed, recounting the whole horrible adventure to Witch. It was like being a small child again, to be burrowed against Witch, breathing in the fragrance of her skin. She always smelled like roses.

"You shouldn't have let him stay here and upset you." Witch kissed Rapunzel's forehead. "I wish you'd rung your bell at once."

"I didn't go with him, though," Rapunzel said.

"No, you didn't. You're much too wise. I'm very proud."

Warmth swelled in Rapunzel's chest. She shut her eyes and relaxed into the very pleasant sensation of having her hair stroked. It was wonderful to be beloved and safe after such a nasty shock. Witch made everything better.

"Did he *ask* you to go with him?" asked Witch after a moment.

"No, it was all wrong," Rapunzel said. "He didn't fall to his knees or ask me to marry him. He just told me to go to Geguul. What is Geguul?" she asked, but Witch seemed to be very far away.

Witch kissed her forehead again. "I'm listening," she said. "Tell me more."

"Well," said Rapunzel, trying to think of more to tell. "Oh yes! He was going to take one of my roses, but he wasn't tall enough to reach the ceiling." She smirked at the memory of his shortness.

Witch's eyes clouded. "Why did he want your roses?" she asked.

"I'm not sure," said Rapunzel. "He said he was finding a cure."

"A cure? Did Jack say that he was ill?"

"No — it was for a fairy!" Rapunzel sat up, remembering that she had left several details out of her story. "A fairy is dying! Jack said I hurt it, but I've never touched a fairy."

"I'd like to get my hands on this Jack," said Witch.

"Why? You wouldn't kill him, would you?"

Witch turned an awful, ashy color. "What?" she whispered.

"Jack said you'd kill him," said Rapunzel in a small voice.

Witch stared at her as though she had never seen her before, and then she put her face in her hands and her hair fell forward, obscuring her.

"I tried to keep you safe." Witch's voice was muffled. "I did everything in my power to protect you — but I've failed."

"But I'm safe!" cried Rapunzel. "Jack was lying. No one cut my hair. And I can *prove* it," she said, realizing that she could.

Witch raised her head at once. "Prove it?" she asked.

"Of course," said Rapunzel. She jumped out of bed and hurried to the window wheel, where she unwound the tail end of her braid. "If Jack was telling the truth, my hair would be cut."

"Rapunzel —" Witch was on her feet.

Rapunzel untied the end of her braid and pulled apart the tail to expose its middle. There, amidst the tapering wisps of gold, was the proof she had expected not to see.

It had been cut. Someone had hacked off a good six inches of one thick lock.

She stared at the shorn chunk of hair.

"But . . . ," she managed, when she could speak. "But I don't remember." She looked up to find Witch likewise staring at her braid, white-faced. "I don't understand. If it's cut . . . *was* there a prince yesterday?"

Rapunzel searched her mind for any hint that such a visitor had come. She tried to recall a face, a voice, a feeling of anger.

"I don't remember," she said, amazed. "I *would* remember if someone cut my hair. But someone did, and I don't. What's wrong with me? Why don't I know what happened?"

Witch's eyes flicked from the ruined lock of hair to the window wheel, and then to the ceiling garden. "A fairy came here, you said?" she asked.

"Why? Could a fairy have —"

"Let me *think*."

Witch had never spoken so sharply to Rapunzel, who drew back, startled. She tied up the end of her braid and replaced it at the window wheel. Witch's eyes were still fixed on the roses that bloomed overhead.

"A fairy," Witch muttered. "It would be a fairy."

Rapunzel burned to know what Witch was thinking, but she didn't dare ask another question. She turned instead to the window and gazed down at the dark world below. It was hard to see now; she could make out only the shapes of tall trees and distant mountains. But Rapunzel knew the view by heart and could fill in the picture with her mind.

The tower stood in the center of a large clearing of hard red dirt. The woods that fringed it were dense and green, full of trees even taller than her tower. Each morning, the sun rose over the tops of the eastern trees, and each evening, it melted its way down the sky until it was hidden behind the western woods. Then the moon rose, soft and white, and pale violet stars shone in the blackness. Tyme was a land of such beauty that Rapunzel had sometimes pined to leave her tower and touch it.

But she knew better. Every beast and peasant below would try to kill her if she went to the ground, and she understood that being killed was something very bad.

"Come sit with me?"

Rapunzel turned from the window to see Witch seated on the edge of the bed, one hand outstretched. Rapunzel went at once to sit beside her. She held Witch's hand tight. "Do you feel well, Witch? You look upset."

"I'm well." Witch covered Rapunzel's hand with her own. "It's you I'm worried about. Rapunzel, there is magic — fairy magic — that can steal human memories."

Rapunzel's hand flew to her mouth. "Steal memories?" she breathed. "But I thought fairies were useless! All my books say —"

"Your books are mostly right," said Witch. "But certain liberties have been taken."

"Liberties?"

"Little changes here and there. I don't like to give you stories that are too frightening, so I alter them a bit."

"Oh!" said Rapunzel, who rather thought her stories were scary enough. "Good."

"And since fairies fly near your balcony from time to time, I didn't want to make you afraid," said Witch. "But one fairy is capable of magic. And she is powerful."

Rapunzel's skin crawled at the idea that a fairy might have done magic on her. "Why haven't you told me this before?" she demanded.

"I thought there was no need," said Witch. "Ever since you were an infant —"

"When you rescued me from the swamps?" Rapunzel said. Her rescue from the ground was a story she knew and loved. It was her favorite bedtime tale.

"Yes." Witch smiled. "Since that day, I've put spells around this tower to stop fairies getting in. And though that fairy got through my spells, she is ill now, or so Jack said. She is even dying, perhaps. And if that is true . . ." Her eyes shone. "She can never trouble you again. Nor will anyone else. Not ever."

"Oh, Witch." Rapunzel hugged her. "I love you."

Witch's arms closed around her. Warm wind blew in through the window, and the moon beamed through the stone arch, making the tower room glow.

"Will you stay a little longer?" Rapunzel asked, her voice muffled against Witch's shoulder.

"Yes. And I'll be back early tomorrow to celebrate your birthday."

"What will you bring me?"

"Something more wonderful than you can guess."

Rapunzel lifted her head, intrigued. "Is it a toy?"

Witch shook her dark head.

"Is it a snack?"

Witch laughed. "Ever so much better than a snack," she said.

Rapunzel bounced in place on the bed. "I must be nearly as old as you now."

"Innocent girl," said Witch, laughing. "You're still a child. I'm ever so old."

"You don't *look* old," Rapunzel insisted. Witch had clear hazel eyes, dark lashes, and a lovely face framed by waves of deep brown hair. She was wonderful to look at.

"That's very kind."

Rapunzel frowned. They had had this conversation before. She had first noticed it on her twelfth birthday — she grew older, and Witch didn't. She wondered how old Jack was, and then realized what she was wondering. "Bother and drat," she said, annoyed.

"What's wrong?" asked Witch, who had gone to the window wheel. She untied the end of Rapunzel's braid and took it apart in her hands.

"Jack." Restless, she went to her toy chest and grabbed her velvet bag. She turned it over into her palm, spilling out a handful of silver jacks and a small bouncing ball, and she sat on the floor to play. She loved the cool heaviness of the jacks in her hand, loved the smoothness of their knobby little X shapes and the rounded points sticking out of their middles. Witch had given them to her on her seventh birthday and taught her how the game went.

Rapunzel scattered the jacks on the floor before her. She bounced the ball and picked up one jack before the ball could touch the ground again. Onesies. She bounced the ball again and picked up two jacks. Twosies. She bounced the ball a third time and scooped up some jacks without looking. She had played so many hundreds of times that she could tell, by weight, exactly how many she held in her hand. Sure enough, when she opened her palm, she counted three jacks.

And then it occurred to her.

"*Jacks*," she muttered.

But it had always been her favorite game, and so Rapunzel bounced the ball and snatched up four jacks with a practiced hand. Foursies. She continued until she cleared fourteensies, but no matter how she focused, Jack would not be gone. Disgusted, she stuffed the jacks and ball back into their bag and shoved it all into the pocket of her robe. "I wish he had never come," she said.

"Do you?" Witch asked, holding up a lock of golden hair to study it in the moonlight.

Rapunzel was silent. Witch bound her hair with cord and ribbon and came to kneel on the floor beside her. "An early birthday present," she said, and opened the curling tail of the braid to show Rapunzel its middle.

Rapunzel stared. There were no rough cuts, no jagged ends. Every hair curled softly over Witch's fingers. It was perfect.

She took the curl into her own hands, and Witch brushed a wisp away from her forehead. With two cool fingertips, she pressed the soft circle of Rapunzel's temple.

"Jack isn't everywhere, the way it seems," Witch said. "He's just in here."

"I know."

"Everything he did and said exists now only in your mind. That's all that makes him real."

Rapunzel nodded and yawned. She was exhausted. It had been a long and trying evening.

"He hurt you," said Witch. "I can't bear to think of how much. He insulted you. He accused you of violence toward another creature. How dare he?" Witch's hand slipped from Rapunzel's temple to cup her cheek. "Do you wish you could forget him?"

Rapunzel sighed. "I'll probably forget him by tomorrow," she said. "I already forgot what happened yesterday."

"Only because the fairy made you."

"Yes, and I don't like it."

Witch withdrew her hand. "You'd rather remember such an awful day?"

"I don't know. It's just . . . so strange." Rapunzel struggled to put into words what she felt. "It's not that I *want* to remember. It's that something happened to *me*, and I can't find it in my head." She strained her mind again in frustration. "Suppose I *did* kill a fairy. Shouldn't I know that?"

"You killed nothing!"

"But Jack said she's dying. If she got hurt in my tower, who else could have hurt her?"

Witch sat back. "Let me set your mind at rest," she said. "*If* the fairy is ill, it isn't because of you. It's because of me. I used powerful magic to protect this tower. And my magic and the fairy's do not mix." Her smile tightened at the corners.

Rapunzel squinted at the blue firelight. "If your magic made the fairies ill," she said, "that must be why Jack came back for the cure. But why would he want to help that fairy?" she asked. "And why would the fairies send *him*?"

Witch looked thoughtful. "I suppose the fairies sent him as their emissary."

"Emissary?"

"He came on their behalf," Witch explained, "because they cannot come themselves."

"Because the magics don't mix?"

"Exactly. You're so clever, darling."

Rapunzel warmed at the pride in Witch's eyes.

"Now get in bed," said Witch, "and I'll tuck you in before I go."

With a few graceful flicks of her fingers, Witch restored everything in the tower to its place. Rapunzel crawled into bed. As she snuggled under her covers, she caught sight of the glass balcony door, and she shivered, remembering how Jack's shadow had looked against the translucent curtain, his hand reaching for the door handle. She wished her mind wouldn't think of it, but even when she closed her eyes, the image wouldn't leave her. She wondered what was worse: to forget something awful, or to remember it.

"Maybe forgetting is better," she mumbled.

Witch sat down at Rapunzel's side and smoothed her hair. "Is that what you want?" she said. "You know you can ask me for anything."

Rapunzel glanced at her. The way Witch talked, it was as though she could make her forget, just as the fairy had. The thought of losing more memories made her stomach curdle.

"What did that fairy want here, anyway?" she asked, turning on her side and curling up. "She must have wanted something, if she pushed through all your magic. . . ." She yawned and clasped Witch's hand. "What if she wants to kill me?"

"Shh." Witch stroked her hand. "No more worries. That fairy didn't come for you at all. She came for me."

Rapunzel sat up, her drowsiness gone, and stared at Witch in horror. "*You?*" she repeated. "She wants to kill you?" She felt cold and light-headed. "But she can't."

Witch looked alarmed. "No, she can't. You needn't worry. Lie down — you were almost asleep; I'm sorry I upset you. Forget the fairy, please."

"Why does she want to kill you?"

Witch's mouth opened in surprise, and Rapunzel leaned in closer. "There *is* a reason!" she said, and then an awful idea occurred to her. "If your magic makes the fairy sick, can hers make *you* sick?" Witch looked dismayed, and Rapunzel pressed on. "If she comes after you again, what will happen? How will you defend yourself if the magics don't mix?" She tightened her grip on Witch's hand. "Isn't there something I can do? Can I be *your* emissary? I'm ever so much taller and cleaner than Jack —"

"Enough." Witch's voice was firm. "I cannot have you worried."

"But I want to help you."

"Then *help* me," said Witch. "Let go of these fears. Be happy. That is all I need."

"How can I be happy if you're in danger?"

"When you are happy, there *is* no danger. Your happiness makes me strong enough for anything." Witch laid her hands on Rapunzel's shoulders and guided her onto the pillows. "Don't let this ruin your birthday."

Rapunzel pushed Witch's hands away and sat back up. "I don't care about my birthday!" she said hotly. "I care about you! I don't want you to be killed!"

Witch winced. On her lovely face, a change was taking place. Between her dark eyebrows, in the smooth, pale skin, a fine line appeared and began to deepen, like a bloodless gash in her brow. Beside this first line, others soon surfaced.

Rapunzel stared at the lines. "What's happening?" she cried. "What are they?"

Witch lifted her hand and moved her fingertips over her forehead. "Wrinkles," she said.

"Why are they happening?"

"Because I'm worried about you."

Rapunzel's stomach clenched. "It's my fault?" she asked. "I did that?"

Witch stood, bent over Rapunzel, and kissed her hair. "No fairy, no matter how powerful, can ever hurt me as much as your pain hurts me."

She withdrew from Rapunzel and went to the window wheel, where she began to unwind the braid, feeding it through the stone arch and watching it drop.

"You're leaving?" asked Rapunzel, pushing off her covers and getting up.

"I'll be back tomorrow."

"Witch, wait." Rapunzel hurried to the window, frightened. "Do wrinkles hurt?" she asked. "Say you're not in pain!"

"I must rest." Witch took Rapunzel's braid in both her hands and swung herself out into the night. She braced her feet against the outer wall and hung there, moonlight illuminating the wrinkles on her brow.

Rapunzel leaned out through the window arch. She could not name the emotion she felt, but it was heavy and sickening. Witch was hurt, and it was her fault.

"Witch, what can I do? Tell me."

"Only be happy." Witch looked weary as she repositioned her hands on the braid.

"But," said Rapunzel, "what if the fairy hurts you? What if Jack comes back, or —"

"If you love me, banish these thoughts. I am always near. And I will do anything to help you, if only you will ask me. Remember that."

"I'll remember," Rapunzel managed. "Good night, Witch."

Witch lowered herself until Rapunzel could see nothing but the crown of her dark head. Either the moonlight was playing tricks, or there were white streaks in Witch's hair.

Then she was gone.

CHAPTER THREE

*R*APUNZEL woke with a shout from a nightmare she could not remember.

Her tower was cold and dark. The fire was dead. Her feet stuck out from under the blankets, freezing; the rest of her was slick with sweat. She curled into a ball and huddled beneath her blankets, disturbed beyond her experience. She thought of Witch climbing down into darkness, wrinkled and in pain, her hair shot through with white, and some of her nightmare came back to her in horrible snatches of color. Her braid severed like dry twigs. Jack's sharp, gleaming grin. Witch sobbing, white-haired, her face gnarled beyond recognition.

"Light!" Rapunzel commanded. The fire flickered awake, and its blue flames were a comfort, but they were not enough to make her feel safe. She pushed down her covers and ran to the window wheel, seized by a sudden, unreasonable panic. Her hair was wound neatly in its place.

With sure, rapid turns of the wooden crank, Rapunzel unwound her hair from the wheel and hefted as much braid as she could carry into her arms. It was bulky and heavy, but she lugged it back to bed with her and yanked up the covers to hide herself, hair and all. She hugged her braid closer for comfort.

A clang of metal on metal sounded just outside the balcony door. Rapunzel screamed and pulled her covers over her head. Jack had returned, and he wanted to help the fairies hurt Witch.

She only cowered for a moment before she remembered: This was *her* tower. She didn't have to be afraid here — *he* did.

Rapunzel threw off her covers, jumped out of bed, and pointed to the fire. "Roar!" she commanded, and it did. "Get bubbling," she shouted to the bathtub, and then she turned to the harp. "You heard me — play! Everything, get up!"

She raced to her silver bell but stopped short, unwilling to ring it. Much as she wanted Witch to come, she couldn't bear the idea of giving her more pain. She would handle this herself, for Witch's sake.

Rapunzel pulled on her robe and tied it tight. She shoved her feet into her slippers. "I know you're there," she shouted, stepping out onto the balcony, where, sure enough, a silver claw gripped the railing. She squinted toward the dark ground but saw no one. The long, slim rope was taut, but the climber was obscured by darkness. "Answer me!"

"Hi there." Jack's disembodied voice floated up from below. "Nice weather we're having."

"*You!*" cried Rapunzel. "I knew it! Get away from here!"

Jack climbed into sight. He scaled the rope with terrifying ease, much faster than Witch ever had.

"Vile peasant!" Rapunzel shouted.

"Guess you remember me." Jack hauled himself higher and reached up to grab the railing.

The second his hand touched the silver rail, his rope vanished with a sizzling sound. Jack's eyes widened; he flailed for a hold, but there was nothing to support him. "Help me!" he gasped.

Rapunzel snatched up the slack of her braid and threw it to him. Jack grabbed it, and she squealed in pain as his weight yanked her halfway over the railing. She pressed hard against the stones with her feet and clung to the railing with both hands. Jack hung below the balcony, clutching her hair and staring up at her.

Rapunzel stared back, her scalp throbbing. "Hurry," she said when he didn't move. "It hurts."

Jack scrambled up her braid and over the balcony railing. When his feet were on firm ground, he backed against the tower wall and wiped sweat out of his eyes.

"Thought you didn't want me here," he said.

"I don't."

"Could've let me fall, then."

Rapunzel massaged her aching scalp. "Well," she said, "I didn't." And since she didn't know why she hadn't, she said nothing else.

Jack shoved his hands into his pockets. "I should've cracked a new rope," he said. "That one was going for thirty hours, and they're only supposed to last twenty-four. I'm usually lucky — sometimes they last for three days. Not this time, I guess." He paused. "Thanks."

A warm wind picked up and blew across the dark balcony, and Rapunzel pulled her robe tighter. It gave her something to do, which was useful since she didn't know what to say. Then she remembered. "I know that you came back to get the cure, but you can't have it."

Jack's eyebrows lifted. "What cure?" he asked.

"The cure for the sick fairy." She folded her arms. "You want to help her. But if she gets better, she'll come back and kill Witch!"

"What are you talking about?" asked Jack. He looked honestly bewildered.

Rapunzel studied him, frowning. "I'm talking about yesterday," she said. "Do *you* not remember yesterday?"

He scratched his head. "I remember visiting you," he said. "But I've never met any fairies. I'm just a peasant."

"Then they took your memory too!" Rapunzel gasped. "*Horrible* fairies! If any of them ever comes back here, I'll . . ." But she wasn't sure what she would do.

"Call your witch?" Jack suggested.

She shook her head. "I can't. Witch might get hurt. If the fairies come back, I'll just take care of them myself."

He cocked an eyebrow. "You will, huh?"

She nodded. "For Witch," she said, "I'd do anything."

Jack glanced past her at the balcony door. "Mind if I go inside, then?" he asked.

"What for?" said Rapunzel. "Since you don't remember the fairies, why did you climb back up here?"

Jack ducked his head. "'Cause it's a beautiful tower," he mumbled. "And I, uh . . . I wanted to see it one last time, before I go home."

Rapunzel felt a surge of pity for him. He had spent his whole life on the ground, dirty and unsafe. Of course he preferred her tower.

"Go on, then," she said indulgently, and she moved out of his way. "It's all right if you want to look. But only for a *minute*. Then you have to go, all right?"

Jack nodded. He pushed open the door and slipped into the fire-lit tower as Rapunzel pulled her braid back onto the balcony, amazed at herself. She had let a stranger climb her hair. Someone other than Witch had held it in his hands. As if that wasn't odd enough, she had gone so far as to allow him into her tower without supervision. She hurried inside to make sure Jack hadn't ransacked her belongings.

He hadn't. Her harp had not been worried; her dressing table stood undisturbed. Instead, Jack stood on the bathtub rim, reaching for the roses. Rapunzel marched up to the bathtub.

"Get down."

Jack looked pleadingly at her. "Can't I have one?" he asked.

"One of my roses? Why?"

He picked at a loose thread that hung from the cuff of his sleeve. "It's just, I've never seen one," he said. He glanced at her. "And they're so . . . you know."

"Beautiful?"

He nodded, looking pained, and Rapunzel felt another surge of pity.

"Well," she said, "I suppose it's all right. You *did* ask. Get down, I'll reach one for you."

Jack leapt to the floor, and Rapunzel climbed up the marble bathtub steps. At the top, she balanced on her tiptoes and snapped the stem of the nearest rose. She offered it to Jack, who cupped it and held it against him with one hand. With the other, he fished in one of his pockets.

"They smell nice too," said Rapunzel, hopping down to the floor. "Smell it. Go on."

Jack did not reply. From one of his vest pockets, he produced a small glass vial, which he used to collect dew from the center of the rose. He got only a few drops of the clear liquid, but it seemed to be all that he needed. He dropped the rose on the floor.

"You said you wanted it!" Rapunzel cried. "Pick it up."

Jack capped the glass vial. He took a pink silk handkerchief from one of his pockets, and Rapunzel made a noise of surprise.

"That handkerchief," she said. "It's mine."

"No, it's not." Jack wrapped the handkerchief around the glass vial several times. "You gave it to me the other day, to carry the fairy."

"But you — you said," stammered Rapunzel, "you said you didn't remember any fairies!"

Jack tucked the silk-wrapped vial into his back pocket and strode onto the balcony. Rapunzel ran after him.

"You lied to me!" she cried, but he didn't answer. He yanked a small round object out of his pocket and slammed it against the silver railing. Just as it had before, a rope exploded from his fist, and a tripod of metal hooks burst from the top end of the rope. Jack hung the hooks from the railing and tossed the end of the rope to the ground, then turned and made his way into the tower once more. Rapunzel didn't even have time to protest before he returned to the balcony, lugging nearly all of her braid in his arms.

"What are you doing?" Rapunzel demanded. "Put down my hair!"

"Whatever you say." Jack dumped the braid over the side of the balcony, and the weight of her plummeting hair pulled at Rapunzel's scalp and made her shout. Jack clapped his hand over her open mouth. "Keep quiet!" he hissed. "The fairies are waiting for me right outside this tower, understand?"

Rapunzel's stomach went cold. She stifled her screams, even when Jack grabbed her braid in his dirty hands and hurdled the silver railing. He planted his boot soles against the tower, and her head bent under his weight. She whimpered and clutched the railing pressing into her stomach. "Use your stupid rope!" she whispered. "It's right there!"

"Nah." Jack shimmied down into the darkness. "This'll work."

Rapunzel tried to yank her braid out of his hands, but his weight was too much for her. She stayed bent over the railing as the darkness swallowed him. Just before he disappeared, he turned up his face to look at her.

"The fairies told me to thank you if you helped," he said. "So thanks." He waggled the little vial with the dew from the rose as his face split into the sharp, gleaming grin that Rapunzel recognized from her nightmare. She gasped.

"If you want the fairy's cure," Jack taunted, "you better come and get it yourself. If you call that witch, you know she'll get hurt. . . ."

He unhooked his wrist and slipped down into the darkness. Moments later, his weight vanished from Rapunzel's braid, and she lifted her head, her heart thumping. She could barely breathe. She was such a fool.

"LIAR!" she screamed. Witch had warned her. Ground people were liars. Rapunzel knew it — she had always known it. She should have guessed what Jack would do. Yet she had failed, and now the fairies would get their cure, and the powerful fairy would wake up again.

And Witch would die.

Panic seized Rapunzel. She clutched the railing and swung one leg over it, and then the other, until she was barely perched, by the toes of her slippers, on a tiny ledge of stone. She looked down and choked. The tower had never seemed so high. She could not think about what she was about to do. She couldn't think or she would stop, and she couldn't stop. Witch's life depended on her.

She released the railing with one hand and grabbed the rope that Jack had left behind. It was splintery and rough. She swallowed a cry of discomfort and made herself let go of the railing with her other hand, the soles of her feet pressed against the tower's outer wall. She had seen Witch do this thousands of times, but that didn't make it any easier. The whole weight of her braid hung down from her scalp, and her neck craned backward.

Rapunzel put one hand under the other and made her way lower. Her arms ached, her neck throbbed, her fingers chafed — she tried to suck her burning fingers — her sweating palms slipped against the rope —

Rapunzel lost her grip and her footing all at once and screamed as she slid uncontrollably downward. Her vision blurred; wind rushed in her ears. She was careening — she would crash — Witch had warned her to be careful —

She clamped her legs together and caught the rope between them. As she skidded a few feet farther, the rope tore into her skin. The pain made her vision gray out, but she gripped the rope with all her might and hung there, trembling.

When she could see clearly, she looked down. Her stomach dropped as though she'd just taken another skid down the rope. There was the ground, just feet away. She stretched down one shaking leg to get her final foothold against the tower, but the toe of her slipper scraped the dirt instead. Rapunzel lost her grip on the rope, tumbled to the ground, and lay there in a heap.

"Great White skies," she rasped, scrambling to her feet to get out of the dirt, which was probably full of poisonous snakes or something else equally dreadful. She stared up at the window from which she'd come, small and distant in the black night. The height of her tower was dizzying. She wanted to call out for Witch — she even opened her mouth to do it — but fear for Witch's safety stopped her voice.

Witch was in danger now, and in danger she would stay until Rapunzel could retrieve the cure that Jack had stolen for the fairies.

There was only one thing to do.

Rapunzel whirled toward the woods and ran after Jack.

She plunged into the forest. Tree branches touched her, and she squealed in fear. Gossamer webs caught at her arms and her face, and many-legged things skittered around her, making her scream. She kept running, her torn skin burning with every step. There was no time to mind the pain, or to fear the beasts, or to notice the sensation of balmy, open air, or even to wonder whether she was going the right way. Jack had a mighty head start.

"MISERABLE PEASANT!" she finally yelled, and then she yelped as she was brought to a painful halt. "My hair!" Her braid was caught somewhere back in the trees. She gripped it with both hands and yanked, but it was snagged, and every moment she was delayed, Jack was getting away.

"COME BACK!" she shouted. "LIAR! BRUTE! EMISSARY!"

Rapunzel tugged and pulled and began to cry. Humid air seeped through her nightgown and robe, and moist dirt filled the toes of her slippers. Through a blur of tears she saw just how big and frightening everything was — the endless space of the woods, the giant trees, the open air. And she was alone.

"TROLL!" she shouted through furious sobs. "IMP! UGLY LITTLE GNOME!"

"Ah, shut up."

Rapunzel clutched her hair to her chest and whirled around, staring into the darkness in every direction until she found the source of the familiar voice. Jack knelt several paces away, grimacing as he dug his bare hands into a thorny plant and worked her braid out of its prison.

"Jack!" Rapunzel's voice was ragged from shouting. "I caught you! I thought I'd fallen too far behind, I thought —"

"You," Jack said, freeing her braid and throwing it into the dirt, "are the loudest person I've ever met." He gathered up the rest of her hair in an unkempt pile, dragged it over to her, and dumped it at her feet.

Rapunzel looked down at the pile in horror. Her braid, which had always been clean and golden, was as battered and filthy as Jack's fingernails. But she would have to deal with that later. The only thing that mattered right now was the glass vial that Jack was carrying.

"Give me the cure," Rapunzel demanded. She seized Jack by the front of his vest so she could search his pockets. Jack grabbed her wrists and fought her.

"Let go!"

"Not — until — you give — me — the cure!"

Jack stepped nimbly back. "I don't have it anymore, all right? I already gave it to a fairy. He was waiting for me."

Rapunzel whipped her head around in fear, but she saw nothing but the darkness and the trees. "Where is he?" she asked.

"He flew ahead to give it to his mate."

"His what?"

"The fairy who's dying. He went to save her life."

Rapunzel gasped. The fairies had their cure. "But those fairies want to kill Witch," she moaned. "They'll hurt her."

"Maybe they have their reasons," said Jack with cool unconcern. "Maybe they're just defending themselves against her. Ever think of that?"

"Don't you *dare* blame Witch," she shouted. "She did nothing to those fairies!"

"Then why did one of them almost die just from being in your tower?"

"That was the fairy's own fault! She shouldn't have pushed her way in!"

Jack shrugged. "Fine," he said. "Have it your way. Just follow me close, all right? We have to get to the Red Glade, fast. It's dangerous out here. Especially for me," he added, and suddenly he looked afraid. "Come on," he said, and he turned and set off into the darkness.

Rapunzel did not move. "The Red Glade?" she repeated.

Jack glanced back over his shoulder. "It's where the Red fairies live," he said. "Let's go."

"Don't be ridiculous! I'll never go where the fairies live!"

"Well, that's where the cure is," said Jack, smirking. "So if you want to save your witch, I guess you'd better hurry."

Rapunzel hesitated. To follow a peasant through the woods, away from her tower and into the lands far, far away — it violated everything that Witch had ever taught her. She knew what Witch would tell her to do. But if Witch came now, she would want to protect Rapunzel, and that would mean going back to the tower while Witch traveled alone to the Red Glade to retrieve the cure. And if Witch went to the Red Glade, where her magic didn't mix with the fairies', she might be killed.

Rapunzel could not allow it. She would go to the Red Glade herself, for Witch's sake. She swallowed hard.

"What will I do with my hair?" she said in a small voice.

Jack raised his dark eyebrows at the dirty, tangled heap of braid that sat at Rapunzel's feet. "Cut it off," he said. "We'll move faster

without it, and I can't afford to lose time. I've wasted enough already."
He strode back to her, pulled a rather large knife from a short sheath
at his belt, and grabbed her braid at shoulder length.

Rapunzel shoved Jack so hard that he landed on his backside in
the dirt, his knife still clenched in his fist.

"What's wrong with you?" he yelled.

"Cut it *off*?" she said. "What do you mean, what's wrong with *me*,
you lying, thieving, hair-cutting —"

"Peasant?" Jack hefted a good portion of Rapunzel's braid into
his arms before she could stop him. "What're you dragging, fifty
pounds of hair?" He dropped it with a thud. "It's useless. Get rid of it."
He raised his knife.

Rapunzel kicked out as hard as she could and caught Jack in the
front of his trousers with the sole of her slipper — just barely, but it
seemed to be enough. He stumbled back with a howl, and his knife
flew off into the trees. "If I see that knife anywhere near my hair again,"
Rapunzel began, "I'll —"

"That was my dagger!" Jack hobbled into the trees. "I don't have
another one!"

"Well, I don't have another braid." Rapunzel swept her braid
back over her shoulder. "So stop trying to chop it off."

Jack made no reply. He emerged from the trees, teeth clenched.
"Great," he said. "It's lost, and I don't have time to go digging it out, so
you better hope we don't run across bandits. Or a Stalker."

"What's a Stalker?" Rapunzel asked.

"Tell you what," said Jack. "If we come across one, I'll feed *you* to it."

Rapunzel looked into the dense and towering woods, which
were forbidding enough in the darkness, even without bandits. But at
least they were empty of sizable creatures — or seemed to be.

"We'll have to carry your stupid braid." He sighed heavily. "Give me half," he said. "You'll take forever if you try to haul it yourself. And hurry *up*."

Rapunzel wound her braid around Jack's shoulders. She crisscrossed it over his back, sashed it around his front, and twined it around his waist like hairy, golden armor. Jack's head stuck out of the hive of hair, looking red and angry.

"I said *half*," he barked.

Rapunzel made a few big loops around herself with the remainder of her braid. Looking furious, Jack set off at a waddling run. Rapunzel skipped to keep up with him, but her skip turned to a hobble when her skin began to burn again where the rope had torn into it.

And then it occurred to her.

"You remember the day that I forgot," she said, coming to a halt and forcing Jack to stop with her. "Don't you? You remember coming to my tower, and a prince cutting my hair, and the fairy being sick and everything?"

From within the hair hive, Jack sliced a contemptuous look at her. "Maybe," he said.

"Tell me the story!" Rapunzel said eagerly. It had bothered her beyond belief not to remember Jack's first visit. The opportunity to have the blanks filled in was too tempting to resist, even if it meant listening to a liar who worked for the fairies.

"You want to know what happened?" Jack asked. "The truth?"

"That's what I said, isn't it?"

"Then come see for yourself," said Jack, veering left off the path and plunging into a dark, dense thicket. He pulled Rapunzel with him, and she hunched her shoulders as the trees closed in around her.

"Where are we going?" she whimpered. "I don't want to go this way."

"Neither did he," said Jack, and he came to a halt. "Look."

Rapunzel stopped beside him. She looked. And then she screamed so loudly that birds flew from the trees.

The man before them was made of stone.

CHAPTER FOUR

RAPUNZEL stumbled back from the horrible statue. "He's real," she said. She wasn't sure how she could tell, but there was no doubt in her mind.

"Yeah, he's real. He's Prince Dash of the Blue Kingdom."

He looked exactly — but *exactly* — like the princes in her storybooks.

"Prince who?" she whispered.

"Prince Dash," said Jack, and he shook his head. "You must be the only girl in Tyme who doesn't know who he is."

"Does he know we're here?" Rapunzel asked. "Can he see us?"

"I don't know. He could be dead."

She hugged herself. "You mean he's killed?"

"If he's not, he probably wants to be."

Rapunzel's heart fluttered. She had never seen anyone dead before, and Prince Dash of the Blue Kingdom was so lifelike that he might have moved at any moment. Though his eyes were made of stone, they were full of fear. She swept her gaze over his beautiful mouth, his billowing stone cape, his broad chest, and the veins that stood out in his large, strong hands. One hand was flung up before his face. In its grip, something golden glinted. Something not stone.

Her hair.

Rapunzel recognized it at once, and a shiver of shock ran through her. Her very own hair, shining in the stone grasp of a strange prince.

So he really had cut it, then. Jack had told the truth.

"That's mine," she said, and her breath came fast. "He *took* it."

She stepped up to the stone prince and yanked on her hair, but it was caught fast. When she tried to get a better grip on it, her fingertips brushed the prince's stone ones, and she recoiled.

"He's warm," she said.

A gust of hot wind blew through the thicket and made the branches rattle. Dried leaves rained down on the prince, scraping his stone limbs and his wide-open eyes.

"Let's get out of here," said Jack, "before the same thing happens to me."

"Why would the fairies hurt *you?*" asked Rapunzel, dragging her eyes away from the statue to look at Jack. "Aren't you their emissary?"

Jack looked silently at her. Then he pushed his way back toward the path, bringing Rapunzel behind him through the dense thicket.

"Ow," she said. "Wait! Can't you hold the branches so they don't — *ow!*"

She ducked and turned to avoid being smacked in the face. When they were walking once more along the narrow dirt path through the woods, Jack spoke. "You really don't get it, do you?"

"Get what?"

He struggled to loosen a thick coil of braid that had wound itself about his neck. "The fairies didn't hurt that prince. The witch did."

"Liar," said Rapunzel. "Witch would never do anything like that."

Jack let out a long, irritated breath. "Look," he said, "I guess I can see how this might be hard for you to believe, but that witch is —"

"Stop calling her *that* witch. She's *Witch*," said Rapunzel. "Now, tell me the story of the other afternoon, with the prince and my hair and the dying fairy. And tell it fast, because as soon as I get the cure back, I'm going to call for Witch and go home."

She waited for him to speak, but he was silent. "Well?" she prompted, but Jack only waddled along faster. He dragged her with him, over rocks and gritty dirt, through plants that scratched her ankles and across a little stream that soaked her slippers and made them squish with each step she took.

"Wait!" she snapped, tripping over a root. "Tell me the story!"

"You won't believe me."

"Selfish peasant!"

"Spoiled brat."

"What does that mean?"

"It means *you*," said Jack. "'Tell the story, tell the story!'" he screeched. "My eight-year-old sister is more mature than you are."

"Mature?" said Rapunzel. "Sister?"

Jack blew out another breath. "Skies," he muttered. "Fine. Here's your stupid story about the other day, all right? I was trying to find the Red fairies, but instead I found your tower. I thought it might be magical —"

"It is."

Jack gave her a look. "Are you going to say something every five seconds?"

Rapunzel pressed her mouth shut.

"I stayed back in the trees," said Jack. "I could see a man standing on the ground by the tower. I didn't know it was Prince Dash, I just saw him holding on to your hair."

"I would *never* let my braid down for a prince!"

"It wasn't in a braid," said Jack. "It was all spread out and hanging over the railing and stuff."

This made sense, and Rapunzel nodded. "Witch washed it that morning and hung it out to dry before she left," she said. "I remember that."

"Congratulations. So while I was standing there watching, Prince Dash cut a piece of your hair off."

"Evil!"

"It's just hair," said Jack, "and you have plenty to spare. But you screamed like he'd cut off your arm, and you started pulling all the hair up onto your balcony really fast. The prince ran for it, right past me, into the woods. When he saw me, he shouted, 'Run, there's a witch!' — and believe me, I ran. But I didn't get far before Rune flew in front of my face and told me to stop."

"Rune?"

"The fairy who needed my help. Stop interrupting!" said Jack. "So, while the prince was cutting your hair, Rune's mate was climbing up it."

"A fairy was *climbing* my *hair?*"

"Yeah. She couldn't fly into your tower, because the magic in there was too thick and she couldn't use her wings. But she wanted to talk to you."

"She was climbing up to kill Witch!" said Rapunzel. "When did *you* get there?"

"Right after that," said Jack. "Rune was panicked. You pulled up your hair while his mate was still climbing, and she didn't come back or give him any sign. He was afraid she would die, so he asked me to rescue her." He lifted his chin. "He said the magic in the tower wouldn't hurt me the way it would hurt him."

Rapunzel picked her way over a fallen log, listening hard. It was just as Witch had told her. "Fairy and witch magic don't mix," she ventured.

"Right," said Jack. "Rune said that the witch who protects you is more powerful than any witch in Tyme, and if I wasn't quick enough, she'd kill me. But he also said that if I rescued his mate, he'd owe me a very great favor. So I couldn't say no." He slowed, his expression tense. "I need their help."

Rapunzel prodded him onward in the tale. "So you climbed up to my tower?"

"Yeah." Jack glanced at her. "Rune's mate was lying on your dressing table, in the middle of a bunch of rose petals, and you were trying to talk to her."

"What did she say?"

"She couldn't talk back. She was really sick. She reached up a hand when she saw me, and then she went unconscious."

"So Rune's mate is the powerful fairy," Rapunzel said, "and she's the one who needs the cure."

Jack frowned at her. "What do you mean, 'the powerful fairy'?"

"Witch told me that one of the fairies has powerful magic."

"Just one?" he said, and he laughed. "There are probably a thousand Red fairies."

The number unsettled Rapunzel. It was larger than she could imagine. She had pictured maybe twenty or thirty fairies at most, which already seemed like an awful lot of creatures all at once. Witch had said they were useless, but that did not put her at ease.

"So then what happened?" she prompted. "The fairy went unconscious, and . . . ?"

"You gave me your pink handkerchief to wrap her up in so I could carry her away. And then," said Jack, with feeling, "you rang your stupid bell, even though I begged you not to. I told you the witch would kill me — I said, 'Please just let me go' — but you said no, which meant I had to *run*. That witch came after me pretty fast after she visited you. She would've caught me, but Rune was waiting for me. He led me into a fairywood, and the witch couldn't follow."

"A fairywood?"

"That's how fairies travel. They go into one group of trees, and they come out in another. They can get all the way across Tyme within a day. Wouldn't that be great?"

Rapunzel didn't really hear him. Jack's story had given her a great deal to think about. She trudged forward, wishing again that she could call for Witch. But she couldn't bear to subject Witch to danger just because she herself had been stupid.

"Will we be there soon? To the fairies? How much longer?"

"I don't know," said Jack. "Rune told me to walk northwest away from the tower and he would come for me as fast as he could. Can't you walk any faster?"

Rapunzel could not. Her shoulder already ached from carrying loops of her braid, which she had to shift to the other arm. The night was intensely hot, which she was unused to; the air in the tower was never thick and wet like this. The ground was as horrible as she had expected.

It was also much bigger than she had imagined. Without a ceiling or walls, space continued forever. It was forty paces across her tower and one hundred twenty-five and a half paces around it, but she lost track of her steps in the woods before she even started counting. Her eyes went everywhere as she walked, her gaze drawn helplessly to the tops of the towering trees.

A rustling in the bushes to the left of the path made both Rapunzel and Jack freeze.

"Quiet," Jack whispered, holding up a hand. "Don't move."

Rapunzel looked to her left. A pair of wide, luminous eyes stared back at her from the darkness. She screamed in terror, the luminous eyes widened, and a toast-colored beast leapt out of the thicket and dashed across the path in front of them, followed closely by a smaller beast of the same color. Both disappeared into the woods.

"Ground monsters!" said Rapunzel. "Vicious, gluttonous beasts! Will they eat us?"

"They're *deer*," Jack said.

Only after he had defended the harmlessness of deer to Rapunzel's satisfaction did they march onward. Finally they reached another clearing ringed by more woods. Rapunzel dropped down to sit on a log.

"What are you doing?" Jack demanded.

She ignored him and looked at the sky, where the moon shone above the pointed peaks of the trees. It was the same size down here as it was in her tower, and she was grateful for something familiar. A sudden wind blew across her face, and she was grateful for that too. It was nice to sit still and let the wind cool her sweating brow and lift the damp hair from her temples.

The wind smelled different here. Not like her tower breezes. It was bigger. Sharper. She took a deep breath of it and decided that, of all the ground things so far, it was the least offensive. Rapunzel lifted her braid from her neck and bent her head to let the wind touch her hot skin.

"We can't stop!" Jack yanked at her braid, pulling her off balance. "Come on!"

Rapunzel braced her hands against the dirt. "Can't I rest for a little while?"

"And let that witch catch up and tear my head off?" said Jack. "No!"

"Her name is *Witch*," Rapunzel said. "And she wouldn't tear off your head. She would just be angry with you for worrying me. Can't you understand that? Don't you have anyone who loves you?"

"I have parents," said Jack. "Like normal people do."

"Well, whatever parents are, they must not care much about you," said Rapunzel. "Or you wouldn't be so awful."

Jack's face fell. For a moment, he looked young and lost, and then he turned away. He unwound a coil of her hair from across his body and dropped it to the ground, and then he unwound another and another. Rapunzel looked on in distress.

"You can't do that!" she said. "I can't carry it all. Wind it back up."

Jack struggled out of the last few coils and shoved the braid down to the ground. He stepped out of the pile of hair and brushed himself off. He adjusted his boots. He cracked his neck. And then he strode into the moonlit clearing and away from Rapunzel, who sat, anchored by her braid, unsure of what to do.

"You can't leave me here," she said.

Jack stopped at the edge of the clearing. He stood very still, except for his hands, which he balled into fists. "No," he said, his voice low, "I can't." He turned to her. "But I wouldn't spend another second with you if I didn't have to."

Rapunzel was prevented from telling him she felt the same way by a humming noise that suddenly seemed to be everywhere. "What is that?" she said. "Jack, what is that?"

The humming grew louder. Closer. Rapunzel whipped her head from left to right but could not see what was making the sound.

"Is that a deer?" she called out, terrified. "You don't sound like a deer —"

"Silence, prisoner child."

The voice was thin and cool. Rapunzel spun toward it, but saw no one. She stared at the not-quite-empty space in front of her. A sliver of light no bigger than her thumb hovered in the air at eye level.

"Are you going to hurt me?" she whispered. "Or help me?"

"You deserve no help." The voice was cold and unpitying. "I am here to take you where you must go. Now follow." Without waiting for her, the sliver of light darted out of sight and into the trees, leaving a shimmering red trail in its wake.

Rapunzel felt as though her knees had turned to water.

"A fairy," she breathed.

"That's Rune," said Jack. "Come on, hurry." Without looking at her, he bent and pulled a good amount of her braid into his arms. Rapunzel did the same, and between them, they carried her hair across the clearing and into the woods.

Rapunzel could hardly believe that she was following a fairy. She hoped he still had the cure with him. Maybe she could get it from him here, now, and never have to see the other fairies at all.

Once among the trees, she had the strange sensation that she was moving very fast, though she knew it was impossible: She was barely managing a trudge. Even so, when they had walked for a few more minutes, she couldn't help thinking that the woods looked and felt different. The air was cool. The trees stood far apart, tall and silver in the moonlight. Mist moved through them at great speed, obscuring the ground, but there was no wind. The trail of red light was gone.

"Stop," said Jack, his voice low.

Rapunzel stopped. The mist in the trees before them was so thick that it could have hidden anything. She heard only a faint and beautiful chiming sound that wasn't a sound at all. It seemed to come not through her ears, but through her skin.

"Where are we?" she whispered.

"A fairywood," said Jack reverently. "Shh."

The mist began to swirl as though churned by a wind. It twisted into dozens of tall white funnels among the trees, and then the funnels burst, along with the trees themselves, making the strange, silver forest disappear in one silent puff of smoke, revealing a vast and empty darkness.

Not empty, Rapunzel realized as the smoke thinned and vanished. *Not empty at all.* Her heart nearly burst with joy at the most familiar sight the ground had yet afforded, and the most beautiful.

Roses. They were everywhere, and they belonged to Witch. Rapunzel knew it at once. No one but Witch could make roses like these. They twisted thickly around the few remaining trees at the outskirts of the clearing, dark and ripe, so alive that they pulsed. They blanketed the ground, filling the air with perfume. In the center of the clearing, a hundred feet away, they rose up in a colossal dome, a dune of blooming roses coiling and twisting in the moonlight, not as high as the tower but so wide that Rapunzel couldn't see how far it stretched.

Rapunzel moved toward the rose dune, but Jack gripped her elbow hard. She batted his hand away. "Stop grabbing me."

"Not that way," Jack hissed. "The fairies can't penetrate the flowers. We have to go underground to get in."

Rapunzel had a sudden, unsettling suspicion. Jack seemed awfully familiar with the place. "Have you been here before?" she asked him.

"Yeah."

She clenched her teeth. "So you *have* seen roses," she said. "Plenty of them."

"Course I have," said Jack. "Everyone has. I couldn't believe you believed me — you've got to be the most gullible person alive." He snickered, and Rapunzel went hot with anger. But then Jack dropped to his knees and pulled her down with him.

"Ow!" she said as her knees banged the dirt. "What was *that* for?"

The answer rose from the ground before them, a slim pillar of clay with a red marble top no bigger than a plate. In the middle of the plate was a little red fairy. Now that he stood still, Rapunzel could see that he had large moon-white wings and a shock of white hair. He wore a bit of silver leaf for his trousers and a sash of white silk around his chest, pinned at his hip with a silver ring. From this ring hung a small but heavy-looking leather pouch. The fairy bowed his head and touched his tiny fingertips to the center of his breast in salute.

"Beanstalker," he said. "You are welcome here. It is a rare mortal that we would bring through the fairywood, but you have earned your passage."

Jack bowed very low. "I brought her like you asked, Rune," he said. "I gave her all the help that was in my power."

Rapunzel reeled. She knew she'd been tricked, but this was worse than she had realized. The fairies had told Jack to bring her, and so he had left the rope on the railing on purpose, to give her a way to get down — and then he had taunted her and *made* her come.

"Did you even need a cure?" she demanded. "Or was that just another lie?"

Rune laughed, and the sound was chilling. "The cure for magic ills must include a drop of the magic that caused them," he said. "The dew was necessary — and effective. Eldest Glyph is conscious."

Rapunzel's heart plummeted. If the powerful fairy was awake, then she had failed Witch in every possible way. "No," she said loudly, as though by the force of her voice she could make it untrue. "She can't be cured, she can't be conscious — that fairy has to die!"

Jack gasped.

"Just as I expected," said Rune. "You are beyond unwelcome here, girl."

"If this is where you fairies live, then I don't want to be welcome here," said Rapunzel, who found that she was breathing fast. "I just wanted to get what Jack stole from me. But since you already used it and woke up your mate, now you'll try to kill Witch. Well, I hope you fail. I hope your mate dies, and I hope you never come back to my tower again, *ever*."

Jack shot her a warning look, but Rapunzel ignored him.

"Do you imagine that Eldest Glyph desired to visit your tower?" asked Rune.

"She came there, didn't she?"

"Yes."

"To hurt Witch? To kill her?" Rapunzel's voice was rising.

"Yes."

She clenched her fists. "And to steal my memory too," she said. "Don't deny it."

"If we *could* take your memory," said Rune, "now would be an excellent time to do it. You are here in anger. You want to hurt us. If we could make you forget your tower, and your witch, then why wouldn't we?"

Rapunzel hesitated. There was no denying the fairy's logic, and yet it made no sense. She looked to Jack for help, but his smirk told her that he was on the fairy's side.

"Because you're powerless!" Rapunzel exclaimed, finding an answer. "You can't do any magic. Your mate is the only one who has power — Witch told me so."

Rune beat his wings and rose up to meet Rapunzel at eye level. He dug one hand into the leather pouch at his hip and withdrew a palmful of red clay, which he began to ply with his fingers, rolling it long and thin before he crushed it between his hands.

"What are you . . . ," Rapunzel began, but the words dried up in her mouth. Her lungs grew tight, and her body felt as though it was deflating. The few remaining trees shot up to an alarming height, and then her vision turned soft and black. Air rushed past her face as though she were careening again down the side of the tower. She tried to scream, but there was only a bizarre zinging sensation throughout her body, followed by a pop in her ears.

When her lungs and vision were restored, Rapunzel looked down to make sure her body was whole. She gasped when she saw that she was kneeling on a giant green leaf, even bigger than her bed in the tower.

Rune descended before her, and Rapunzel swayed in terror at the size of him. He was as big as she was, and his wings were half the size of the massive leaf. Either Rune had grown enormous, or he had made Rapunzel the same size as a fairy.

He landed in front of her, and his features came into sharp focus for the first time. Rapunzel saw that he looked human, except that his skin was red and marked all over with strange patterns that looked like they were drawn on with black ink.

"Did you shrink me?" she whispered.

"How could I?" said Rune, smiling as he rolled the ball of red clay in his fingers. "I am powerless. Or perhaps your witch is a liar. Will you believe her words, or your own senses?"

Rapunzel barely heard him. Witch thought there was only one powerful fairy to worry about, but Rapunzel saw the truth now. There were two.

She had to get home. She had to warn Witch.

"Rapunzel!"

She turned toward Jack's voice and saw that he too was now fairy-size, some distance away. The sight of him filled Rapunzel with relief. At least he was familiar.

"It feels strange the first time," Jack said, shoving his hair out of his eyes as he jogged toward her. "But you get used to it." He gave Rapunzel's shoulder a pat, as though he had never tricked her, and he laughed. "You look like you swallowed a bug," he said. "Don't worry, you won't stay this size forever."

Incredulous, Rapunzel turned her eyes back to Rune.

"It is time for you to enter the Red Glade," he said, watching her closely. "To face the damage you have done."

Rapunzel pushed herself to her feet. "I'm not going anywhere with you," she said. She meant to say it furiously, but the words came out small and afraid. She didn't want to go and meet a thousand fairies. She couldn't steal back the cure; the powerful fairy was already awake. She had failed Witch, and she could not fix her mistake. Not by herself.

The only thing to do was go home.

As Rapunzel opened her mouth to call for Witch, a shock of pain erupted in her lungs and traveled up into her brain, sharp and hot, making her ears ring. She fell to her knees on the giant green leaf, clutching her throat with one hand and her forehead with the other.

"If you call the witch," Rune said quietly, "I will kill you and feel no remorse. I would have killed you already, but I was sworn to bring you here alive — unless you summon her." One of his hands was clenched, and as he squeezed his fingers tighter, clay oozed from between them. Rapunzel's head throbbed. She opened her mouth again to cry for Witch, but her voice was gone. It appeared that Rune now held it in his fist.

Jack apparently heard none of this. "Come on," he called, waving to her from the bottom of the clay pillar on which Rune had risen from the ground.

"Go," said Rune.

Rapunzel had no choice. She made her way over the massive leaves, crawling across sticks and rocks that were half her height. When she reached Jack, the fairy platform descended to ground level, and they both stepped onto it. Rapunzel looked over her shoulder to find Rune standing on the platform behind her. She glared at him, since it was all she could do.

"Prepare yourself, prisoner child," Rune said.

Then the platform descended, and the clay swallowed them.

Chapter Five

No sooner had the clay closed overhead than it opened before them into a long, narrow passageway, lit by small cages of twined copper threads that glowed with strange light. Rune unclenched his fist and rolled the clay into a ball, allowing Rapunzel her voice back.

"You won't be able to summon the witch in here," he said. "We are not conquered — yet."

He flew forward, and Rapunzel and Jack followed behind, each taking as much hair as they could carry. Rapunzel glanced around the passageway, hugging her braid for comfort. Here were walls and ceilings again, but these were made of clay. Her head began to throb. Her stomach hurt.

"I feel sick," she whispered. She had only been sick a few times in her life, but she remembered the occasions clearly. They were the few unpleasant memories she had.

"It must be the magic," said Jack. "Because fairy and witch stuff don't mix."

"But I'm not magic."

Jack shrugged. "You've been around witch magic for a long time," he said. "You're probably full of it."

Rapunzel hoped it was true. Maybe if she had enough of Witch's magic with her, she could summon her. She watched Rune fly ahead until she thought he was out of earshot. "Witch," she whispered. "Witch, please help me. Witch, please come for me."

She held her breath in hope. In her storybooks, whenever she called for Witch, the air whirled, the ground shook, and Witch appeared out of nowhere to sweep her away from danger and take her safely home.

One minute passed. Then two. Rapunzel swallowed hard to keep the sick feeling down.

"I don't want to go any farther," she said, hovering behind Jack as they came to the very end of the passage. "They'll hurt me. Rune wants to kill me."

"No, he doesn't."

"Yes, he does. You didn't hear him. He said he would kill me, and he took my voice, and he hurt me." Rapunzel edged backward down the tunnel. "Help me go home," she said, wincing against a wave of nausea. "Please, Jack, I don't want to stay. I'm afraid."

Jack glanced at her. "I promised them I'd help," he said. "I'm sorry."

He sounded like he almost was.

And then he was thrust aside by several pairs of grasping red hands that reached into the passageway from the outside. The hands seized Rapunzel by her braid and yanked her forward into their grasp. She sobbed and thrashed as they dragged her past Jack and into the dim light.

"LET ME GO!" she screamed. "WITCH, WITCH, HELP ME —"

"Silence!" shouted one fairy voice.

"Kill her!" shouted another. "End it here!"

"You know that we cannot." Rune did not sound happy about it. He stood before Rapunzel, lifted one hand, and made a sharp, twisting gesture. Rapunzel's braid whipped instantly around her in tight coils, gagging her and securing her arms to her sides. Her hair tasted of filth, and she choked, her eyes watering as she looked frantically around to understand where she was. Red grass as tall as trees surrounded her, and the sky was dark overhead. More copper-caged lights illuminated the glade, hovering among the giant grasses and casting weird shadows over the fairies who surrounded her. They were all red, like Rune, some with lighter and some with darker skin, some with pink wings and hair, others with orange or brown. If their faces had not been hideous with hatred, they might even have been beautiful.

"Bring her to the Centercourt," said Rune.

Jack followed Rune with one look behind him at Rapunzel. He wasn't smirking now. In fact, he looked anxious, which made her more afraid — and then he was gone, hidden by the tall grass ahead. The end of Rapunzel's braid hung from her like a leash, and the other fairies dragged her forward to follow Rune. She tripped, then tried to rise, but it was impossible without her hands to help her; she fell into the dirt. Tears streamed down her cheeks, but the fairies yanked her to her feet and flew onward, bringing her stumbling behind them.

In minutes, they had brought her to a wide-open space around which a thousand fairies stood muttering and watching her. Rapunzel nearly fainted at the sight of so many creatures together at once. Rune's minions dragged her to a stake in the center of the circle, and they lashed her to it with the remainder of her hair. Then they backed away into the masses, and Rapunzel stood trapped, unable even to sob, her heart beating as rapidly as Rune's wings, her tears coursing without pause. It was worse than anything that had ever happened in her books, and she had no hope of being saved by Witch.

Rapunzel searched for Jack, and found him standing just behind Rune at the head of one of the huddled fairy groups. He looked frightened.

"Destroy her!" cried one fairy voice. "While we have the chance!" said another. "We must save ourselves!" "She is the source of ruin!" The voices chimed together until it seemed the entire glade clamored for Rapunzel to be killed on the spot.

"No!" said Jack, but no one listened.

"No!" Rapunzel tried to shout, but the word stuck in her braid.

"No," said a weak voice that cut through the rest of the noise. A hush fell over the fairies. "Let me see her."

Rapunzel craned her neck to see who was speaking.

The fairies parted in front of her, revealing a red marble dais on which a fairy wearing a pale blue sheath rested in what appeared to be a large cupped hand made of soft red clay. Her hair was the color of a cloudless sky, and so was one of her wings. The other wing hung, dull gray and broken, down to the ground beside the hand.

This fairy tried to sit forward, but was too weak. She stretched one hand toward Rune, who flew to her and clasped it at once. With his other hand, he supported her back and helped her to sit up. The fairy looked at Rapunzel with blue eyes that spoke of many things Rapunzel could not fathom. Rapunzel stared at her, breathing hard against her gag.

"Poor prisoner child," said the fairy. "Rune, untie her."

"Eldest Glyph, if I let her go, and she runs, or strikes out —"

"Untie her," Glyph repeated. "She has nowhere to run, and she cannot harm us here. She does not even know her crime. To bind her like this is senseless and cruel."

"Compassion blinds you," said Rune. "She wants you dead. This is a matter of survival."

Glyph ran her fingertips over the soft clay on which she sat, and then she made a gesture in the air as though moving aside an invisible curtain. Rapunzel's braid tumbled to the ground. She dropped to her knees in the midst of all her hair.

When she looked up again, Glyph had fallen back against the clay, her breath coming in heavy gasps, her eyebrows drawn together. Rune turned on Rapunzel. "She shows you kindness," he spat, "after you whipped and broke her and would have let her die. You poisoned her!"

"I didn't!" cried Rapunzel. "I've never seen her before!"

"Yes, you have." Jack's voice was quiet. "You just don't remember it."

"Poor prisoner child," Glyph said again. She opened her eyes and beckoned to Rapunzel with a weak hand. "Will you come to me?"

Rapunzel wasn't given a choice. The fairies pressed in on her, forcing her toward the dais and up its steps, then shoved her to her knees beside Glyph. The dais smelled of dying roses, and Rapunzel could see why: On a small table next to the fairy, the little glass vial of stolen dew lay empty on her pink handkerchief. Beside it, a large clay bowl smoked, giving off a pungently sweet scent that was not altogether pleasant.

"Give the child space," Glyph said, and the fairies eased off at once, though with a murmur of dissent. Glyph placed her red hand on the crown of Rapunzel's head, then snatched her fingers away as though they'd been burned.

"Witch magic," she whispered, her eyes wide. She flexed her hand and paused. "Tell me, prisoner child, what do you think is happening here tonight?"

"I *know* what's happening," Rapunzel retorted. "You're the powerful fairy who came to my tower." She wiped spit and tears from her mouth. "But you got sick from Witch's magic, and you needed dew from my roses to make the cure, so Jack tricked me to get it, and Rune woke you up. And now you'll kill Witch if you can."

"She knows this much," said Glyph in surprise. The fairies murmured low among themselves.

"Of course I know!" Being free of her bonds, Rapunzel was less frightened, which left her room for anger. "I know you came to my tower — I know everything!"

"You know only what Envearia wants you to know," said Rune.

"Who is Envearia?" said Rapunzel.

"You see?" said Rune to Glyph. "Do not confuse her little knowledge with actual understanding. She doesn't even know the witch's name."

Rapunzel started. "It's just Witch," she said.

"She calls her Witch as a child says Mother," said Rune in disgust.

"Mother?" Rapunzel repeated.

"Where *is* her mother?" asked Jack. "Does she have one? I mean, of course she *had* one, but did the witch kill her parents, or kidnap Rapunzel, or —"

"Kidnap," scoffed Rune. "No. It was a bargain. Envearia has played it very well. She has learned from her mistakes, and now she gains power year to year, and crushes us all in her fist as her magic grows."

"You frighten her," said Glyph, watching Rapunzel's face. "This is too much at once."

"What is?" Rapunzel cried, overwhelmed. "Why are you calling her Envearia? What is a mother?"

"Her innocence is evident in every word she speaks," said Glyph. "Treating her with violence will teach her that *we* are the ones to be feared. We will not be safe —"

"Until this girl is destroyed and Envearia is forced to flee and start again," said Rune. "And you know it. As for her *innocence*" — he said the word as though it tasted foul in his mouth — "it is high time to shatter it. We must kill her, Glyph."

Rapunzel shrank from the ugliness in his look.

"No," said Glyph, breathing so rapidly that even her dead wing seemed to beat a little. "I do not give my consent to kill her. While I live, the child lives."

Rune looked at Glyph with eyes full of an emotion that Rapunzel could not name. It was hard and soft at once. He touched Glyph's cheek, and then the withered edge of her dull gray wing. "You live."

"I live," said Glyph. "For now."

Rune tensed and pointed to Rapunzel. "For now," he repeated. "But as long as this child lives for Envearia, nothing more can be done to help you. I refuse to trade your life for a life that has brought such suffering upon us!"

At his words, the fairies raised their voices together in passionate agreement.

"The child is not to blame for our suffering, or even for mine," said Glyph. "She does not know what she is. My injury was an accident. She doesn't even remember my visit — just touching her forehead, I felt so much witch magic that I would guess she has forgotten half the last year of her life."

Rapunzel jerked.

"LIAR!" she shouted. "I remember the whole year, it's just one day that I forgot!" She had put Witch in more danger than ever, coming here. For surely Witch would figure out where she was, and she would come to save her, and then they would both be killed.

"I'm hurting her," she mumbled, and her tears began to rise as she thought of the ugly wrinkles on Witch's face, and the streaks of white in her hair, and how much worse it would all get now that she had left her tower. "I'm hurting her. If only I'd listened — I should have asked her to help me. She'll be so frightened — oh, Witch, Witch, I'm sorry. . . ."

Rapunzel wept.

"Poor thing," said Glyph kindly, but her kindness only reminded Rapunzel of Witch and made her cry harder.

"Listen," Glyph said to Rapunzel, "and hear me. Two days ago, I came to the witch's tower. While a prince called to you, I tried to climb your hair."

"Jack told me about that," Rapunzel managed, hiccuping in an effort to stem her sobs.

"Ah, but he doesn't know all of it," said Glyph. "Do you know what happened when I reached you?"

Rapunzel shook her head.

"I was smashed to the stones of your balcony as you collected your hair," said Glyph. "My wing snapped and died, as you see. You didn't know I was there, and you cannot be blamed for it. When you found me, you were alarmed — and kind." She raised her voice, and beads of sweat stood out on her red brow. "I hope you are all listening," she said, her words carrying across the silent Centercourt. "This child was gentle. She sought my comfort."

Glyph continued in a quieter voice, as though telling Rapunzel a bedtime story. "You took me in your hands and carried me inside. You were curious to meet another creature and anxious to do something to help, so you laid me in a clump of the witch's flowers and fed me dew from her roses. I was too weak to refuse, and I could not use my voice — the magic in the tower was too strong. You could not know that it would all be poison to me."

Rapunzel already felt sick to her stomach; now she felt as though sickness were spreading into her heart. She couldn't remember any of what Glyph was telling her. But somehow, she knew that the story was the truth. She *had* poisoned a fairy — she *had* whipped and broken her. Maybe not on purpose — but still.

She covered her face with her hands.

"She acts as though she cares," said Rune. "Yet she knows nothing of pain, while you . . ." He made a sound of despair. "You cannot fly! Why do you protect her? Why?"

"There are more important things than flight," said Glyph, clasping Rune's hand tightly in her own. "And while I . . ." She drew a deep breath. "While I do regret the loss . . ."

Her voice broke, and a terrible silence fell across the Centercourt. No one moved until Glyph spoke again.

"The sacrifice was not made in vain," she said. "The Beanstalker rescued me from the tower and brought me here. And now that you have come, prisoner child, I have what I wanted when I first climbed the tower."

"What *did* you want?" Rapunzel asked.

"To speak with you," said Glyph. "To tell you things and see if you can hear them, or if you are beyond all hope. I have faith that you are young enough yet to be salvaged, and my faith has grown since I met you, for though you are selfish and ignorant, your heart is good."

Rapunzel pushed herself to her knees. She wiped her face on the sleeve of her robe and hiccuped. She didn't know what it meant to be salvaged, but it didn't sound very nice.

"Why do you all call me prisoner child?"

"Because that is what you have always been," said Glyph. "A prisoner in a tower."

"I'm not a prisoner," Rapunzel said. "I love my tower."

"Love is a slippery word. Are you sure you understand it?"

Rapunzel nodded. "Witch loves me," she said, "and I love her. I only came down here to help her — but I failed."

"You have failed no one."

"Yes, I have," said Rapunzel. "You're alive. I wish I hadn't shown you compassion. I wouldn't have helped you if I'd known you want to kill Witch. I would have wanted you to die."

Jack sucked in a sharp breath, along with the rest of the fairies in the Centercourt.

"Do you hear?" said Rune. "Do you see?"

"I see a creature more truthful than most I have met," said Glyph, her clear eyes on Rapunzel. "Prisoner child, I know you wish to return to your tower. I cannot allow it. But you are tired in body and mind, and I wish to give you some comfort. Tell me what you need."

Rapunzel gazed at Glyph. Everything was dreadful, and it was no good attempting to sort out the truth from the lies; she could hardly remember half of what had been said in the first place. What did she need? "I'm all dirty," she said plaintively. "And I've felt sick ever since I shrank."

"Do you want sympathy?" asked Rune at once. "You have been ill for an hour. Imagine your pain lasting near a decade. While Envearia's magic crushes in around us, not one of us has a single day of ease. We are poisoned, weakened, unable to —"

"Rune." Something in Glyph's tone silenced him. "I cannot take our guests to the lake to bathe," she said. "I am not well enough. One of you, volunteer."

A plump, pretty fairy with short pink braids burst from the middle of the crowd, scattering several fairies in her wake. "I will, Eldest Glyph," she said, but she wasn't looking at Rapunzel at all. She fluttered straight up to Jack and hovered nose to nose with him. "Come with *me*," she said, and flashed him a dazzling, red-lipped smile. Jack looked surprised, but not displeased. He even smiled back a little.

"Go with Trompe," said Glyph. "And when you have bathed, eat and rest. It is daybreak now, but both of you must sleep."

Daybreak. Rapunzel realized it must be true; the light was dim, but a few pale morning rays filtered into the glade, dappling the Centercourt and the fairies' faces. It was nothing like the glorious sunrises she had known in her tower; down here, the world remained in shadow.

"How long will you allow her among us — free, unchained?" Rune demanded in a low voice, leaning toward Glyph so that the rest of the thronging fairies could not hear him. "When will you decide what should be done with her?"

What should be *done* with her. Rapunzel shuddered at the coldness of this statement. In her books, the punishments devised for her by ground people were always cruel.

"Tonight, I will decide what must be done," said Glyph. "Tomorrow, I will share my decision."

Rune looked uneasy. So did Jack. He cleared his throat. "It's, uh, really nice of you to let me stay and everything," he said to Glyph. "But I've got to head north. I'm running out of time. I don't know if Rune told you about, ah, our deal?"

"I know what you seek."

"Oh." Jack shifted his weight. "So since I've done what he asked me to do . . ."

"You may yet be needed," said Glyph. "I will tell you more once you have slept."

Jack didn't seem to know what to say to this.

"Until then," said Glyph to Rapunzel, "I hope that you will be at home among us."

"I won't," said Rapunzel. "But . . ." She hesitated, then decided a little politeness was forgivable. "Thank you," she said, "for not killing me."

Glyph's good wing shimmered.

Chapter Six

"T O the lake," said Trompe. She grabbed Jack's hand and zoomed into the sky with him in tow. Jack dangled from Trompe's grip as they sped over the tall red grasses and out of sight.

Rapunzel followed only with her eyes. She remained trapped where she was as she worked out how to carry her hair, and finally had to resort to making giant loops of braid and hanging them over her neck and shoulders. The fairies tittered as she struggled. Hunched under the weight, she made her way slowly through the crowd in the direction Jack and Trompe had disappeared and into the grasses outside the Centercourt.

Hovering among the tall blades were more coppery cages of light, each one no bigger than her fist. She paused and looked around to be sure that the high grass concealed her from fairy eyes. When she was sure that no one was watching, she reached up to touch one of the lights. The copper cage was cool; still, the light gave off comfortable warmth. Rapunzel couldn't help thinking it was pretty.

So were the shining globes, windowed and lit from within, that hung suspended in the air overhead. Some of the globes were made of colored glass, others of glittering metal. A few dangled so low that their curving underbellies brushed the grass; others sat so high that they reflected in the sky.

Rapunzel blinked at the odd sight. Things couldn't reflect against the sky. Except it wasn't a real sky, she realized, squinting up at it. Far overhead curved a dome that appeared to be made of countless tiny bits of colored glass. They were set meticulously together, which was how the dome reflected the hanging globes. It had to be glass; the whole sky was somewhat transparent.

When Rapunzel looked closely, she could make out the shadowy outlines of the twisting vines and roses that covered the dome outside. Morning light pushed weakly through the flowers, but mostly they were dense enough to block out the sun. In a few places, Witch's roses had even cracked the glass sky. Vines with flowers snaked through the jagged holes, and Rapunzel caught her breath in longing. It looked so like her ceiling garden at home. In fact, the more she looked, the more cracks in the glass she found, and the more roses she saw, the tendrils of their vines patterning the inside of the dome, their blooms darker red than any of those in Rapunzel's tower.

Of course, if they *were* Witch's roses, then it was Witch who was blocking out the fairies' sun. And if Witch's roses were magical, and her magic made the fairies ill, then Rapunzel supposed, with some reluctance, that it made sense for the fairies to be angry. Still, it was their fault. Witch wouldn't have needed to protect herself if the fairies hadn't wanted to kill her.

Tired of such thoughts, Rapunzel pushed her way out of the grasses and was glad to see that she had walked in the right direction. Jack stood several paces ahead with Trompe, looking down a sloping hill that led to a shining mass of water. Rapunzel stopped to gaze at its rippling surface. It must have been a thousand times the size of her bathtub.

"You can bathe here, in the lake," said Trompe, her eyes on Jack. "Go ahead."

Jack dropped his knapsack on the ground and stripped off his patchy vest. He unlaced his boots and kicked them off. He grabbed the hem of his shirt to pull it over his head, but glanced from Trompe to Rapunzel and stopped. "Just a sec," he mumbled, and he hid himself from their view behind a wall of tall, red grasses. Rapunzel heard the sounds of a few soft thuds, followed by a loud splash.

"Hoo!" shouted Jack. "Feels good!"

Rapunzel believed it. She couldn't wait to be clean. She unwound her braid from her arms and neck and dropped it to the ground, then stripped off her robe and nightgown and stepped out of her slippers. The red clay ground was cool and spongy beneath her bare feet. She picked up the tail end of her hair and began the long process of unbraiding it. As her braid came apart, she found plenty to disgust her: rocks, sticks, and leaves were all tangled in her tresses.

"How ugly you are."

Rapunzel looked up from her braid to find Trompe staring at her.

"Ugly?" Rapunzel said. "You can't be speaking to *me*."

"Your skin is all white," said Trompe in distaste. "And no wings. And your hair."

"What *about* my hair?"

"It's silly," said Trompe, and she flew up to Rapunzel and gave her nose a hard, painful tweak. She laughed like a little bell and soared out over the lake.

Rapunzel was furious. The horrible little fairy hadn't even given her a chance to retort that her hair wasn't silly, and of *course* she didn't have wings. She stomped down to the water's edge and stepped into the lake. Cold water closed over her feet, and she screamed.

"What's wrong?" Jack called from the other side of the tall grass.

"It's freezing!" cried Rapunzel. She eased her legs into the water, inch by excruciating inch, and longed for her warm bath at home. When the water reached the tops of her legs, she stopped, afraid to go farther in and feel such a chill on her bare stomach. Instead, she busied herself dragging all her hair down the bank and into the lake, where she hoped it might get clean.

"It's easier if you jump in all at once," Jack called.

She glared at the grass wall that hid him. "No it isn't."

"Fine, don't believe me," came Jack's reply. "Suffer."

Rapunzel had no wish to suffer. She dropped into the water, and icy cold consumed her. She jumped up, sputtering, and shrieked when the air lashed her skin. She dropped down into the water again and shivered, hugging herself.

"Better, right?" called Jack.

Rapunzel looked up to see that he had already swum out to the middle of the lake. Curious, she took a step toward him. She floated in her bathtub all the time, and she had read about swimming. It couldn't be too hard. She took another step, but when she put her foot down again, she found nothing. The lake floor sloped steeply into deeper water.

Quickly, she tried to take a step back, but lost her balance. The water covered her mouth. When her toes touched mud again, she curled them into it to anchor herself and managed to bob above the surface. Her lungs burned, her nose stung, and she coughed until her throat was raw. Shaken and hacking, she inched up the muddy incline until she stood in the shallows.

Trompe hovered before her, just out of reach, laughing so hard she had to hold her belly in both hands.

Rapunzel looked away, exhausted. Her eyes itched with tears. She splashed water on her face to make them go away, but she could not wash off the heavy, awful feeling that came with them. She cleaned her skin and hair as best she could without soap or a cloth, and walked out of the lake, covered in gooseflesh. She pulled her nightgown, robe, and slippers back on. They were uncomfortable against her damp skin, but there was nothing she could do about it.

It took a long time to pile her loose, wet hair into the skirt of her nightgown. When she was done, Rapunzel pushed the grass wall apart. Trompe waited on the other side, fluttering very close to Jack. His shirt was untucked, his knapsack and belt were slung over his arm, and his black hair was plastered to his head.

"Good swim, huh?" he asked, glancing at Rapunzel.

Rapunzel didn't answer. Her skirtful of hair was heavy and tangled, and it hurt her arms to lug it along as she trudged behind Jack and Trompe. They reached a stone globe that hovered alone overhead, and Trompe held up a little ball of clay. This she lowered slowly, and as she did, the globe came floating down. It flattened the grass as it came to rest on the clay, and Trompe dropped her hands, looking drained. Rapunzel noted the change in her with pleasure.

Jack climbed into the globe and Rapunzel followed. "Wow," said Jack, staring around. "This is amazing."

The furnishings were plain: a flat floor, two beds, and a tiny table set with a full meal and two plates. But the inner walls of the round room were painted to look like the fairy glade: The sky graced the rounded ceiling, the grasses and the lake surrounded them on the walls, and the floor beneath their feet looked like rich, red clay. The painting was so real that it seemed as if they were still outside.

"Beautiful," murmured Rapunzel in spite of herself.

"I painted it," said Trompe, who hovered in the doorway, smirking at Rapunzel for a moment. "Sleep well, Beanstalker," she said sweetly as she fluttered into the globe. "If Glyph wants you later on, I'll fetch you." She brushed the tip of her nose against Jack's, and color rose in his cheeks.

"Sounds good," he said. "See you then."

Trompe flitted out of the painted globe, closing the door with a flick of her wing as she went.

The silence that followed was a welcome one. Jack went about eating his meal as Rapunzel crawled onto one of the beds, which had a window beside it. The room was big enough for two, but her hair made a definite third. Since there was nowhere else to put it, and since she had no way of untangling it, she pushed the whole wet mass out the window and watched it drop into the red grasses outside. She sat uncomfortably against the curving wall, stuck her legs out on the bed, and shut her eyes.

"Owoodoin'?" asked Jack after several minutes. He had plunked down on the other bed and continued shoveling in the food the fairies had left for them. He swallowed. "How you doing?" he repeated. "You all right?"

"No thanks to you," Rapunzel said bitterly, opening her eyes. "You *brought* me here."

Jack wiped his mouth. "I had to," he said. "But I swear, I had no idea they'd be so rough on you. Aren't you eating anything?"

Rapunzel pushed herself to the edge of the bed and looked at the fairy food that sat on the little bedside table between them. Her stomach rumbled. Tentatively, she sniffed a spoonful of what looked like mealy mush. It smelled strange, but not bad, and Rapunzel was too hungry to be suspicious of it for long. She dug ravenously into it, shoving as much into her mouth as she could fit.

Moments later, her stomach lurched, and she dropped to her knees between the beds. Her mouth opened, her whole body heaved, and the food she had eaten flooded onto the floor at Jack's feet, spattering across his boots. He cried out and jumped up.

"You can't eat fairy stuff," he said. "Great." He lifted one boot and then the other, his lip curling. "These'll stink for days," he complained. "You couldn't aim the other way?"

Rapunzel remained limp on the floor, unable to answer. She had never lost a meal before. Tears slid from her eyes for what felt like the thousandth time that day.

"Don't cry," said Jack. "You're sick, that's all."

Rapunzel's tears continued. "It's m-my b-birthday" was all she said. It was all she could think of. She should have been at home, with Witch, eating a birthday feast and opening her presents. Instead she was wet with sick, surrounded by fairies who hated her.

"It's your birthday?" Jack sounded surprised. "Why didn't you say so?"

"I th-thought I'd be h-home by now."

Jack said nothing. He grabbed her under the armpits, helped her to her feet, and sat her on the bed.

"I'll get that," he said, glancing at the sick. "Lie down."

Rapunzel obeyed. The bed was harder than she was used to, and there was no canopy overhead except Trompe's painting. She turned on her side and closed her eyes.

She heard the little door of the globe open and shut a couple of times. Jack muttered to himself while he cleaned up the floor, and then everything was silent. Rapunzel had drifted halfway into sleep by the time the door opened once more. Jack tapped her on the shoulder and she jumped, unready for the touch.

"Want your present?" Jack asked.

Rapunzel rolled onto her back and looked up at him. "Present?" she said uncertainly. "But you didn't even know it was my birthday."

Jack held out Rapunzel's pink handkerchief, which he'd tied into a parcel.

"You're giving me something that's already mine?" She sighed a little. "Well, thank you," she said. "I suppose."

"No, stupid," said Jack. "Open it." He thrust the parcel closer, and it quivered and shook. There was something inside the handkerchief — something dark and jumpy.

"I don't want to open that!"

"I'll do it." Jack untied the bundle, and Rapunzel pushed herself up onto her elbows. When the handkerchief was open, she stared at the thing in Jack's hand.

In the middle of his palm sat a squat, moist, green little creature with darker green splotches on its skin. On each of its two front feet were four funny, gelatinous little toes with knobby ends; its knees stuck out to its sides; the line of its mouth was long and uncertain; its chin was a round yellow gut; and its golden eyes were wide and round and shiny, with bright black pupils.

"Ribbit," it said.

Rapunzel drew back.

"It won't hurt you," said Jack, offering the little creature to Rapunzel once more.

The creature gave a hop and looked imploringly at Rapunzel. It hopped again and again, pausing only to look up at her with big, mooning eyes.

"What does it want me to do?" asked Rapunzel in a whisper. She didn't want to startle it. "It looks like it wants me to do something."

"Sure. Pet him."

"It'll probably bite me, or poison me, or —"

"If it did those things, would I be holding it?"

Rapunzel bit her lip. With one finger, she reached out to touch the creature, which sat still and let her prod it. "Ooh," she squealed, touching it again. "It's clammy." And yet it didn't bother her. The texture was interesting, different from anything she'd ever felt. "Where did you get it?"

"Outside," said Jack. "It jumped up on my leg and tried to get in my pocket. Never seen a frog do that before."

"Frog?"

"That's what it's called," Jack said. "You like it?"

"Frog," Rapunzel repeated. Even the word was squat and moist and green. "Frog frog."

"Ribbit," said Frog.

"Ribbit," said Rapunzel, and she giggled.

Jack laughed too. "Take him," he said. "I think he likes you."

"Does he?" Rapunzel sat up straighter. It would be a nice change if someone around here liked her. "All right, then . . . Come here, Frog." She cupped her palms together and, to her delight, Frog hopped into her hands. His gelatinous toes curled against her skin. His moist belly beat against her fingers.

"Do you like me?" Rapunzel asked Frog. "Or are you with the fairies?"

Frog's eyes bulged. He hopped a frantic pattern in her palm. Rapunzel wasn't sure what it meant. "If you like me, hop right now," she said.

Frog hopped in place, his eyes wide above the uncertain line of his mouth. Behind Rapunzel, Jack was laughing.

"You can't tell anything from that," he said. "Frogs hop all the time. You know he likes you because he isn't hopping *away*."

But Rapunzel had a feeling that Frog understood her, and it was good to have an ally, however small. She held Frog near her mouth and whispered, "I like you too."

Frog's yellow gut-chin expanded.

"He must be tiny if he's a normal-size frog to us," said Jack. "You should name him."

"His name is Frog. There's no other right word."

"You used to think the only right word for *me* was prince."

Rapunzel looked up at Jack and laughed before she could help it. It seemed ages ago that she had called Jack "Prince." "Then I'll call him Prince Frog," she said.

"You would," said Jack.

With tender hands, Rapunzel settled Prince Frog onto a corner of her pillow. She rested her head beside him. Wakefulness gave way to a heavy, drowsy sensation in all her limbs, and if she hadn't felt queasy, she would have been quite comfortable. She looked across at Jack.

"The world feels like it's spinning," she said.

Prince Frog gave a sympathetic croak and hopped onto her forehead. His cool, damp weight gave Rapunzel immediate, if not complete, relief.

"Thank you," she sighed, and closed her eyes. She heard Jack climb into his bed, followed by the sound of his long, loud yawn.

"Happy birthday," he said.

It was too late for that, she thought; it had been a miserable birthday. Still, with Jack being kind and Prince Frog sitting on her brow, things felt less dire than they had just an hour ago. Rapunzel wished that she were falling asleep at home, in her own bed. At home, she always said good night to the blue fire, and the starry canopy, and the silver harp. It was a happy ritual.

"Good night, Jack," she said instead. "Good night, Prince Frog."

"Night."

"Ribbit."

That was different. The things in her tower never answered back.

Then there was nothing left to think about. Or, if there was, it didn't matter. She was fast asleep.

CHAPTER SEVEN

*R*APUNZEL slumbered for a day and a night. She woke disturbed and disoriented, and when she rolled over in bed, her hand hit a wall, and her stomach bunched. There was no wall beside her bed — or there shouldn't have been. Not if she was at home.

She opened her eyes, and Trompe's painted ceiling came into focus. Rapunzel moaned softly. Never had she woken in an unfamiliar place. She sat up and flattened her back as much as possible against the curving wall, nervous that Rune or Trompe might have crept in while she slept, but there were no fairies present. There was only Jack, snoring in the other bed, and the little green lump of Prince Frog asleep in a puddle of water on the bedside table, where a goblet had been knocked over.

And her nightgown was clean. Rapunzel gazed down at her white lace cuffs in surprise. Her robe was clean too, and had been folded and hung over the end of the bed. Rapunzel wondered how the fairies had managed it and why they had done something kind for her. Perhaps they had cleaned her braid too. She turned to the window through which she had dumped the wet mass of her hair — and she froze.

Her hair was gone.

Rapunzel stared at the windowsill where her braid should have been and waited for it to appear. Her hair could not be gone. It *could not.*

"Jack!" she shouted.

Jack made an unintelligible noise but remained otherwise motionless. Prince Frog, however, woke with a start and sprang across the bed and onto the windowsill. Rapunzel jumped up and stubbed her toes on something cold and hard. She shrieked, and Jack opened one bleary eye.

"My hair!" screamed Rapunzel. "It's gone, it's gone, the fairies took it!"

Jack rubbed his eyes. "Good," he said, and slumped into his pillow again.

Rapunzel grabbed his arm and shook him as hard as she could. "Good?" she cried. *"Good?"*

"I'M SLEEPING!" Jack bellowed. He flung his pillow at her, missed, and flopped back onto his bed with a groan.

Rapunzel grabbed her head with both hands. The hair on her scalp had been smoothed back and bound at the nape of her neck. Frantic, she reached behind her neck to find the rest of it, and to her immense relief, she grabbed a thick cord of braid, which hung between her shoulder blades. She reached behind her waist and felt the plait continue.

But that was only a small portion of her hair. Fearing the worst, Rapunzel looked at her feet. Propped against the bed was the thing she'd stubbed her toes on: a circular contraption somewhat smaller than her window wheel at home. It was made of shining bronze, with two thick fabric straps on its back. Coiled around the spool on its front was what appeared to be the rest of her braid — all of which was still attached to her head.

"My *hair*," cried Rapunzel, and she dropped to her knees beside the circular object and wrapped her arms around it. She buried her face in the coiled braid.

"Insane," Jack muttered. "You got tied up with it, and you still don't want to cut it off?"

"I want to *see* all of it!"

No sooner had Rapunzel said this than the fairies' wheel whirred and the end of her braid shot off the spool, straight into her hands. Rapunzel tugged to unwind it further, and as she piled it into her lap, she relaxed. It was still there. Moreover, it was clean.

"All right," she said, breathing a sigh of relief. "Wind back up, please."

The fairies' wheel spun again, and the braid flew out of her hands. In seconds, the entire thing was wound. Rapunzel gave the wheel a grateful pat.

Jack glanced at the wheel first and then at Rapunzel. "How did you know it would do that?"

"Witch makes things like this for me," she said. "I wonder why fairy and witch magic won't mix. They aren't very different." She lugged the fairies' hair wheel into her arms and was happy to find it lighter than she expected. The braid was still heavy, but the bronze wheel itself didn't seem to weigh very much.

Jack watched her, looking pensive. "Eldest Glyph's waiting for us," he said. "She sent for me last night while you were sleeping, and she . . . talked to me. I'm supposed to bring you to her when you wake up."

Rapunzel hugged her hair wheel. "What did she tell you?" she asked in a small voice.

Jack shook his head. "She's letting you go," he said. But something in his voice suggested that this was not quite the truth.

"What's wrong?" Rapunzel demanded. "Is she going to make me stay tiny, like a fairy?"

"No, she's making us both big again," said Jack.

Rapunzel's heart leapt — once she was big again, she could get home to Witch without being eaten or crushed. Or so she hoped. She pulled on her robe and tied it shut, then grabbed the braid wheel by the straps and hefted it into her arms. "All right," she said. "I'm ready."

"No you're not," said Jack. "The wheel goes on your back, see? Stick your arms through those straps."

Feeling silly for not having realized their use, Rapunzel worked her arms into the straps. They were wide and padded against her shoulders, and the braid wheel rested comfortably against her back, as though it had been designed to fit her shape. She set Prince Frog upon her shoulder and followed Jack out of their sleeping globe.

Outside, the fairy glade looked different. Fewer roses pushed through the dome today, and sunlight poured through several of the cracks.

"It doesn't make sense," Rapunzel said, squinting up at one of the roses.

Jack glanced at her. "What?"

"Why did you have to get dew from my rose? There are thousands of roses right here."

"They're not the same." Jack bent over to pluck something out of the dirt. It was leafy and dark, and he held it carefully by one large petal. "Take a look," he said as he laid it in her palm.

It was a rose, Rapunzel realized, but like no rose she knew. Needle-sharp thorns crusted the stem, leaving nowhere for fingers to hold it, and the oversize petals were tough, thick, and leathery. At the rose's heart was a small ring of what looked like sharp white teeth, which seemed to pulse as though it breathed. Thick, pungent sap leaked from the center of the ring, making the teeth glisten.

"Ever seen a rose like that?" asked Jack.

"No." Rapunzel tipped it into the dirt. "To think I thought they were Witch's."

"They are."

Rapunzel looked down in disbelief. If that horrid thing was Witch's rose, then it was ill. Could that mean Witch was also suffering? Her mind presented her with the awful image of Witch, arriving at the tower for Rapunzel's birthday feast, only to find her missing. How Witch must have felt and what she must have done, Rapunzel could not imagine.

They made their way to the Centercourt, where Glyph curled in her chair on the dais. Rune stood beside her, watching them with narrow eyes as they approached.

"Good morning," said Glyph, who was slack and sweating, looking sicker than she had yesterday. "How do you find your hair, prisoner child?"

"I did find it, thank you," said Rapunzel, looking uneasily at Rune. She shifted her shoulders and adjusted her new straps, feeling the weight of the hair wheel shift on her back as she did so.

"I hope the wheel is comfortable," Glyph said. "Do the straps fit?"

"Oh — yes." Rapunzel swallowed.

"We would have made your braid lighter, but Envearia's magic prevented it. If you wish to keep your hair, you will have to carry it. But the wheel should help, and it will last as long as you wish to journey."

"I don't wish to journey," said Rapunzel, surprised. "I wish to go home."

"No." Rune advanced on her in one swift step, and Rapunzel stepped back. "Not while I can prevent you. And I will watch your every step. I will not rest."

"Jack said you would let me go!" cried Rapunzel.

"You will go, but not back to Envearia," Rune declared. "If you call for her or set foot toward the tower, I will kill you."

"Enough." Glyph's voice was quiet.

Rune clenched his fists. "I believe that you are making a fatal mistake," he said to her. "I am opposed to this plan — fully opposed."

"I know."

"If she makes you regret this, it will be too late."

"I have faith."

Rune gazed on Glyph, his face full of emotions Rapunzel had no power to name. She had never seen anyone look that way before. She was shocked when Rune laid a tender kiss on Glyph's brow.

"Prepare the exit," Glyph murmured. "Ready yourself to follow her. If she will not learn, then I give you leave to do as you must."

Rune nodded. He flew into the grasses, out of sight.

Glyph fixed Rapunzel with a look that was drawn and resolute. "I have made my decision," she said. "If you obey me, Rune will not harm you. If not . . ."

She left her sentence unfinished, but Rapunzel understood. "I won't obey you if you want me to hurt Witch," she said.

"Do as I ask, and I will not lay a hand on your witch," said Glyph. "Nor will I strike out with magic against her. This I promise you."

Rapunzel crossed her arms. "You might have hurt her already," she said. "You could have attacked her while I was asleep. . . ." She stopped, arrested by her own awful idea.

"Envearia is alive and well."

"I don't believe you!"

"Even so, you must do as I bid you."

"Then you have to let me send her a message and tell her I'm not hurt!" Rapunzel said, imagining how sick and frightened Witch must already be. Just a little worry had caused her to get wrinkles and white hair — what would a lot of worry do? "I don't want her to think I'm dead."

"She knows you are well, prisoner child," said Glyph quietly. "She cannot help but know. Now listen, and I will tell you where to go."

"If I can't go to my tower, where should I go?"

"You must journey to the center of Tyme," said Glyph. "The Beanstalker will guide you. He has already agreed to help you in this task."

Jack said nothing. His jaw was tense.

"The center of Tyme?" said Rapunzel. "But that's easy. We're already in the center."

Jack glanced at her in disbelief. "We're south of almost everything," he said. "Don't you even know where you *live*?"

"Of course," said Rapunzel confidently; Witch had taught her this. "The Redlands is in the middle, and then there are the lands far, far away."

"Haven't you ever seen a *map*?"

"Enough," said Glyph, silencing Rapunzel before she could make a retort. "You will travel north to the First Wood to find the Woodmother. It will take you some weeks, I think, to reach the place where she dwells."

"Weeks?" repeated Rapunzel in dismay. "Where *is* the First Wood?"

"It cannot be fixed on a map," said Glyph. "I have given the Beanstalker what guidance I can. Most who seek the Woodmother never find her, but once you reach her realm, I believe she will sense you and . . . find you worthy."

"Worthy of what?"

Glyph's eyes shone. "You deserve to know who you are," she said. "You deserve to understand what Envearia is."

"What do you mean . . . what she is?"

"If I told you, you would not hear me," said Glyph. "She has made sure of that. No — you must journey. You must experience. Or you must die."

Glyph spoke the last so quietly and with such sadness in her soft blue gaze that Rapunzel grew cold. The fairy meant what she said.

"But what if I can't find the Woodmother?" Rapunzel demanded. "You said most people never do. Will Rune kill me if I don't?"

"I will send word to the Woodmother that you are coming," said Glyph. "She will seek you, I know it." She reached for Rapunzel's hands and took them in her weak red grip. "Look around you as you travel," she said. "Listen and be willing to hear. Because the Redlands itself is at stake, prisoner child, and when it is threatened, so is Tyme."

Rapunzel was so surprised that she forgot to pull her hands away. Glyph held on to them as she spoke to Jack. "Beanstalker," she said, "remember. The prisoner child will have many questions —

always tell her the truth. Do this and stay with her, and I will ask nothing further from you. I will give you the help you seek before your time runs out."

Jack was pale. But he nodded.

"Then make your way." Glyph released Rapunzel's hands and brought her fingertips to her chest in salute. Her arm trembled with the effort. She slumped back against the clay bed, and two fairies with red sashes slipped out of the tall grass behind her. They surveyed Rapunzel, then turned their backs on her with decided emphasis and tended to Glyph.

Jack and Rapunzel walked out of the Centercourt and into the tunnel down which they had first come. At the end of the tunnel, Rune waited, his eyes like silver fire in the dim light.

"What Glyph desires me to give you, you do not deserve," he said.

In his fingertips, he rolled a pebble-size ball of red clay, which he lifted to his mouth, puffing out his cheeks. His white wings flared and his red skin dulled with effort as he blew air into the little clay ball. It expanded as it filled with his breath, becoming a translucent globe, while the edges of his wings grew so bright that Rapunzel finally had to shut her eyes against the light.

When she opened them again, Rune was leaning against the clay wall, panting. In one hand, he cradled a bubble of glass no bigger than a large marble.

"A lifebreath," he rasped.

He thrust it toward Rapunzel, who took it. It was so light, she could barely feel it in her hand. The glass was whisper-thin; she feared it would dissolve between her fingertips. A wisp of white smoke twisted and funneled inside the bubble, a tiny, shining windstorm.

"The lifebreath will restore any injured mortal creature," said

Rune. "It can even rescue one from the brink of death. If you need it, break it near the victim's mouth. You cannot crush it by accident. But do not waste it thinking that I can give you another — we can make very few in our lifetimes, and this is my last."

"Thank you," said Jack, sounding awed.

"You, Beanstalker, are welcome," said Rune. "You have stood between us and ruin."

The platform lifted them out of the Red Glade and into the fairy-wood once more. Rapunzel and Jack stepped down onto the giant leaves that paved the dirt around them. Rune remained on the platform.

"Stand back," he commanded. He took clay from the pouch at his hip and began to roll it between his palms, making it longer and thinner.

A tingling sensation started in the tips of Rapunzel's toes. It rushed up her legs and she wobbled, unsteady on her feet. Soon her middle was tingling too, and then her arms, and finally her head. The world streaked around her like a tunnel of falling stars, and then came to a slow, rolling stop. Her vision dawned, and she blinked.

"I'm big!" she cried when she realized what had happened. "I'm myself again!"

Prince Frog had grown bigger as well, to about the size of her fist. He leapt from her shoulder to crush a spider on the ground, and croaked with evident delight at his change in size.

An instant later, Jack stood beside Rapunzel at his regular size and height. Below them on the platform, Rune fell to his knees. He raised one shaking hand to his forehead.

"Go north," he gasped, "and do not turn back. I will be watching every step. One movement toward the tower — one breath to call Envearia — and I will not forgive."

Thick mist swept in, obscuring the platform on which Rune knelt and blotting out the dome of roses that marked the fairies' glade. The mist twisted into funnels and burst. When it dissipated, the glade was gone. They were alone again in the strange silver woods.

Jack fished a circle of metal and glass out of one of his pockets. The arrow under the glass swung around in a circle, then stopped on the letter N.

"North," said Jack. He pointed along a path that disappeared among the trees, and Rapunzel stifled a sigh. She had no choice but to do what Glyph had told her: walk for weeks to find the Woodmother so that she could learn whatever it was she was supposed to know. At least now that she was out of the Red Glade, her queasiness was gone, and even though she knew that Rune was watching her, he was out of her sight. She could try to forget him.

She scooped up Prince Frog, who hopped onto her shoulder. "It's only for a few weeks," she said under her breath. "Then I'll be back, and Witch will be safe. We'll live happily ever after, just like in all my books." Thinking this way, her heart grew lighter, and so did her steps, until she was walking along at Jack's pace despite the weight of her hair.

"Now," she said, "where are we going?"

CHAPTER EIGHT

*T*HEY were headed north toward Yellow Country, Jack told her as they walked. It was a country famous for its farms and its food, and the capital, Cornucopia, was a big, merry marketplace where all the farmers and gourmets sold their goods. There were meat pie vendors and pig-roasting pits and toasted cheese sandwiches; there were fresh chunks of honeycomb and lemon custards and chocolate-dipped cheesecakes. Farmers sold apples and strawberries and tomatoes and pumpkins, everything was cooked with the freshest herbs and dished up with the most delightful chutneys, and it all smelled sensational.

Jack had to stop several times in his description of Cornucopia to define his words. Rapunzel had never heard of Yellow Country, or a marketplace, or pig-roasting pits. Jack was patient about her questions. In some cases, he didn't wait for her to ask but launched into long, unprompted explanations. He described the food in such detail that Rapunzel's appetite roared up for the first time since she had vomited — another word Jack was happy to teach her.

"I'm starving," she said.

"No you're not," said Jack. "You've never starved ten seconds in your life, I bet. Or did the witch sometimes forget to leave food up in your tower?" He looked at her with interest.

"Of course she didn't," Rapunzel scoffed. "Witch brings me whatever I want. I just ring my bell."

"Must be nice," said Jack.

"It's very nice," she said, ignoring the insincerity of his tone. She thought of Witch's wonderful cooking, and the sandwiches and soups and meats that would have been her fare at home, and her stomach rumbled. "I'm *hungry*," she said. "I haven't eaten in forever, and I vomited everything up."

Jack dug into his pocket and pulled out a toasty-brown acorn. He offered it to Rapunzel.

"I'm hungrier than that," she said.

Jack stopped walking, and Rapunzel almost tripped right into him. "You don't know what this is?" he demanded, shaking the acorn in her face.

"It's an acorn," said Rapunzel, stepping back to avoid getting smacked on the nose with it.

"It's Ubiquitous Instant Bread," said Jack. "Crack it on a stone."

"You-bick-wit-us?"

"Ubiquitous," said Jack again. "Don't tell me you've never seen one of these."

"Of course I have," said Rapunzel, and she snatched the acorn to study it. "You've pulled them out of your pockets before and turned them into ropes."

"Different ones turn into different things," said Jack. "You've never even heard of . . . Wow." He pushed his hair back and shook his head. "Everyone uses this stuff. Ubiquitous! It's everywhere! Come on, you've really never heard of it?"

Rapunzel shook her head.

"Well, go on," Jack said. "Crack it."

She crouched beside a stone and tapped the acorn against its surface.

"No," he said. "*Crack* it."

She tapped again, harder. Still, nothing happened.

"Just give it here," Jack said, sighing. "I'll —"

Rapunzel gave the acorn a mighty whack against the stone. It made a loud, satisfying crack, and she squealed as the acorn in her fingers exploded into a heavy, round, crusty loaf of warm and fragrant bread.

"Amazing!" she said.

"Ubiquitous," said Jack. "Split it with me."

Rapunzel tore the loaf in two and kept the bigger half.

"I should've given you some the other night, instead of letting you eat fairy stuff," said Jack, looking a bit sorry as he took his share. "I just didn't think of it."

Too hungry to care, Rapunzel followed him deeper into the woods, munching the bread until it was gone. She offered a handful of crusty crumbs to Prince Frog, who wasn't interested. She licked them off her hand.

"Still hungry," she said.

"We have to ration the supplies," said Jack. "It'll take almost a week to reach Cornucopia."

"Ration?"

"Just eat a little at a time."

Rapunzel didn't like this definition. She decided to ask another question instead. "Is it hard to learn to swim?"

"Why, can't you do it? Course you can't," Jack said. "Hmm. That could be a problem. We'll be crossing a river soon — rivers are like lakes, except they're really long, and the water moves fast," he explained before Rapunzel could tell him that she'd already read about rivers in her books. "There are bridges, but it's better if we don't have to use official crossing points."

"Why?"

"Because we don't have papers proving who we are or what our business is."

"Do you need papers to cross rivers?"

"Sometimes. It depends."

Rapunzel remembered the sensation of slipping underwater and being unable to breathe. Would she have to walk through the rivers? Would they be too deep for her? If the water moved fast, would it suck her in? She thought of the lifebreath Rune had given them and was glad that at least she had that much protection — though she hated to be grateful to Rune, who would have killed her already if Glyph hadn't stopped him.

Rapunzel wondered why Rune listened to Glyph, anyway. He could have ignored her if he'd wanted to. Glyph had been sick, after all, and with a broken wing too.

"What's the feeling I get when I see Glyph's wing?" she asked suddenly, troubled by the memory of the dull gray thing hanging limp and broken from Glyph's body.

"What feeling?" asked Jack. "Describe it."

"I feel . . ." Rapunzel searched for words. "Like it's all my fault," she finished, thinking of Witch's wrinkles and her streaks of white hair. Those had been all her fault too, and they'd probably only gotten worse.

"Bad feeling?" Jack asked, his eyes ahead on the path. "Heavy? Kind of sits right here?" He rested one of his fists under his rib cage and closed his other hand over the back of his neck.

"That's it!" Rapunzel said. She touched her stomach and neck in echo. "That's the feeling."

"That's guilt," said Jack. He dropped his hands and kept walking. "You've never felt that before?" He laughed, but the sound was short. "That's some tower."

"It's an awful feeling. I hope there's not a worse one."

"There's grief."

On Rapunzel's shoulder, Prince Frog concurred with a silent, sober hop.

"Grief?"

"It's mostly how you feel if someone you love dies. Or leaves."

"What does it feel like?"

"I can't tell you that."

"You have to," said Rapunzel, marching alongside him. "Glyph said you have to tell me the truth, no matter what I ask."

"And the truth is, I can't tell you," said Jack. He shrugged. "You either know how it feels or you don't."

They soon emerged from the silent silver fairywood and reentered the noisy forests of the Redlands, which Rapunzel had never seen by day — not from the ground, anyway. She was surprised to find that the dense woods weren't riddled with scuttling poisonous things at all. The delicate webs that had caught at her in the darkness were easy to avoid now; they shimmered by daylight, outlined in dew. Clusters of tiny yellow flowers bloomed in patches of sunlight. Birdsong filled the branches overhead. She looked up into the great, dark-green needles of the shockingly tall trees and decided that they were very pretty. It was lovely to see how the rays of sunlight split apart as they came through the treetops and filtered down in long, sparkling beams.

Jack brightened with every step northward, as though walking in the woods was the sort of thing that suited him exactly. Rapunzel could not feel the same way; the wheel that held her braid was beginning to press on her.

"Cheer up," said Jack, happening to glance at her when she was wincing. "It's not so bad. Everywhere's got to be interesting to you — you've spent your whole life in one room."

"I have a room *and* a balcony."

"Guess you've seen it all then," said Jack. "Come on, ask some more questions. Anything you want. There's plenty I can tell you, if you want to know."

Rapunzel considered. She *did* have questions.

"What's a mother?" she asked.

"Crop *rot*," said Jack in a low voice. "What a question. You really don't know?"

"I wouldn't ask if I knew!"

"All right, all right, it's just . . ." Jack shrugged. "A mother is . . . a woman," he said, scratching his head. "And a father is a man. They're parents. They have children. You're supposed to grow up with your parents, unless they die or something bad happens."

"Oh. So . . . Witch is my mother?"

Jack looked offended. "No!"

"Why not? I grew up with her."

"But she's not your real mother."

It was Rapunzel's turn to take offense. "Don't be stupid," she said. "Of course she's real."

"No, she's . . ." Jack seemed to be fighting for words. "Skies," he finally said. "This is harder to explain than I thought. See, your real parents are the ones who . . . who *had* you."

"*Had* me?"

"Yeah. Parents . . ." The lump in his throat bobbed. "They make children together."

"Make them how?" asked Rapunzel.

"I'm . . ." He turned his face away from her. "I'm not the right person to ask."

"But you know all about it, don't you?"

Jack's neck flushed pink. "Not *all* about it."

"Well, tell me what you know, then."

He said nothing.

"You have to," said Rapunzel. "Glyph said."

Finally Jack broke down and described, in a few short sentences, without making eye contact, how parents go about making children. His voice cracked, and when he was finished, he strode off ahead of her and put several paces' distance between them. Rapunzel was disgusted.

"So some other mother made me," she said when she caught up with him. She ignored his pained wince. "And then Witch found me in the swamps. So that other mother must have left me lying around, but Witch took care of me. Doesn't that make her my *real* mother, and the other mother a fake one?"

He didn't seem to know how to answer.

"Do all parents make their own children?" Rapunzel pressed. "Aren't there any parents who don't?"

"Some kids get adopted," he admitted. "Their parents can't take care of them for some reason, so other people do it instead."

"Are the people who adopt them still real parents?"

"Of course, if they take good care of them and love them and stuff."

"Then Witch adopted me, and she's my real mother! She loved me and took care of me. Nobody else did."

He was quiet, frowning.

"What about fairies?" Rapunzel demanded after a moment, still thinking about the strange things Jack had told her. "Do Glyph and Rune —"

"Oh, don't," said Jack. "Just don't."

"Do you get to pick who you make children with?"

He gawked at her. "Of course you do. What else?"

"Well, I certainly wouldn't pick Rune. Glyph was the best of all those fairies, and he was the worst. What would she want him for?"

Jack shrugged. "He cares about her."

"*Cares* about her? He never agreed with her once!"

"You don't always agree with the people you care about."

"Witch always agrees with *me*. And Rune was so nasty."

"He's scared," said Jack. "People can be nasty when they're scared."

"*I* wouldn't be," said Rapunzel.

"Really?" He raised his voice and shrieked, "LIAR! BRUTE! EMISSARY!"

Rapunzel bit her lip.

"TROLL!" He went on, seeming to enjoy himself. He danced his hands about and tossed his hair. "IMP! UGLY LITTLE GNOME!"

"I shouldn't have called you ugly," said Rapunzel. "I'm sorry about that."

Jack only laughed. "My sister calls me worse," he said.

"You've said 'sister' before — is it some sort of beast?"

"Yeah," he said with a snicker, but he quickly shook his head. "You'll just get confused if I joke," he said. "Children who come from the same parents are called sisters and brothers. Girls are sisters, boys are brothers. They grow up together, usually. My sister and I have shared a room since she was born."

They had come to the top of a hill, and Jack stopped for a moment. Rapunzel took the opportunity to adjust the straps of her hair wheel, which were now cutting into her shoulders. She saw only another long stretch of tall woods ahead, overshadowed by dark gray clouds.

"If you have a sister, does that make you a brother?" she asked.

"Yeah." Jack gazed out at the clouds for a long moment, and then he set off down the long hill ahead. "So," he said as he strode along, "what other questions do you have?"

The lightness of his tone didn't match his expression, and Rapunzel looked suspiciously at him. "Something's wrong," she said. "What is it?"

"Nothing."

"Liar."

"Just ask another question, all right?" Jack's voice was tight. "Leave it alone."

"Then there *is* something wrong!"

But though she continued to press him, Jack would not share one word of whatever it was that troubled him — not even when Rapunzel reminded him that he *had* to tell her everything she asked, because Glyph had said so.

"This is my business," Jack said shortly. And then he sped up until he reached a pace Rapunzel could not hope to match. Balancing carefully to offset the weight on her back, she followed him down the long hillside and into the gloomy woods. The air was hot and moist, and her nightgown stuck to her damp skin. Jack stayed far enough ahead to prevent conversation, and all she could think about was the pain in her back and feet.

They walked another hour and came to a stream. Jack bent down to the brown water, cupped his hand, and drank. Rapunzel drank a very small sip, afraid it would taste as bad as it looked. When it tasted fine, if rather warm, she copied Jack and scooped water from the stream into her mouth. She drank for some time before she was finished, and wiped her mouth with her sleeve. She hadn't realized how thirsty she was.

Prince Frog leapt into the cloudy water, belly up and little feet splayed, looking very green and relaxed. He seemed to love to be wet, and Rapunzel decided to soak one of her pockets for him. She reached into the pockets of her robe to turn them out.

To her surprise, they weren't empty. In one, she found her bag of jacks; in the other, Rune's lifebreath. She held out the bubble to Jack.

"You have more pockets to put things in," she said.

Jack stowed the lifebreath in his vest as Rapunzel dipped her pocket into the stream. She picked up Prince Frog.

"There you are," she said, slipping him into her wet pocket.

Prince Frog croaked gratefully.

All day they walked, through thickets and across muddy streams, and with each step Rapunzel's braid grew heavier. Her pace became a slow walk. Her slow walk became a trudge. When the sun began to set, they reached a wide, grassy field. At the far end of the field, where the grass gave way to rocks, she saw a crack in the ground. The rocks ended and dropped off into nothing.

Rapunzel stayed away from the edge. From where she was, she couldn't tell how deep the crack went.

"Can we stop here for now?" she asked. "I can't walk anymore."

"Hang on a sec," said Jack with enthusiasm. He approached the crack in the ground and surveyed it, then cast a wide grin over his shoulder at Rapunzel. "Can you believe this?" he asked. "We're already at the Golden River! That fairywood saved us over two days of walking. Good thing too — now we'll have enough food to last till Cornucopia."

Rapunzel picked her way carefully to the edge of the crack and looked down into it.

"Yellow Country is right on the other side of the river," Jack said. "Might as well go across now and make camp under those willows. See them?"

Rapunzel didn't. Her eyes were fixed on the churning river.

"That's a lot of water," she said.

"It's okay," said Jack. "I've got this." And he pulled a dark brown acorn out of his pocket.

"Oh good." Rapunzel reached for it. "Is it time for dinner?"

"This one's not bread," he said. "It's a Ubiquitous Instant Bridge."

"Bridge?"

"It goes across things, so you can get from one side to the other." Jack swept his hand in a rainbow arc. "Like this. And you can walk on it."

Rapunzel looked at the little acorn in Jack's fingers. "*That's* going to be a whole bridge?"

"Sure is."

"But what if it disappears like your rope did? Won't we fall and die?"

"Nah, the fall wouldn't be that bad," said Jack, squinting at the water. "It can't be more than fifteen feet. Twenty, tops."

"But if I fall, I'll go underwater with no breath."

"Drown, you mean," said Jack, flipping the acorn into the air and catching it again. "Don't worry. Some people say Ubiquitous acorns crash all the time, but I say they're cracking them wrong. Ubiquitous always lasts for me."

"What do you mean, they crash? Into the ground?"

"No, crashing's when they stop working all of a sudden and they disappear," said Jack. "With some products it's hilarious — like the ball gowns and stuff."

Rapunzel stared at the furious river. "There must be another way."

"There is." Jack shrugged. "But I don't want to take it. There aren't many crossing points out of the Redlands — the Golden River runs along the entire northern border. It's a day's walk to the nearest bridge."

Rapunzel sagged at the idea of carrying her braid for an extra day.

"Then . . . I suppose we have to cross," she said. "Please don't let me drown."

"Just get ready to run, all right?"

Rapunzel took a deep breath and tensed. She fixed her eyes on the other side of the chasm and thought of nothing but getting across it.

"All right," she said. "Crack it."

But there came no cracking sound.

"Crack it," she repeated. "Go on, I'm ready."

Jack stared over her shoulder toward the woods, motionless.

"What's the matter?" asked Rapunzel.

"Stalker," Jack whispered.

Rapunzel whirled around to see what he meant, but all she saw were trees. Trees — and an odd shimmering patch of air that was moving along the border of the woods.

"Show yourself," said Jack, his voice quavering. "Unless I'm wrong," he added. "I hope I'm wrong. . . ."

The shimmering patch of air solidified.

A hundred paces away, at the edge of the woods, stood a monstrous beast, with golden fur and a snarling, fanged mouth. Even on all fours, it was taller than they. It clawed at the rocky dirt and bared its dripping fangs. It pinned bloodred eyes on Rapunzel and shut its jaws with a sickening snap.

Prince Frog quivered in Rapunzel's pocket. Then she realized it was she who was shaking.

The Stalker suddenly crouched, snarled, and leapt thirty paces toward them with frightening ease. Rapunzel's shaking worsened when she saw that its mouth was easily wider than her head.

"Do something," she said hoarsely.

"You're the one who lost my dagger," Jack hissed. "*You* do something."

"I . . ." Rapunzel licked her lips. "I can call for —"

She was about to say *Witch*. But a faint red light shimmered in the woods beyond the Stalker, and Rapunzel knew that Rune had heard her.

Jack must have seen it too. "Rune!" he called out. "Help!"

The Stalker sprang forward again, and Rapunzel stumbled back and shrieked in terror. Another pounce and the Stalker would be upon them.

"Rune!" shouted Jack again as Rapunzel glanced over her shoulder. If the Stalker leapt again, they would have nowhere left to run. One more step and they would fall straight over the precipice.

Into the *river*.

Rapunzel had a sudden, wild idea.

"Jack!" she whispered, angling her back to him. "Take my braid."

The wheel of hair whirred, and the end of her braid shot into Jack's hands.

"Hold on to it," Rapunzel said, barely moving her mouth. "When the Stalker jumps at us again, we'll run in opposite directions —"

"And trip it into the water!"

Jack had barely said the last word when the Stalker crouched down once more and sprang toward the two of them with a ravenous roar.

"Go!" shouted Jack, and they shot apart. Rapunzel gasped as the Stalker slammed into her hair and her braid went taut against her scalp. The Stalker's hind legs were caught on the braid; it stumbled, snarling — and then it lost its balance.

So did Rapunzel. The weight of the Stalker knocked her off one foot; she teetered backward toward the crack in the ground. She heard the Stalker roar in fury, saw it tip over the edge of the cliff and fall, flailing and spitting, into the chasm.

And then she screamed as she too fell from the precipice and dropped like a stone toward the river.

Rapunzel hit the water with a smack that knocked the breath out of her. Its roar filled her ears as the river pulled her under and carried her away. She opened her eyes and scrambled for something to hold, but the water was dark and empty; there was only a faint gleam above her. She kicked and lurched, beating her way toward the light, but every thrash of her arms drove her deeper into the river. Her lungs tightened; her chest pounded. Her mind went red.

She would die like this, she thought. She could call for Witch now — Rune's threats meant nothing if she was only going to die here anyway. She opened her mouth, but it was too late; she could not get air. Her brain softened into darkness.

The sensation of every hair in her scalp being yanked at once brought her back to her senses for one horrible second — everything was splitting agony. And then there was another wrenching yank, and Rapunzel's head cleared the surface of the water. She sucked in the most fantastic breath that she had ever breathed.

"Rapunzel!" shouted Jack from high above as he pulled her by her braid through the rushing water.

Weak with pain and fear, Rapunzel could only breathe and tremble. That was enough.

"Grab your braid! Come on, you've got to climb it — I tied the end to a tree, I've got you!"

When Rapunzel was close enough to the wall, she took her braid in shaking hands and leaned her forehead against it. Jack had said the chasm was fifteen or twenty feet deep — she could never climb so high. She lolled against the stone valley wall, the water pulling at her as it rushed past.

"Try!" Jack shouted. "Come on, Rapunzel — brace your feet on the wall."

"I can't," Rapunzel whispered to her wet braid. She gave a tiny sob. "I can't."

"Ribbit," said Prince Frog from her shoulder.

"Oh," she choked. "Prince Frog — you didn't drown."

Prince Frog gazed at her as if to say that frogs did not drown very often, and nudged her jaw with his clammy head. "Ribbit," he insisted.

For him, perhaps she could. Rapunzel braced her feet on the stones and, for the first time, looked up.

Jack hung partway over the precipice, the braid clasped in his hands. His face was white against the black of his hair. "RAPUNZEL!" he screamed. "CLIMB!"

Startled into action, Rapunzel reached up, gripped her braid, and hauled herself a foot out of the water.

A furious roar erupted behind her. She looked back over her shoulder.

The Stalker was there, clutching an outcropping of rock. Its head disappeared beneath the roiling water, then surfaced again, its red eyes wide, its dripping jaws no more than a few feet from Rapunzel's waist. It struggled toward her along the rock.

Energy unlike any Rapunzel had ever felt surged through her limbs. Finding her strength had tripled, she pulled and pulled, putting hand over hand, until her feet cleared the surface of the water.

"USE YOUR LEGS!" Jack tried to pull the braid up, and Rapunzel with it, but only hefted her a few inches farther. "HURRY! IT'S BEHIND YOU!"

Rapunzel felt hot breath at her ankles, the snap of teeth closing just at her heel. She screamed, shoved her right foot into a crevice in the stones, and pushed up with her legs. Jack was right. It was faster. She shoved her left foot into a pocket between two jutting rocks and pushed up again. Her limbs trembled with power that felt almost like magic.

She looked down. The Stalker was a few feet below her now. It scrabbled at the valley wall, flailing to reach her with its claws and teeth. Terrified, Rapunzel climbed on.

"LOOK OUT!"

Rapunzel looked down. Below her, the Stalker bared its fangs and lunged for Rapunzel's dangling braid.

"PULL UP YOUR HAIR!" Jack shouted.

Rapunzel shrieked, clamped her braid between her feet, and pulled her knees up as high as she could, yanking her braid out of the Stalker's reach. She could only hold the position for a second, but it was long enough. The Stalker scrambled for balance, made one last leaping, desperate effort, and missed her hair by inches. With a howl, it fell backward into the river and was swept away by the churning foam.

Rapunzel hung from her braid, breathing in long, uneven gasps, until she felt ready to make her way upward. The strange, surging energy in her limbs had ebbed away, leaving her as weak as jelly.

"You can do it," Jack called.

Rapunzel pushed as much as she could with her legs as Jack tugged her braid. When she reached the rocks at the top, she was careful, not wanting to grab hold of anything that might come loose and send her plunging straight back down again. Finally, her knees hit the safety of the grass, and she fell onto it, her heart racing, her cheek pressed to the cool dirt. Prince Frog stayed close as Jack untied her anchored braid and returned with most of her hair. He pulled the rest up from where it still hung toward the river, and then he sat heavily beside Rapunzel, panting. With effort, Rapunzel turned her head and looked up at him. He was sweating so much that his hair was wet. He massaged his upper arms and rubbed his hands, which looked red and raw.

"Thank you," Rapunzel said.

Jack glanced at her. He nodded, and she considered him with some admiration. He had climbed up her whole tower — and he'd done it three times. He must be very strong. And Witch, who had climbed her tower every day for years and years, must be the very strongest person in the world.

Jack wiped his forehead and flicked the moisture from his hand. "Would've been nice if Rune had helped me," he muttered. "I know he heard me."

"Yes, but he wants me to die."

He raised his eyebrows. "I guess," he said. "You sound so matter-of-fact about it."

"Well, it's a fact."

Jack eyed her for another moment, and then he grinned a little. "You're going to have some good stories to tell after this, you know that?" he said. "Of how you conquered a Stalker and climbed your own hair out of a ravine, in spite of the fairy who wants you dead."

"That's an *awful* story."

"That's what makes it good," said Jack. "My father always said that about adventures. The parts that are worst in the doing are best in the telling." He gazed out across the river, and his grin faded into a thoughtful expression.

With effort, Rapunzel pushed herself up to sit. Jack stood and fished the Ubiquitous Instant Bridge out of his pocket. He held it up.

"Ready?"

Rapunzel braced her hands on the ground and tried to get to her feet. Her head pounded where every hair had been pulled. When she stood, her knees wavered a little, and Jack grabbed her arms to steady her.

"You sure you're all right?" he asked.

"I — I think so," she said, glancing at her braid. It was frayed all over from scraping against the cliff's edge, but just now, she had no energy to worry about it. "Wind up, please," she said. The wheel spun and the hair coiled.

Jack cracked the acorn against a rock.

A narrow rope bridge appeared, spanning the river valley. Rapunzel tucked Prince Frog safely into her pocket and went across first. The bridge swayed each time she stepped on the wooden slats. She did not look down or back, and she did not breathe until her feet touched the ground on the other side. Jack crossed it twice as fast as she had done, but he needn't have hurried. Though it looked rickety, the bridge stood firm long after they had crossed it.

"So here we are," said Jack. "Welcome to Yellow Country."

Rapunzel took a deep breath. She could have sworn that the air was different here than it had been on the other side of the bridge. It was spiced. Sweet. She breathed again, enjoying the way it tasted. On her shoulder, Prince Frog seemed to be doing exactly the same.

"Come on," Jack said, and they continued toward the willow trees to make camp.

CHAPTER NINE

RAPUNZEL woke halfway through the night, roused by the throbbing of every muscle in her body. She *ached*. She was stiff from sleeping for the first time without pillows or a mattress. She was sore from all the walking and braid-carrying she had done the day before. She was bruised and battered from climbing up the rocks and smacking her arms and legs against them. Worst of all, her neck seemed to be frozen in place from having been jerked out of the river by her hair. She tossed on the ground and tried to find a comfortable position to lie in, but it was no use. She barely slept for the rest of the night, and when the sun rose, she was almost as tired as when she'd first lain down.

Still, once she and Jack had eaten a bit of bread for breakfast, Rapunzel walked all day. Her hair, still wet from the river, grew heavier with every step. Whenever she complained about it, Jack volunteered to cut it off, and so, eventually, she stopped complaining. She tried to be glad that at least it was no longer humid and hot, as it had been in the Redlands. Yellow Country was much more temperate and often cooled by winds.

Rapunzel's second day in Yellow Country was more excruciating than the first, and she wanted to cry out for Witch every minute. What kept her marching was her fear of Rune, whose shimmering trail of red light she spied several times. She wondered if Witch was trying to follow her; she knew that Witch would look frantically for her. But as long as Rune was watching, Witch probably could not approach.

Jack checked his compass from time to time, explaining the world to Rapunzel as they walked. He pointed out horses, crops, and farmhouses and told her how people lived by working the land; he showed her where trails led off the main road toward smaller villages. But nothing he said, no matter how interesting, could tear Rapunzel's mind from the pain in her feet for very long. When they made camp that night, she felt as though they were nothing but two big, pulpy bruises, throbbing at the ends of her legs. Jack told her that traveling would get easier as she got stronger, but it hadn't happened yet.

The next day, they descended into a wide, shallow valley divided into farms; but though Rapunzel found the landscape fascinating, she could think of very little besides the pain in her back and feet.

"I can't go any farther," she whimpered when they reached the other side of the valley. She looked at the top of the hill, miserable with exhaustion. "And don't tell me to cut my hair," she said before Jack could make his usual reply. "You know I won't."

He sighed but said nothing, and sat next to her on the side of the road while she rested her feet.

"Tess used to hate walking up the mountain," he said.

"Who's Tess?"

"My sister. That's her name. Anyway, our village is way, way up in the Peaks, so we have to walk two leagues down the mountainside to the nearest town for supplies, and the path home is straight back up again. Tess used to complain the whole way. She'd cry and beg me to carry her. Which was fine when she could still ride on my back, but then she got too heavy."

"So what did she do?" asked Rapunzel, curious.

"She started playing this game."

"What kind of game?"

"If you keep going, I'll show you."

This was too tempting to resist. She stood again on her sore feet and walked up the hill beside Jack.

"So," he said, "what you do is, whenever you feel like you want to complain, you have to make yourself say something good instead. Tess always says stuff she's happy about, or stuff she's looking forward to."

"Seeing Witch," Rapunzel said instantly.

"Right . . . but maybe try to branch out a little more," said Jack. "Like, Tess will say she's happy it's sunny out, or she's happy we're having eggs for supper."

"Oh." Rapunzel thought about it. "I'm happy that Rune didn't kill me," she offered.

Jack snickered. "Good one," he said. "I'm happy the bridge didn't crash."

"I'm happy you have Ubiquitous Instant Bread."

"I'm happy the Stalker didn't eat us."

In this way, they climbed the hill, and Rapunzel realized that Tess's game was a good one; it was easier to endure the walking when she was busy thinking of things to be glad about. Still, she could not trick her feet into believing they were painless forever. She was nearly in tears by the time Jack looked at the sky and said that they should make camp again.

Dusky blue evening fell over the fields and the world grew quickly darker; the moon and stars could not be seen. They chose a level expanse of grass in a little copse of trees, and Rapunzel had just begun to shrug off her wheel of hair for the night when water started to fall from nowhere and splash her with little cold drops. She shrieked and took cover beneath a tree.

"What is that?" she shouted, searching the sky. But it was empty except for branches — and Jack was laughing.

"You've never seen *rain*?" he asked.

Rapunzel remained close to the tree trunk. "I've seen it," she said, "but it stays outside. Witch doesn't want it to hurt me."

"Rain won't hurt you." Jack stood in it and tilted up his chin. "And you'd better get used to it. It rains plenty in Yellow Country; that's why they've got such great crops. Come on, feel it."

Prince Frog boinged into the drops, but Rapunzel only watched with a sinking heart as rain pelted the grass where they were to sleep. She had already been dreading another night sleeping on the ground; now it would be more uncomfortable than ever. "I've been wet enough since I left my tower," she said. "I want to stay dry."

"There's nothing we can do about it," said Jack. "I don't have an umbrella."

"A what?"

"A little dome on a stick. You hold it over your head so the rain can't get on you."

"Oh." Rapunzel pursed her lips in thought. "You don't have a Ubiquitous one?"

"I used it on the way to the Redlands. How did you know Ubiquitous makes umbrellas?"

"If they make bridges, it can't be hard to make domes," said Rapunzel. "It can't be hard. . . ."

She glanced at the bendy branches of the willow tree overhead. They hung and swayed in the rain, which was falling faster. If she wanted a dry place to sleep, she would have to act quickly.

She grabbed the end of a branch in one hand and reached out to grasp another branch from a neighboring tree. The branches were slim, but not bendy enough to be tied in a knot.

"What are you doing?" Jack asked.

"Do you still have my pink handkerchief?"

Jack did, and Rapunzel used it to lash the branches together. Rain fell on her hands and face, and she decided it was refreshing, but she still didn't think she'd like to sleep in it. She strode a few paces away and grabbed another pair of branches.

"What are you doing?" Jack repeated.

"Making a brella."

"*Um*brella."

Rapunzel ignored him. "What can we tie these with?"

Jack, who looked interested in the experiment, lashed the branches together with his belt. The two of them stood in the space between the tied branches, which was no wider than Rapunzel's balcony.

"What now?"

"We hang a canopy over these," said Rapunzel, "and we can sleep under it without getting wet."

"Nice one!" said Jack, looking impressed. Rapunzel was proud of herself. Witch, she thought, would have been proud of her too, for figuring this out all on her own.

"What should we use for a canopy?" she asked.

Jack eyed her. "Your hair would work, if we took it out of the braid."

Rapunzel hesitated — then nodded. Even after three days of walking, her braid remained damp from the river; a little rain wasn't going to make it any worse. Having to braid it up again was better than having to sleep on wet grass.

"Unwind," she said. Her heavy braid uncoiled from her throbbing back, and Rapunzel's shoulders slumped in relief. Jack untied the ribbon that secured the end of her hair and stuck it into one of his pockets before beginning to undo her braid.

"Wow," he said as her hair came apart in long, damp waves.

"What?"

Jack didn't answer. He continued to loosen the braid, looping it over his elbow as he freed long sections of it that never seemed to end. "Think you've got enough of this stuff?" he muttered. "I didn't know hair could even grow this long."

"It's magic."

"Why would anyone use magic to make all this hair?"

"I asked Witch to do it," said Rapunzel. "When I was little, it used to go down to my feet, and it was so pretty that I asked if I could have more. I asked if I could have so much hair that it went all the way down to the ground outside the tower. Witch said it was a wonderful idea."

Rapunzel slipped off the wheel the fairies had given her. Though every muscle rebelled, she lowered herself to the ground and lay down in the grass. Jack gave her an odd look.

"I'm making sure I have enough slack to lie down and sleep," she explained, tugging a bit of hair away from him.

"Oh," said Jack. "Well, you stay there, then." He ducked under one set of tied branches and passed the loops of her hair over it, then carried it all to the other set of branches and passed the loops over that one too. As he traveled back and forth, the golden hair began to form a thick canopy above Rapunzel in the damp grass. She listened to the soft thudding of the rain and imagined that she was in her own bed, and that stars might begin to twinkle in her hair.

When Jack ran out of hair, he secured the end to the branch and spent a few minutes spreading it out evenly on one side of the canopy and then the other. Finally he ducked beneath it and lay down beside Rapunzel. A moment later, the soft sound of rain became harder, and the branches all around them began to thrash. But their canopy remained secure, and they were, if not dry, then much drier than they would have been.

"See?" Rapunzel said when they had been quiet for a long time. "My hair isn't useless."

Jack shifted beside her. "Not completely," he agreed. Rapunzel heard a crack, and then she smelled bread. Jack handed her half the loaf, and they propped themselves up to eat.

"It's nice to get the wheel off my back," she admitted, tearing off a chunk of bread with her teeth and wishing it was something different. She was getting sick of bread. It didn't seem to have flavor anymore.

"I don't know how you stand it," said Jack. "Won't you ever cut it off?"

"If I had cut it off, we couldn't have tripped the Stalker," Rapunzel pointed out to him for the twentieth time. "*And* we'd be sleeping in the rain."

Jack shrugged. "We should get you something to carry it in, at least," he said. "Cornucopia's not far now — about a league and a half from here. We'll probably get to town by noon tomorrow. A town's a place where lots of people live."

"I know. I've read about towns." Rapunzel gazed up at her hair. "They're full of diseased peasants who will want to sell me into slavery."

Jack burst out laughing. "What kinds of books were you reading in that tower?" he asked.

Rapunzel chewed her tasteless bread. Jack mocked her as often as he explained things to her, and since she couldn't get away from him, she tried to ignore him when he was insulting. She longed to get back to Witch, who would listen to her without laughing.

Thinking of Witch made Rapunzel depressed. It was nearly a week now since she and Witch had seen each other, longer by far than the longest separation they had known. Sometimes, Witch would go away for a couple or even three days, but that was the very most. Usually she visited Rapunzel every day.

"I miss her," she mumbled, picking bits of crust off her bread.

"Hm?"

"Nothing." Rapunzel knew better than to tell Jack that she missed Witch. She had done it last night, and he had replied so cuttingly that she had no desire to do it again.

"What'd you say?" Jack insisted.

Rapunzel shrugged. "So the First Wood is on the other side of Yellow Country?" she asked, though Jack had already told her this.

"I think I have a map in here somewhere," said Jack, perking up at the question. "You should have a look at it."

Rapunzel swallowed the last of her bread. "Map?"

He stuffed the rest of his bread in his mouth and fished a tiny lantern from his knapsack and a folded square of paper from his vest pocket. The paper was a picture, he told her, that represented where places were.

"We're here," he said, and put his fingertip on the map over the large, slanting words *Yellow Country*, and near the much smaller, cursive word *Cornucopia*. There were other cursive words written inside the Realm of Yellow's border. Jack explained that they were all towns and villages.

"Where's my tower?"

Jack dragged his finger toward the bottom of the map, over *Redlands*, to a place in the southeast of that country, near the border of a country called Grey. There were no towns near where Jack was pointing. Her tower must have been the only place for many leagues.

It was funny, she thought. The Redlands really was south of everything. She wondered why Witch had said that they were in the middle.

"Where's the Red Glade?" Rapunzel asked, studying the Redlands. "I don't see it."

Jack pointed to the words *Fortress of Bole*. "Bole's the capital of the Redlands," he said. "Most fairy glades are near the capital cities, I think, but they're not on maps. They're hidden and tricky to find — for people who aren't fairies, at least."

"Where else have we been?"

He traced his fingertip over the path they had taken, showing her where they had seen the stone prince, and the Golden River where they had met the Stalker, and the places they had camped so far in Yellow Country.

"And the First Wood, where the Woodmother is?"

Jack tapped the center of the map, and Rapunzel traced a path with her finger from where they now sat all the way up to the place marked *Independence*, which Jack said was the capital of Commonwealth Green. "Glyph told me the First Wood's usually near that area," he said.

Rapunzel measured the distance with her fingers. It was three times as far as they'd already traveled. "We have to walk for that long?" she asked, discouraged.

"Commonwealth Green's a big country," said Jack. "It used to be a province of the Pink Empire, but it's independent now."

"Pink Empire?"

"Here." Jack touched the northernmost country, a sprawling mass labeled *New Pink*. "But they're not conquerors anymore," he said. "Not since the old rulers went to sleep."

Rapunzel only half listened. She had found the words *Violet Peaks*, and she brushed them with her finger, tracing the mountains that bordered Tyme all along the east, from north to south. "You're from the Violet Peaks," she said to Jack. "You said so, didn't you?"

"Good memory," said Jack, and Rapunzel grew warm with pleasure.

"Do you live in a tower?" she asked.

Jack chuckled. "Are you serious?" he said, but he didn't wait for an answer. "No. People live in houses and stuff on the ground — like those farmhouses we passed. My family lives in a . . . cottage."

"Cottage?"

Jack shrugged. "If you want to call it that." He toyed with one ragged corner of the map. "Didn't you get lonely in that tower?" he asked. "Or scared?"

"Why would I?"

"I don't know. Was the witch always there?"

"No."

"And you don't have sisters or brothers or anything. Or even a pet."

Rapunzel shrugged. "No, I guess not." In fact, a pet would be very nice to have. She would take Prince Frog with her when she went home. She was sure Witch wouldn't mind.

"I'd go crazy all by myself in one room," said Jack. "What did you *do* up there all day?"

"I ran on the balcony, and I read books. I played dress-up and puzzles and things."

"By yourself?"

Rapunzel nodded. "Don't you ever play by yourself?"

Jack rolled the corner of the map between his fingertips. "I mostly play with Tess," he said. "I watch her all the time, so I taught her to read and play jacks and stuff."

"You play jacks?" she said, somewhat startled. "So do I!"

Jack smiled. "Tess and I have this map game," he said. "You close your eyes and point somewhere on the map, and that's the place you'll live when you're grown up."

"Really? Is it?"

"Well, no . . . it's pretend. You know. For kids. My sister likes it."

"Can we play?" she asked.

"Sure. Close your eyes. No peeking," he added after a moment.

"I wasn't!" Rapunzel stopped trying to see and squeezed her eyes shut.

"Now move your finger in a circle."

She made a wide circle in the air with her index finger, and felt Jack's hand on hers, guiding it downward. "Has to be over the map," he said. "Now, put your finger down!"

Rapunzel planted her fingertip on the map, and she opened her eyes.

She had landed on *Maple Valley*. It was a place in Commonwealth Green, not far from the capital, and Rapunzel lifted her fingertip, not sure what to think. The game was pretend, she knew, yet it felt suddenly real and serious. She had never imagined where she would live when she was all grown up. She had never imagined living anywhere but the tower.

There were so many places on the map.

"My turn," Jack said, and he closed his eyes and made circles with his finger until his fingertip landed on *Quintessential*. He looked pleased when he saw it. He told Rapunzel it was the capital of the Blue Kingdom — a huge, important city with a massive palace. "I'm going to travel there one day," he said. "I've always wanted to see it."

Prince Frog leapt right onto the map and landed on a place marked *Olive Isles*. These looked like several tiny countries all sitting in the middle of blue space. "Islands," Jack explained. "They're part of Tyme, but the whole country is surrounded by the Tranquil Sea."

"What is the Tranquil Sea?"

"Salt water," said Jack. "As far as your eyes can see. Water that stretches forever. It's supposed to be beautiful."

Prince Frog croaked and looked down at the painted sea beneath his gelatinous toes.

"Prince Frog wishes it were real water," said Rapunzel, giggling as she moved him off the map and into her pocket, where he could stay damp. She had continued to wet her pocket for him at every opportunity. "Or you can keep playing in the rain," she told him, patting him again through her pocket.

"When we get to Commonwealth Green," said Jack, "you'll have visited three countries, out of thirteen."

"Three whole countries before I go home." Rapunzel was amazed by the prospect.

Jack lifted his eyebrows. "Before you go home?" he asked. "You'd go back and live in a tower after seeing all of this?"

"Of course," said Rapunzel. Her eyes trailed over the rest of the map, and she absorbed all she could. *Orange. Crimson Realm. Republic of Brown.*

"How could you stand it, now that you've been out?" Jack demanded. "How could you stay locked up?"

"I wasn't locked up," she said. "Witch lets me do whatever I want. I just didn't want to leave."

"But there are so many places to go," said Jack. "The Lilac Lakes, and the jewel mines of Crimson, and the beaches in Orange, where the Bardwyrms write poems in the air — don't you want to see all that?"

Rapunzel could not conceive of the things he was describing. "What's out here?" she asked, drawing a circle in the air around the outside of the map. "Past the Violet Peaks and the Tranquil Sea?"

"The Beyond."

"What's that?"

"Everybody guesses, but no one knows," said Jack. "That's what my father said."

Rapunzel found it a strange answer, but was forced to accept it. When she asked Jack for more information, he had none to give.

"Why are there only twelve countries on the map?" she asked. "You said thirteen, didn't you?"

"The thirteenth country is Geguul."

Rapunzel turned to him. "You told me to go there! What is it?"

"It's the country in the sky, where the White Fairy lives."

"In the sky!" she repeated. "Is it beautiful?"

"No," said Jack.

"How do you know?"

"I've been there."

Prince Frog wriggled out of Rapunzel's pocket, leapt onto Jack's knee, and sat staring up at him with eyes like saucers.

"Tell me the story!" Rapunzel cried, delighted. It sounded exactly like the sort of thing that Witch would put into a book for her. "How did you get to the sky? Were there beasts there? Ogres, maybe?"

"I don't want to talk about it."

"Please? You have to!"

Jack didn't answer directly. "Up until forty-seven days ago," he said, "I lived here." He unrolled the map again and touched a tiny cursive word written among the eastern ridges of the Violet Peaks: *Dearth*. "I helped my mother work our farm — just a few cows and goats."

"Like the ones we saw on the farms we passed?"

"Yeah, but not as healthy as the ones you see around here," said Jack. "Where I'm from, it's pretty rough. After our animals got sick about a year ago, it got worse. No one would buy what was left, and we couldn't even trade them. People knew they were diseased." Jack pushed his hand through his hair. "We've always been poor," he said. "I'm used to being poor. But until my father left, we'd never been starving."

"Buy?" said Rapunzel, not sure she understood. "Trade?"

Jack shook his head a little. "You're lucky," he said, petting Prince Frog once with his thumb. "You've had magic giving you whatever you want. Everyone else needs money. See, you give people money, and they give you what you need. To get money, either you can sell something — which means someone else takes that thing in exchange for money — or you can get paid to do things."

"That sounds simple."

Jack laughed, but did not sound happy. "You'll see when we get to Cornucopia."

"Why? Will we have to trade and buy things there?"

"If we want to eat, yeah."

"What do you mean?" asked Rapunzel, alarmed. She pushed herself back up onto her elbows. "Of course we want to eat."

"Well, food costs money."

"Do you have money?"

"No. I had a golden egg, but I traded it to get supplies for my trip to the Red Glade. Since I've had to travel with you, we've eaten everything twice as fast — and I wasn't planning to go to the First Wood. I thought I'd be going straight home after seeing the fairies. After we eat breakfast tomorrow, we'll be out of bread."

Rapunzel lay back down, thinking hard. It had been bad enough eating just bread and water for the last four days. Their lack of food scared her.

"We'll just have to find some money," she said. "I'll get some. I'll do something."

Jack looked up at the canopy of hair that protected them. "We could get a lot of money for your hair, I bet," he mused.

Rapunzel crossed her arms behind her head. "Never," she said, and yawned.

"So what's your big plan?"

She didn't have an answer. "You never told me how you got to the sky," she said instead. "Finish your story."

"Later," said Jack.

Rapunzel decided not to press him, and he said nothing more. When she fell asleep, Jack was still sitting up with Prince Frog beside him, staring out into the darkness and the rain.

CHAPTER TEN

RAPUNZEL awoke to the sound of birds chirping and the smell of damp leaves. She glanced over at Jack, who was fast asleep on his back, his mouth open, his chest rising and falling.

"Wake up," she said. "Help me get my hair down."

"Ngh," he said, and curled up in protest.

Rapunzel stood. Her body was stiff, and her bones felt like they were creaking. Worse yet, her stomach felt tight and empty.

It was a nasty job unwinding her wet hair from the branches, and a worse one plaiting it up again. When Jack woke, he wasn't much help. Sighing, he held her hair off the ground as she twisted it into a misshapen braid. It took so long that her fingers grew sore, but she finished and slid her shoulder straps on. When her hair rolled onto the wheel, Rapunzel's back began to ache at once. They had not walked long before she was forced to slow down. "How much farther to Cornucopia?" she asked, stopping beside a tree to lift her right foot, trying to give it a rest.

"About a league," said Jack. He cupped his hand above his eyes and squinted up into the sun. "We'll get there in time to eat lunch — if you can get us some money, that is." He smirked.

Rapunzel twisted her left ankle in circles and gritted her teeth. "My feet," she said.

"You need boots," said Jack. "You could use some clothes too. You can't go wandering around in your nightgown forever."

"How do I get clothes?"

Jack pushed back his hair. "Money," he said.

Rapunzel was beginning to think that money was stupid. "Does anything not take money?" she asked.

He shrugged. "Water's free," he said. "We can forage for berries and roots."

"*Roots?*"

"Can't be too picky." He scratched his head. "We can fish, but it'll work better if I can buy real hooks and line. We could use your hair for line, I guess. It's not quite strong enough, but I could wind a few pieces together. And I can always catch a rabbit or something. It's just that all that stuff takes time," he finished, sounding anxious. "I don't have time."

Rapunzel didn't know what half the things were that he had just mentioned, but she wasn't in the mood for explanations. She put her left foot down and winced when it throbbed, but started walking again with determination. They were close to Cornucopia, and some-how, in town, she would find a way to get enough money for lunch and boots.

They had not even walked another hour before she had to stop again.

"I have to rest," she said, and slid to the ground. She rolled onto her side and cried a little when the weight of her hair slumped onto the grass and off her.

Jack stood over her, looking uncomfortable. "I guess I could carry it," he said.

When she stood up again a few minutes later, Rapunzel gladly passed the wheel off to him. Without its weight on her back, she felt so much lighter that she would have skipped for joy if her feet hadn't been so blistered. They didn't speak again until the woods thinned and they reached a long, grassy slope, which spilled down into clusters of tidy little thatch-roofed buildings. Warm, fragrant, delicious scents wafted across the fields and up the slope. Moved by hunger, Rapunzel hurried toward the buildings, dragging Jack and the hair-wheel along with her.

"Wait," he yelped, and though Rapunzel did not want to, Jack dug in his heels and brought her to a halt. "We have to hide your hair before we get into town — and your nightgown, for that matter. You look like a lunatic." He shrugged off the wheel of hair and helped Rapunzel into it. "Put this on," he said, pulling a thin cloak out of his knapsack. He flung the cloak over the wheel of hair, and Rapunzel tied it closed in front. "You look like you have a hunchback," he said, sounding more than a little amused. "But believe me, that's better."

They ran down the rest of the slope, toward the wonderful smells. Soon they were wandering among long lanes of short, boxlike houses all pressed together, with people milling in and out of their windowed doors.

"Look at all the people!" Rapunzel whispered, nudging Jack. "What are they doing?"

"Those are shops," said Jack. "People buy things in them."

"Can we get food in them?"

"If you have money."

Rapunzel bounced on her sore toes. "It smells so good," she said.

Prince Frog wriggled out of Rapunzel's pocket and stared around with his wide golden eyes. Rapunzel put him on her shoulder.

"How do I get money?" she asked.

"See that fountain?" said Jack, pointing down a long road toward a great expanse of green. Just before it there stood a round, stone-walled pool of water, very like Rapunzel's marble bathtub at home. Water spilled from a high-up stone dish, down into another, bigger dish, and then into another, even bigger one, which sat in the middle of the water.

"Is it for taking baths in?" asked Rapunzel. Almost a week of walking had left her uncomfortably grimy.

"No," said Jack as they approached it. "It's a public fountain. Just stay here so I can find you again, all right? I'll be back as soon as I can. I'll go faster on my own."

"Should I try to get money?"

But Jack had already disappeared into the crowd.

Rapunzel stood for a minute at the edge of the square, watching all the people. There were short people and tall people and people in between. There were people with black hair and white hair and brown hair; people with toasty-brown skin and peachy-pale skin, wrinkly skin and spotty skin. There were skinny people and fat people, old people and young people, people in feathered hats, people in aprons, and people carrying big wicker baskets full of fruits and vegetables. There were so many kinds of people that Rapunzel couldn't count them all.

What they had in common, she realized, was that they all wanted to look at her. Everyone who passed gave her a long, incredulous stare. Men and women alike swept their eyes over Rapunzel's dirty slippers and the hump on her back, wearing looks of disdain, disgust, and pity. Children huddled to whisper, point, and laugh.

They had something else in common, Rapunzel noticed. Nearly everyone who passed her was either carrying food or eating it. All of them must have had money.

Almost salivating at the smells that mingled around her in the air, Rapunzel approached a woman who was sitting on a bench, licking a large spoonful of custard.

"Do you have any money?" she asked. "I'm hungry."

The woman drew back. She looked at Rapunzel's cloaked hump and ruined slippers. She looked at Prince Frog on her shoulder. And then she gathered up her skirts and her custard and hurried away.

A fat woman in an apron leaned out of the custard shop. "Get on with you now," she said to Rapunzel. "Stop scaring away business! Shoo! Shoo!" When Rapunzel didn't move, the woman swatted at her with a large wooden spoon. "Filthy beggar!" she cried. "We work for our livings here."

Rapunzel moved away from the shop, undaunted, and wandered down the road, reading the signs. The Cursed-Tongue Bait Shop didn't sound like it had much promise, and neither did Tully's Tack and Saddle. Between these shops stood a waist-high pillar of dark stone topped with a cheerful yellow box that repeatedly emitted the words *Hear ye! Hear ye!* Through a small glass door in the box, Rapunzel saw a stack of paper. She wished it were a stack of food. At the end of the road was a place called Shepard's Alehouse that looked more interesting — a lot of people sat inside on stools, drinking from big metal mugs and laughing at the tops of their lungs. Across from the alehouse was a very pretty corner shop, neat and tidy, marked with a copper sign shaped like an oven that read *Copper Door Confectionery*. This shop overflowed with visitors; the candy inside it must have been delicious.

"Hello, freckly!" A man stood beside the confectionery, in front of a little red door with a painted window that read *The Muffin Man*. He grinned at Rapunzel when she caught his eyes. "Free samples!" he called, beckoning to her with pudgy fingers. His cheeks were round and red. He held a platter laden with bite-size muffins.

Rapunzel hurried toward him and took one. She shoved it into her mouth and closed her eyes to relish the taste. It was airy, sweet, and wonderful.

"Feckly?" she managed through her mouthful.

The man tapped a fingertip to the end of Rapunzel's nose. "Freckles!" he cried. "They're cheerful! They make you look hungry!"

"I am hungry," said Rapunzel, taking another sample and popping it into her mouth. "I've been journeying for four days with nothing but bread to eat."

"Tut tut," said the man, "not a good idea. You need fuel for a journey like that." He pointed to a menu that stood by the door. "Try our sausage and eggs for three thorns!"

"Thorns?"

"That's what it costs, freckly." The man's eyes twinkled for a moment, but when Rapunzel ate a third tiny muffin, the twinkling faded. "If you're a beggar, you can just move along," he said. "I thought you looked ratty — you and your frog."

Prince Frog croaked reproachfully. The man put down his tray and picked up a broom. Before he could swat at her, Rapunzel hurried away among the shops. It was misery to see food everywhere and know that she was not allowed to touch it.

"Look at her, Clover."

"Oh, I'm looking. She's a carriage wreck."

"Those *shoes*. And what's under that cloak?"

Rapunzel turned around, aware that the conversation must be about her. Two people stood there, a man and a woman. Both were young, but older than she was, and both had deep brown skin. The woman's hair stood out like a massive, frizzy black hat on one side of her head; on the other side, tight white curls covered her scalp. The man wore a long coat with one sleeve missing; the skin of his exposed arm was purple, and coppery sparks crackled from his fingertips. Rapunzel looked inquisitively at this spectacle, while the man and woman gazed upon her with dismay.

"Are you all right?" asked the young woman, lifting an eyebrow.

"No," said Rapunzel. "I don't have any money."

The young man held out his hand. In it were two flat, bronze things, each about the size of an eye. "Take these and buy yourself some shoes. Burn those things you're wearing." He made a gesture with his purple hand when he said this, and fiery orange light sparked from his fingers.

Rapunzel took the bronze things and held one up. "Is this money?" she asked.

The young man frowned at her. "Of course. They're Hawthornes."

"Food in the park's cheaper," added the young woman, jabbing a thumb over her shoulder.

"Thank you," said Rapunzel. Clutching the coins in her hand, she ran back along the streets she'd come down until she found the fountain where she was supposed to meet Jack.

He wasn't there. Rapunzel sat on the fountain's edge to rest her aching feet, her stomach gurgling so loudly that she could hear it over the rushing water. She wondered how long she would have to wait. She smelled hot buttered corn, sweet apple tarts, sizzling sausages, and fresh cake. It was all she could do to keep from drooling.

When Jack returned, Rapunzel stood at once, ready to go and buy food at last. But he sat down on the rim of the fountain and slouched over his knees.

"I couldn't get a job," he muttered.

"It's all right, I have money."

Jack raised his head. "You do? How?"

"A man gave it to me."

"How much did he give you?"

"This much," said Rapunzel, and she showed him the two bronze coins. "Is that enough to eat with?"

Jack's mouth fell open and he plucked the coins out of Rapunzel's palm. "Somebody just *gave* you these?" he asked. "For no reason?"

"He said that I should get new shoes and burn my slippers. And I do want some better shoes," she said, wiggling her aching feet one at a time. "But first, let's eat. Come on, Prince Frog," she said, and Prince Frog, who had been swimming in the whirling fountain, bounced into Rapunzel's hand, then up her arm and onto her shoulder.

They made their way to the park, which was a crowded but jolly place where people played music and games, and floated in a lazy river. Rapunzel might have found all this worth looking at if she had not been so hungry; as it was, she hurried straight toward the long, tented rows that Jack called food booths. There, hundreds of people wandered about, sucking lemon ice through peppermint-stick straws, or munching turkey legs, or gulping from tankards. Pale, furry little creatures scurried around on their hind legs, picking up garbage and scraps of food in their front paws and eating the remainders before tidying the trash into neat piles. Jack said that the creatures were called Brownies, and Rapunzel was surprised. She had thought that brownies were a chocolate dessert.

The idea of chocolate dessert was too much to bear. Rapunzel headed toward the closest booth, where whole chickens were roasting on spits, licked by flames. She pushed her way across the crowded path, following the marvelous smell.

"Hold on," said Jack. "Don't you want to get a look at everything before you decide?"

Rapunzel did not. "I'll buy a chicken," she said to the aproned man in the booth.

"A quarter or a half chicken?" he asked.

"A chicken," Rapunzel repeated. The man wrapped one up in paper and handed the greasy, bulky package over.

"Five thorns," he said.

Jack handed over one of the bronze coins, and the man in the apron gave back a handful of little gold coins.

"A Hawthorne is twenty thorns," Jack explained to Rapunzel. "So we get fifteen back."

He bought himself two skewers of meat and potatoes, and as they looked for a place to sit, Rapunzel saw a tall white thing with a sign on it that said *Wine by the Skin (or Half Skin)*. Jack told her that the tall white thing was a tent and that wine was something she wouldn't like.

"But I want to taste it," said Rapunzel, watching as a girl with a long, dark tail of hair ladled pretty, garnet-colored liquid through a funnel into the same kind of pouch that Jack wore at his belt.

"Just get a half skin, then," said Jack, taking the pouch off his belt and dumping the water into the grass. "You can use mine."

Rapunzel took it and brought it to the dark-haired girl, who put a ladleful of purple liquid into the skin. A half skin of wine cost one thorn, and Rapunzel handed over one of her little gold coins, happy to be able to pay for something without begging.

They took their food and drinks and found a grassy meadow beyond the booths and tents where they could sit under a tree. It wasn't until they had eaten their fill and were picking at the last of the meat that Rapunzel tried her half skin of wine.

"Blech!" she yelled, and spat blackish-purple stuff everywhere. "It's bitter!" She smacked her tongue against the roof of her mouth in distaste.

"Told you," said Jack. Rapunzel tossed the skin into the grass. Wine flooded from it, gushing around Prince Frog's legs to form a puddle. He leapt out of it, bouncing repeatedly to shake purple droplets from himself — and then he bounced into a tree and gave a dazed croak.

Rapunzel leaned against the tree, watching several little bright yellow birds flitter around in the grass. She was full. She was sitting down. Her hair was off her back; the wheel lay beside her on the ground, covered with the cloak. As far as she was concerned, they could camp right here tonight. And maybe tomorrow night.

Prince Frog tottered over sideways and flopped down beside Rapunzel, who sprawled out beside him, gazing up at the sky. She never wanted to move again.

"I wish I had a lemon custard," she said. "I saw people eating them."

"Go get one, then."

Rapunzel groaned. "I *can't* put my hair on yet," she said.

Jack finished the last piece of meat on his skewer. "It's time," he said. "We need to get supplies while all the shops are still open."

They got to their feet, and Rapunzel stowed a very wobbly Prince Frog away in her pocket. With a little moan of effort, she strapped on the hair wheel, and Jack covered it again with the cloak. They made their way toward the north side of the park, where Jack said the equipment shops were located.

The heart of the park had no food tents but was even more crowded with people. In the center was a large, raised wooden platform with a few wide, shallow steps leading up on all sides. A dense crowd surrounded it. Atop the platform were men and women, all wearing sashes across their chests that said things like *Village Champion of Plenty*. Most of them clutched small pouches in their hands, looking disappointed.

Two of the sashed people, however, knelt on an even higher stage that rose from the center of the platform. When she realized what they were doing, Rapunzel stopped and stared.

They were playing jacks. To her surprise, it was the same as the game she had played by herself in her tower, except that they were playing it together, and instead of trying to beat their own scores, they were trying to beat each other.

"It's a championship," said Jack, stopping beside her in the thick of the crowd. "Too bad we don't have time to watch."

"A championship?"

"You're a champion if you're the best at something," said Jack. "These are some of the best people in jacks. People compete all over the country to be Village Champions, and then they come here to see if they can beat the Capital Champion."

Jack pointed to the high stage, and Rapunzel read the champions' sashes. The Capital Champion of Cornucopia was playing against the Village Champion of Chutney Falls.

"If he beats her," said Jack, nodding to the champion from Chutney Falls, "he gets to represent Yellow in the All-Tyme Championships next summer. It's a big deal."

Rapunzel watched the competition closely. She had never seen anyone else play the game, but Witch had always praised her for being good at jacks. The Village Champion of Chutney Falls bounced his ball high into the air. He picked up nine jacks without touching any of the others, and then, with great speed, he made a vertical circle around the falling ball with the hand that held the jacks.

"Around the world," murmured Rapunzel. "I can do that up to twelvesies."

The Village Champion then tried to catch the ball in the same hand before it bounced. When he missed instead and knocked the ball out of the ring, a loud *ooooh* sounded from the crowd around them. He looked very unhappy as he watched his opponent.

The Capital Champion of Cornucopia threw her ball into the air. She gathered nine jacks without touching any of the others. She circled her hand twice around the ball, then caught it, and smiled at the crowd.

"Capital Champion wins!" shouted a man in a yellow jacket, and the crowd sent up a whooping cheer. The whole park seemed to be shouting and waving.

"IS THERE ANOTHER CHALLENGER?"

Rapunzel turned and looked toward the booming voice. A man with a thick double chin and a capacious belly sat opposite the jacks players on a grand platform, in a beautiful chair with a high back. His skin was dark, and his hat was tall, with a wide brim that went all the way around, a deep cleft in the top, and a golden band encircling the middle. This band was embellished in the front by an emblem that looked like two sheaves of wheat crossing.

"That's Governor Calabaza and his family," said Jack. "He's in charge of Yellow. See the armed guards all around there?"

Rapunzel swept her eyes across them, fascinated by the spiky sticks they carried.

"That's the governor's daughter in front," said Jack, "and his sons are just behind."

Rapunzel studied Calabaza's daughter, who wore a burnt-orange dress that showed her muscular upper arms. Her skin was deep brown, and she had a mass of extremely curly hair swept back by a bright copper hair band.

"The Nexus is right next to the governor," Jack went on.

"Is that his name?" asked Rapunzel. "The Nexus?"

"No, it's his title — he's Nexus of Yellow. Most countries have a Nexus. See his amulet? Means he's Exalted."

The amulet was pretty; it gleamed from its resting place against the Nexus's embroidered tunic. "Exalted?" Rapunzel asked.

Jack's eyes widened. "I keep thinking I'm used to you not knowing stuff," he said, shaking his head. "The Exalted are really important. They're people like us, but they're full of magic."

"Magic like Witch?" asked Rapunzel, looking curiously at the Nexus's tanned face, straw-colored hair, and the clear glass circles he wore over his eyes. "Or magic like the fairies?"

"Neither," said Jack. "The Exalted are humans who are born magical, and they all have different talents. Some of them advise governors and queens, others are healers or inventors, and some of them fight magical problems all over Tyme."

"What magical problems?"

"Threats to people's safety," said Jack. "Like Stalkers. The Exalted Council tries to protect everyone. They slay mimics and tooth harpies and wi—" He stopped short and gave Rapunzel a nervous look, but before Rapunzel could ask him what the matter was, Governor Calabaza spoke again in his booming voice.

"THEN LET THE CONTEST BE ENDED," he roared, "IF NO CHALLENGER REMAINS!"

"What does that mean?" asked Rapunzel.

"If no one else wants to play jacks, then the Capital Champion wins," said Jack.

"But I want to play!"

Rapunzel said it more loudly than she'd intended to. The crowd had quieted somewhat, and everyone turned to look at her. Calabaza's daughter shaded her eyes to glance down at Rapunzel. So did Calabaza himself.

"And who are you?" he asked.

"Rapunzel," said Rapunzel. "Your lordship," she added after glancing at Jack, who was frantically whispering the words to her.

"Are you a Village Champion?" asked Calabaza, studying the hump of her cloak.

"No."

The whole crowd murmured at once. One of the governor's sons said something to the other two about laying a wager. People whispered to one another and giggled, and Rapunzel was reminded of the Red Glade and the tittering of hundreds of fairies.

"Can I still play?" Rapunzel asked. "Do I have to be a Village Champion?"

"Not at all," said Calabaza, grinning. "I've just never known anyone else to try it."

"Because it's ridiculous," Jack muttered under his breath. "You have to be good to compete with these people."

Before Rapunzel could reply to this, Calabaza's voice boomed again. "ONE LAST BRAVE SOUL!" he cried, and the crowd went wild with noise. "MAKE WAY FOR THE FINAL CHALLENGER!"

Rapunzel didn't know what to do, but it didn't matter. Several people in the crowd shoved her, all at once, onto the platform steps, which were so wide that she had to take two strides across each one. She climbed them with purpose, feeling under her cloak and in the pocket of her robe for her jacks.

Atop the platform, the village champions parted to give her room, and Rapunzel walked all the way up to the high stage in the middle, with the jacks ring. Kneeling on the other side was the Capital Champion of Cornucopia. Her brown hair was pulled sleekly back, and she wore a long green dress that Rapunzel thought very pretty.

"I'm Carmella," said the Capital Champion, raking her eyes over Rapunzel's hump and looking satisfied. "Do you challenge me?"

Rapunzel guessed she did. "Yes," she said. "What do I do?"

"What do you mean?"

"I've never done this before. I've just played jacks on my own."

The crowd below gave a roar of laughter, and Rapunzel glanced down at Jack, who covered his face with his hands.

Carmella smiled and held up her hand to quiet the crowd. "First, you must kneel at the ringside," she said to Rapunzel, "facing me."

Rapunzel did. It was a little awkward with the weight on her back, but she managed to get into a good position.

"We start with Commons," said Carmella. "Onesies and so on. Are you familiar with the game, or will you need a lesson?" she asked, casting a knowing look at the crowd, which bellowed with laughter again.

Rapunzel narrowed her eyes. "I know the game," she said.

"Lovely," said Carmella. "Now take your jacks from the umpire."

A man in a yellow jacket held out a small bag to Rapunzel, but she didn't take them. "I've got my own jacks," she said, removing her set from her pocket.

"Are they regulation?" asked the umpire, and he whisked them out of her hand. He went to a little scale on the side of the platform, where he poured them out and weighed them, and then held each one to a ruler. He tested the ball next, and when he was satisfied, he brought the bag back to Rapunzel, who took it.

"All clean," said the umpire. "Challenger starts!"

When Rapunzel didn't do anything, Carmella gestured to the ring. "He means you, dear," she said. "Time to play."

Rapunzel scattered her jacks. They gleamed silver in the sunlight, and Carmella stared at them with her mouth open. "Those are precious," she said, knitting her dark eyebrows together. "And you say you're not a champion?"

"Yes, I say that," said Rapunzel, digging the ball out of her velvet pouch and bouncing it in the ring before Carmella could say another word. Rapunzel picked up one jack before the ball landed.

"Onesies," she said.

Carmella bounced her own ball and completed onesies with her own jacks, which appeared to be carved from some hard, white substance. "And how did you come by such valuable jacks?"

Rapunzel pulled twosies. "They were a birthday gift," she said.

"You must be very well connected to receive such gifts," said Carmella. "Who is your family? Perhaps I've heard of them."

"I don't know what you mean."

Carmella raised an eyebrow and flashed another quick smile at the crowd. Their laughter resurged, and Rapunzel glared across the ring at her opponent. She had never wanted to beat someone at a game until now.

They said nothing else to each other until each had cleared sevensies, at which point Rapunzel realized that it had been half an hour since she had checked on Prince Frog.

"One minute," she said to Carmella, and she dug her hand into her pocket. Prince Frog wasn't there. Rapunzel looked around the platform and searched the steps. When there was no sign of any frog, she began to panic.

"Prince Frog!" she cried, and stood.

Carmella looked up at her. "Do you wish to forfeit the match?"

"No, I lost my frog —" Rapunzel began, but she was interrupted by a rather loud croak from across the crowd. She looked over the throng of people, toward the platform where the royal family were enthroned.

There was Prince Frog, still stumbling sideways rather than hopping, beside the feet of Governor Calabaza's daughter. How he had managed to get through the crowd without getting squashed, Rapunzel didn't know.

"Prince Frog!" she said. "Come back here right now! I'm in a championship!"

Prince Frog leapt onto the governor's daughter's lap. She gasped, and the crowd chuckled.

"Jack, get him!" said Rapunzel. But Jack was nowhere to be seen.

Calabaza's daughter looked up from Prince Frog and called out to Rapunzel, "Want me to hold him for you?"

Prince Frog gave a croak of deep satisfaction.

"Fine," Rapunzel shouted back. "But he likes to be wet, so if you'd dip your pocket in some water and put him in there, he'd be happier."

Calabaza's daughter quirked an eyebrow, but she gestured for a goblet of water, into which she dipped the pocket of her orange dress. The crowd applauded, Calabaza's daughter laughed, and Prince Frog wriggled into her pocket without delay.

"BACK TO THE CONTEST!" cried Calabaza, and Rapunzel knelt at the ringside once more. She bounced her ball and scooped eight jacks.

Soon, they had cleared elevensies. Carmella smiled again.

"And now it gets interesting," she said.

Rapunzel pulled twelvesies with ease. "What does?" she asked.

Carmella's smile faded. She cleared twelvesies, and the champions on the platform below them murmured as they watched. They were no longer whispering or pointing.

Rapunzel pulled thirteensies. "What does?" she repeated. "Get interesting, I mean."

"The *game*," said Carmella, who was concentrating now. She gave her ball a hard bounce and managed to scoop thirteen jacks. The crowd gasped, then whooped and cheered.

"Really?" asked Rapunzel. "How does it?" She bounced her ball and picked up fourteen jacks. She didn't have to count them; she could feel the number in her hand. But fourteen was as high as she was usually able to catch. The ceiling of her tower wouldn't allow her to bounce the ball high enough to catch fifteen jacks in time.

Rapunzel counted her jacks and laid them in the ring. "Fourteen," she announced, and laughed when the crowd cheered.

"I do not appreciate your mocking me," Carmella hissed.

"Mocking you?" Rapunzel repeated. "What did I say?"

Carmella shut her mouth. She glanced down at the crowd below. And then she bounced her ball, hard and high, and scooped a number of jacks into her hand. The ball bounced, and she counted her jacks aloud as she laid them in the ring.

"Fourteen," she said.

The crowd roared, and Carmella's expression relaxed into a generous smile.

"Now," she said. "If you miss, and I do not, I win. If we both miss, we will move on to Variations — ups, downs, double ups and double downs, and so forth."

Rapunzel understood. "And if I don't miss, and you do?" she asked.

A hush fell over the crowd below.

Carmella's smile tightened. "Then you win," she said. "Go ahead."

Rapunzel flexed her hand. She threw her ball hard against the ground — there was no roof here, so she could get all the height she needed. The ball soared into the air, and Rapunzel swept a handful of jacks. She felt them; there were too many. She dropped one into the ring before the ball bounced.

Rapunzel opened her hand and counted out her jacks.

"Fifteen," she said, setting the last silver jack down with a click.

The crowd erupted. Carmella barely concealed a snarl. Rapunzel searched the cheering crowd until she found Jack, who had finally resurfaced near the platform. When he caught her eyes, his expression made Rapunzel feel warm. It was a little like the way Witch looked at her sometimes.

Rapunzel's heart gave a sudden twinge. She had barely thought of Witch at all since coming to Cornucopia. She wished that Witch could see her now, competing against a champion. Witch would have been so proud of her.

Carmella waited until the crowd had settled. The moment their attention was on her again, she dashed her ball to the ground. It shot into the air, and she grabbed her jacks. She opened her hand and looked at them, counted under her breath, dropped one jack, shook her head and picked it up again —

Her ball bounced. Carmella clenched her fist, and her eyes darted to Rapunzel's. One by one, she counted out her jacks, keeping her hand clutched around them.

Rapunzel held her breath. After laying down her thirteenth jack, Carmella tightened her fist again for a moment before slowly uncurling her fingers.

In her palm, there was only one jack.

A marvelous sensation, like buzzing, liquid heat, spread outward from Rapunzel's chest, filling her limbs and head. She had *won*.

Carmella placed her final jack in the ring. "Fourteen," she said, her voice flat.

"Challenger wins!" cried the umpire.

"HAIL THE NEW CHAMPION!" cried Governor Calabaza.

The park exploded in a frenzy of delirious noise as Rapunzel gathered her jacks, grinning so hard she thought her cheeks would split. Ground people weren't so bad when they were cheering, she thought. She saw one of Calabaza's sons collecting silver coins from the other two, and then she caught sight of Jack, who had thrown both fists into the air and was hollering himself hoarse. She laughed in delight.

"Beaten at Commons," said Carmella, staring at the ring, her voice low under the roar of the crowd. She raised her eyes to Rapunzel. "Where do you hail from?" she asked. "Where did you learn to play?"

"In my tower," said Rapunzel, still unable to stop smiling.

"And where is that?"

"In the Redlands."

Carmella's eyes widened. She stood up. "WAIT!" she cried, and the crowd turned to her. She pointed at Rapunzel. "The challenger is not from Yellow Country; she is from a tower in the Redlands!" Her voice was triumphant. "The contest does not stand!"

The crowd was quick to turn. Whistles and cheers became jeers and boos; people cried "Cheater!" and "Hunchback!" and threw things at the platform. Eggs, tomatoes, and even a fish splattered against Rapunzel, staining her cloak and stinging her eyes. The joy of victory evaporated, and she covered her head with her arms.

"ENOUGH!" cried Calabaza.

A final egg cracked against the wooden steps. The crowd fell silent.

Calabaza leaned forward in his throne and looked across the crowd at Rapunzel. "Is it true?" he asked her, and his voice did not boom now. It was timid. "Are you from . . ." He hesitated. "From a tower in the Redlands?"

"Yes," said Rapunzel. "Why?"

Calabaza's dark eyes flashed. "The Bargaining," he said.

Everyone in attendance went silent. The Nexus looked grim, and the governor's children gaped. All eyes turned to Rapunzel.

"The Bargaining," Carmella repeated in a whisper, staring at Rapunzel. She looked thunderstruck. "I was a child of nine when it happened; I lived near the house. . . ."

Rapunzel felt sudden, grasping hands on the back of her neck, and she cried out in alarm as Jack's cloak was torn from her throat. Her hair was exposed, and the crowd gasped with one voice.

"There's a wheel of hair on her back!" shouted the man who had stripped her of her cloak. He pointed at her. "She's no hunchback! The child has a braid as long as the tower is tall, just like the stories!"

"She's the witch's child!" shrieked a woman.

Screams went up around the park, and people scattered in every direction. Rapunzel knelt on the stage, looking down on the panicked crowd and understanding only that she was responsible for their terror. What the Bargaining was, or why they were afraid, she didn't know. She hugged herself and wished that she could call for Witch.

"What should I do?" she murmured.

"You should collect your winnings," said Carmella, still staring at her. "If you are the witch's child, then you hail from Yellow Country."

CHAPTER ELEVEN

CALABAZA'S guards seized Rapunzel. "Let me go!" she shouted, trying to wriggle out of their grip as they wrenched her to her feet. She nearly shook one of them off, but the guard caught her arm, twisted it behind her back, and pinned it there.

The guards marched Rapunzel down from the wooden plat-form. They steered her through the thinning crowd of villagers and straight to Governor Calabaza, who looked out at the fleeing crowds as though he wished he could have joined them.

"Well, don't hurt her," said Calabaza's daughter as the guards dragged a wincing Rapunzel before them. "Father," she said sharply, "tell them to let her go."

"All right, Delicata — let her go, let her go." Calabaza waved at the guards, who released Rapunzel. His daughter stepped back again.

"What do you want?" Rapunzel demanded. "Are you going to kill me? The last time people dragged me around, it was in the Red Glade, and all the fairies wanted me dead."

Calabaza looked amazed. Behind him, one of his sons snickered. "No, no killing," said Calabaza. "Certainly not." He adjusted his hat to scratch his bald head. "I only wanted to ask: Does Envearia know you're here?"

"If you mean Witch," said Rapunzel, who couldn't help thinking that it was very strange to have heard that name again, from a new source, "then no, she doesn't."

"Then she didn't let you out of the tower."

"She didn't have to let me out," said Rapunzel. "I climbed down."

"You escaped," said Calabaza. Sweat stood out on his brow.

"I didn't *have* to escape," said Rapunzel. "I just left."

"You . . . weren't imprisoned?" He looked bewildered. "She wasn't cruel to you?"

"Cruel? Witch?" Rapunzel laughed at him. "Of course not," she said. "She loves me."

His eyebrows shot up. "Well, that's not so bad, is it?" he asked.

"Exactly," said Rapunzel. "Now, can I go, please? I'm on my way to the First Wood."

"Certainly, you may go," said the governor. "Accept the apology of Yellow Country, and . . . yes, be on your way, of course, the First Wood, whatever you like."

"The apology of Yellow Country?"

"For not intervening," said Calabaza, "at the time of the Bargaining. Your mother asked for help, and I was sorry, of course — children of my own, you know, and I felt for her, I did — but what could I do? There was nothing I could do. Envearia won you fair and square, and then she took you into another country, out of my power. Nothing I could do. Leave the magic to the magical, you understand. No good can come from interfering. . . . Isn't that right, Nexus Burdock?"

Calabaza looked up at the Nexus, who colored slightly. "Interference was not deemed prudent," he said.

"Give her the winnings, Nexus," Delicata said. "You've got them, don't you?"

Nexus Burdock gave Rapunzel a lopsided smile. In spite of the amulet that shone from his breast, reminding her of his magical importance, he appeared friendly and kind. "It doesn't make up for what you've endured," he said, holding out a leather pouch. "No amount of money can erase your past. But it *can* help to build your future."

"I don't want to erase my past," said Rapunzel, thinking of the memories she had lost already. "And what do you mean about building my future? What am I supposed to build?"

Nexus Burdock looked mildly surprised, but sympathetic too. "That's up to you," he said. "You're free. You can choose any path you wish."

She took the pouch he offered her. It was heavy, and its contents clinked.

"Well said, well said!" Calabaza clapped his hands against the arms of his chair. "Congratulations to the new Capital Champion of Cornucopia! And now, to the carriages!"

The party began to disperse. Delicata hung back for a moment.

"I'm glad you'll represent Yellow at the ATC next summer," she said warmly to Rapunzel. "You're really good. Don't slack off just because you've had a victory, all right? Keep practicing. The champion from Brown has won the last three tournaments in a row, and it's time he got thrashed."

"ATC?" Rapunzel repeated.

Delicata's eyebrows shot up. "Of course you don't know," she said with a shake of her head. "The All-Tyme Championships. We'll send an invitation and explain everything, but where should we send . . . That is, are you still living at that tower, or —"

"Deli," Calabaza barked, looking quickly around the park as if expecting someone to appear at any moment. "No more."

"All right — but don't forget your friend," she said, and she extracted Prince Frog from her pocket. He looked a bit greener than usual. Rapunzel took him, but he slipped out of her grasp and flung himself onto the platform, where he hopped once more toward Delicata's skirt.

"Come *back*, Prince Frog," said Rapunzel. "Wait — Governor! I mean, your lordship!"

Calabaza turned with obvious reluctance. "Yes?"

"What's the Bargaining?" she asked. "And what do you mean about my mother?"

Before he could answer, one of Calabaza's sons let out a powerful shriek. "It's in my hair!" he screamed, batting at his head.

Guards ran toward him. Calabaza looked terrified.

"It's down my back!" shrieked the boy, waving his arms in the air. "It's in my sleeve —"

As Rapunzel watched, Prince Frog wriggled out from between the boy's neck and his shirt collar. The instant he appeared, one of the guards smacked him away with such force that Prince Frog flew through the air with a miserable, rasping croak.

"Prince Frog!" cried Rapunzel, and she pelted down the steps of the platform. Calabaza's other sons roared with laughter. She dove toward the place where Prince Frog was falling and just barely caught him in her outstretched fingers. He shuddered in her hands.

"*Ground* people," said Rapunzel, getting to her feet and snatching up the pouch of money, which she had dropped in her rush. She glanced at Calabaza, but he was paying no attention to her; guards escorted his party away in a great hurry. Prince Frog wriggled from her hands again and hopped after them.

"Prince Frog!" Rapunzel crouched and scooped him up again. "What's *wrong* with you?"

"Rapunzel!" Jack appeared out of the thinning crowd. "You won! I can't believe you won — you get to go to the All-Tyme Championships." He looked at her with new respect. "I'm sort of sorry you won at Commons, actually; it would've been great to see you beat her with some tricks. Can you do any variations? Like backhand catches, or flips, or —"

"Yes," Rapunzel interrupted, getting a grip on Prince Frog, who was still struggling to get out of her hands. "I can do all of it. Here — take the money, would you?"

Jack took the pouch, unlaced it, and dug into it. He brought out a fistful of gold, bronze, and copper coins, which he let sift through his fingers and fall, clinking, back into the pouch. There was a silver piece as well, which he gazed at in wonder. He flipped it in his fingers and looked up at Rapunzel.

"You were born here, huh?" he asked. "What's the Bargaining? People got out of here so fast, you'd think there were giants after them."

Rapunzel was uneasy. She wished she knew the answers. She *should* have known them. It was wrong that so many strangers knew things about her that she didn't.

"I didn't know I was born here," she said. "*Stop it*, Prince Frog. Is that enough money to get boots?"

Jack cinched the pouch and held it out to Rapunzel. "It's ten times more money than I've ever seen in one place," he said. "We can get all the supplies we need."

"You carry it."

He looked all too happy to stow the pouch in his knapsack.

"Hold Prince Frog too," Rapunzel said. His struggles had grown so desperate that she feared she would hurt him if she clutched him any harder. "Do you have a pocket that buttons? He's being a very bad frog."

Jack opened a large pocket in his vest. He pulled out a handful of things and shoved them into his knapsack, then took Prince Frog, stowed him in the pocket, and buttoned it. The pocket bulged and strained, and Prince Frog croaked from within it.

Rapunzel adjusted her wheel on her back and sighed.

"You know what you need?" said Jack. "A wagon. It rolls, and you pull it with a handle." He pantomimed for Rapunzel's benefit. "You could put your hair in it."

The idea of putting her hair somewhere other than her back was so welcome to Rapunzel that she readily agreed, and they set off together toward the shops, which sat on the opposite bank of the river that flowed alongside the park.

First they bought a wagon. Rapunzel laid the hair wheel in the rectangular bed with a sigh of relief, then lifted the wagon handle and pulled it along behind her through the few remaining shoppers. All of them stared at her — not particularly nice stares, but not hostile and scary ones like the fairies had given her. Rapunzel tried to smile at a few of the people who passed her, but every time she managed to meet someone's eyes, they glanced immediately away.

"Might as well give up," Jack said to her, flicking back his hair. "When people don't want to get involved in your problems, they just pretend not to see you."

Next, Jack bought a sword. It was sharp and light, and Rapunzel admired it as Jack buckled the scabbard to his belt. When he was finished, he straightened up and put his hand on the hilt.

"You look more like a prince now," said Rapunzel, thinking of the illustrations in her books. Jack lifted his chin into the air. "Should I get a sword too?" she asked.

He helped her to find a sturdy dagger, a useful leather belt with pouches, and a water skin of her own. They also found gloves and cloaks, which Jack said they would need by the time they got to the center of Green, where it was bound to be much colder. He stowed their purchases in the wagon with her hair, paid for it all with a flourish, and led the way to the biggest shop Rapunzel had yet seen. It took up an entire street at the very top of the park, and its long, tall window-panes glinted in the sunlight. Bright golden letters shone in an arc above the great double doors: *UBIQUITOUS.*

"Ubiquitous!" said Rapunzel, running up to the shop with her wagon rattling behind her. "Oh . . . ," she breathed as she stared through one of the enormous windows. "Look at it all!"

The Ubiquitous shop was enormous. Hundreds of polished barrels gleamed within, stacked sideways along every wall and all the way up to the vaulted ceilings. Tall, rolling ladders made it possible to climb to the very highest rows. In each barrel end was a little glass door with a shining copper handle, and beside each door hung a palm-size copper shovel, just the right size for scooping out a handful of something.

"Are all of those barrels full of acorns?" asked Rapunzel, squinting to see through the glass doors.

"Yep," said Jack as he strode toward the front doors. "This is just what we need."

Rapunzel followed him. "Will they have bread and ropes and bridges?"

"They'll have everything you can think of, and things you've never heard of."

A sudden burst of energetic noise erupted from across the street. Rapunzel turned to see what the sound was, and when she saw who was making it, she gripped Jack's arm.

"Blue fairies," he whispered.

Two of them. They were as big as humans, and they were different shades of blue, with small wings that glittered in the sun. The woman fairy was laughing as though she had never heard anything so funny in her life — a low, husky laugh, which made her sequined dress sparkle on her short, curvaceous frame.

"You are too *much*," she said to a human woman who stood by the door of the building from which they'd just emerged. "I'd just eat you up if I weren't already so fat, I swear I would." The woman said something in reply, and the fairy answered, "No, *you're* fabulous. Pleasure doing business with you. Ta, babe."

The woman shut the door. The instant it closed, the fairy stopped laughing and scowled. She heaved a gusty sigh of annoyance and pushed a hand through her short spikes of frosty blue hair.

"I hate this town," she muttered. "Can that aunt be more provincial? The girl just wants to marry a merman in an underwater ceremony. Like it's the first time *that's* ever happened. Did you take notes?"

"Yes, Jules," said the other fairy. His posture was impeccable; his voice was flat. "I'll organize it."

"Perfect. If I don't take ten minutes for my*self*, I'll lose my *mind*." Jules rubbed her blue temples with her fingertips. "I mean, honestly," she groaned, "when's the last time I did anything just for *me*?"

The fairy beside her did not answer. He was reading what looked like a very long list, and his lips were pressed together.

"We'll get some work done tonight, sound good? I *swear* I won't keep you as late as yesterday. Ta, babe." Jules fluttered her glittering wings until they were moving so fast that Rapunzel could no longer see them, and she rose several inches into the air. She flew off down the road, leaving the other fairy behind.

"*We'll* get some work done," this fairy said to no one in particular. He grimaced at the list in his hands, then stalked to the front door of the Ubiquitous shop. He stopped at Jack's elbow without sparing a glance for either of them, and Rapunzel stared at him, half-frightened, half-fascinated. He was taller than she by a few inches, with pale blond hair that was cut short all over his head except in the very front, where a thick plume of it fell in a perfect wave over half of his forehead, partly obscuring one eye. His suit and cloak were crisp, cream-colored velvet, his black boots were high-heeled, and his wings were taut. He put out his blue hand with a sharp gesture, blew the doors of the Ubiquitous shop open with a bang, and went inside. Rapunzel and Jack exchanged glances, then hurried into the shop after the fairy. Rapunzel barely had time to yank her wagon in behind her before the doors slammed shut.

The Ubiquitous shop was cavernous in size, with every surface polished to gleaming. It was empty of people except for the shopkeeper. He stood up when they entered, blinked first at the Blue fairy and then at Rapunzel, and then ducked down behind the counter, out of sight.

The Blue fairy took a large wicker basket from the front of the shop and clicked his way over to a wall of polished barrels, filled with acorns of all hues. Rapunzel pulled her wagon to the closest section, over which swung a little gilt sign that read *New Additions*. Rapunzel read one of the tiny copper plaques above the little glass doors: *Writing quills — 3 thorns*.

Rapunzel withdrew an acorn and turned it over in her hand. It was pumpkin-orange, with a quill stamped on it.

"Why didn't your acorns have pictures?" she asked Jack, who was also surveying the newest Ubiquitous products.

"I think they sell different stuff in the Violet Peaks," he said. "It's a lot cheaper there — that means it costs less money."

"What does this one do?" asked Rapunzel, putting back the quill and picking up a small glassy-looking acorn from a bin marked *Spectacles (Nearsighted) — 5 thorns*. Jack explained, and Rapunzel realized that she had just seen spectacles a moment ago.

"Oh!" she said. "Like the Nexus was wearing. Where can you get one of those amulets he had? They're pretty."

The Blue fairy paused in his acorn collecting. He turned his head toward Rapunzel, and she wished she'd kept her voice low.

"You can't *get* an amulet," said Jack. "I told you, you have to be born Exalted. Hey, there's the aisle we need." He pointed to a sign that read *Adventure*. "That'll be tents and lanterns and stuff; come on."

He went, but Rapunzel didn't follow. Instead, she looked up at the signs, amazed by how many aisles there were and not sure where to start. *Fashion . . . Tools . . . Housewares . . .* It all sounded interesting, but when her eyes fell on *Edibles*, Rapunzel forgot everything else and hurried toward the food. She was full now, but she had felt hunger this morning, and she had no intention of feeling it again. She was delighted to find acorns that would crack into all sorts of good things, like cheese and apples, sausage and eggs, rice pudding, hot chocolate, and tea. She scooped shovelfuls of everything into the wagon.

"Hungry?" came a dry voice from her shoulder.

Rapunzel jumped. The Blue fairy stood beside her. She took two steps back and watched him warily. His own expression was a mixture of mockery and suspicion.

"Any particular reason that you're out shopping in your nightgown?" he asked, folding his velvet-clad arms.

Rapunzel tried to take another step back and nearly fell over her wagon. She stood with her calves pressed against it, hugging herself. "Don't kill me," she whispered.

The fairy looked mildly amused. "That's not my line of business," he said. "My name's Serge. What's yours?"

"Rapunzel," she whispered.

"Funny name." Serge swept his eyes over her dirty clothes and slippers. "You ran away from home," he said, "didn't you?"

The question was so unexpected that Rapunzel was surprised by emotion. "I didn't want to," she whispered, wiping her eyes with the blackened lace cuffs of her robe.

"Sure you didn't." Serge eyed her tearful face with disdain. "Go home."

"I can't," Rapunzel said, sniffling and scrubbing at her cheeks. "I'm not allowed. They won't let me go back."

Serge looked halfway surprised by this. "Who won't let you?" he asked. "Your parents?"

"The fairies."

His eyebrows arched. "Yellow fairies won't let you go home?"

"No, the fairies in the Redlands."

"*Red* fairies? But they'd never . . ."

His eyes followed her braid to the wagon, where it was buried under a heap of cloaks, supplies, and Ubiquitous acorns.

"You don't . . . happen to have a hundred feet of hair under there," he asked slowly, "do you?"

Rapunzel nodded, and Serge's wings wilted.

"Great White skies," he said. "It's been fifteen years."

At this moment, Jack rounded the end of the *Edibles* aisle. When he saw Rapunzel wiping away tears, he strode up. "What is it?" he asked in a low voice, glancing toward Serge. "You all right?"

Serge was still staring at her braid. "Ra*punzel*," he said. "I knew I'd heard that name."

"You know her?" Jack asked, stepping forward. "You've heard of her too?"

"Sure." Serge gave Jack an appraising look and shrugged. "It's *the* fashionable dare. Find the tower, try to get the girl to come down. Most people aren't stupid enough to cross a witch, especially Envearia, but you get your thrill seekers. . . ." He cocked his head to one side and studied Rapunzel with interest. "How did you get out of the tower?" he asked.

"I climbed down a Ubiquitous rope," said Rapunzel.

Serge whistled. "Bet Envearia wasn't expecting *that*," he said. "Did she come after you? Ah, but that might spoil things, hmm? Tricky, tricky. I wonder what her plan is?"

"She can't come after me," said Rapunzel. "Rune — the Red fairy — he says he'll kill me if I call for her. He's following me to make sure."

"Interesting," said Serge with a flicker of his wings. "Following you where?"

"To the First Wood."

At this, Serge let out a peal of shocked laughter. "Well, if you're not just one surprise after another," he said. "Envearia might have made a perfect bargain with your parents, but I'll bet she never counted on this."

Rapunzel's heartbeat quickened. "What parents?" she asked. "Governor Calabaza said something about me having a mother, but I don't!"

Serge's blue face paled. "You don't know?" he asked. "You don't know —"

"*What?*"

But he didn't seem to be able to make himself answer. "How do you think Envearia got you?" he asked instead.

"Witch rescued me," Rapunzel said. "From the swamplands. What were you going to say about parents?" When Serge remained speechless, she stamped her sore, slippered foot on the polished wooden floor. "If you're not going to answer me, then go away and let me get some shoes. I'm so *tired* of you fairies! You're all horrible and confusing!"

"Don't hold it against her," Jack said to Serge. "The witch never told her anything real. She didn't even know what parents were till I explained it."

Serge considered him. "And *you* are?"

"Jack Byre of the Violet Peaks," said Jack. "I rescued her from the tower."

Rapunzel opened her mouth in indignation. He had done nothing of the kind.

"And when I met her," Jack went on, "she didn't want to leave at all — Envearia had her thinking she'd get eaten by beasts, and she was too scared to come with me."

"That's not true!" said Rapunzel, rounding on him. "I didn't want to leave my tower because I love it."

"You were brainwashed."

"No, Witch never washed out my brain. She said it was the fairies who took my memory!"

"Took your memory?" Serge peered at Rapunzel. "Is that how Envearia keeps you from asking questions? She wipes your mind?"

"Yes," said Jack.

"No," shouted Rapunzel at the same moment. "You don't know anything," she said to Jack. "Witch would never hurt me. You don't understand."

"She lied to you."

"No —"

"You *know* she did," Jack insisted. "She told you towns were full of diseased peasants who would sell you into slavery, but Cornucopia isn't. She told you the Redlands was in the center, but it's not —"

"She told me there were beasts, which there are, and horrible people, which there *are* —"

"She never told you about your parents, or that you were born in Yellow."

Rapunzel felt as though she could not breathe. It was true — Witch had never told her. Why had she kept such secrets?

"You don't understand," she repeated.

"Let's all take a moment," said Serge, holding up a blue hand. He was silent for a space, and Rapunzel hugged herself while she waited for him to speak. She could not look at Jack.

"I think I see how it is," said Serge finally. "Maybe I can explain a few things, but we'll take it slowly. First things first." He guided Rapunzel into the middle of the shop. "Stand there a minute and let me fix you up." He stepped back and studied her. "Technically, I'm not supposed to do this — you're not on the List. But you're a special case, wouldn't you say?" He tapped his finger in the air toward her feet. "What you need is real shoes."

"I know that," mumbled Rapunzel, wiping her nose. "I'm getting Ubiquitous ones."

"No you're not," Serge said. "They only last twenty-four hours."

"Then why are they for sale?"

"They're for one-night events: balls, parties, that sort of thing. You're a tall one, aren't you?" Putting his hand flat, he touched the top of her head and then drew his hand toward his own face until he touched his eyebrows. "And you've got some big feet there too. . . . So. Shoes for a long journey." Serge looked at her ruined slippers. "Take those off," he commanded.

"Do you want me to burn them?" Rapunzel asked as she peeled a filthy slipper from her foot.

"I wasn't going to say it," said Serge, "but yes." When both Rapunzel's slippers were off her feet, he flicked his fingers in the air, and a bit of what looked like blue glitter flew from his fingertips. The slippers were incinerated in a burst of bright flame and a puff of blue smoke.

Serge exhaled with satisfaction, closed his eyes, and pressed his mouth shut. Rapunzel watched him curiously.

"What are you doing?"

"Designing. Shh — a minute, please."

"Designing what?"

"Shoes." Serge's eyes snapped open. He swept his fingers through the air, drew them into a fist, and opened them to reveal a palm that was covered in the same blue, glittery dust that had flown from his fingertips before. He looked down at his hand in surprise. "I forgot what it's like when I actually *want* to do this," he said. "Anything in your pockets?"

When Rapunzel checked, she found her jacks, which Serge told her to put in one of her belt pouches. And then, with a sharp swish of his arm, he flung the dust at her. A cloud of pale blue smoke burst around Rapunzel, enveloping her from head to toe. When it cleared, she looked down at herself — and gasped.

Her tattered nightclothes had been replaced by a long tunic with billowing sleeves and a fitted vest with many useful pockets — rather like Jack's, but not shabby — cinched around by her leather belt. Her trousers fit her well but were stretchy, giving her room to crouch or climb. The entire outfit was made from fine, heavy fabrics in greens, browns, and tans, expertly tailored to her height and figure, and soft against her skin.

Best of all, her feet and calves were now encased in high, thick-soled boots made of dark green leather, with shining buckles at the ankles and calf tops. The inner soles were lined with soft fleece that cushioned Rapunzel's blistered feet, almost relieving them of pain. She bounced on her toes and took a few steps, and then she put her hands over her face and cried just a little in relief.

"You don't like them?" Serge asked. "I suppose I could've gone trendier, but you'll be hiking — and all the ladies in Blue are dressing like gentlemen this season, so I thought —"

"I like them *so* much," blurted Rapunzel. "They're the most comfortable shoes I've ever worn."

Serge's wings flared.

It was a long time before Rapunzel could do anything but admire her shoes. She paced the shop from end to end, delighted. "Will they crash?" she asked, holding up one booted foot.

"Never," said Serge. He flicked his gaze to Jack, whose vest pocket still bulged from time to time as Prince Frog continued his losing struggle. Serge's attention, however, was fixed on Jack's battered boots. "You could use some new shoes yourself," he said. "You've about worn those through. How about it?"

Jack's face lit. "Yeah — I mean, thanks," he said. "If it's all right."

He was soon shod in striking black boots that Rapunzel thought went very well with his sword and made him look even more princely — though he didn't deserve to know that. He shouldn't have said those things about Witch. Even if Witch *had* hidden things — which Rapunzel had to admit was true; Witch had hidden things — she must have had good reasons.

What were the reasons?

Troubled, Rapunzel approached the counter to pay for their acorns. Mostly they'd selected camping equipment and food, but Jack had also gathered a handful of miniature acorns that glittered, pale green and blue and gold. As he showed them to Rapunzel, his hair fell over his eyes and partly obscured the pink in his cheeks. "Costumes to bring back for Tess," he said. "From the kids' section. She's never been in a shop like this; there's nothing like it in the Peaks."

"Costumes?" asked Rapunzel. "For playing dress-up?"

"Fairy wings, a tiara, glass slippers — that kind of stuff. We don't have to buy them," he said hastily. "I can put them back."

"No, let's buy them! Where are they? I want some too."

Paying for it all was a little difficult, as the shopkeeper remained cowering under the counter, but Rapunzel remembered what Jack had told her about Hawthornes. As Serge watched, she laid out the right coins.

"So you know how to count," said Serge. "Can you read too? Envearia taught you?"

"Of course she did," said Rapunzel, insulted. She tucked the remaining money into a pouch in her belt, stowed the acorns under the cloaks in the wagon, and held the wagon handle out to Jack.

"We have to take turns pulling," she said, "since both our things are in it."

Jack took the wagon handle from her, and they followed Serge out of the shop.

"If you're looking for the First Wood, then I'm going your way, at least for a little while," said Serge. "I know a shortcut."

They headed north out of the town center, through another cluster of houses that spilled out into great swaths of farmland. Tyme stretched endlessly ahead, and many leagues of travel remained before they would reach the First Wood, but the distance didn't worry Rapunzel now. Wagons were wonderful inventions, and boots were the best shoes in the world. She could not believe she had come all this way in slippers with her hair on her back.

But though her feet were comfortable, her mind was not. Her thoughts fixed on her mother and father, the Bargaining, and Envearia. Envearia — that had to be Witch's name. The Red fairies, Governor Calabaza, and now Serge had all called her the same thing. Rapunzel wondered why Witch had never told her that she had another name.

They passed the outer limits of Cornucopia. Lush farmlands rolled onward before them, empty and quiet. A light rain fell, pattering against the dirt road and refreshing Rapunzel's skin. Serge ushered them toward a copse of trees at the bottom of the road, which he said was the shortcut.

The three of them walked into it, and Rapunzel realized at once that she was in another fairywood. Like the one in the Redlands, it was silent and full of slender, silvery trees and the strange, not-quite-sound of faint chiming. When they walked out of it again, the landscape ahead was foreign. Gone were the gently rolling farmlands. Ahead were high hills of shining green, planted thickly with trees. The sky was cold, clear blue, and the temperature had plummeted, but Rapunzel decided she liked the chill air. It tasted of pine and made her feel alive all over, just like the green hills ahead.

"Have we left Yellow Country?" she asked. "Is this Commonwealth Green?"

"It is," said Serge. "I'd say I just put you several days ahead of schedule — no, don't thank me, it's the least I can do. Now, you must have questions."

Rapunzel drew a deep breath as they started to climb the first hill.

"What do you know about my mother and father?"

"Not much," Serge replied. "They had a house on the border of Yellow. Envearia had the house behind it, just inside the border of Green. Their gardens were separated by a fence."

"Witch lived in Commonwealth Green?" asked Rapunzel. "Is her house still there?"

"It's empty now," said Serge. "Or so I hear."

"Did my parents know her?"

Serge shook his head. "They moved into their house right before you were born," he said. "The way I heard it, behind your parents' house, Envearia had a fantastic garden full of vegetables and salad greens. And since your mother was pregnant with you, she started to crave those greens."

Rapunzel knew only what Jack had told her about pregnancy, which wasn't much. "She was very big?" she asked, extending her arms away from her stomach in a circle. "And she was hungrier than usual, because she was so big?"

"Right," said Serge. "So she sent your father over the fence to get some of the greens from Envearia's garden —"

"To steal them?"

"Well . . . yes," Serge admitted. "And Envearia caught him. She told him he could have the greens, but that she wanted you in exchange. Your dad was so frightened of Envearia that he agreed. And so, when you were born, Envearia took you from your parents, whisked you away to the Redlands, and put you in the tower. People around here called it the Bargaining."

Rapunzel frowned. "Why was everyone so afraid, then?" she asked. "The Bargaining was only a trade."

Serge and Jack looked incredulously at her.

"But *you* got traded!" said Jack. "She took you from your parents!"

"Why should I have wanted to stay with them, if they were willing to give me away for a salad?" asked Rapunzel. "At least Witch wanted me. I'd rather be with someone who wants me."

Neither Jack nor Serge had any reply to this.

"Now I understand why Witch didn't tell me," said Rapunzel. "She didn't want me to feel hurt because my parents didn't want me. She never wants me to be hurt."

"Oh, really?" Jack snapped. "Is that why she messes with your brain?"

Rapunzel shot a glare at him. "How many times do I have to tell you — it was the *fairies*."

"You can tell me all you want, but you'll still be wrong. You *saw* Prince Dash holding that piece of your hair. You *know* the witch went after him for cutting it."

Serge stopped walking with a jerk. "What about Prince Dash?" he demanded. "Did Envearia hurt him?"

"She turned him to stone," said Jack. "He's a statue in the Redwoods, between the tower and the Red Glade."

"Is he alive?"

"I don't know. I couldn't tell."

"He'll have to be found," Serge said. "I've got to go."

"But you can't go!" cried Rapunzel. "I still have questions!"

"The king and queen might not even know he's missing," Serge said. "I need to get back to Quintessential."

"But where are my mother and father?"

Serge's wings tensed.

"What is it?" asked Rapunzel. "Please, tell me."

The fairy drew a deep breath, laid a blue hand on her shoulder, and spoke with gentle directness. "Your parents died," he said. "A long time ago. I'm so sorry."

The words passed through Rapunzel like water. She felt vaguely disappointed.

"They're killed, then?" she asked.

"Well . . ." Serge frowned. "Yes."

Rapunzel toed the grass with her boot. "So where are they?" she asked. She wondered what they looked like.

Serge's frown deepened. "I'm sorry you don't understand," he said, "but I don't have any more time. Jack, you take over from here." He squeezed Rapunzel's shoulder. "You'll be fine. Just stay on the ground — and don't agree to any more mind wipes."

He let go of Rapunzel, snapped his fingers, and vanished. Nothing but a faint cloud of blue smoke remained where Serge had stood.

CHAPTER TWELVE

JACK looked gravely at Rapunzel.

"I'm sorry," he said.

Rapunzel was taken aback. He sounded unlike himself.

"What for?" she asked him.

"Because your parents died," he said, as though that were obvious.

She shrugged a little. "I didn't know them," she said.

"Aren't you sad at *all*?"

"No." Rapunzel didn't like his expression. "Stop looking at me like that," she said. "How am I supposed to feel?"

"Awful," Jack said. "Your parents *died*."

"Well, I don't understand why you want me to feel awful about *their* being dead, when they didn't care a thing about me," said Rapunzel. "But you don't think I should worry about Witch, when she's the one who loves me."

For the second time that afternoon, Jack had no ready response. "Let's go," he said after a moment. He jerked his thumb toward the wagon. "Your turn."

As Rapunzel reached out for the wagon handle, she noticed that Jack's front pocket had gone still. "Oh — Prince Frog!" she said, putting her hand to her mouth. "I hope he's all right — take him out, would you? See if he'll stay put."

Jack unbuttoned his pocket and pulled out a rather wilted Prince Frog, whom he placed on his shoulder. Prince Frog sat slumped there, his golden eyes fixed dully on the distance, and he made no attempt to hop anywhere as Rapunzel and Jack hiked into the north.

"Why did you ask Serge where your parents were," asked Jack, "*after* he told you they were dead?"

"Well, they're killed, aren't they?"

"And why do you keep calling it that?"

"Because in my books, if people get killed, they're dead."

"But some people don't get killed. Some people just die."

This was a new idea, and Rapunzel rejected it. "You can't just *die*," she said scornfully. "You have to drown, or get your head chopped off, or *something*."

"No," said Jack, "if you're lucky, you get nice and old, and you die in your sleep."

"How old?"

"Like eighty or ninety. People who are fairy-born live longer than that, but regular people usually don't. My mom's parents died at sixty-three and seventy-one."

"Why? Did something crush them?"

"No!" Jack laughed. "They just got old."

"What does that matter?"

"Because when you get old, you wear out, I guess," he said. "You get sick more easily. And one day you die."

They crested another hill. The sun had begun to set, and the trees around them stood out sharply against the sky.

"One day I die?" echoed Rapunzel. "How do you know?"

"Because everyone dies."

"Not Witch. She's ever so old, and *she* never dies."

"She's a witch," said Jack.

"Well, if Witch doesn't die, then I won't either," said Rapunzel. "Not unless I get killed."

"What does that even mean to you?" Jack replied in exasperation.

"When a person is killed, it means they're very hurt," said Rapunzel. "Like when I almost drowned. It's very, very bad."

"Yeah, it's bad," said Jack with a snort. "It means your body stops working."

"Like Prince Dash!" said Rapunzel. "Like a frozen statue."

"It's not the same." Jack stooped to pick up a long stick from the ground. "I'm trying to remember how I explained this to Tess," he said. "But I don't think I ever had to. Nobody had to explain it to me either — I saw animals die on the farm, and I guess it just made sense after a while."

"What did?"

"Death," said Jack. "Look. When you die, it means . . . well, it means you're gone for good. Your body gets buried under the ground, and the rest of you goes into the Beyond."

"The rest of me?"

"The part that isn't physical."

"Oh." Rapunzel thought about this for a little while. "You mean my feelings?"

"Sort of, yeah. Some people call it a soul. Some people call it the shard of the Black. Some people don't believe there's a Beyond at all — they think we just rot, and that's it."

"Are they right?"

"I don't think so. But who knows?"

"Doesn't anybody know?"

Jack shrugged. "Some people say they do," he said. "My mom believes in the Beyond. She says she can feel it. My dad said it's better left a mystery, and I agree with him."

"What about Tess?"

Jack shot her a surprised, grateful look. "Tess thinks everyone in the Beyond is happy," he said. "And at peace. And that they're together with the people they love."

This, Rapunzel liked. "If I die," she said, still not convinced she ever would, "do you think I could meet my parents in the Beyond?"

"Maybe. If it works like that." Jack looked sideways at her. "I thought you didn't care about your parents."

"I don't, I just . . ."

"Yeah?"

"I don't know. I'd like to at least meet them."

Jack looked somewhat relieved to hear this.

They headed up the next hill. It was very steep, but Rapunzel's thoughts were so deep and strange and new that she barely felt the climb. She had a mother and father, but she couldn't know them. Her parents' bodies were buried in the ground, and the rest of them was in the Beyond, where she could not go. Maybe they were happy there.

She wondered how they had died. She wondered what had happened before that, when they were still alive. Governor Calabaza had said that her mother had gone to him for help after the Bargaining. But why? Her mother hadn't wanted her, had she? Serge had made it clear that her parents had traded her to Witch, fair and square.

She found that she couldn't help imagining what her life might have been like if there had been no Bargaining. She would have grown up in Yellow — what an odd thought. She would have had to find ways to get money for food and clothes. She might have learned to swim. She might have lived near Cornucopia and been in lots of jacks contests. She might have played with other children.

How different her tower was. Everything in it was beautiful and easy. Everything belonged only to her. There was no need to worry over money or clothing or hunger, no need to learn how to swim. Things had been perfect since before she could remember.

Though lately, her memory hadn't been quite reliable.

Rapunzel rubbed her head. She tried to think back to her birthday, a year ago, and was almost not surprised when her memory seemed too short. She had no sense of whether certain days were missing or whether anything unusual had passed, but she didn't believe she remembered *enough* to fill a year.

It was impossible that Witch would have wiped her mind and lied about it. Wasn't it? Witch might have kept secrets from her, but that didn't change the fact that she loved her. The fairies *must* have wiped her mind themselves. But if that was true, then why hadn't they done it again, in the Red Glade? Rune had asked her that — if he could have done it, why wouldn't he? Maybe he had been trying to confuse her.

Perhaps he had been trying to trick her into this. Into doubting Witch.

Her thoughts circled in this way for an hour. When it was time to stop and camp, Rapunzel was sorry; although she was exhausted, she would rather have kept walking until she burned out her thoughts altogether.

"Look at that, would you?" said Jack.

Rapunzel stood still and watched the sun drop beyond the

horizon. The sky darkened for a dramatic moment, then shone with pink light. It was as pretty as any sunset she had seen from the top of the tower, and she liked watching it from here, in the brisk, cool wind, listening to the rustling of the trees that grew in small thickets all over the hills.

"This is my favorite weather," said Jack. "Clear and cold."

Rapunzel thought it might be her favorite too, but saying so felt somehow traitorous. The weather at home never felt like this.

"So the Blue Kingdom is that way," she said, nodding to the sunset. "And the sea?"

"Yeah," said Jack. "When I go there, I'll work on one of the ships to get passage out to the Olive Isles."

"Ships?" asked Rapunzel.

And so Jack explained ships and sails to Rapunzel as they cracked their Ubiquitous acorns and made their surroundings comfortable. First they cracked a little green tent and made it comfortable with pillows and woolly blankets. Jack pulled a tiny lantern from his knapsack and hung it from a hook inside the tent's peak, and Rapunzel parked the wagon outside the tent door and unwound enough of her hair from the wheel to let her lie down and sleep. They took off their boots and vests, and settled down to eat sausages and cheese and drink mugs of hot chocolate that steamed in the cold night air. When they finally crawled into the tent, their teeth chattered, and they dove under the blankets. Jack told stories of things he'd seen and read and heard about — stories he said Tess had always liked to hear — and Rapunzel mostly let him talk. He seemed happiest when he was telling stories and explaining things, so he didn't mind her silence, and she had much to consider and little to say.

She lay on her back, staring up at the lantern and petting Prince Frog, who camped on her stomach. She thought about Witch, and about everything that had happened since Jack came to the tower. And then she thought of Serge, telling her not to agree to any more mind wipes.

"I won't," Rapunzel mumbled to herself.

"Won't what?" said Jack. "Are you even listening to me?"

"Yes," said Rapunzel. "Go on about mermaids."

She let go of her troubling thoughts as Jack told stories of women with fish tails, who could breathe underwater and wore jewels in their scales. Rapunzel listened to his voice until she fell asleep.

In the morning, they consulted their map. The last village they'd passed was Bayberry. If they headed slightly northwest today, then tomorrow they could follow the main road north along the Mimicry River. The air was frosty, and Rapunzel reached for her cloak, but Jack cautioned her away.

"You'll get hot enough walking," he said.

He was right. They walked all day, over green hills and past two small villages, until Rapunzel's tunic was damp with sweat. At sunset, they descended into a valley that dropped more sharply than any they'd seen so far in Green. The rocky road wound back and forth in a long, snaking pattern, and when they reached the bottom, Rapunzel didn't know which idea she disliked more — to climb up to the other side immediately or to wait and do it first thing in the morning.

They decided to camp in the valley. They had another friendly evening together, and Jack taught Rapunzel how to build a fire without any help from Ubiquitous acorns, which was a very good distraction from her thoughts. But though she settled down and fell asleep that night in moderate comfort, she did not wake up in the same way.

Someone clamped a hand over her mouth.

Rapunzel came fully awake at once with every muscle tensed, her scream stuck in her throat. She opened her eyes. It was barely light out, certainly not time to be awake yet, but Jack was kneeling beside her, practically smothering her with his palm. She smacked at him, but he caught her smacking hand in his free one and gripped it.

"Shh." He waited for Rapunzel to relax before he lifted his hand. "Listen."

There was rustling outside the tent, and the sounds of two people whispering. Rapunzel saw the shadows and light of a lantern swinging and heard a tinny clang, as though something had dropped into the wagon, which was parked outside the tent with all their things in it.

Including her hair. Rapunzel sat up, ready to scream down the valley, but Jack covered her mouth again and shook his head.

"Bandits," he whispered, his mouth very close to her ear so that he made almost no noise. He was shaking as he put his hand to the hilt of his sword. "I'll sneak up on them and save our stuff. Don't move again — if you do, your braid will move in the wagon, and they'll see it."

Rapunzel stayed where she was as Jack crept out of the tent and became a silhouette on the wall. She watched him crouch and look around the corner.

"NO!" he yelled. His shadow lunged toward the two whisperers, who were standing near the wagon. There were two shouts — a crash — and the light flickered out. Rapunzel could see no more. She crawled out of the tent and ran around the side in her stocking feet. Jack was pulling on his boots in a hurry, his sword thrown across the top of the wagon.

"We've been robbed," he panted, stuffing Ubiquitous acorns into his pockets. "I'm going after them."

"I'm going with you!"

"You can't!" Jack shouted as he sprinted away from her toward the steep northern wall of the valley. "They got your boots!"

It was true. Her boots were gone.

Rapunzel cursed, picking up one foot and then the other. The ground was covered in frost; her stocking bottoms were already wet through, and it was bitingly cold. The idea of journeying onward in bare feet was unthinkable.

Panicked, she squinted after Jack. He had reached the valley wall. Above him, in the growing light of very early morning, Rapunzel saw a large man running along the snaking roads that led to the top of the steep hill. Far ahead of him, a thin man was carrying something that was just about the right shape and size to be her boots. She realized with a sinking heart that he looked too far away to be caught.

There was an echoing *crack!* and Jack tossed a grappling hook straight up. It anchored in the rocks, and he began to climb the rope up the valley wall, able to clear its height faster than either of the bandits, who had to run back and forth along the road. Rapunzel watched, breathless. She had seen Witch scale her tower many times, and she had seen Jack do it too, but until she had clambered out of the river herself, she had never appreciated how much effort it took.

Jack climbed on. Above him, the larger bandit had run high enough that he met with the top of the rope. He took hold of the hook and tried to yank it out of the rock wall, but Jack vaulted onto the road. He pulled his sword and swung it at the large bandit, who dropped something and backed away.

Jack snatched what was dropped, cracked another rope in almost the same moment, and tossed the grappling hook up again. It lodged in the dirt just below the path where the thin bandit was running. That bandit was moving more slowly now, Rapunzel noticed, her heart in her throat.

Jack raced up his rope, getting closer to the second bandit every moment. This time, when he came to the pathway, he pulled himself onto it and tore along the winding road after the thin man. Jack caught him at the top of the valley, where Rapunzel lost sight of them both as they stumbled away from the edge. She heard faint, distant shouting — and then nothing at all.

Barefoot or not, she had to follow Jack. She folded the tent, packed the wagon haphazardly, swept Prince Frog onto her shoulder strap, and ran toward the bottom of the road, pulling the wagon behind her. She raced up the first few legs of the winding road, jogged along the next few, and was reduced to a winded walk before she was halfway there. She winced with every uncomfortable, wet, cold step. The large man had already disappeared over the sloping top of the valley and was gone.

As early dawn became morning, Rapunzel willed herself to keep going, promising her feet that it wouldn't be much longer. She looked toward the top of the hill, beginning to fear the silence. She hadn't heard anything since Jack had disappeared.

"Jack!" she called. Her voice echoed between the steep valley walls. "Are you all right?"

There was no answer.

"Jack!" she cried again. "Where are you?"

At the top of the valley, now just a few turns of the road above her, a familiar figure staggered into the morning light, clutching a pair of boots by their buckled straps. He held them aloft. And then he doubled over, dropped the boots, and braced his hands on his knees.

Rapunzel ran toward him without another thought of her feet.

"Jack!" she cried, rattling up to him with the wagon and grabbing his arms to pull him up straight. "You got my boots! You climbed so fast! I can't believe you caught them both!"

Jack fought for breath. He was slick with sweat, his hands were rope-burned, and there were streaks of blood across one cheek and down one of his arms, where the sleeve had torn. Rapunzel stared at the blood. She had never seen so much.

In spite of it all, Jack managed a brilliant smile.

"What happened?" she demanded, strapping on her boots as Jack licked his thumb and rubbed the blood off his arm. "Are you all right? Did they run off? How did you get the boots? What did that other man take?"

Jack breathed heavily and said nothing. But he pulled Rapunzel's belt from where he had slung it over his shoulder, and he held it out to her.

"So that's what he dropped!" Rapunzel cinched the belt around her waist and checked to see that her dagger and money were still in it. When Jack had recovered, he strapped on his knapsack.

"It's a good thing we've got Prince Frog," he said, cracking his neck on one side and then the other as they trekked over the top of the hill. Around them, the sky grew brighter every moment. "He bounced on my head till I woke up. That's why I heard the bandits." He gave Prince Frog an affectionate look.

"He's a very good frog," said Rapunzel. "But what did the bandits get away with? I know they got acorns — I saw, when I packed the wagon."

"They got about half of them," said Jack. "We should've kept them in the tent; it was stupid of us. They must've gone for those first and grabbed the rest of it second — your belt, your boots. I kept my belt in the tent, and you should do the same."

"I will from now on," said Rapunzel. "All the money's in there."

"*What?*" Jack yelled. "I thought you kept it in your pocket! Rapunzel, you can't just leave money out in the wagon —"

"Well, I said I *won't* anymore!" she shot back, marching on. "Anyway, are you hurt?" she asked. "There's blood."

"I'm all right," he replied, touching the scratch on his cheek and looking at the blood on his fingers before he wiped them on his vest. "It wasn't bad. They weren't much worse than the chicken thieves we get around home."

"I'm so glad you caught them. You really were amazing when you climbed."

Jack smiled again, but there was a little less brilliance to it. He almost looked guilty.

"Try to stay calm, all right?" he said. "Before the bandits ran off, they . . ."

He slowed to a stop and gestured to the wagon.

"After they got the acorns, they went for something else," he said. He looked distinctly nervous. "They didn't get it, but they tried. Look, I told you it was valuable. You should be flattered people like it so much, right? Don't scream when you see it."

Rapunzel looked at the wagon, not understanding. What else was there to steal? The cloaks? The mittens?

"My hair," she gasped. Her heart pitched in her chest. She crouched beside the wagon and spoke to the hair wheel. "Unwind to the same place you did last night," she commanded, and her hair shot off the wheel. It whirred to the point that Rapunzel had requested and stopped.

Her heart stopped with it.

There, where the braid fed into the wheel, someone had sliced into her hair, deep enough to sever a very thick lock — almost a third of her braid. The hewn hank of hair stuck out like bundled straw from the rest of the twisting mass. The cut had been made perhaps fifteen feet from the crown of her head; the severed chunk was plaited into the rest of her hair now, but as soon as she unbraided it, almost a third of her hair would be gone.

Rapunzel touched the blunt ends with trembling fingertips. For the first time since Cornucopia, she longed to call for Witch. Witch could fix it. Witch could make it all right.

It *was* all right, she told herself, still crouched beside her ruined hair. It *had* to be all right. She couldn't go back to the tower now; they had come too far, and Rune was surely still watching. She had no choice but to go on.

"I'm not going to scream," she said, and she pushed herself to her feet. "Wind up," she said, and winced when the severed lock frayed a little as it was whipped back onto the wheel with the rest of her braid.

"I tried to stop them," said Jack. "I should have gone out earlier, I knew it."

"It's all right," said Rapunzel. "Is that why you yelled 'no' at the bandits? To stop them from cutting my braid?"

He nodded. A satisfying suspicion struck Rapunzel.

"But you're always telling me to cut it off," she said.

Jack shifted his weight and looked away from her. "We might as well keep walking," he said. "Get a head start on the day."

"You like my hair!" said Rapunzel triumphantly.

He seemed to have gone temporarily deaf. "Let's get on the road," he said, picking up the wagon handle and setting off.

"You didn't let them cut it off," sang Rapunzel, skipping after him. "You think it's beautiful, admit it. You love my hair, *admit* it!"

"Shut up or I'll change my mind," he said, and Rapunzel fell silent, beaming.

CHAPTER THIRTEEN

*T*HE acorns the bandits had stolen included all the sausages, a good deal of the other food, and many of the ropes and tents. To keep from despairing over the loss of so many supplies, Rapunzel decided to play Tess's game while she walked. She tried to think of something to be glad about, and found it very easy. A flood of ideas quickly came to her.

"I'm happy I won the jacks contest," she said, and prodded Jack. "Your turn."

"It's Tess's birthday today, actually," he said, smiling slightly. "She's nine. We should eat some cake in her honor, if there are any good acorns left."

"There aren't," said Rapunzel. "That's why I'm playing the happiness game."

"That's what Tess calls it too," said Jack, glancing at the sky. "All right, I've got one. I'm happy Serge showed us another fairywood and saved us more time."

"I'm happy he made us such comfortable boots."

"I'm happy we didn't *lose* the boots."

"I'm happy you're faster than a bandit!"

Rapunzel didn't quite hear what Jack said next. Her attention shifted to another sound, one that seemed out of place among the early morning noises of birds and breeze. She turned her head toward the sound, but saw nothing behind them except the empty road.

"What is it?" asked Jack, glancing back as well. "Do you hear something?"

"Shh." Rapunzel listened hard. Prince Frog heard it too, and he leapt from Rapunzel's shoulder and put his belly to the ground, looking warily in the direction from which they had come.

Four horses trotted over the peak of the hilltop, pulling a cart behind them. The front of the cart held a bench, on which sat a large man with a large beard.

"Quick," said Jack, and he retreated into the trees that lined the road, tugging Rapunzel with him.

"What's wrong?" she said.

"I want to get a look at him before he sees us."

"Why?"

"Because you never know."

They stayed in the trees, and as the wagon drew nearer, Rapunzel read the words that were painted along its high-walled back.

DELECTABLE DELIVERY SERVICE
Serving Bayberry, Hickory Hills, and Shagbark
~ Reliable since 1010 ~

Rapunzel took a step toward it. If there was something delectable in the wagon, perhaps they could replace some of their lost supplies. Jack caught her hand and kept her with him.

"Don't," he said, his voice low.

"We just lost most of our food," said Rapunzel. "We ought to at least talk to him."

Jack considered this and agreed that she was probably right. Together they approached the road. The wagon slowed and stopped in front of them. Rapunzel was a little frightened of the horses; she had never seen them up close and hadn't realized what big round eyes they had, or how tall they were, or how hard they stamped. She stayed away from them and addressed herself to the bearded man who sat alone on the wagon's front seat.

"Do you have delectable things in there?" she asked, pointing to the back half of the wagon.

The man nodded.

"Can I buy some, then?" asked Rapunzel. "I have a bag of money. I won it in a contest."

Jack looked warningly at her. The wagon driver didn't answer right away. His eyes traveled Rapunzel's braid from where it started at her neck to where it ended in the little wagon, wrapped around the fairy wheel. Prince Frog had just hopped in and was settling down in the middle of the hair coil.

"We've been robbed," Rapunzel went on. "Bandits took our food."

The driver looked at her. Behind his beard, his face was difficult to read. "Where are you off to?" he asked. "North country?"

His voice was a low rumble, almost even a growl. Rapunzel was unsettled by it and the intensity of his gaze.

"We're just camping," Jack said, eyeing the driver. "Why do you ask?"

"Because I'm headed north," he said. "As far as White Pine Ridge." His eyes were dark under his heavy eyebrows. "Why don't I offer you a ride?"

"A ride, huh?" Jack's voice was clipped. "Thanks, but we're not going much farther."

"If you're going even as far as Hickory Hills, it's five days' walk." The driver leaned his large forearm on the raised side of his seat and looked down at them. "I can get you there in three."

"We're actually headed south," said Jack, with a quick look at Rapunzel. "Isn't that right?"

But Rapunzel was doing quick calculations.

"How far north is White Pine Ridge?" she asked.

"Center of Green," the driver answered, shifting his dark eyes to her. "More than two weeks on foot."

"But you could get us there in a little over a week."

"Sharp girl."

Rapunzel's heart beat quickly. The center of Green, right near the First Wood, was where she wanted to be. If she could get there faster, then Witch would be safe from the fairies sooner, and she could return to her tower, as Glyph had promised.

The driver's dark eyes glimmered. He extended his large, rough hand. "Name's Greve," he said. "Hop in. I've only done the Bayberry drop-off this trip, so there's just enough room in the back for one of you. The other one sits with me."

"That's a nice offer," said Jack, grabbing Rapunzel's belt before she could hop onto the wagon seat. He gave her a piercing look. "But we'll need a minute."

"Take your time." Leaning heavily on the side of the seat, Greve got down from the wagon. He was as big as the two of them combined, and so tall that Rapunzel had to tilt back her head to look up at him. "Need to take a break, in any case." He flicked his eyes from Rapunzel to Jack. "And there's no point in stealing my wagon," he said. "Everyone on this route recognizes it."

Greve pulled a walking stick down from the wagon seat. He seemed to depend on the stick as he limped off, favoring one leg. His massive boots crunched out a lopsided rhythm in the frosty grass.

When they could no longer see him, Jack let go of Rapunzel's belt.

"Why'd you tell him anything?" he demanded. "Can't you see he's strange? We're not riding with him."

"Of course we are!" said Rapunzel. "He can take us right where we need to go — in a week instead of two! Jack, it's such a lucky thing he found us."

"*Found* us is exactly my problem," said Jack, squinting over Rapunzel's shoulder toward the trees where Greve had gone. "How did he know we were going north? And look at his wagon — his last delivery's in Shagbark, not White Pine Ridge."

"Maybe he saw us from the other side of the valley," said Rapunzel. "He could have been coming down one side while we were climbing the other — in fact, he must have been. He would have seen us walking north."

"Maybe," said Jack. "But something's not right. It's too convenient."

"It's *so* convenient."

"And the way he looked at you — I'm telling you, he recognizes your hair. He was too quick to offer us a ride."

Prince Frog gave a loud, wary croak.

"We need to walk south until he's out of sight."

"Jack, we don't have food. He does, and he'll take us straight into the towns too."

"No."

Rapunzel clenched her fists in frustration. "You don't get to decide by yourself!" she burst out. "I'm the one who has to find the

First Wood, and *I* say we go in the wagon. I just want to go home," she pleaded when Jack's eyes flashed. "Witch is hurting while I'm gone, I know it. If I can get home a week earlier, then I have to do it."

"But Rapunzel, listen —"

"No, *you* listen; I've listened to you a hundred times. I'm going with Greve."

"And if I won't go with you?" threatened Jack.

"You have to," said Rapunzel. "Glyph said if you stay with me, then she'll help you. Which you *still* haven't explained to me, by the way."

Jack rubbed his temples with his thumb and forefinger. "Fine," he said. "We can ride with Greve, but I don't like it. And *I'm* sitting up front."

"You didn't even want to go!" cried Rapunzel. "Now you want the front?" She dashed toward the seat before Jack could steal it.

He grabbed her by the belt again, bringing her to a jerking halt. "I don't want the front because it's *fun*," he hissed. "If Greve turns out to be a bad kind of guy, then you shouldn't be alone with him."

"Why not? I'm not afraid of him," she said, wiggling out of Jack's grip. "He can't even walk right. Didn't you see him with his stick?"

"But he's big," said Jack.

"Well, I'm bigger than you," said Rapunzel, tossing her head. "So you're the one who should be scared of him."

"You've got all that hair. If it turns out we have to get away from Greve, you should be where he can't grab your braid and you can get a head start."

Rapunzel humphed. But perhaps he did have a point.

"Fine," she said. "Take the front. But if Greve turns out to be all right, then you have to trade places tomorrow."

Greve limped into view. He climbed into the wagon and looked down at them.

"We'll go with you," said Rapunzel.

"Good." The word was a low rumble. "I'll expect help with my deliveries in exchange. It's hard work, but you both look strong enough. Deal?"

"Deal," said Jack, sounding surprised. He was visibly more at ease as he walked with Rapunzel to the back end of the wagon, and she understood why. If Greve wanted something from them, it made more sense that he'd offer them a ride.

They unlatched the wagon's high door and lowered it. Jack helped Rapunzel lift their little wagon into Greve's big one. As soon as she had clambered in after it, Jack raised and latched the door again. From the sound of his footsteps, she knew he was walking to the front of the wagon, but she couldn't see him or Greve. The walls were too high. There was nothing to look at in the back of the wagon but wooden walls, wooden crates, and sky.

Rapunzel cushioned the planks beneath her with Ubiquitous pillows from last night's camp, wrapped herself up in her cloak, and lay down, looking up. The wagon clattered into motion; the horses' hooves beat on the ground, and the wheels rolled.

The motion of the wagon lulled her. She was sleepy, she realized, yawning. The bandits had startled them so early that she had only had a few hours' rest. Cold air blew across her face, and she blinked in the early morning light. Overhead, white clouds swept by . . . then blended together . . . then faded to darkness as her eyelids drifted shut.

How long she slept, she wasn't sure, but when she woke, the sun had already passed overhead and was full in the sky. She guessed it was midafternoon. Midafternoon of the . . . eighth day. Rapunzel counted on her fingers and realized she was right. She had slept seven nights out of her tower. She couldn't believe it was such a short time. If Witch had told her that she could have done so many things in just eight days, she would never have believed her.

They helped Greve with his deliveries in a village called Methley Plum, unpacking everything from dried flowers and spices to enormous wheels of cheese from the crates. When they reconvened at Greve's wagon, Rapunzel was carrying a parcel of iced cakes that she had purchased from the baker. She and Jack sat in the back of the wagon to eat them. Prince Frog chased down and devoured several big, spindly spiders that had been disturbed by the moving of the crates, and they were all quite content by the time Greve limped out of the butcher's. He pocketed his jingling money pouch and crossed the cobbled street.

"Appreciate the help," said Greve. "We'll be in Littleleaf by nightfall. Might be a bit late to find a room by the time we get there."

He was right. By the time they arrived in Littleleaf, the stars were bright violet in the deep, black sky.

"Not a bad night for camping," said Greve, leading the horses off the road and nearer to the trees. He went about unhitching them from the wagon.

"You won't fit in our tent," said Rapunzel, "but we have extras." She held out a Ubiquitous acorn. "Would you like one?"

"I've got my own," he said. When he had finished watering and tying up the horses, he pulled a folded tent from beneath the seat of the wagon and went about pitching it. He moved slowly, leaning on his stick as he limped from one corner of the tent to the next. Jack and Rapunzel cracked their own tent, and Rapunzel strapped on her hair again and began to build a fire. The orange flames made long, jumping shadows against the tall trees.

"Glad to see you don't need Ubiquitous for everything," growled Greve, hobbling up to them once his tent was in order. He set a sack on the ground and knelt beside it, bracing a hand on the dirt. "Hungry?"

They nodded.

"Then find me three long sticks."

Rapunzel and Jack found three long, slim, sturdy branches.

"Bought a few things in town," Greve said as he speared a few small squares of meat on each of the three sticks. He handed the skewered meat to Rapunzel and Jack.

They roasted their suppers. Jack didn't say much, and Greve only looked into the fire as he ate, focused on something Rapunzel couldn't see. When they finished eating, he threw his stick into the fire and watched it crackle into ash. Then he looked at Rapunzel.

"You've got a lot of hair," he said. His voice was startlingly low in the quiet night. Rapunzel shivered.

"Yes," she said. "What about it?"

Greve studied the hair wheel, which lay on the ground beside Rapunzel. "Must've taken a long time to grow."

Rapunzel narrowed her eyes and watched him, waiting for him to say something else. Something about the Bargaining, or Witch.

Greve got to his feet, balanced on his stick, and nodded to them both. "Sleep well" was all he said before he limped to his tent and crawled in. The flap fell shut.

Chapter Fourteen

*T*HEY traveled four days with Greve, and made enough deliveries to clear a great deal of space in the wagon. It grew colder each day as they moved farther north, and Prince Frog didn't seem to like it. He stayed burrowed under the woolly blankets and rarely appeared, even to pounce on spiders.

"We might get to Shagbark before nightfall," Jack told Rapunzel. They were sitting together in the back of the wagon as they traveled. The tip of Jack's nose was ruddy with cold, and his breath clouded in the air as he spoke. He unrolled the map so that they could trace how far they had come. "Tomorrow midday, at the latest."

"And then we're nearly to Independence, and the First Wood."

"Nearly."

Rapunzel's heart fluttered. Soon, she could go home.

Night fell before they reached Shagbark, and they pitched camp in a moonlit valley. In the morning, light filtered into the tent. Rapunzel pushed herself up to sit and saw that Jack had gone out already. She buckled her boots, grabbed Prince Frog, and pushed open the tent flap. One shock of cold air was enough to send her scuttling for her cloak, and then she marched out into the frosty morning — and stopped short.

Overnight, the world had exploded into color. Rapunzel stood agape, staring at trees the likes of which she had never seen. Their leaves were wide and bright — oranges, yellows, and reds as vivid as flames, each color crisp against the cold blue sky. The trees blanketed the hills that surrounded them, and Rapunzel turned in circles, awe-struck. It was like the world had caught fire.

Jack crunched up to her through some fallen leaves and stood beside her to admire the long, bright valley.

"I wish the trees near my tower looked like this," Rapunzel mur-mured. "They're always dark green."

"So don't go back," said Jack. "Stay here, if you like it better."

Rapunzel marveled at the view. It was the first time she had ever believed that there might be any place she *could* like better.

Greve folded his tent and limped toward the wagon.

"We ought to pack up," said Jack, and threw open the tent.

They had just finished packing when a loud crash sounded from Greve's big wagon. Both Rapunzel and Jack whirled toward it. Greve stood in the wagon bed, pinned against the remaining crates by a large plank of wood that looked as big as the wagon bottom. They dashed over to him. Jack leapt into the wagon. The plank was taller than he was, and when he pulled it toward him, it nearly sent him over back-ward. Rapunzel climbed up and helped him steady it; it was much heavier than it looked.

"We'll need to lift it," said Greve, rubbing his right thumb, which looked purple. "I want it secured on top before it rains."

Rapunzel realized that the heavy wooden plank was meant to cover the top of the wagon. It had been standing on its side between the crates and the wagon wall. She hadn't noticed it before.

"It's going to rain?" Jack squinted up at the morning sky. "Doesn't look like it."

"I've made a few trips through Green in my day," said Greve. "I know the skies."

They helped Greve lift the wagon cover into place, and he secured it on all sides with padlocks. When they were finished, the wagon looked like one giant crate. Rapunzel didn't like the thought of crawling into it.

"I want to see the trees," she said. "Can't I sit up front?"

"If I turn out to be wrong about the weather, you can," said Greve. "But if you're soaked to the bone, you won't be much help with deliveries. Now hop in."

Rapunzel and Jack fetched all their things, including Prince Frog, and packed them into the wagon. She climbed in after them with a sigh, sorry that she wouldn't have another morning of watching the sky fly past. She gazed again at the spectacular trees.

"What are they called?" she asked, pointing. "The trees. I've never seen this kind."

"Maple," said Greve. He motioned to Jack, who was still standing outside the wagon, looking at the sky. "Go on," he said. "Let's be on our way."

But Jack didn't move.

"Rapunzel," he said, "get out of that wagon."

He said it calmly, but a chill ran through her. She came at once to the edge, remembered Prince Frog, and crawled into the wagon again to get him.

"What's the trouble?" Greve asked pleasantly, but somehow his face wasn't pleasant at all.

"This isn't Shagbark," said Jack. "You've brought us to Maple Valley, and it's not exactly on your route. Whatever you want with us, you can forget it. Rapunzel, get *out* of there."

"I'm coming," she said, reaching into the bundled blankets and closing her hands around Prince Frog.

It was too late. Behind her, there were the sounds of a sudden scuffle. Jack cursed. Rapunzel spun around on her knees to see that Greve had dropped his walking stick and taken hold of Jack around the middle, pinning his arms to his sides. Jack struggled, kicking and thrashing.

"Let him go!" cried Rapunzel, scrambling to the edge of the wagon to help.

She wasn't quick enough. Greve threw Jack in the back and slammed the gate into place. They heard the scrape of metal and the thunking click of a padlock being shut.

"LET US OUT!" Jack threw himself against the wooden door. It rattled, but the wood was heavy and the locks were tight, and it gave no sign of breaking. Jack hurled himself against it again, while Rapunzel sat in the giant crate that they had helped to build, frightened and unsure of what had happened.

"What's Maple Valley?" she asked. "Is it bad?"

There was the sound of a cracking whip and a loud "YAH!" from Greve. The wagon jerked into sudden motion; Rapunzel was thrown from her knees to sprawl on the wagon floor, while Jack stumbled against the locked door with a crash. There were so few crates left now that the horses were able to run, and they pulled the wagon swiftly onward.

Jack dropped to his knees and looked up at the ceiling of

wood above them. He ripped the map out of his knapsack and unrolled it.

"Look." He jabbed his finger at Commonwealth Green, west of the Mimicry River. There, nearly twenty leagues southwest of Shagbark, were two small, cursive words: *Maple Valley.*

Rapunzel pushed herself up from the floor. "It's where I put my finger when we played the map game!" she exclaimed. She looked from Maple Valley to Independence and measured the distance with her eyes. "Oh no . . . we're farther south than we were yesterday. He took us backward. . . ."

"Forget that," said Jack. "What's he *doing* with us?"

Rapunzel put the map aside and stroked Prince Frog, who looked up at her with fear in his round, golden eyes.

"No wonder he told us we could stay back here yesterday," Jack fumed. "He didn't want us to see where he was headed. He must have turned west right after Hickory Hills."

"It's all right," she said to Prince Frog. "Don't worry."

"Don't worry?" Jack gave a harsh laugh. "I wonder if Greve even has a limp, or if it was just a ruse to make us comfortable." He slammed his fists down on either side of him, making Prince Frog jump. "I can't believe I got swindled into building my own cage." He leapt to his feet and pounded hard on the wooden wall that separated them from the front seat of the wagon. "You know the *skies*, huh?" he bellowed at Greve. "What are we worth to you?"

"Worth?" Rapunzel repeated. The skin of her neck crawled. "What do you —"

"He'll sell us," said Jack, turning on her. "We've been kidnapped. He must have a deal with someone out this way."

It was a nightmare straight out of Witch's worst warnings. Rapunzel huddled against the wagon wall and hugged herself, leaving Prince Frog to hop in a worried circle on her thigh. *Witch*, she thought, because she could not shout it. *Witch*.

"Sell us to whom?" she whispered.

"Anyone," said Jack, glancing with real anxiety now at Rapunzel. "I bet there are people who'd pay a lot of money for you."

"For me?" Rapunzel's voice was very small. "Why?"

Jack didn't answer. "Rune!" he called out, and when there came no reply from the fairy, he tried again, louder. "RUNE!" he bellowed. "Come on, I know you can hear me — help us!"

"If he didn't help us with the Stalker, then why would he help us now?" said Rapunzel. "He's not allowed to kill me, but he's not going to stop someone else from doing it."

Jack knelt beside her, looking grim. "No one's getting killed, all right? We'll get out of this."

The wagon pitched and rattled as they careened onward.

"If I could call for Witch, she'd save us."

"She'd save *you*," said Jack. "Not me. And we can save ourselves. One of us just has to think of something."

"But I can't think of anything!"

"You thought of tripping the Stalker, didn't you? You thought of making a canopy. You won a jacks tournament and got us money too."

Rapunzel drew herself up a little. Hearing Jack recite her accomplishments nearly distracted her from the bleakness of their circumstance.

"That's true," she said. "I did. All right, I'll think of something."

They scanned the inside of the wagon. There was nothing that could help them.

"I do have my dagger," she said when they had rumbled along in silence for several minutes.

"And I have my sword," said Jack, perking up. "Let's hack our way out."

They got to their feet and grabbed their weapons. Rapunzel had to hunch more than Jack did to keep from hitting her head. She tried to drive the dagger straight into the wall, but when she struck, the blow was painful to her fingers, and the blade stuck in the wood and was hard to pull out again. Jack thwacked at the sides with violent energy, but his luck was no better. The sword was too light; the wood, too dense.

"When Greve lets us out," said Rapunzel, yanking her dagger from the wood, "we'll just have to attack him."

"He's — stronger — than he seemed," said Jack, thudding to the floor. He leaned against the wagon wall to catch his breath. "When he pinned my arms, I couldn't move them at all."

"So we'll cut his arms off."

Jack laughed, but when he looked up at her, his eyes were sober. "Don't do anything too violent," he warned. "Not unless there turns out to be no other way. You could get into a lot of trouble for chopping an arm off. There are laws."

"Like what?"

"Well, you CAN'T KIDNAP PEOPLE," Jack shouted toward the front of the wagon.

"Can you steal?"

His head snapped toward her. "If you don't get caught," he said.

"But it's against the law?"

"Letting people starve should be against the law," Jack muttered.

Pondering this, Rapunzel realized that she was hungry. She looked at the undelivered crates. "Is it stealing," she asked, "to eat things that belong to someone who kidnaps you?"

Jack raised an eyebrow at her. "You're catching on," he said, and he crawled toward the crates. "We should go through these anyway," he said, pulling one toward him and opening it. "Maybe there's something useful inside."

They opened every crate and ate whatever they wanted: jars of apricot and strawberry preserves, parcels of fudge, dried figs, smoked ham, and pickled garlic. There were several crates of wine as well, which Rapunzel wanted nothing to do with. But they found nothing else useful, nothing that would help them to escape. The last crates were filled with sacks of rice and dried beans.

"We could throw a sack of rice at him when he opens the door," said Rapunzel.

"Or wine bottles," said Jack.

"Or just shove all the crates at him."

Jack looked quickly at her, his black eyes gleaming. "There it is," he said. "There's the idea." He glanced at the front of the wagon and beckoned Rapunzel closer. She knelt at once and leaned in. "We could pack up the crates again and stack them at the back door, right against the edge. When he opens the door —"

"We can push them over! But Jack, will it crush him?"

"It won't kill him," said Jack. "But it'll slow him down. If he really does have a limp, we'll have plenty of time to get away. Even if he doesn't, we'll still have a better chance."

"But it'll take so long," said Rapunzel. "My hair, and Prince Frog, and the wagon —"

"Let's get ready then," said Jack, rolling up his sleeves in spite of the cold.

They worked swiftly together. Jack packed the crates and slid them toward the back of the wagon, where he stacked them up to the ceiling against the door. Rapunzel pocketed Prince Frog, stuffed their remaining acorns into her vest pockets, loaded whatever else would fit into Jack's knapsack, and hefted the hair wheel onto her back. It pained her to leave the little wagon, but there might not be time to get it out.

They had just finished their preparations when the horses' clopping hooves lightened their rhythm and the wagon slowed. Rapunzel pressed her face to the slatted wooden side of the wagon and peered through one of the cracks.

They were in a town — leaving a town, it looked like — and heading up a steep hill into more fantastic trees. Rapunzel watched a stretch of fiery orange and bright golden woods roll past, unbroken, for several minutes. The wagon turned left off the main road, and Greve drove them forward, in among the trees.

The wagon stopped.

Rapunzel and Jack took their places and braced their hands against the crates. They heard the sounds of Greve getting down from the wagon. They heard the thump of his stick and his heavy, lopsided footsteps as he came around to the back. They heard the scrape of a key in the padlock . . . the click of it being popped open . . . the creak of the back door as it was lowered . . .

"NOW!" cried Jack, and they shoved the wall of crates at Greve. The boxes tumbled off the wagon, and Rapunzel heard Greve shout with pain as he was pinned beneath them.

"Let's go!" said Jack, jumping out of the wagon. Rapunzel stepped down with less ease, now that she had the burden of her hair again. Once outside, she saw that Greve had brought them right up to a small house built of shining white stones. It stood alone at the top of the hill. Beneath its peaked roof was a large triangle of delicately carved stone, wrought like lace around a circular window. Rapunzel stared at it.

"Come on!" said Jack. "What are you doing?"

The door of the white house flew open. At the top of the front steps stood a tawny woman in a long apron, wearing her brown hair in a net.

Her eyes fell on Greve. "White skies," she cried, and ran down the steps. "What have you done to him?" She fell to her knees and pulled the crates away from Greve's head and chest. Blood gushed from his lip, and he groaned but did not stir.

"Same thing we'll do to you if you get in our way," Jack said to the woman. "Let's go, Rapunzel."

"Rapunzel." The woman looked up from the crates.

Rapunzel felt a stab of fear. The woman knew her. Greve *had* brought them here on purpose.

"Having trouble, Skye?"

The voice was deep and unfamiliar, and it came from right behind Rapunzel. She and Jack both whirled. They looked in dismay at a man as large as Greve but younger, with no beard and no limp. He was carrying an ax, and its blade glinted in the sunlight. He glanced past them at Greve. "Did they attack him?" he asked, his voice dropping lower. "Is he —"

"He'll be fine — Edam, that's Natty's girl, look. Look at her hair."

The man nearly fumbled his ax. He stared at Rapunzel. "*No,*" he said.

"Yes . . ." The low growl came from Greve, who winced as he moved. "Didn't tell them where I was taking them," he said, struggling to sit up. "Not their fault. Had to make sure she'd come."

"Make sure *why?*" Jack asked, taking a step back from Edam and his ax and throwing out his arm in front of Rapunzel. "Who are you people? What do you want with her?"

Skye put her arm around Greve. She helped him to his feet and handed him his stick.

"What's your name, boy?" said Edam, flipping the handle of his ax in his palm as he looked at Jack. "What's your business with this girl?"

Jack flushed. "I have no *business* with her," he said, taking another step back and bringing Rapunzel with him. "I'm just . . . with her."

"Are you now? Since when?"

"We don't owe you explanations," Jack said harshly. "And we've had about enough of being locked up. So if that's your plan —"

"No one's going to lock her up here," interrupted Edam.

"Where is here?" asked Rapunzel.

None of them made any move toward her or Jack. They didn't seem interested in killing them or selling them into slavery. They were only watching her with great curiosity and something like . . . Rapunzel couldn't quite name it. But she was sure that they had no desire to hurt her.

"Natty's girl," said Edam, shaking his head a little. "Out of the blue."

"Who is Natty?" asked Rapunzel. "Does Witch have another name?"

Skye inhaled sharply, and her wide brown eyes brimmed with tears. She put her hands over her face and began to cry in earnest.

Greve put a bruised hand on Skye's shoulder and fixed his dark eyes on Rapunzel.

"Natty was your mother," he said.

Before Rapunzel had gotten over the shock, Greve leaned on his stick and limped more slowly than usual toward the door.

"This was her home," he said as he went. "Now come on inside. Your grandmother's been waiting a long time to meet you."

CHAPTER FIFTEEN

GRANDMOTHER.

"Your mother's mother," Jack told her, watching her with black eyes almost as curious as everyone else's. He no longer seemed worried that Greve would cheat them. On the contrary, he hung behind Rapunzel and apologized to Edam and Skye for what they had done with the crates.

"Apologize to the old man, if you want," said Edam. "But it sounds to me like he left you no choice. Only a fool or a coward would let a man lock him up without a fight."

Jack seemed to feel better at this.

If Greve heard the exchange, he didn't acknowledge it. He limped up the steps and onto the white porch. He pushed the door open and looked over his shoulder at Rapunzel.

"After you," he growled.

Rapunzel walked in.

The room was larger than it looked from outside, and warm and well lit. Windows stretched nearly from floor to ceiling on either side of her, framing the bright trees outside and allowing sunlight to pour in. The furniture was simple and sturdy, nothing like the elegance Rapunzel had grown used to in her tower, but there was something inviting in the curve of the rocking chair's wide arms and in the worn, quilted cushions of the sofa. Glass lamps stood on corner tables with graceful legs. Samples of intricate lacework in small, polished frames looked down from the wall above the great fireplace, within which flames crackled, baking the room. Even the books looked cozy and comfortable; they filled the shelves in the walls, and the lettering on their thick, weathered bindings glinted in the firelight. A slim, dark book drew Rapunzel's eye, and she stepped closer to read the tarnished golden title on its spine: *Fairies, Willcrafters, and Witches: A Mortal's Guide to Magic.*

Rapunzel removed the book from the shelf at once and flipped through it for mention of her own name. To her surprise, the book wasn't about her at all. A few chapters of it were about witches. Not her own Witch either, but witches in general. Rapunzel was derailed momentarily by the idea of more than one Witch. She had never imagined there were others. But since more than one mother existed, she supposed that it made sense that there was more than one Witch, and she wondered if there were other Rapunzels, in other towers.

Rapunzel shelved the book and looked across the room. To the right of the fireplace, the space opened into a clean, spacious kitchen full of gleaming copper pots and a big-bellied oven. To the left of the fireplace, she saw a narrow, lamplit hallway with three wooden doors. At the end of the hallway were stairs. Perhaps they went up to the room with the peaked roof, where the stone looked like lace around the window.

"It's nice," said Jack, beside her. "Really nice," he added a bit wistfully. "Tess would like it."

"I like it too," Rapunzel said. The whole house seemed to want her to belong to it. She would have liked to curl up on the quilted cushions and read a book in front of the fire, as though she were at home. She *felt* at home. But that was wrong — her tower was home. She thought of Witch, and her stomach twisted.

Rapunzel heard the door of the house close and looked around to see that everyone had followed her inside. Edam glanced at her but tended to Skye, who was still weeping.

"I'm sorry," Skye said, looking up at Rapunzel. "But you could be Natty back from the dead. What will Purl do when she sees you? How will she stand it?"

"I'll get her." Greve limped past Rapunzel, down the hallway, and knocked on the first door. There was the sound of a sharp rap in reply, and Greve let himself in. Rapunzel tried to see into the room, but caught only the flicker of lamplight, more lace, and more books before Greve closed the door behind him.

"How long have you been out of that tower?" asked Edam.

"Twelve days," said Rapunzel.

"You must be tired. Hungry. What can I get for you?"

Rapunzel's eyes drifted to the room into which Greve had disappeared, and she wondered if her grandmother was in it.

"I want to meet my grandmother," she said.

"My dad's waking her now."

"Is she asleep?" Rapunzel was surprised. "It's the middle of the day."

"She . . ." Skye sniffled and lowered her voice. "She's fragile these days. She's gotten old so fast these last few years. We're not sure how much longer she'll last."

"Last?" asked Rapunzel, frowning as she remembered what Jack had told her about people growing old and wearing out. "Is she dying?"

"Hard to say," said Edam. "She's been ill, off and on. Stays in bed most of the time. It took her years to give up on you, but that's what she's done."

"Give up on me?"

"On ever getting you home," said Skye. "Fighting for you kept her strong. She read every book, talked to everyone she thought could help her, supported every movement to impose more laws and controls on magical folks. And then she stopped trying."

Jack was listening to Skye with interest. "Are you Rapunzel's aunt?" he asked.

Skye shook her head. "I'm just a neighbor — but Natty was like my sister," she said. "Best friends since we were barely toddling. I never wanted her to move down to Yellow with Rem. The only good that came out of the whole mess was that I met Edam — he lived next door to them. He's the one who drove Natty back home after the Bargaining. After Rem . . ." She looked at Rapunzel. "After he passed," she said.

"Passed what?" asked Rapunzel.

"Died," said Jack, his attention still on Skye. "So her father died first. His name was Rem, you said? Rem what? What's Rapunzel's last name?"

"LeRoux."

The room stilled. A new voice had spoken — a quiet, wavering voice, but one full of command nonetheless. Rapunzel's eyes darted to the lamplit corridor.

A woman in a long white nightdress stood in the doorway, supported by Greve's strong arm. She looked as though she had once been tall, but she stooped now, and she leaned her shaking hand on a straight white cane with a silver tip. Her skin was as wrinkled as a piece of crumpled parchment that had been smoothed out. Only her eyes, piercing blue, had anything of strength still in them. But it wasn't her eyes that caught Rapunzel's attention.

It was her hair.

Her grandmother's hair was as silver as a polished coin. It was bound at the nape of her neck and cascaded from its binding in a long, soft tail, like a stream of water in moonlight. The tapering curl at its end brushed the wooden floorboards with a shushing sound. Rapunzel had seen enough in her travels to know that hair was different from person to person. But she had never found anyone's hair, other than her own, to be worth staring at.

"Lottie," whispered Rapunzel's grandmother, her voice shaking. "Is it you?"

Rapunzel had no idea what she meant.

"Is your braid a hundred feet long?"

Rapunzel nodded. As she became used to her grandmother's wrinkles, she found she could see past them, and the features they had clouded came into clearer focus. Her grandmother's eyes were like mirrors of Rapunzel's. Her nose was the same. The lift at the corners of her mouth was the same.

"May I see it?"

Rapunzel barely knew what she was talking about. It was Jack who slipped behind her and helped her to pull her arms out of the wheel straps. He held the wheel and asked it to spin, and Rapunzel's braid came loose. The coils made a golden hill on the floor.

Skye and Edam stood together by the fire, hands clasped. Greve neither moved nor spoke.

Rapunzel and her grandmother looked at each other across the room, each gazing at the other, each studying the other's hair, clothing, and face. Rapunzel's throat was dry; she wanted to speak, to ask questions, but her grandmother's blue eyes burned with an emotion so fierce and raw that Rapunzel could not find her voice.

"Lottie," her grandmother finally whispered, and she swayed where she stood. "My granddaughter. My Charlotte." She drew a sharp, trembling breath, and the sound that came from her frightened Rapunzel. Her grandmother's eyes watered and spilled over; tears ran down her cheeks in strange patterns, following the map of wrinkles that covered her face. She moved toward Rapunzel, who tried to step back, but there was nowhere to go. Her grandmother threw thin arms around her and clutched Rapunzel to herself with another low, passionate sob. She held and rocked her, repeating "Charlotte, Charlotte . . ."

Rapunzel was terrified. She wanted to feel something kinder — she could see how much her arrival meant to her grandmother, and she suspected that it ought to mean just as much to her, but it didn't. She tried to pull away, but found that there was more strength in the old woman than there appeared to be. She looked toward Jack, who watched them with sadness in his face.

"I don't understand!" said Rapunzel. "Who is Charlotte?"

"*You* are," he said.

Rapunzel's grandmother pulled back and seized Rapunzel's hands. Her grip was tight and uncomfortable.

"Your mother would have named you Charlotte," she said, through the tears that continued to stream down her face. "Lottie, if you were a girl, she said. If you were a boy, she would have named you after Rem. My poor daughter. She never had a chance to call you anything."

"If you wanted to meet me so much, then why are you so unhappy?" said Rapunzel, trying to pull her hands out of her grandmother's papery grip.

"I have never felt such happiness. Oh, my own Charlotte —"

"Stop calling me that!" She jerked her hands free. "My name is Rapunzel."

Her grandmother's tears slowed. She stared at Rapunzel with her powerfully blue eyes, and there was a new expression in them now, one Rapunzel was not sure she liked any better than the crying. There was pity in her gaze. Pity — and fury.

"I believe I need to sit down," she said. "Greve?"

Greve helped Rapunzel's grandmother into the rocking chair. She dried her eyes with a handkerchief, and Greve draped her long, silver tail of hair over the arm of the chair. It pooled on the floor.

Now that her grandmother's expression was composed, Rapunzel was struck again by how much the woman's features reminded her of her own. It was so strange.

"Will you sit? Near me?" her grandmother asked.

Edam brought a chair from the kitchen. As Rapunzel sat beside her grandmother, she caught sight of Jack behind the sofa, where he put down the hair wheel and retreated toward the wall. She wished he would come nearer.

"Can't Jack sit with me?" she asked.

Her grandmother's eyes shifted to him, and Jack straightened up.

"Jack Byre of the Violet Peaks," he said, bowing slightly. "I'm her friend."

Rapunzel looked gratefully at him. She had only ever had Witch for a friend before. It was a comfort to have Jack too, and to have him here with her.

"Very well," said her grandmother, her frail fingers trembling as they tapped the top of her white cane. She kept her eyes on Jack as he came around the sofa. Edam brought another chair from the kitchen, and then he pulled the sofa closer, and the rest of them settled on it as Jack took his seat. The room was quiet except for the crackling of the fire. With all eyes upon her, Rapunzel's grandmother drew a shaking breath and began to speak.

"My name is Purl Tattersby," she said, her gaze level with Rapunzel's. "And I have rehearsed many speeches in hopes of this moment, but I never imagined just how much you would look like my daughter. I am sorry if I frightened you. But you are all that I have left of Natalie, and I have hoped for so long. . . ."

Purl's voice trailed away, but her eyes stayed fixed on Rapunzel's face as she lifted the silver tip of her white cane and pointed it at Edam.

"My book," she said.

Edam was up at once, running his fingers along the spines of the books that filled the shelves to the left of the fireplace. When he came to a fairly unimpressive, slim, green-spined book, he pushed it with his fingertips.

There was a soft click. A small door, made to look like several tall book spines, swung open, and Edam reached into the hidden cabinet he had revealed. When he withdrew his hand, he held what looked like a large diary of rough paper, its pages full to bursting. Scrolls, old papers, and other small objects stuck out from in between the pages. With great care, Edam placed the book in Purl Tattersby's waiting hands.

She opened it. Rapunzel sat on the edge of her chair, unable to look away from the well-worn cover and stuffed pages. It was a book about her, she knew — one that she had never read — and she barely managed to stop herself from reaching out and snatching it. It took all her patience to wait as her grandmother unfolded the delicate spectacles that hung from the long chain about her neck and balanced the thin frames on the bridge of her nose.

"I always thought," Purl said, "that it would be a waste of copper to commission a portrait of Natty. She was a pretty girl, but I didn't want her vain as a peacock, and in any case, I saw her every day. What would I need a great oil portrait for? Ah, hindsight." She opened the book in her lap and turned the first page.

"This is the only likeness I can give you," she said, offering it to Rapunzel. "Done just before they left."

Rapunzel took the book at once, and her heart slowed down to a strange, slurring rhythm as she looked at a small watercolor painting of her mother.

It had to be her mother. The golden hair, the laughing mouth, the sharp blue eyes. Freckles dusted her nose and cheeks, and her stomach protruded roundly underneath a loose white gown. She held her massive belly in her arms, leaning against the man who stood behind her in the painting. He was handsome, broad-shouldered and striking, and taller than Rapunzel's mother. His hair and eyes were dark, his smile white. Under the painting were words in careful script: *Natalie and Remoulade LeRoux, Summer 1072.*

"LeRoux," said Rapunzel, testing the name in her mouth as she brushed a fingertip over the man's small, painted face. "This is my father?"

"Aye," said Purl. "Handsome boy. With a way of pleasing and a head for business — and wasn't Natty gone on him? He was older and had his pick of sweethearts. I never thought he'd give a second look to Natty, lovesick puppy that she was. Still, from the time she was old enough to go down for Market Day, she pined after him, and when she came into her own beauty, at about your age" — Purl paused, tilted her head, and nodded at Rapunzel — "Rem noticed her too. I never thought she ought to marry him, though I understood. He was the finest young man in Maple Valley and had great plans to make his fortune in Yellow. He was famous in these parts for making sauces that could melt a man's stomach, just the way his smile could melt a woman's heart."

Rapunzel was alarmed at the idea of stomachs and hearts being melted, but Jack was quick to explain that it was just a way of putting things. Purl regarded Jack shrewdly for a moment.

"After they married," she continued, turning her eyes to Rapunzel once more, "they lived here, with me, while Rem pulled together his business interests. Natty was seven months along with you when Rem got his 'good news.'" Purl's blue eyes were hard as metal. "They'd granted him a license for Market Park in Cornucopia. He'd gotten one of the best spots, he said — just north of the center, near the riverbank. But if he wanted it, he would have to go at once. Of course he wouldn't hear of waiting until the next season. And of course, Natty wouldn't hear of staying behind without him."

"Even though we begged her," Skye burst in from her place on the sofa beside Edam. Her cheeks were feverishly pink. "Begged her for two solid weeks. 'Rem's not thinking right,' I told her. 'He should put off the business till you're safe and the child is sturdy — and if he won't, then *you* must. Let him go to Yellow if he wants, but you stay here until that baby is born and both of you are well enough to travel.' That's what I told her. Oh, if she had listened . . ."

Rapunzel turned her eyes back to the book and looked again at her father's watercolor likeness. He was as handsome as a storybook prince, and his painted smile seemed to say that he knew it.

"If she had listened," repeated Purl, gazing at Rapunzel without seeming to see her. "But whatever Rem wanted, Natty wanted. She went away with him, so pregnant that she was lucky not to give birth on the side of the road." She snorted softly. "But they arrived intact. And they moved into a house Rem had rented on the border of Yellow country."

Rapunzel looked up from the book. "And Witch lived in the house just behind them . . . ," she said slowly, realizing that she knew the next part of the story.

Her grandmother was looking narrowly at her now. "That's right."

"Their back gardens were separated by a fence."

"They were."

"And Witch grew the most wonderful salad greens," said Rapunzel, warming to the tale, "and my mother began to crave them, because I was inside her. My father went over the fence to steal them, but Witch caught him in the garden, and she told him he could take the greens, but that, in exchange, he would have to give me to her when I was born. And he did."

Purl's chest rose and fell rapidly. "How do you know all this?" she asked.

"A Blue fairy told us in Cornucopia," said Jack.

"His name was Serge," added Rapunzel. "Do you know him?"

"I do not," said Purl, still looking rattled. "But the story is famous enough among fairies. Among the Exalted too. And witches."

"And the people in Cornucopia," said Rapunzel, remembering how they had run from her. "They seemed to know all about it."

"They know." It was the first Greve had spoken in quite some time, and his deep voice was hoarse. "No one who lived there during the Bargaining will ever forget it."

"Can *you* tell me why the Bargaining frightened people?" The question had never been answered to Rapunzel's satisfaction, and she angled her chair away from the fire, toward Greve. "If it was a trade, and my father wanted to give me away, then I don't understand why it was so terrible."

No one answered. All eyes registered shock except Jack's, and he was quick to speak.

"You have to understand," he told them, "Rapunzel didn't know what parents *were* until she left the tower. She didn't know she was from Yellow. She didn't know much at all." He looked at her as though to apologize for saying so, but for once, Rapunzel had no desire to fight him.

"You want to know why it was terrible?" Greve pinned his dark eyes on Rapunzel. "I can tell you. I was there."

Rapunzel nodded, but the look in his eyes sent a chill through her in spite of the fire's warmth. Edam stood up and paced away to the window, where he turned his back on the room.

Greve set his jaw. "Envearia owned both houses," he said. "Your parents' house and her own — but she only lived in one of them. The other was vacant, for rent. It stood empty for years until Rem and Natty came. I lived next door to the rental house with Edam. He's my son, and he was nineteen at the time. We didn't notice Envearia much; she didn't make herself neighborly. She never went into town, never mixed in the neighborhood. Never had a booth in Market Park, when her garden was easily the best in Cornucopia.

"I had my suspicions she might be a witch," Greve went on. "People thought I was paranoid. My daughter, Brie, had been killed by the Witch of the Woods several years before, and I guess folks thought I was inclined to see witches everywhere after that. And maybe I was."

At the window, Edam clenched his fists. Jack looked sickened.

"So I had my eye on Envearia," said Greve. "But others believed she was just an old woman who preferred to be alone."

"Old woman?" Rapunzel shook her head. "Witch *says* she's ever so old, but I'm sure she's only teasing. She looks too young."

Purl leaned back in her chair and began to rock. "Envearia is over one hundred and seventy years old," she said.

Rapunzel's head snapped toward her. "*What?*" She looked to Jack for assistance, but he offered none.

Greve went on speaking. "Fifteen years ago, I found out the vacant house behind Envearia's had been rented," he said. "It made me uneasy. Why rent it then, after so many years? What was she up to?" He frowned. "When your parents moved in, and I saw Natty pregnant out to here . . . I wondered if Envearia was after the child. Wasn't much I could do about it if she was, except send for help from the governor — which I did. He didn't reply. Two weeks after your parents arrived, I was at home when Natty started her labor. She howled for hours."

Looking red-faced but determined, Jack explained childbirth, more with gestures than words. Rapunzel made a noise of disgust.

"Well, no *wonder* she screamed" was all she could think to say.

Purl Tattersby gave a crackling laugh and looked fondly at Rapunzel. Rapunzel wasn't sure what was funny, but to be looked at with such obvious approval was very nice.

"What happened after my mother's labor?" she asked.

"By then, it was dark." Greve's low voice rumbled through the quiet room. "I went over to check on the new family, see if they needed anything. Barely saw the midwife as she ran past me out of Rem and Natty's house. She left the front door wide open and every lamp blazing. The place looked as if it was on fire. I was on the front steps when I heard your mother scream."

The rocking chair stilled, and Purl stared straight ahead, her features taut. Skye went to Edam at the window. She touched his shoulder, but he stood like stone.

"I've never heard anything like it again." Greve looked into the fire. "The sound a woman makes when her child is ripped from her."

The hairs rose on the back of Rapunzel's neck, and Jack met her look with one that said he too was disturbed. No one spoke.

"Then I saw her," Greve said. "Envearia. She came to the door where I stood, and she was carrying a bundle of sheets and lace. It wriggled and cried. I . . . I knew she had Natty's infant. And I knew I'd been right. She was a witch." Greve shuddered. "I couldn't stand by and let her take you. I tried to grab you from her — I told her she'd have to leave empty-handed, that I wouldn't let her pass. She just laughed and took a deep breath like she was taking a drink of you. I could only think of my girl, Brie. How I never knew what had happened to her until it was too late — how I never got a chance to fight for her. So I tried to strike Envearia, but I never made contact. She raised her hand and threw me across the road without touching me, and I haven't been the same since." He gestured to the leg that didn't work. "I couldn't save you."

"Don't blame yourself," snapped Purl. "You did more than anyone else ever has. You risked your life, didn't you? And what else is there?"

The room was silent. Rapunzel hugged herself, not certain why the story made her feel so cold. Perhaps it was that Witch had managed to stay young in spite of her age — but Rapunzel could understand wanting to remain beautiful. No, it was something else that troubled her. She looked intently at Purl and tried to get her mind around it.

But looking at her grandmother only made her think of how pretty her mother had been in that painting, and how happy, with her arms around her belly, smiling and radiant. Not long after, she had given birth to Rapunzel. And on the same night, she had given the scream that Greve could not forget. It all sounded very dreadful, and yet it made no sense.

"But *why* did my mother scream when Witch took me?" she asked.

"Because she wanted to hold you," said Purl. "She wanted to raise you, laugh with you, dry your tears, help you to learn, see you become a woman. Such was her *right*. And it was stolen from her."

"But she traded me!"

"Ah . . ." Purl pressed her lips shut. "No. Your father traded you. Within a week of living in that house, he traded you. But he never told Natty what he'd done. She had no idea that her unborn infant had been bartered away until you were snatched from her arms."

"But — but didn't she send my father over the fence to get the greens from Witch's garden?" Rapunzel asked urgently, needing to make it right. "She *wanted* him to steal, didn't she?"

"That was Rem's story," said Purl, her voice hard. "And Natty backed him up till the day she died. Loyal even after . . ." She shook her silver head. "We will never know how the witch's bargain was really struck. But your mother wanted you, Rapunzel. That you must believe. She wanted you so much that it killed her."

Rapunzel sat quietly, trying to absorb what she had just learned. She could not deny that some of what they said was true. Her experiences matched these tales. She believed that she was from Yellow. She believed herself the daughter of Rem and Natty LeRoux. She believed that her father had traded her to Witch. All of it made sense; none of it made Witch a villain.

But if her mother had wanted to keep her, then it made the bargain cruel.

And Witch had struck the bargain.

"How did my mother die?" she asked. Her voice jerked, not quite in her control. "And my father? How did he die?"

Purl slumped back in her chair with her eyes half-shut.

"Let me." Edam turned from the window. "The news spread fast," he told Rapunzel. "Rem tried to start his business in Market Park, but no one would go near him. Witch Bargainer, they called him. Some had lost children to the Witch of the Woods, but those children had been tricked. No one else had willingly and knowingly traded their children away. The people thought Rem was a monster. He wasn't in business two weeks before he broke his neck one night, falling from his horse. He was drunk. Some said he'd been drunk since the Bargaining."

"He wanted to die," said Skye quietly.

"Aye, and then so did Natty. She was half-dead already — the news almost finished her. She had to be carried to his funeral, and afterward, I brought her home. Here."

"But she was broken." Skye's eyes were full of tears again. "Mind and heart. She didn't last six months. The first fever she took was the one that killed her."

"She had nothing left to fight for," said Edam.

"Why didn't she come and get me?" Rapunzel demanded. She pushed Purl's book onto the table, stood up, and glared around at them. "She just sat down and died? She didn't even try? She couldn't have wanted me so much."

"She did try." Purl's eyes had now fallen shut. "Her letter from the governor is there in the book. She went to him for help, and received . . . a most efficient reply."

Rapunzel snatched up the book and turned its pages. Stuffed in between the first few sheets was a royal scroll, its wax seal broken, its ink faded with age. At the top of the scroll, in embossed, gilt lettering, were the words *Yellow Country ~ Official Correspondence*. At the bottom, in the same kind of script, was the stamped signature: *Royal Governor Calabaza of Yellow Country*.

Between the head and foot of the note, Rapunzel read, in perfect, black calligraphy:

> *Dear Citizen of Yellow Country,*
>
> *Thank you for your inquiry. While his Lordship the Governor of Yellow Country cannot attend individually to every subject's request, rest assured that your thoughts and suggestions are of deepest concern and that your best interests as a citizen of this great country are always under close consideration. Governor Calabaza thanks you for your participation in the community and hopes that you will continue to share your views.*

Rapunzel let the letter curl up with a snap. She clenched her fist around it.

"He said he was sorry for her," she said. "He said no good could come from interfering."

"Leave the magic to the magical," Greve muttered.

"Yes, he said that too."

"Who did?" asked Purl.

"Governor Calabaza," said Rapunzel. "I met him at the jacks tournament in Cornucopia."

Everyone stared at her.

"She won," Jack said. "She'll be competing in the All-Tyme Championship next summer. She's got amazing skill."

"You *won*?" Edam's face, which had been stony throughout the tale of Rapunzel's parents, now brightened. "You're a Capital Champion? Truly? She's a champion, Skye! Did you hear? Competing in the ATC and all!"

"I heard," Skye muttered. "Really, Edam, does this seem like a good time?"

"There's no bad time to be a sportsman! We'll all attend, of course. For once, I've got a reason to pay for the good seats —"

But Edam's exclamations were cut short. "Well, well." Purl folded her hands. She examined Rapunzel for a long moment. "You may look like a copy of your mother," she said, "but you are your own woman, aren't you?"

Rapunzel looked down at herself. "I'm not sure what you mean. I belong to myself, yes."

"Precisely. To yourself, and not to any man — or any witch." Purl gave a queer little smile. "You have courage. Strength . . ." Her voice trailed off, and she leaned back in her chair. Her papery eyelids fluttered shut.

"Don't try to do it all at once," said Greve in a low voice. "You'll exhaust yourself."

"She'll be getting tired anyway, Purl," said Skye. "We should let her have a bath and get to bed, poor thing — and her friend, as well."

"She'll be hungry too," said Edam, rubbing his hands together. "I'll cook her up something hearty, all right? Something fit for a Capital Champion."

"But she's barely said a word about her own life yet," said Purl, opening her eyes again and fixing them on Rapunzel. "You must tell me everything. How Envearia treated you all those years, how you came to leave the tower, how you managed to travel so far north —"

"Time for all of that tomorrow," said Greve. "Just now, you rest."

"One more hour —"

"Do you want to get sicker now that she's come home? Or do you want to get well and spend time with her?"

Purl sighed in defeat. "Skye," she said, "make up the bed in Natty's old room. Jack may stay here, by the fire — get the pallet from the shed. Tomorrow we'll go into town and get you everything you need, Charlo —" She stopped. "Rapunzel. What matters tonight is that you've finally come home to stay."

"Stay?" Rapunzel got to her feet, confused. "Here?"

"Here." In Purl's blue eyes was a terrible longing, an ache that seemed to wrap itself around Rapunzel's heart and make her ache too.

"But . . ."

"But? Don't you want to stay?"

Rapunzel was alarmed to discover that she did want to stay — she wanted to be here in this cozy house, listening to Purl and looking at her silver hair, hearing about her mother and father, and learning more about Witch.

But Witch was still in danger. And Rune would never allow Rapunzel to stay here in any case. She was sure he would do something terrible if she stopped for too long. She had been sent to the First Wood, and there she must go.

"I can't stay," she said. "I have to save Witch. If I don't get to the First Wood, then the Red fairies will —"

"You want to *save* Envearia?" Greve interrupted. "After all you've just heard? Weren't you listening, girl?"

"Yes, but Rune is following us, and if I don't do what Glyph said —"

"You *can't* leave!" Skye exclaimed. "You just arrived!"

"If I don't go, the fairies will kill Witch!"

"So let them kill her." Edam's face was cold again. "You're not going back to that tower." He took a step toward her. Rapunzel backed away.

"You can't tell me what to do," she said shrilly, panic rising in her chest. "I have to go to the First Wood — Jack, help me!"

"I can't stay here either," said Jack, getting to his feet. "Wish I could, but I've sworn to help Rapunzel get where she's going."

"Have you?" said Purl, fixing sharp eyes on him. "And just what is your stake in the business? What precisely is your interest in my granddaughter?"

"The Red fairies will help him if he helps me," said Rapunzel.

"Help him with what?"

Rapunzel opened her mouth to reply and realized that she did not know the answer. She had asked Jack about it, but he had never told her.

All eyes, including Rapunzel's, were focused on Jack. When he spoke, it was with obvious reluctance.

"I have to bring something to a giantess in Geguul," he said in a voice so low that it didn't sound like his. "The fairies will help me do it, but only if I help Rapunzel. So we can't stay."

Purl's eyebrows flew up until they were nearly lost in her silver hair.

"A giantess," she repeated. "In Geguul."

Even the fire seemed to stand still. No one knew how to reply except Prince Frog, who gave a long, slow croak.

"Are you a witch, boy?" Greve's growl was a shock in the silence, and Jack jumped.

"No!"

"Then how do you have dealings in Geguul? No mortal can go there and back again without White hatching, can they?"

"I got there by accident," Jack said, putting his hands up in protest.

"No one climbs the highest Peaks into the White Fairy's lair by accident."

"I didn't go that way," said Jack. "I swear. There was this giant beanstalk —"

"Beanstalker!" Rapunzel cried, remembering what Glyph and Rune had called him. "I knew I forgot to ask you about something."

"A giant beanstalk?" said Edam with contempt. "Start making sense, would you?"

"I know it sounds crazy," said Jack, "but you have to believe me. If I were a witch, why would Red fairies help me?"

"How do we know Red fairies *are* helping you?" Edam countered. "You could be lying."

"He's not lying," said Rapunzel. "I was there. The leader of the Red fairies, Eldest Glyph — she's the one who promised to help him. She said we have to go to the First Wood together."

Purl looked first at Rapunzel and then at Jack for a long, hard moment. Then she rapped the tip of her cane against the floor, and the whole room seemed to start. "Oh, for the love of trees, Edam," she said, waving her cane at him, "back off and stop scaring my granddaughter. Greve, get away from that door. You've held these youngsters prisoner enough for one day. Rapunzel may come and go from *this* house as she pleases."

"But —" said Edam, with a face full of passion.

"I won't trap her," said Purl. "I'm no witch. Rapunzel, I hope that you and Jack will break your journey here with us tonight. I very much wish you to stay longer and speak with me, but I will not force you."

Rapunzel looked at Jack, who cast his eyes around the room and studied each of its inhabitants coolly. Then he nodded.

"We can stay one night," said Rapunzel. "We would have had to camp anyway. I don't think Rune will stop us as long as we leave tomorrow."

As she said this, she thought she saw a trail of red light out of the corner of her eye. She turned quickly to the nearest window, but the light had already vanished, and all she could see were the shapes of trees in the darkness, outlined against the starry sky.

"Then it's settled," said Purl. "Greve, you help me back to bed. Edam, fix them something to eat — and don't plague Rapunzel with questions, any of you. Not one more word about witches or towers until morning."

CHAPTER SIXTEEN

*T*HE evening began in strained quiet. Edam prepared supper almost without a word, and Jack seemed inclined to stay out of everyone's way. He sat in the farthest corner of the living room, out of sight of the kitchen, thumbing through the same book about magic that Rapunzel had been looking at earlier.

Once Purl was tucked away in bed, she called for Rapunzel and asked if she would kiss her good night. Rapunzel did it, feeling rather strange as she put her mouth to her grandmother's wrinkled cheek. Purl looked so hungrily at her that Rapunzel was relieved when it was time to put out the lamp. She was even more relieved when she emerged from Purl's room to find that Greve had gone back to his own house next door, leaving her and Jack with Edam and Skye.

Edam relaxed a little after that. He couldn't resist asking Rapunzel about the jacks tournament, and Rapunzel was quite happy to recount every play of it to him, which he very much appeared to enjoy. By the end of her tale, supper was ready, and the four of them sat down to a real, non-Ubiquitous meal, complete with fennel salad, cheese soup, and roast beef, and followed by a slice of chocolate cake so delicious that Rapunzel secretly believed Edam might be as good a cook as Witch.

Afterward, Rapunzel bathed for the first time in what felt like forever, and she washed her itchy scalp with lots of strong, nice-smelling lavender soap. Prince Frog refused to splash in the bathtub; he stayed far away and entertained himself by eating dead bugs from the windowsill. When she was clean and dry, she put on a long, soft flannel nightdress that Skye said she had made for Natty when she was first pregnant. When Skye left her, Rapunzel pulled the downy covers up to her chin and lay there in her mother's old bedroom, feeling nearly as safe and secure as if she were in her own tower.

She had questions. Strange questions. Why had Witch grown that garden? Why had she tricked Rem LeRoux and taken Rapunzel away from a mother who wanted her? Was it that Witch loved her so much that she'd been willing to hurt people to get her? But *why* had she loved her? Rapunzel hadn't even been born yet, when the bargain was struck — what had made Witch want to bring her home to the tower and care for her?

At dawn, she woke to the sensation of a hand clasping her own. She opened her eyes to find Purl sitting on the edge of the bed, wrapped in a fleecy dressing gown. She gazed down at Rapunzel with an expression quite different from yesterday's hungry, aching looks. Her wrinkled face was quiet; her bright blue eyes were curious.

"Good morning," she said.

Rapunzel sat up a little, squinting. "It's early," she said, peering at the window. Outside, the sky was still pale purple.

"I had an unexpected visitor last night," said Purl. "Rune, he called himself."

Now Rapunzel sat up straight. "What happened?" she demanded. "Are you all right?"

Purl squeezed her hand. "He did nothing alarming — other than appear. That was enough, I can tell you." She snorted. "No — he only told me that you and Jack were telling the truth about this First Wood business, that you must leave me today at dawn, and that I have no choice but to let you go." She paused. "It's difficult, you see. I've had to let you go before, without a choice. I'm afraid I'll never see you again. And our meeting was such a brief one."

"I'll come back," said Rapunzel impulsively. "Once I've been to the First Wood and I've had a chance to talk to Witch, I'll come back here again."

Purl looked doubtful.

"I will," said Rapunzel, and she meant it. "I like it here. I want to visit for a long time, and I want to hear everything about my mother and father, and you —"

"You truly intend to go back to Envearia?" her grandmother said.

"I have to," said Rapunzel. "I have so many questions."

"Can't I answer them?"

"I don't know. Can you tell me why Witch was willing to cause so much unhappiness?"

"Witches possess the magic of the White," said Purl, "and the White is cruel."

"But Witch *isn't* cruel," said Rapunzel. "I wish someone would believe me. I wish you could know how kind she is, and how much she loves me."

Purl let go of her hand. "You'd better wear this," she said, and reached behind her neck to unfasten a long, dull chain of what looked like silver, but without any gleam. She hung it around Rapunzel's neck. It was fine, but heavy. "Iron," said Purl. "It dampens magic, and it inflicts painful injury on witches. It's worth a fortune, so wear it under your clothes, where it won't tempt the bad sorts."

Rapunzel reached up to remove it. If it would hurt Witch, then she didn't want it.

Purl stopped her hand. "If you believe anything we've told you here, then wear it," she said. She braced herself on the edge of the bed and pushed herself carefully to her feet. "Now, wake your friend. The sooner you finish this errand of yours, the sooner you'll come back to visit me — and you will come back?" she asked with sudden urgency. "Promise me?"

At the look on Purl's face, Rapunzel's chest tightened. She did not fully understand the tears that stung her own eyes, but she felt with fierce certainty that she must and would return here. She owed it to Purl, who had waited for so long. She owed it to herself too. She could never know the mother who had wanted her — but she could know her mother's mother. That was something.

"I promise," she whispered.

Once Jack was awake, Purl fed the two of them a hot, sturdy breakfast of porridge and eggs, and then they were off, plunging northeastward into the frosty dawn, toward Independence and the First Wood. Jack pulled the wagon, Prince Frog burrowed into Rapunzel's front pocket, and Rapunzel stopped and looked back at her grandmother's home.

Purl stood on the front step, leaning on her cane, her tail of hair shining silvery pink in the dawn light. She raised her hand in parting. As Rapunzel raised her hand in reply, her heart gave a sharp pang, and she decided she had better not look back anymore. She turned away and started walking again. The faster they made it to the First Wood, the better.

"How many more days until we reach Independence?" she asked

when they had put the distance of a league or so between themselves and Purl's house.

"Six? Hopefully not longer." Jack sighed. "I never imagined I'd miss home so much, but I'll sure be glad when this is over and I get back to the Peaks."

"You didn't think you'd miss your home?" asked Rapunzel, surprised. "I thought you liked playing with Tess."

"I do. But I've always wanted to adventure," he said. "I'm like my dad that way. When Tess and I play make-believe — I mean, when I help Tess play make-believe," he corrected himself, looking a bit pink, "she always plays a fairy godmother, and she grants me wishes and lets me go wherever I want, with all the money I can carry."

"A fairy what?"

"A fairy godmother — they're fairies who help people."

"Like Serge!"

"Exactly," said Jack. "Tess loves pretending to be a fairy," he added, smiling. "She usually makes a gown out of old feed sacks, and we make wings and a crown out of leaves and stuff. If my mother's not there, Tess gets up on the kitchen table so that she can pretend she's flying." He laughed. "She's going to love those Ubiquitous costumes you bought her."

"The bandits didn't get them?"

"Nah, I kept those ones in my belt."

They walked on for many hours, stopping only for lunch, and then again when it was time to set up camp for the night. Rapunzel barely noticed the quiet. Her brain was full, her body weary. She was shocked at how exhausted she became after just a day of walking.

Riding in Greve's wagon had let her forget her sore feet and aching muscles, which were now all throbbing again. Still, the pain helped to keep her thoughts from gathering too close together.

She slept heavily that night and woke to find sunlight streaming through the trees and Jack bending over her, his face full of worry.

"What is it?" she asked.

"You were crying in your sleep," Jack said. "Are you all right?"

"I . . . don't know." Rapunzel pushed herself to her elbows and winced when she found that her head was pounding as hard as any of her muscles. "My head," she moaned, and reached up to rub it, shutting her eyes against the painful sunlight. "Please let's not walk today."

"We have to," said Jack. "Rune's still watching us."

They pushed on. As they walked, the throbbing in Rapunzel's head distracted her from the ache in her feet. But it could not distract her from her thoughts. She had no interest in the father who had traded her, but she did not understand why Witch would not have let her at least meet her mother. Her mother had wanted to raise her and love her, yet Witch had taken her away, even though her mother had screamed. Even though she had gone to the governor for help.

Why?

It was the heaviest question of all. Why had Witch taken her? Why had she told Rapunzel that she had rescued her from the swamps? Why had she raised her in a tower, so far from the place where she was born? Why had she said that fairies were useless? Why had she never mentioned Rapunzel's parents or said that her name was Envearia? Why had she never told Rapunzel that her own last name was LeRoux?

So engrossed was Rapunzel in these questions that she did not notice how cold the air had grown until her breath was coming from her mouth in great white puffs. Surprised, she flexed her fingers and found that they were stiff from cold. She and Jack stopped their march for half an hour to eat lunch and dress more warmly. They donned their mittens, slung cloaks over their shoulders, and pulled up the hoods. Thus protected, they continued their winding path through the woods and down the hills.

It was twilight before they came to a good campsite. Sleep came quickly, and so did jumbled dreams. When she woke the next morning, her head ached as though it would split. But when Jack expressed concern, she only brushed him off and picked up the wagon handle, wanting to walk in spite of the pain. The sooner they finished their journey, the better. She would have no peace until she spoke with Witch.

They walked for an hour, Rapunzel still lost in thought. She became conscious of the cold white flakes that tumbled all around her only when they began to fall thickly. She looked up into the sky and then down at the ground in surprise, watching as a white blanket formed at her feet.

"What's this?" she asked. "Salt?"

Jack laughed. "It's snow. Snow's like rain, but it's soft and cold. You'll love it."

"Why would I love it?" she asked as it caught in her eyelashes and stung her cheeks. She pulled the hood of her cloak farther forward. "It's freezing."

"You'll love it anyway," said Jack, grinning. "Because I have a surprise. Wouldn't you like to stop walking for a while?"

"Well, yes," Rapunzel admitted. "But we can't."

"We can't stop *moving* . . . and when we find some open space and have a little more snow, we won't have to," said Jack mysteriously.

About an hour later, they came to the edge of the forest and studied the map once more. From here, Rapunzel saw, it was just short of twenty leagues to Independence. Jack folded the map and looked ahead. A smooth expanse of untouched white snow stretched before them into the distance.

"I didn't think we'd see this much snow," he said, surveying it with a delight Rapunzel did not share. "I was hoping — but it's not even quite winter yet, and we're not far north enough. This is pretty intense weather for this time of year."

"It's going to make it harder to walk, isn't it?" said Rapunzel, sighing.

"We're not going to walk." He produced a gleaming silver Ubiquitous acorn. Rapunzel recognized it as by far the most expensive one from the Cornucopia shop — a Hawthorne all on its own. And Jack had bought two of them. She held out her hand.

Jack hesitated. "Actually, do you mind if I do it?" he asked. "I've always wanted to crack one of these."

"All right," said Rapunzel, who was now very curious. "Go ahead."

Jack knelt beside a small rock that protruded from the snow. He raised his hand and brought the silver acorn down with a mighty CRACK.

Rapunzel shrieked and leapt back. Whatever it was he had cracked, it quickly filled the space between them, a strange, flat contraption with metal railings and leather straps leading from its front. Attached to the straps were round collars. To Rapunzel's amazement, translucent creatures materialized as well, their necks secured by the collars, their bodies covered in silvery, transparent fur.

"Dogs!" breathed Rapunzel. There were six of them, all attached to the flat thing, all sniffing one another and scratching themselves. "Are they real?" She had seen pictures of ferocious dogs in her books, but they had always looked solid in the pictures — not see-through like these.

"They're real enough for a little while," said Jack. "Real as magic can make them, anyway. A Ubiquitous Instant Dogsled!" He paced around it, admiring. "I can't tell you how many times I've wished I could afford one of these."

Jack loaded their wagon onto the sled. He sat down and gestured for Rapunzel to join him.

"How does it work?" she asked, climbing in.

"Like this," said Jack, lifting a long leather thing that was coiled at the front of the sled, just behind the dogs. He flicked his wrist, and the leather thing lashed upward into the air and came down with a cracking sound. "YAH!" he shouted, and the dogs took off at once, racing across the snowy expanse. Wind blew Rapunzel's hood off, exposing her face to the freezing cold, and she shrieked and laughed together.

"Fantastic!" Jack yelled. "I knew these sleds were supposed to be fast, but this is incredible! We'll make it to the First Wood in half the time!"

"Won't the sled crash in twenty-four hours?" Rapunzel shouted.

"No!" Jack's hair flew straight back from his face as he grinned into the snow and wind.

"Why not?"

"I don't know! I can just feel it. This sled will take us a long way."

Rapunzel believed it. Commonwealth Green raced past them in a blur as the Ubiquitous dogs pulled the sled forward, faster and faster, until they were almost flying. "I love it!" she cried, and Jack thumped her on the back with his fist.

Rapunzel's heart was lighter than it had been since she had left her tower. "I'm coming, Witch," she whispered, and the words were whipped away by the rushing wind before Jack heard them. "I'm coming."

By evening, the snow had stopped and the clouds had rolled away, leaving a canopy of starry darkness. Only one tent remained, so they did not crack it — they had to save it for bad weather, Jack said. The night was cold, but blankets made it bearable, and they made camp on the sled to keep from freezing on the snow. The Ubiquitous sled dogs did not seem to feel cold or hunger; they curled up in the snow and went to sleep.

"Let's get all the use we can out of this sled," said Jack. "We'll just sleep a few hours, all right? Then we'll keep going, and whenever the sled crashes, we'll take another break."

Rapunzel agreed. She made a fire near the sled and delighted in the way the firelight danced across the whiteness of the snow all around them. Jack got dinner out of the wagon, and for the first time Rapunzel noticed that their current stash of food did not come from acorns. He passed her a bright pink apple, a chunk of soft bread all laced with herbs and oil, and a little brick of cheese.

"Where did you get these things, anyway?" she asked.

"Purl must have packed them in the wagon while we were having breakfast the other day," Jack replied. "She really loaded us up."

Rapunzel folded the bread around the cheese and said a silent thank-you to Purl before tucking in.

"You believed her, didn't you?" said Jack through a mouthful of cheese. "About your mother and everything?"

Rapunzel's bread suddenly felt too thick in her mouth. She swallowed, with effort, and looked down at her apple.

"I don't want to talk about it," she said.

"Come on," said Jack. "You've barely said two words about everything that happened at your grandmother's house, and her story goes along exactly with what Governor Calabaza said, and with what Serge told you —"

"I know."

"And that woman in the picture looked an awful lot like you —"

"I *know*."

"Then you won't really go back to Envearia, will you?" said Jack. "I mean, you can't, can you? Knowing what you know?"

"I don't know what I know." Rapunzel twirled the apple in her hands, watching firelight bounce from its taut pink skin. "Except I know — I *know* — that Witch loves me."

"Rapunzel, you can't seriously believe —"

"You asked what I think, so listen."

Jack closed his mouth.

"I didn't know Natty LeRoux," said Rapunzel. "Witch is my only mother. She's taken care of me my entire life. That's love, isn't it? Even if she didn't tell the truth about everything —"

"So you *admit* —" Jack began, but at the look Rapunzel gave him, he fell silent again. He hunched forward and frowned at the fire, his hair falling into his eyes. "Do you know where witches go when they die?" he asked eventually.

Rapunzel was surprised. "I thought you said they didn't die."

"Not like humans, they don't," Jack said. "Remember how I told you what happens when we die?"

"Our bodies get buried, but the part of us that isn't physical goes into the Beyond?"

"Yes." He spoke slowly. "But witches don't get to go to the Beyond."

"Where do they go?" said Rapunzel, leaning toward him.

"They go to Geguul," said Jack. "The White Fairy takes them."

A cold wind blew across the dark and snowy plain. Rapunzel put her apple aside and drew her blanket close around her.

"Tell me about Geguul," she said. "What was it like?"

Jack looked pained.

"Please — at Purl's house you said we were friends, didn't you?"

"We are," said Jack. "But I did something bad, Rapunzel. Really bad."

"Worse than tricking me out of my tower?"

"So much worse," said Jack, and he hugged himself. He looked afraid.

Rapunzel moved to sit beside him and gave him half of her blanket. He huddled under it with her.

"I told you how, before I started traveling, I lived with my mother in Dearth." His voice was strange. Unreadable. "My mother and Tess."

He stared at the fire before continuing.

"Fifty-eight days ago," he said, "I was sitting outside our house. It's not much of a house — it's not like your grandmother's place. I was milking the cow when these things that looked like shiny white beans dropped from the sky and into the milk pail. I fished them out, and they sparkled like diamonds or something. But while I held them, they changed. They turned brown. They looked kind of like seeds."

Rapunzel understood seeds. Witch used them to start her roses. "Did you plant them?" she asked.

"I threw them in the dirt, and I guess they planted themselves. That night, while I was asleep, a beanstalk grew in our yard."

"Beanstalker!" Rapunzel burst out.

"Right. See, beans usually grow on vines about this tall," said Jack, showing her with his hand. "But the beanstalk in our yard went all the way to the sky and pierced the clouds. It had leaves almost as big as me. I tried climbing on them, and they held me up, no problem, just like steps. So I climbed higher, and for a couple hours I was just picking beans and throwing them down. They were huge, and I figured we could eat them. I didn't realize I'd gotten to the top of the beanstalk until I saw whiteness everywhere, and mist. The ground looked like clouds."

"Really?" Rapunzel was fascinated. "You walked on *top* of the clouds?"

"No, I stayed on the beanstalk. I wasn't sure what to do, or whether it was smart to do anything — I guess I realized that I might have found Geguul, but it didn't seem possible. I thought maybe I'd found some other magic place, somewhere nobody had ever discovered, and if I explored it, I might find something good."

"Something like what?"

"Something I could trade for money. My father had been dead for a year, and the farm was in bad shape. Like I told you, we were starving. Tess usually got something to eat, but my mother and I had to take turns skipping our meals to make that happen."

Rapunzel stared at him. "Your father died?" she said. "You never told me."

Jack shrugged. "He went exploring," he said. "He found a map that he thought would lead him to treasure deep in the caves of the Violet Peaks. So he pulled together some people and supplies from around Dearth, and he led an expedition to find the treasure."

"And what did he find?"

"Nothing." Jack's voice was flat. "There was a cave-in — some rocks inside the mountain fell. He was crushed, and his party came back without him."

Rapunzel did not know what to say to this.

Jack pressed on. "The point is," he said, "I climbed the beanstalk. It was pretty empty up there in the clouds, but there was this big white cave nearby, all surrounded by white mist. And when I say big cave, I mean huge. *Huge*," he repeated, throwing out his arms to show her. "You could fit ten houses in it. That's when I knew it had to be Geguul. Only a giant could live in a cave like that."

"And a giant . . . is a very big beast?"

"Giants are shaped like humans," said Jack, "except they're ten times taller, and they're all white. Dead white."

"Like snow?"

"Like snow," Jack agreed. "Their skin, their nails, their tongues — white as snow. And they have no hair. They look like they're made of lumps of white clay. Except their eyes." He gave a faint shudder. "Their eyes have color. Their eyes look human."

"Did you meet one? Is that how you know?"

"Yes," said Jack, and then he stopped talking again for a minute and looked as though he was trying to piece the next parts of his story together.

"In the mist," he said, "right next to the top of the beanstalk, someone had left three treasures. One was a silver harp a lot like the one in your tower. One was a golden goose — really golden, but alive, and it laid an egg made of solid gold right there in front of me. The third was a bag of coins. And I should have thought a lot harder about what I was doing, but I didn't. I was stupid. I picked up the goose to look at it. The second I did, a giantess came out of the cave nearby and told me not to move. I've never been so scared in my life."

"Not even of the Stalker?"

Jack laughed humorlessly. "Giants make Stalkers look like kittens," he said. "I thought the giantess would kill me. But she . . . she was . . ." He paused. "She had kind eyes," he said. "She didn't want to hurt me. She said that since I had taken something precious from her, I would have to do as she asked, or she would take what was most precious from me. I told her I didn't steal anything, but she said, 'You are standing on a thing of the ground while holding a thing of the sky that you were not invited to hold.' I tried putting the goose down, but it was too late. She said I had to take it with me, that it was mine now, so I owed her a treasure in exchange. She'd tricked me. She put those treasures there hoping someone would pick one up."

The story was too fantastic to be real, but Rapunzel knew, from the way Jack spoke, that every word was truth. "What did she want?" asked Rapunzel. "Something the Red fairies have to give you?"

Jack nodded. "The giantess wants to die," he said. "She said it's agony, living in Geguul. She said she wishes she'd never been White-hatched, that it wasn't worth it — that she just wants to die like a regular human and go to the Beyond."

"White . . . hatched?"

"It's what happens when someone goes up to the White Fairy and gets magic power from her. 'White-hatching' — I guess it got shortened to 'witch.' Anyway, part of the deal when people White-hatch is that they go to Geguul when they die. When that happens, the White Fairy turns them into giants and just sort of . . . keeps them."

"Will the White Fairy turn Witch into a giant?" asked Rapunzel in a small voice. "How long will she keep her?"

"Forever."

"And the giants are unhappy in Geguul?"

"The one I met was."

"So unhappy that she wants to die?"

"Yeah. She said that the Red fairies were the only ones who might know how to help her. So she sent me to find them, and she gave me seven fortnights to come back. Ninety-eight days." His voice was quiet. "She'll lower the beanstalk at the end of each fortnight, and if I'm not back to climb it and give her what she wants by the seventh time, then the beanstalk will wither and I'll lose my chance. I'll owe her whatever is most precious to me."

"That means . . ." Rapunzel calculated. "You've got forty-one days left."

Jack nodded.

"And you have to go south again to the Red fairies and then go all the way north to the Violet Peaks in just forty-one days?" She finally understood why Jack needed the fairies to help him. They could give him what he needed for the giantess, and then they could take him home through fairywoods to get him there fast. "What's the giantess going to take if you don't make it back in time?"

Jack spoke, but his voice was so faint that Rapunzel didn't hear him. He cleared his throat and spoke again.

"Tess," he said.

CHAPTER SEVENTEEN

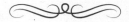

A chill that had nothing to do with the snow passed through Rapunzel. Distressed, she tried to touch Jack's arm, but he pulled away. She withdrew her hand, and her fingers fluttered to her heart instead.

There, beneath her fingertips, she felt a strange, frozen lump.

Rapunzel looked down. In the vest pocket over her heart, there was a familiar bulge. But the bulge was motionless.

"Prince Frog," she gasped.

Her fingers fumbled uselessly as she worked to unbutton her pocket. The fear that gripped her made her clumsy and stupid. She couldn't believe it. She had forgotten all about Prince Frog. Her mind had been so full that she hadn't checked on him since Maple Valley, and he had not moved, or croaked, or bounced, or done anything at all since they had left Purl's. How could she not have noticed? The weather had grown ever colder, and now they were surrounded by snow, and she had done nothing to keep him warm.

"Help me," she yelped, and Jack grabbed the front of her vest and threaded the button through its hole. Rapunzel dug into the open pocket and let out a cry when her fingers closed around Prince Frog's frozen form. She withdrew his squat little body from her vest and felt for the beating of his belly or the trembling of his gut chin.

His eyes were shut. He was cold and still.

"Oh, my frog," she whimpered, and she stumbled from the sled to kneel beside the fire, where she could see him better. She laid him on her knee and rubbed his icy flesh until it was somewhat clammy again. When he did not stir, she laid her cheek against his back. "Jack, what do I do?" she pleaded when Prince Frog did not respond.

Jack knelt beside her, his face grim. "I don't think we can do anything."

"Of course we can!" Rapunzel cupped his little body in her hands and held him out to Jack. "We have to!"

Jack felt Prince Frog with his hand for a moment, then shook his head.

"I'm sorry," he said.

"Don't be sorry — do something!"

"I can't. When something dies, it's just dead."

"No!" shouted Rapunzel. "You take that back!"

Jack only looked at her, and it was much worse than if he had argued. Rapunzel's pulse thudded with such force that she felt like she was rattling.

"I'm sorry," Jack said again. "I really am."

"You shut up!" she spat. "He isn't dead, you're wrong!"

"If he isn't breathing," Jack said, "then he's dead."

"BREATHING!" Rapunzel leapt to her feet and clutched Prince Frog's inert body to her heart. "Oh, Jack! Yes! It's a perfect idea — hurry, hurry, get it out!"

"Get what out?"

"The lifebreath that Rune gave us! We'll break it near Prince Frog's mouth, and it will save him! Hurry, before it's too late!"

"It might already be too late," said Jack. "Rune said it could bring someone back from the brink of death, right? Not from death itself."

"It will work, I *know* it will, please, Jack, hurry —"

Jack hesitated. He took a deep breath. "Rapunzel . . . look. I hate to say this . . . but we might need the lifebreath for ourselves before this is all over. We can't just spend it on a frog."

"*Can't just spend it on a frog?*" Rapunzel shrieked, the pitch of her voice rising with every word. "You give me that lifebreath and you give it to me now!"

"You'll regret it later if I do," said Jack.

"You'll regret it now if you don't!" Rapunzel held Prince Frog to her chest, which rose and fell rapidly. "I will never forgive you, and I won't go another step on this journey, and I don't care what Rune does about it, do you hear me, I don't care!"

When she said this, she thought she saw a trail of red sparks out of the corner of her eye, and she knew that Rune was watching. But at this moment, she felt she would face anything at all, if only she could wake Prince Frog.

Jack narrowed his eyes, but he got to his feet and pulled the lifebreath out of his vest. The wisp of whiteness still whirled inside the little glass bubble.

"You're going to wish we hadn't done this," he said. "I'm telling you."

"Break the glass!" Rapunzel commanded, thrusting Prince Frog toward Jack. "Do it now!"

Jack held the fragile bubble near Prince Frog's mouth and crushed it in his fingers. It crumbled into glittering red dust, releasing the wisp. It twisted and turned, then fled into one of Prince Frog's nostrils.

Rapunzel held her breath and watched Prince Frog's body for signs of life. She waited for his belly to move, or for his eyes to open, or for his gut chin to wobble.

Nothing happened.

"It's too late," said Jack. "We shouldn't have used it —"

"*SHHH!*"

Apart from that sound, Rapunzel did not stir. She knelt there in the snow, hearing her own heartbeat in her ears, holding Prince Frog and wishing with all her might for him to open his eyes and look at her. The fire crackled cheerfully, and the sound was terrible and out of place. Jack did not venture another word.

Rapunzel's shins were half-frozen in the snow. She would have to get up soon. She couldn't pretend any longer. Wanting him back would not make Prince Frog spring to life. He was gone. He was there, right there in her hands — but he was gone.

So this was death. And she had caused it.

Guilt and grief struck her together, and she knew what they were, but that did not make them easier to endure. "Sweet frog," she managed. "Forgive me." She laid her face against his cold little back and began to cry. But the tears gave Rapunzel no relief; they seemed to pour from the empty place in her heart that Prince Frog had occupied. They came and came, and she huddled beside the fire, still cupping Prince Frog in her hands, unwilling to let him go. Her sobs filled the dark night around them, and she thought her heart would break apart inside her.

"Is everything all right?" asked a voice that did not belong to Rapunzel or Jack. "What's the matter here?"

Jack sprang to his feet. He whirled around, brandishing his sword, and nearly stabbed the man who had come up behind them.

The man was tall and broad, older than Jack by a handful of years. He wore a dark orange cape that fell to the snow and was embroidered with intricate designs in copper thread and fastened with an ornate copper hook. In this hook was set a large orange jewel that glimmered in the light of the fire. The man's hair too was flaming orange, and his face was plastered all over with freckles.

"I'm looking for my dog," said the man. "Have you seen him? Big, red, likes to lick people. I thought I heard his bark coming from this direction, but now I see your Ubiquitous dogs —"

"Who are you?" Jack demanded, keeping his sword out.

"He's a p-prince," Rapunzel managed through her tears. Other than the freckles, the man fit the images in her storybooks perfectly, from his cape to his heavy, buckled boots. She wiped her eyes with one hand and kept the other curled around Prince Frog's body.

"Prince Mick the Magnificent of Orange," said the prince. He bowed sideways to avoid the point of Jack's sword. Jack quickly sheathed it.

"Forgive me, your highness," he said, bowing low.

"It's dark," said Prince Mick. "You're right to be careful." He straightened as several men and women came up behind him, also dressed in capes and heavy boots, with swords at their belts.

"Sir, Trusty must have run farther than usual," said one of them. "We haven't seen him yet. But we'll split up to cover more ground, and I'm sure we'll have him back at camp in no time."

"Thank you," said Prince Mick, and though he appeared a bit anxious, he turned a smile upon Rapunzel. "Now. What's the matter?"

Rapunzel only sniffled. She didn't care about princes. She didn't care about anything.

Prince Mick crouched down beside her and lowered his voice. "I came this way partly to search for Trusty, and partly because I heard you crying," he said. "Were you attacked? Are you in trouble?"

Rapunzel looked down at Prince Frog in her hand. "It's my frog," she said. "He's . . . he's . . ." But her voice broke and she could not say it.

"Dead," Jack supplied.

"Ah," said Prince Mick. "And this frog was a friend?"

Rapunzel nodded.

"I've lost friends like that," said Prince Mick. "I had a beautiful russet hound who died when I was eight, and I still think of him every day. What happened to your frog?"

"H-he froze. In my pocket."

Prince Mick held out his large, freckled hand. "May I hold him?"

"Can you save him?"

"No — I'm sorry."

Sorry again. Rapunzel was beginning to hate the word.

"But I can give him a royal burial," said Prince Mick. "Stay in the Orange camp tonight, both of you, as my guests. We'll celebrate and mourn your friend together. You ought to come with me in any case — it's much safer to camp in a group than out here on your own."

"No," said Rapunzel, keeping hold of Prince Frog and staring into the fire again.

"You can't say no," Jack whispered. "He's a prince."

"I don't care."

"I understand your feelings," said Prince Mick. "I wish I could help, but it's beyond my power. Although, maybe . . ." He paused. "Hmm. But it's best not to interrupt."

Rapunzel looked swiftly up at him. "Interrupt who?" she said. "Is there someone who can help him?"

"The Exalted Council has a camp nearby," said Prince Mick, frowning. "If healing the frog *is* possible, one of them would know how to do it. However, he does seem to be past hope, and the Exalted are very —"

"Let's go," said Rapunzel, already on her feet. She pressed Prince Frog into Jack's hands, strapped on her hair, and snatched Prince Frog again. "Take me to the Exalted."

"You can't command royalty," whispered Jack.

"It's fine," said Prince Mick, scratching the orange stubble that lined his jaw. "Well. If we're going to go, we might as well be quick!" He gestured to the small company of servants who had joined him, and they put out Rapunzel's fire, packed the wagon into the sled, and led the sled dogs back toward the Orange camp.

Rapunzel and Jack followed Prince Mick into the darkness in another direction, their footsteps crunching on the snow.

"Why are the Exalted camped around here, your highness?" asked Jack, struggling to keep up with Prince Mick's massive strides. "Has there been some kind of trouble?"

"No trouble," replied Prince Mick. "Commonwealth Green is about to celebrate the seventy-fifth anniversary of their independence from the Pink Empire. People from all over Tyme will meet in the capital to celebrate with Green and support them as they prepare for the Hundred-Year Day."

"Hundred-Year Day?" asked Rapunzel, out of habit. She stroked Prince Frog's unresponsive little body with her thumbs, growing more agitated with every step.

"I'll let my sister tell you all about it," said the prince. "She'll be beside herself with joy to have an audience. Ah — this must be it."

There was nothing before them but darkness and snow and a pair of cloaked figures standing a short distance ahead. Rapunzel broke into a run. When she reached the two cloaked people, she thrust Prince Frog toward them. One was a woman, the other a densely bearded man. Both of them had dark purple stains on their faces — the woman's looked like a patch over her right eye, while the man's covered half his nose, vanished into his beard, and reappeared on his lips — and both of them raised their eyebrows at Prince Frog.

"State your name and your business," said the woman.

"Rapunzel. I'm looking for someone who can fix my frog."

"Fix your *frog?*" The bearded man glared at her. "This is an official embassy of the Exalted Council, not some wandering passel of animal healers."

"Perhaps you could make an exception," said Prince Mick, coming up behind Rapunzel. He placed his freckled hand on her shoulder. "As a special favor to me."

"And who are *you?*"

"Prince Mick the Magnificent of Orange." He bowed slightly. "At your service."

"Oh!" The bearded man gave such a violent and awkward bow that he nearly tripped. He wobbled as he straightened up, holding his hands out for balance. "I beg your pardon, your highness — couldn't see you — do forgive me. . . ."

He bumbled on for a few moments more. The woman gave a neat, silent bow, turned away, and vanished into the darkness.

"Where did she go?" asked Rapunzel, holding Prince Frog close to her chest.

"Into the camp," said the bearded man. "But they — they're all in a meeting — that's why I didn't show you in immediately."

The darkness behind him wavered and shimmered, and an arcing doorway materialized. Pale silver light spilled through it into the snowy night. The woman with the purple-skinned eye appeared in the archway and beckoned to Prince Mick.

"Welcome, your royal highness," she said. "Won't you come in?"

Prince Mick stepped into the silver light and passed into the camp. Rapunzel went after him, clutching Prince Frog. Behind her, Jack sucked in a breath of awe.

The camp was full of light. It was not bright or glaring; Rapunzel didn't have to squint against it. It was simply everywhere, as though the camp existed inside of a bright bubble. Rapunzel could see the wall of this bubble, in which the door still stood, but the wall was soft and hazy; the trees and snow were still visible through it. Black tents stood in a wide ring just within the outer rim of the campground. In among these tents were carriages and horses, being tended by servants who wore glowing orbs of white light at their belts. In the center of the camp was what looked like a large pool lined with rocks, full of the same silver light that had spilled through the doorway. The light moved like water, and sometimes, droplets of it jumped like little fish, making tiny arcs of light as they dove back into the pool. As Rapunzel watched, the silver light changed to soft purple, and then again to glimmering red. She became aware of a humming sound that sounded almost, but not quite, like a voice. It was as though the light itself were singing one long, soft, unbroken note.

"Your royal highness."

Rapunzel turned toward the low voice. It belonged to a man who was both older and handsomer than Prince Mick, and though the man inclined his dark head to the prince, it was Prince Mick who bowed lower.

"Exalted Keene, Nexus of Lilac, Superlative of the Exalted Council," Prince Mick said. "It's an honor."

"The honor is all mine." Nexus Keene gestured toward the pool of light. "It's a cold night — come and warm yourselves."

They followed him toward the rock pool, which was now full of rich orange light, like a melted sunset. As they moved closer to the pool, Rapunzel realized that it radiated warmth, just like a fire.

"What brings you here so late?" asked Keene, holding out his hands to the light. He wore an ornate ring on each hand, and these gleamed in the orange glow, as did the silver threads of hair at his temples. His lustrous amulet rested against the leather of his heavy coat.

Prince Mick shifted his weight. "I didn't intend to trouble you — forgive me if I've interrupted critical business. I only hoped to speak with one of your apprentices, perhaps."

"Don't make yourself uneasy. Tell me what I can do for you."

"It's my frog!" cried Rapunzel, who could wait no longer.

Nexus Keene looked at her for the first time. He cocked one heavy, dark eyebrow.

"Is it?" he asked. "Do tell me."

Rapunzel held out her hands to the Nexus and uncurled her fingers to reveal Prince Frog. The light in the pool turned green, casting a sickly glow over Prince Frog's lifeless little body. "This is my frog," she managed. "He froze. I don't want him to be dead."

Keene glanced at Prince Frog, and then at Rapunzel again. His gaze flicked from her face to the straps of her hair wheel, and his eyes narrowed. "I see," he said.

"Can you help him?" Rapunzel's voice trembled, and she knew she would cry again at any moment. "Will you look at him?"

"I will."

As he took Prince Frog into his hands, surprise flashed across Nexus Keene's handsome features, but it was gone so quickly that Rapunzel thought she might have imagined it. He turned the frog over and frowned at his belly. He pressed his clammy underside with two fingertips. He lifted Prince Frog to his ear.

"I must have silence," he said.

Rapunzel fell absolutely still. She held her breath.

The Nexus listened for a minute or two, and then he nodded.

"This frog is alive," he said.

Rapunzel gasped. "He's alive?" she said. "Are you sure? How do you know? He's so cold, and he isn't breathing, and his heart —"

"He is hibernating," said Keene, holding Prince Frog out to her. "It is what frogs do in the cold months. It is a very deep sleep, but he will wake when the weather is warmer."

"He's just sleeping?" Rapunzel hardly dared believe it. She took Prince Frog in careful, loving hands. "I didn't freeze him to death? I don't have to bury him?"

Keene smiled a little. "He would be happier if he could burrow beneath the mud at the bottom of a pond, or sleep in a pile of leaves," he said, "in the usual way of hibernating frogs."

"I have the perfect thing!" said Rapunzel breathlessly. "Hold him, Jack."

Jack managed to get Prince Frog safely away from Rapunzel, who was so excited that she nearly dropped him in her haste.

"Unwind to the place where you were cut by the bandits!" she commanded, and her braid shot off the wheel and made a massive pile on the ground behind her. She took the plaits apart until she had released the long, shorn lock of hair that the bandits had cut. She pulled the lock away from the rest of the braid and thrust it toward Jack.

"We can put Prince Frog under that," she said. "Wrap him up, would you?"

She began braiding what remained of her hair, not even minding any longer that it had been cut. If Prince Frog needed it, then that was all right.

"Your *hair*."

She glanced up from her braiding to find Prince Mick staring at her.

"Rapunzel," he said in an awed voice. "I didn't recognize you . . . but then I barely saw your face when I visited the tower."

"I saw her," said Keene. His eyes traveled the length of Rapunzel's braid. "I went into the tower room to speak with her."

"You both visited my tower?" She looked at Nexus Keene. "You were *in* my tower?"

"You don't remember?" Prince Mick asked. "I came to free you, but you summoned the witch. I barely escaped."

Rapunzel's insides felt cold. "When was this?" she asked.

"It's been several months," said Prince Mick. "But how can you not remember? You were furious — you called me a disgusting liar. You said I was just like every prince in every book, and that you would never leave your tower to be eaten by trolls or roasted alive by peasants."

Rapunzel's fingers tightened on her braid. "That sounds just like her!" Jack exclaimed, echoing her thoughts.

"But . . ." Her head pounded. "But I really don't remember." She did, however, remember what Glyph had said about how many of her memories might have been stolen. And here was proof that her memory really had been taken more than once. But how?

You know how.

The voice surprised her. It came from within. Rapunzel tried to ignore it but couldn't.

You know exactly how. Can you admit it?

"Do you remember me, child?" asked Nexus Keene, whose eyes had not left her. When Rapunzel shook her head, he smiled slightly. "Just two months ago, I offered to rescue you, and I told you about your grandmother, who had petitioned me for assistance."

Rapunzel dropped her braid.

"I *knew* about Purl?" she asked. "You told me about her?"

"I did."

"And then what?" Rapunzel demanded. "When you told me about Purl, what did I say?"

"You said you didn't need rescuing, and that there were no such things as grandmothers in any of your books, and that if I did not leave at once, you would call for your witch."

Rapunzel could hardly believe it. She hadn't been interested in hearing more about Purl? She hadn't even tried to understand what her grandmother was? How could she have been so uninterested, just weeks ago?

But of course she had been. Purl had meant nothing to her. What Nexus Keene said was true: There were no grandmothers in any of her books. There were no mothers either. Or fathers. No Blue fairies or kind peasants, no jacks contests or Exalted Councils, no countries, frogs, or giants.

Nothing real.

Unsettled beyond anything she had yet experienced, Rapunzel looked away from Keene. She told her hair to wind up, and she strapped it to her back, ready to leave.

"Why didn't you destroy the witch, Nexus?" asked Prince Mick. "I mean no criticism, of course, but your reputation as a witch slayer is known to everyone in Tyme. Why not rescue the poor girl, whether or not she wanted to escape?"

A *witch* slayer. Rapunzel glanced back at the Nexus. "Did you come to my tower to rescue me?" she demanded. "Or to kill Witch?"

"Both," Keene replied. "But I could not kill Envearia. She is no common witch. Her power is unprecedented."

Prince Mick frowned. "Is she a genuine threat, then?" he asked quietly. "The Redlands is the neighbor and ally of Orange — we'll join Chieftain Fleet in ousting this witch, if need be."

"I thank you for your willingness," said Keene, "but Envearia will be handled by the Exalted Council. She may be powerful enough to defend herself from me alone, but many councillors together will bring her down. I intended to return to the Redlands and finish the business after the summit in Independence." His eyes narrowed at Rapunzel. "But here you are, young lady," he said. "So Envearia must be dead already. Who killed her?"

Rapunzel shivered. He talked of Witch's death, and of killing her, as though they were nothing at all. It was the same way the Red fairies talked.

"Envearia's alive, Nexus," said Jack when Rapunzel wouldn't answer.

"Alive?" said Nexus Keene curiously. His eyes gleamed. "Then truly, this witch is like nothing I have encountered."

As he spoke, the pool of light beside them erupted into a glaring beam that shot up into the sky. Rapunzel winced at its sudden brightness.

"Someone is at the perimeter," said Nexus Keene, turning swiftly toward the still-open door of the camp. He stretched out a hand, but before he could act, a dog as tall as Rapunzel's waist came bounding through the opening, barking joyfully.

"Trusty!" cried Prince Mick, and the dog ran to him and braced his big front paws against his chest. He licked the prince's chin with slobbering enthusiasm as Nexus Keene looked on with an expression of mingled amusement and disbelief.

"Terribly sorry, Nexus," said Prince Mick, who seemed torn between delight and embarrassment; he rubbed Trusty's head and tried to get him to sit, to no avail. "We'll get out of your way. My apologies again for interrupting a meeting of the council — and for, ah, the canine intrusion."

"Not at all," said Keene, returning his eyes to Rapunzel.

Rapunzel didn't want to be looked at. She took from Jack's arms the great pile of loose golden hair that swaddled Prince Frog, and she cradled it against her. "Thank you for saving my frog," she said, and then, to prevent any more conversation, she turned away from the rock pool and walked toward the archway. Behind her, she heard Prince Mick and Jack departing with more formality. She supposed Jack had probably bowed, like he had with Prince Mick. She supposed she should have done the same thing. She wondered when she would learn all the things she was supposed to learn, or if she would ever be able to. Maybe she was permanently behind and could never catch up.

Maybe she would know a lot more if she could remember things.

The camp of the Exalted Council vanished behind them as they left it, and they were surrounded again by the darkness. Rapunzel searched her mind as she tramped across the snow. If Prince Mick and Nexus Keene had both come to her tower, then surely there must be some trace of their visits. She gritted her teeth, trying with all her might to dredge up any flicker of memory, but all she produced was a dull ache in her head. The longer she tried to force her memories to return, the fiercer her headache became.

Perhaps all of them were liars, she thought recklessly. They had lied to her to confuse her — that was what princes on the ground always did in her books.

There is only one liar. You know who it is.

Rapunzel pushed the merciless voice away and thought of Prince Frog. He was alive. She hugged his nest of hair as Jack and Prince Mick caught up to her.

The Orange camp did not sing with magic and light, but it was still splendid. There were several large, circular tents, all striped orange and gold with flags flying from their peaked tops, erected around a massive fire. Among the tents, many white-cloaked and gold-belted attendants were engaged in merry activity. They drank from golden flagons, toasted cheese and bread on long sticks, and sang and danced to delightful, lilting music.

The girl who made the music stood with one foot propped on a chair. With her left hand, she held to her chin an instrument made of glossy wood. With her right, she rapidly drew a long, slender rod back and forth across the instrument's strings. Her skin, like Prince Mick's, was densely freckled, and her short, corkscrew curls of orange hair danced as she played. She appeared no older than Rapunzel, who watched her, mesmerized. When the girl finished, the singers and dancers sent up a mighty cheer and begged her for another song as Prince Mick settled by the great fire with Trusty at his knee. Rapunzel and Jack sat near him, Rapunzel still holding Prince Frog.

"Daigh!" Mick called, and he waved for the girl with the glossy instrument to join them. She looked like she had come from the same mother and father that he did, so Rapunzel knew she must be his sister.

"Do all brothers and sisters look so much alike?" she asked, leaning toward Jack.

"No," said Jack, "but lots do."

Struck by this idea, Rapunzel studied Jack's face. Perhaps his sister, Tess, had the same black eyes, or the same sharp grin. Imagining this, she remembered with a shock what Jack had told her by the fire, before they'd met Prince Mick. Tess was in grave danger, and Jack had barely six weeks to return to Geguul and save her. Uneasy, she scooted just a bit closer to him. She didn't want him or his sister to go to Geguul. She didn't want Witch to go there either.

Princess Daigh walked lightly to them, her curls bouncing. "Have a seat," said Prince Mick, giving Trusty a scratch behind the ears. "I found a pair of travelers who might interest you. Can you tell who the girl is, without an introduction?"

"Really, Mick," said his sister with a laugh. "You dragged a pair of travelers here as a puzzle for me?" Princess Daigh met Rapunzel's eyes. "I guess he didn't ask you if you *mind* being the subject of this game."

Rapunzel shook her head. "I don't mind."

"Well then, that's all right." Princess Daigh sat near her brother. Her eyes traveled along Rapunzel's braid, which hung partly askew from the hair wheel. "This is too easy," she said, "except that it can't possibly be — the girl in the tower?"

Rapunzel's stomach sank. "We've met?" she asked.

"No," said Princess Daigh. "I could've gotten you down from the tower, though. After Mick tried it, I begged for a chance to visit you. But I'm not allowed until I'm eighteen, and now you're already rescued, so I've lost my chance. Not that I'm sorry to see you free!" she added, brightening. She looked at Jack. "Who are you?" she asked.

"Jack Byre of the Violet Peaks, your highness."

Princess Daigh looked delighted. "And so, all the wealthy and well-armed nobles in Tyme were chased away. In the end, it was a boy from the Peaks without a connection in the world — I'm assuming, my apologies if I've got it wrong. . . ."

Jack gave a half smile. "You've got it right, your highness."

"My point," said Princess Daigh, "is that *you* rescued her. What did you use? How did you get her down?"

"Ubiquitous rope and grappling hook," said Jack.

"And with Ubiquitous at that." Princess Daigh threw back her head and laughed.

Rapunzel decided it was her turn to speak. "I wasn't rescued," she said. "And he didn't get me down — I climbed down by myself."

"Fine with me," said Princess Daigh. "I'm only too glad to give you all the credit. How do you like the world outside the tower? You've traveled a fair bit of it, it looks like."

"I like it sometimes," said Rapunzel honestly. "Sometimes, it's not very nice."

"True enough," said Princess Daigh. "What brings you to Commonwealth Green?"

"We're going to the First Wood," said Rapunzel, "to find the Woodmother."

"The Splinterwood!" Princess Daigh's eyes widened. "Really? The First Tree, some call her — the ancient tree from which all others grew."

"Then you've heard of her!" said Rapunzel. "Do you know where she is?"

Princess Daigh cocked her head to one side. "Do you remember the Bardwyrm ballad from Origins of Tyme class?" she asked her brother. And she recited:

> *"The first wood and the last wood*
> *Memory of Tyme*
> *Roots that anchor not in soil*
> *Whom she seeks, she finds."*

"My dad used to say that," said Jack slowly. "I'd forgotten it. He sang it when I was a kid. And it makes sense, doesn't it? We can't seek the Woodmother — she has to seek us. Glyph said something about that, remember, Rapunzel? She said the Woodmother would sense you."

Prince Mick shook his head. "I'm afraid you're on a hopeless quest," he said. "I've never heard of anyone actually meeting the Splinterwood. The old story's just an old story."

"I don't believe that for a second," said Princess Daigh. "The Splinterwood is real."

"You don't know that, Daigh."

"I'd bet my royal rear end on it. The myths of the Dissolution are all based on truths. It's just a matter of knowing which angle to look at. There *was* a first tree, after all. One of the trees in Tyme had to be first."

"Which proves nothing," said Prince Mick. "That tree might be, and probably is, long dead."

"Or she might be alive," countered Princess Daigh. "And she might hold the memory of Tyme — imagine that. What if there is a tree, alive in the world, that remembers *everything*?"

"You'll have to pardon my sister," said Prince Mick. "She's what we call a romantic historian."

"Harsh words!" cried Princess Daigh. "If there's no Splinterwood, then explain all this snow to me, would you? It's not even winter, and we're too far south."

Jack sat up straight. "Of course!" he cried. "I remember — it's a legend, isn't it? The First Wood brings winter with her wherever she goes. That means we must be really close now — closer than we thought."

"You speak like an educated man," said Daigh approvingly to Jack. "I'd heard there were no decent schools in the Peaks. I'm glad to know that's not the case."

"Oh, it's the case," said Jack. "There was no school anywhere near my village."

"No school at all!" She looked horrified. "What, not even a bad one?"

"My dad said a bad school's worse than no school," said Jack. "He taught me everything himself. How to read and write and do sums, history and geography, all of it."

"And how did he come by his education?"

"He was raised in Crimson. Had to hide in the Peaks because of bad debts. They weren't his," Jack added hastily. "He never did anything. But one of the Crimson royals decided to go after him —"

"Enough said." Daigh rolled her eyes. "The Crimson Realm is a political nightmare. I'd prefer to live in the Peaks, if it came right down to it."

Jack looked as though he doubted this but was too polite to say anything.

"Well, I hope you find what you're searching for," said Prince Mick. "And now, Daigh, if you don't mind a change of subject?" He paused, and his eyes twinkled. "It's come to my attention that our young friend Rapunzel has never heard of the Hundred-Year Day."

"Sundragons!" Princess Daigh shot to her feet.

"Now you're in for it," said Prince Mick, laughing. "The least I can do is make sure you're fed while she talks." He beckoned to his attendants.

"Have you really never heard?" Princess Daigh fairly flew to Rapunzel's side, and she perched beside her next to the fire. "I can tell you everything — everything," she said. "I'll start with the bit I think you might like best. In New Pink — the Pink Empire, as was — there's a princess in a tower in an enchanted sleep."

"In a tower?" said Rapunzel with interest. "Really? Does a witch take care of her?"

"No," said Princess Daigh. "She's been asleep for nearly ninety-nine years. Her name is Rose."

Fascinated, Rapunzel hung on Princess Daigh's every word as she told the story of an ancient family, great wars, terrible fairies, and a princess who had inherited a legacy of blood.

They were a long time by the fire, eating a fine supper and listening to Daigh's tales. Afterward, Rapunzel went to sleep in a gold-and-orange tent, and dreamed, for once, of a tower not her own — a tower of resplendent beauty, trapped behind a wall of briars, where a princess slept unknowing.

CHAPTER EIGHTEEN

AT dawn, Rapunzel was roused by gentle servants and given a warm washcloth and a hot breakfast. When she emerged from the tent, she blinked around at the beauty of the early morning. The snow reflected the sky, making everything glow pale pink. The world was still but for the movement of the icy wind; Rapunzel pulled her cloak tightly around her and put up the hood to ward off the chill. Jack emerged from his tent a moment later, and they made their way across camp to the Ubiquitous sled. The ghostly dogs stood at the ready, stretching and pawing the snow.

When they reached the sled, Rapunzel and Jack were amazed to find it now full of provisions both for nourishment and comfort — food and drink, lanterns, firewood, soft but heavy blankets, and splendid cushions to sit on. There was even a small wooden trunk with several holes the size of fingertips bored through the wood. Prince Frog fit perfectly inside it, along with a little nest of hair to keep him warm, which Jack cut from the severed lock of Rapunzel's braid.

"I hope this makes your quest a little more comfortable!"

Rapunzel turned to find Princess Daigh striding toward them in the dawn light, the copper threads in her long cloak glinting. She carried a little book covered in leather as white and freckled as her own skin.

* "Oh good," she said, nodding at the little wooden trunk. "You found it. Did you put your frog inside? My brother bored the holes last night, so the frog will get plenty of air. I hope it's all right."

"It's perfect," said Rapunzel. "Thank you both so much."

"You're too generous, your highness," said Jack, bowing. "How can we repay you?"

"You can validate my theory." Princess Daigh grinned. "Visit me in Orange after the Splinterwood finds you, and tell me everything you learn. I'd rather you traveled with us so that I can see it happen, but it's my theory that she won't seek you out while you're in a big group."

"Then you really think we'll find her?" asked Rapunzel.

"I do." Princess Daigh flipped open the little leather-bound book. "Rapunzel is spelled Z-E-L, right? Not Z-L-E."

Rapunzel peeked into the journal and saw her name scrawled there, along with much else. "That's right," she said. "Why do you ask?"

"Posterity," said Princess Daigh, snapping the journal shut. "I'll want to record our meeting for the university archives." She held out two little sparkly things, one to Rapunzel and the other to Jack. "Take these," she said. "They mark you as royal messengers. Orange is a friend to nearly every country. Say that you're in my service and you'll usually find assistance. Food, shelter, horses — whatever you need."

Rapunzel inspected the sparkly thing, which was an orange jewel half the size of her pinky fingernail, attached to a long copper pin. She saw that Jack had already affixed his to his cloak, so she did the same, admiring the way it twinkled when she moved. "It's so pretty," she said. "And you've given us so much. I wish I had something to give you."

Princess Daigh glanced at the long lock of hair that Jack still held in his hand, left over from the frog's nest. "Well," she said slowly, "if you're willing to part with a little of your hair, it would be a tremendous gift to the university museum. . . ." She bit her lip. "Sorry, I realize that's an intimate request, but —"

"Take it," said Rapunzel.

"Really? The whole thing?"

Rapunzel nodded, and Princess Daigh collected the ruined lock, coiling it into big loops over her arm to get it out of the snow. "May the sun shine upon you both," she said. "Farewell, Rapunzel — farewell, Jack!"

They climbed into the Ubiquitous dogsled, and Jack took the whip into his hand. When he cracked it, the dogs leapt into motion and hurtled northward. As they fled across the snowy plain, the gold-and-orange tents of the Orange camp became smaller and smaller until they vanished altogether into the red glow of sunrise. Rapunzel turned from the view with a great sigh and settled down into the soft blankets that now lined the sled.

At lunchtime, Jack stopped the dogs. They said little as they ate from the stores that Princess Daigh and Prince Mick had given them.

"I'm so tired," said Rapunzel, yawning. "I don't know why. We haven't walked all day."

"So am I," said Jack, and he looked it. His face was drawn, and there were circles under his eyes. Rapunzel realized that although she had been traveling for over a fortnight, Jack had been traveling far longer — for almost sixty days now. No wonder he was exhausted.

"This snow has to mean we're close to the First Wood," said Jack, folding up the map. "Maybe we'll even get lucky and find it today."

"I hope so," said Rapunzel, and she looked at the silvery dogs, who seemed to be enjoying sniffing one another and licking their own fur. "Don't crash," she warned them. She very much appreciated not having to walk.

But although the dogs did carry them for far longer than twenty-four hours, at sunset, the sled crashed with a POP so loud and unexpected that Rapunzel screamed and Jack gave a frightened yelp. The dogs vanished before them, the sled disappeared below, and there was a series of muffled thuds as the two of them, with all their belongings, flew forward onto the soft snow.

"Prince Frog," said Rapunzel at once, and she crawled to the wooden trunk. Once she had checked it and found Prince Frog safe, she helped Jack pile their things in the wagon again. But they had too many things now to fit, and items kept sliding off the heap.

"I hate to leave the cushions," said Jack, "but we don't need them if we're not on the sled."

"I'll carry my braid, and then they'll fit," said Rapunzel, taking up the wheel.

"It's heavy, though," said Jack. "You won't be able to walk far, will you?"

"I can walk," said Rapunzel. "Anyway, if we're riding back on the other sled, we'll need the cushions then, right?"

"Well, we won't *need* them," said Jack. "But it'd be nice to have them. If your hair gets too heavy, just say so, all right?"

"I will," said Rapunzel. "Let's go."

In the falling twilight, they continued their march toward Independence, and Rapunzel realized that walking in snow was more difficult than other kinds of walking. Even walking uphill was not as hard as this. She had to pick up her feet higher than usual with each step, and she sank into the snow as soon as she put her foot down. It wasn't even half an hour before she felt ready to sit down and quit. But she had said she could do it, and she didn't want to take it back, so she made herself keep moving.

"Wish we had skis," said Jack, perhaps an hour into their walk. "Or snowshoes. I should have thought of that earlier — oh well."

"We can play — the happiness game," Rapunzel said, panting as she pulled her boot out of the snow. "I'm happy Prince Frog is alive."

Jack shrugged one shoulder. "Me too," he said. "But I don't want to play this."

"Because it makes you think about Tess?"

He was quiet.

"She's going to be all right," said Rapunzel. "She *is*, Jack. You found the Red fairies, and they'll fix it with the giantess. Glyph said she'd help you no matter what, as long as you stay with me and answer my questions — and you have. You're going to save Tess, I know it."

Jack nodded and stopped walking. "Thanks," he said, his voice low. "I appreciate that. Want to camp here?"

They found a patch of ground that was higher than the rest and not entirely covered in snow. Rapunzel shrugged off her wheel and loosened her hair from it, then helped Jack clear away rocks to make room for a sleeping area. They made a fire with one of the bundles of wood that had been given to them, but it was still a cold night, and Rapunzel missed the company of the Ubiquitous dogs. There had been something very comforting about them, even if they hadn't been real.

"Maybe we can get new dogs," she said as they set up their beds. "What do you think?"

"What, for the journey back? We've already got some, remember? We bought two Ubiquitous Instant Dogsleds."

"No, not Ubiquitous ones. I mean to keep," said Rapunzel. "Like Prince Mick with Trusty. We could get a friendly dog too, couldn't we?"

"To keep where? In your tower?"

"No, I mean . . ." Rapunzel stopped. She wasn't sure what she meant. "I guess you could keep the dog with you," she said. "While I spend some time with Witch. And then when I come down again, we could take it traveling with us."

"Traveling? With *us*?" Jack, who had been laying out the blankets, now sat back on his heels and looked at her. "Are you saying you want to keep traveling with me even when we're done finding the Woodmother?"

Rapunzel looked around, taking in the night. The sky had grown dark, with the pale violet stars scattering light across the blackness. The snow was blue in the darkness, and the wind whistled quietly around them. Firelight played on Jack's face and made all their belongings glow, and the wood crackled as it burned, giving off a pungent smell that stoked Rapunzel's appetite and made her want to cook things. She never would have known a night like this in her tower. And it was beautiful.

"I do want to travel," she said. "After I go home and make sure Witch is all right, I want to go back to Purl's house, and then I want to see all the places you've told me about — the Tranquil Sea, and the Olive Isles, and everything. We're invited to Orange too, so we should go there. And I'm supposed to compete in the jacks championship, so I'll need to go back to Yellow Country next summer, won't I?"

Jack said nothing. He only looked at her.

"Well, won't I?" said Rapunzel. "I want to go to the Violet Peaks with you too. I want to meet Tess."

Jack smiled a little. "Thanks," he said. "But I don't know."

Rapunzel's heart sank. "You don't want to travel together?" she asked. "Why? Because of my hair?"

"No! No." Jack took a deep breath. "You think you'll be allowed to come and go from that tower whenever you want," he said. "But I don't think Envearia will let you. In fact, I'm sure she won't."

"You're wrong," said Rapunzel. "And even if you were right, it wouldn't matter. When I want to leave, I'll just climb down again."

"How? With what?"

Rapunzel shrugged. "I'd find a way."

Jack tilted his head and considered her for a long moment. "Rapunzel, what would you do if you knew Envearia was using you? Would you still go back?"

"Using me for what?"

He dug into his knapsack. "Nexus Keene gave me this last night, after you walked away," he said, and he tossed a small, dark book onto the blanket in front of her. On its front, in tarnished golden lettering, it said *Witches: A Master Slayer's Comprehensive Guide to Identifying, Understanding, and Exterminating the Abominations of the White ~ by Exalted Nebenson, Witch Slayer and Beloved of the Black.*

Rapunzel's heartbeat quickened. She picked up the book, opened it to the table of contents, and ran her finger quickly over the topics. *The Origin of Witches . . . White-Hatching . . . Consuming Innocence . . . Bargaining Power . . .*

She felt sick to her stomach. She didn't want to know.

"I read the part about innocence before I went to sleep last night," said Jack. "Start with that. It'll explain some things."

He prepared dinner for them, but Rapunzel's appetite had crashed like it was Ubiquitous. She wrapped a blanket around herself and moved closer to the fire, where she could see better. She opened the book and began to read.

PART III:
CONSUMING INNOCENCE
How Witches Gain Power and Live to Unnatural Old Age

Once the White-hatching bargain is complete, a new-made witch leaves Geguul and is returned to Tyme on the great unfurled leaf of some abhorrent plant belonging to the White. The witch appears no different, and may even seem frightened and pitiful, but on no account show the creature mercy; on the contrary, take your opportunity to kill it while it is weak. Know this: that witches are unmortal beings, lost forever to the Black, corrupted at their very cores by the White's demented magic. Being less than human, they are capable of the most savage and execrable crimes. It is the duty of the Exalted Council to exterminate them wherever they are found.

Fortunately, a witch has no special immunity. It can be killed like any creature. Burning, drowning, stoning, throat-slitting, shooting with arrows, pushing from heights, suffocating, hanging, bludgeoning, disemboweling, and beheading are only a few of the viable methods of execution, and I can attest personally to all of their efficacy, having used every one of these techniques. But be warned: An experienced witch can protect itself against any of these mortal means, so long as it has magic. Therefore, the first rational step in slaying a witch — particularly one who is older and more cunning — is to deprive the witch of its well-spring of power so that it cannot defend itself.

Innocence is this wellspring. It is the purity of innocence that fuels a witch's magic, and the most pristine source of this purity lies in little children. Witches therefore gain power

270

through that foulest of methods: child-eating. When constantly nourished by the flesh and blood of the innocent, the power of a witch is limitless. The Witch of the Woods, who died by fire in 1056, is said to have eaten nearly five hundred children during her seventy-five-year reign of terror.

It is important to recognize that the older a child is, the less innocence remains for a witch to consume. The more inexperienced the child, the more power the witch achieves. Infants, therefore, are the most vulnerable targets, and the children of Tyme will only be safe once every White-hatched monstrosity is slain and sent back to its foul birthing place in Geguul.

The old stories of witches snatching babies from their beds and boiling them for supper, however, are exaggerated. Witches, like anyone else, may kidnap babies from their beds, but they gain next to nothing by doing so. Taking a child by force grants the witch only a brief, weak ability. To gain deep and lasting power, the source of a witch's power must be obtained through a fair bargain — a disturbing echo of the bargain every witch strikes with the White Fairy upon being White-hatched. If the child is still a baby, incapable of reason, then a bargain must be struck with the child's parents.

Rapunzel stopped reading. Her throat was dry and her fingers ached from clutching the book so tightly.

Innocence was fuel for magic. And Witch had always told her that she was the most innocent girl who ever lived. She had said it made her perfect.

Did that make her Witch's fuel?

Yes.

"But she didn't eat me," said Rapunzel, although she couldn't believe she was thinking such a thing. "Witch didn't eat me — it doesn't make sense. She can't be feeding off my innocence if she didn't eat me. This book says so."

"Well, whatever she does," said Jack, "she's using you. She bargained with your parents, didn't she? She didn't have to take you by force, right?"

Rapunzel slammed the book shut and threw it onto the blankets.

"Aren't you going to read the rest?" Jack demanded.

She covered her face with her hands.

"You have to!" he yelled. "You're throwing yourself in prison if you go back to that tower. Why won't you listen to me?"

"I'm listening! But this book only says *what* witches do. It can't tell me *why*."

"Why what? Why Envearia kept you in a tower and lied to you? Why she wiped your memory? Why she used you?"

"Yes!"

"So you admit that she messed with your mind?"

"Yes — yes, I admit it!"

Rapunzel's breath came hard and fast. She felt lighter and heavier all at once. She uncovered her face, threw her shoulders back, and looked Jack straight in the eyes.

"I admit it," she repeated. "Witch took my memories. She lied to me and kept secrets from me. And if that book is true, then she tricked my father into giving me up so that she could . . . use me," she said. "To make her magic stronger. But I still miss her. I'm worried about her. I love her. And there is *nothing* you can say, and no book you can show me, that will make me stop believing she loves me too."

Jack said nothing for a long time. The fire danced and crackled before them, filling the long silence. When he spoke, his voice was hard.

"Then my answer is no."

Rapunzel looked at him in confusion. "No what?"

He met her eyes. "No, I don't want to travel together," he said. "When we're finished with the First Wood, we're finished."

Rapunzel drew back, struck. "You mean . . . we're not friends?" she managed. "You don't like me anymore?"

"I won't watch you hurt yourself."

"But —"

"*No.* You already forgot me once," he said. "And maybe I didn't care then, but I'd care now, all right? I don't want to visit that tower again and find out that you don't remember me."

A fierce wind blew across their camp. The fire sputtered and went out, plunging them into darkness. The wind died down again as quickly as it had risen, leaving the night abruptly and uncomfortably still. There were no stars in the sky overhead, and Rapunzel could not see Jack's face, though he was only a few feet away.

There was a scrape of flint on tinder, followed by a spark of light. The fire caught quickly and flickered back to life as Jack tended it.

A great shadow fell over him.

Rapunzel followed the shadow with her eyes. Strange, oily movements undulated in the darkness just beyond the firelight, almost as though the darkness itself was moving. She squinted, trying to see what was there. Whatever it was, it was big. Far bigger than they were. Rapunzel put her hand on her dagger.

Jack saw her do it, followed her gaze, and was on his feet in a flash. He drew his sword. "Who is it?" His voice was rough. "Show yourself."

Their campfire roared as if in reply and blazed higher and brighter than any fire Rapunzel had ever seen. She and Jack leapt back. Its glow widened, casting a broad light across the snow and into the sky.

Illuminated before them was a tree.

A monstrous tree.

A black and twisting, terrible tree.

Its roots sprawled across the ground and stretched far out into the darkness. Its trunk was wider and higher than Rapunzel's tower, and a head of enormous, tangled branches filled the sky. Against the darkness and the stars, the black branches appeared to be moving. Slithering.

"Crop *rot*," Jack whispered.

"That tree wasn't there before," Rapunzel said weakly. "Was it?"

Jack shook his head, staring up. The hand that gripped his sword had fallen to his side, and the tip of the blade dragged in the snow.

The tree did not come closer, but its branches moved continuously. It loomed there, dark and terrifying, as the silence thickened around them. Rapunzel could hear only her own breath. She felt a strange pressure, first inside her head and then inside her body, as though the tree was waiting for her to do something. To say something.

"Are . . . are you the Woodmother?" she managed.

The tree did not reply.

"Or . . . or the First Tree? Or the Splinterwood?"

The tree was silent, but the slithering of its branches quickened.

Rapunzel felt the pressure growing inside her arms and legs, and she knew that guessing the name of the tree was not what it wanted from her. It wanted . . . it wanted . . .

"Rapunzel, don't!"

But Rapunzel walked up to the tree and extended her hand. She had to touch its trunk — she *had* to. That was what it wanted. That was why she had come. To reach the First Wood. To find the Woodmother. For Witch.

She stretched her fingers toward the black bark.

"NO!"

Jack tried to pull her back, but he was a moment too late. Rapunzel's fingertips brushed the rough bark. It crumbled like ash, and her fingers sank into the tree up to her knuckles. She tried to pull them out.

They would not come.

Rapunzel pulled again, but as she tried to twist her fingers free, they sank in deeper, until her hand disappeared up to the wrist. She tugged, struggling at the same time against the strange, heavy haze in her mind. She was stuck in the tree. Stuck in the tree . . .

Stuck in the tree.

Rapunzel came to her senses with a jerk and tried to extricate her hand, but it was stuck fast, lost inside the tree's black trunk. She could not see it. To her horror, she could not feel it either. She could not wiggle her fingers, could not stretch them. It was as though her hand was simply gone. Absorbed.

"Jack!" she screamed, yanking at the stump of her wrist and screaming again when this motion only served to bury her arm up to the elbow in the tree. Jack grabbed her around the waist and pulled, but the added force did nothing. Rapunzel pressed her other hand flat against the trunk in an effort to shove herself backward. That hand disappeared into the strange, ashen bark along with the first.

"Let go!" screamed Rapunzel, flailing. "Let go!" She tried to kick the tree and only succeeded in lodging the toe of one boot inside it.

She lost her footing, stumbled forward, and plunged in all the way to one shoulder. She screamed as her face nearly brushed the black bark.

Jack grabbed her by her hair and restrained her.

"It's eating me!" she wept, terrified beyond reason. "Jack, it's eating me, it's killing me —"

"Stop touching it!" he cried. "Rapunzel, don't move! I'll get help — I'll go back to the Orange camp —"

"Let her go."

The voice that spoke did not belong to Rapunzel or Jack, and Rapunzel knew it instantly. She would never forget it. It was the first voice that had ever been cruel to her.

"Rune," she gasped.

He fluttered into view before her eyes, white wings shimmering.

"Surrender," he said quietly. "Let the Woodmother take you."

"*This* is what you sent her to do?" Jack shouted. "Get eaten? I never agreed to help with this. Get her out of there!"

"Glyph did not send her here to die," said Rune. "The Woodmother will not kill her."

Rapunzel strained her muscles and craned her neck, but her whole weight leaned toward the tree, making it impossible to resist sinking in. Her boot tip was gone; the tree had her entire foot and part of her knee and thigh, and the bark was climbing her limbs now, actively seeking her, drawing her inexorably in.

"Please, Rune!" Rapunzel wriggled her trapped shoulder, trying to keep it free, but it only sank in farther, past her armpit. Her neck was next. "Help me."

"I cannot," said Rune.

Hot tears spilled from Rapunzel's eyes and down her cheeks. She wanted to sob — to scream — but if she moved, she would be lost.

"I did what you asked of me," she whispered.

"Let the Woodmother take you, prisoner child," Rune said again. "I will travel back quickly through the fairywoods to tell Glyph that you have done as you promised. As for you, Beanstalker, come back to the Red Glade and claim your reward. We stand ready to help you."

"I'll chop this thing open," said Jack. "I'll get you out, I swear —"

"No, Beanstalker. She must do what she has come to do, and you must keep your appointment with Geguul."

Rune's voice was very close to her ear. Rapunzel could hear his wings buzzing, but she could not turn to look at him. Her face was a finger's width from the deeply scored bark that covered the great tree's trunk.

"You traveled farther than I thought you could." Rune's voice was quiet. "Now you will go where few have ever gone. May the Woodmother open your eyes."

"Will I ever get out?" Rapunzel gasped. "Please say I'll get out."

"Farewell, prisoner child."

Rapunzel's nose brushed the blackness, and then her lips, and then she could ask no more questions. She closed her eyes and went limp.

The Woodmother swallowed her.

CHAPTER NINETEEN

RAPUNZEL blinked, but couldn't see her own eyelids as they closed and opened. She tried to speak, but no
noise issued from her mouth. Within the Woodmother, the darkness
muffled sound as well as sight.

But she could wiggle her fingers.

Rapunzel sagged in relief. She could wiggle her fingers — her
body wasn't gone. She tapped her toes, shook her legs, shrugged
her shoulders — yes. She could even touch her face. She was all in
one piece; nothing had been eaten by the tree.

Or everything had.

Rapunzel reached out into the darkness, expecting to feel the
inside of the walls of the tree, but there was nothing to feel. No rough
bark, no crumbling ash. She took a few slow and careful steps in a
random direction, then reached out again. Nothing.

Rapunzel crouched to touch the ground. At least she had to be
standing on something. But there was nothing solid underfoot.

"Let me out!" she cried silently. "I'm afraid!"

The blackness around her stirred in a slow circle, and she felt
herself revolving with it.

"Stop!" she tried to shout. "Please stop!"

The stirring stopped. Rapunzel gasped. The revolving darkness had turned her toward her braid. She could see it, and only it, glowing gold in the blackness, as though it were lit from within. It looked as though it had been severed about ten feet from her head.

Rapunzel choked. She seized her hair with both hands. As she pulled her hair close to her face to inspect it, the braid grew longer, as though she were pulling it out of the darkness.

It hadn't been cut off, she realized. Most of it just hadn't fallen into the tree with her. The rest of her braid was still somewhere outside the Woodmother, lying on the snow. She began to pull on it, hand over hand, and sure enough, it piled up in front of her. When she got nearly to the end, the braid went taut with resistance. She wondered if it was snagged on something out there.

She had no sooner thought this than the darkness around her drained away like ink. She stood beneath the stars again, on the dark and snowy plain, as though the Woodmother had never come. Jack stood five paces from her, his heels digging into the snow, his hands gripping the end of her braid. The fairy wheel lay abandoned beside him. Beside that, half-buried in the snow, was the iron chain that Purl had given her. It was tangled up in a wet little heap, as though the Woodmother had spat it out.

"Jack!" Rapunzel shouted, but her voice still made no sound.

Jack did not reply. He twisted her braid around his hand and leaned back, his arms shuddering, his feet making trenches in the snow where he was trying to find purchase.

"Come on," he muttered. "Come on."

"Jack, I'm here! I'm right here!" she cried voicelessly.

He only clenched his jaw and pulled harder. His hair was damp with effort. Sweat trickled from his temples. Rapunzel jerked her braid toward her, trying to get it away from him.

"Jack, look, don't you see? It's all right!"

Jack would not budge. "Let her go!" he yelled.

Rapunzel dropped her braid and ran toward him. With no more resistance to pull against, Jack flailed and fell backward. Rapunzel fell to her knees in the snow beside him and grabbed his shoulders.

Her hands went right through him.

She looked at her hands in shock. They seemed substantial enough. She tried once more to touch Jack, and this time she was less surprised when her hands passed through him. He could not see, hear, or feel her. Slowly, Rapunzel realized that she couldn't feel the cold of the snow through the knees of her trousers. She couldn't sense the night wind. She couldn't smell smoke from the fire.

She wasn't here with Jack at all. She was still inside the tree.

At least most of her was.

Rapunzel got to her feet and picked up her braid. She pulled it toward her, out of Jack's reach.

"No!" he shouted. He knelt up and reached for the tail end of the braid, but Rapunzel tugged the last few inches into the Woodmother with her, leaving Jack alone. He made a desolate sound and slumped there on his knees in the snow.

Rapunzel looked up at the great black tree that loomed over Jack's kneeling shape, and she watched its wide, dark branches against the night sky. She didn't understand how she could be *in* the tree and still see it standing there.

"What do you want me to do?" she asked, still voiceless. The tree said nothing.

It was Jack who spoke.

"I have to go home," he said, as if the tree were Rapunzel. He gathered her iron chain from the snow where it had fallen, and clenched it in his fingers. His face was white and bruised with exhaustion. "I don't know how long it'll take you to get out of there, or even if you'll get out." His voice was choked. "Rune said he'll come back for me after he checks on Glyph — he's taking me to the Red Glade to get what I need for the giantess. If you're not out of there by the time he's back, then I have to go with him. I have to make sure Tess doesn't end up in Geguul. But I don't want to leave you like this."

Rapunzel wished she could tell him that she understood. Of course he had to help Tess. She only wondered how she would ever see him again. Perhaps she could travel to the Violet Peaks and find his home in Dearth.

She had no sooner considered this than the scene before her blurred, and the starry, snowy night began to shift and swirl as though made of fog. After a few seconds, the fog blew away, leaving Rapunzel in a world that was rocky and gray. The sky was gray. The dirt was gray. The ramshackle cottage before her was gray. Only the sky had any color in it; it was the vivid violet of early twilight, and it cast a purplish hue over everything.

Jack was still there, but he wasn't kneeling. He stood in the doorway of the cottage, trembling all over. He wore his knapsack, as usual, and his vest. In his fist was something golden — something about the size and shape of an egg. He shoved it into his knapsack and knocked the cottage door shut with his elbow. His breathing was rapid and uneven as he hurried down the two rough stones that served as doorsteps and raced across the rocky dirt, away from the cottage.

"Where are you going?"

The voice was harsh, and Rapunzel turned to the cottage door to see who had spoken. A woman stepped out and caught up to Jack in a flash. She was not old, but her face and body were bony, and her skin was stretched tight across her features. Her hair was black, and long strands of it hung straight as pins where they had come loose from a tight bun at the nape of her neck. Her dark, lidless eyes were exactly like Jack's.

"Can't explain," said Jack. "No time. I have to go — I'm sorry, Mother. I'll be back before seven fortnights —"

"Seven *fortnights*?" cried Jack's mother. "But we need you here. How'll I manage this place without you for three full months?"

He lowered his voice. "You'll have money," he said. "There's a goose in the cottage, on my bed — it lays golden eggs. Keep it hidden; don't let thieves get ahold of it."

"*Golden eggs?*" His mother grabbed him by the vest. "What have you done? I saw that awful plant in the yard this morning; I saw where it went. Tell me you had the sense not to climb it, Jack, please."

"I climbed it," said Jack flatly. "It went to Geguul."

His mother shuddered. "No," she moaned. "How many times have I told you, no matter how bad it gets for us, even if we're half-dead of hunger, never trade yourself to the White —"

"I didn't," said Jack. "I never saw the White Fairy, and I'm not a witch. A giant tricked me into a bargain instead, and now I have to go to the Redlands, or —"

"The Redlands?" shrieked his mother. "I'll never see you again if you go that far!"

"Yes you will," said Jack. "But I have to go *now*. Trust me — it's for all our sakes."

"That's exactly what your father said before he left us to find that treasure. And I begged him not to go, I warned him those caves were full of enchantments and confusion, but he was so sure he could help us —"

"This is different," said Jack. "If I don't do this, then . . ."

The cottage door banged open again and a small girl came running barefoot across the dirt. She was dusty and patchily dressed, and she flung herself at Jack, who crouched and caught her. Rapunzel knew that she was Tess. Like Jack and his mother, her hair was glossy black, but her eyes were wide, long-lashed, and bright blue. Rapunzel wondered if they looked as much like her father's as Jack's eyes looked like his mother's.

"Don't go!" Tess clung to Jack. "Where are you going, Jackie? Don't go, don't."

"Tess." Jack's voice was full of guilt and fear. He looked her in the face. "Listen to me," he said, his voice shaking. "I'm leaving for seven fortnights. How long is that?"

"Fourteen weeks," said Tess.

"Good," said Jack. "And that's ninety-eight days. So you can count those days, and by the time you're finished counting, I'll be home. I promise you." He scrubbed a bit of dirt from under her eye with the pad of his thumb. "You do your reading and writing every day while I'm gone, all right? Promise me."

Tess shook her head. Her small hands gripped his collar. "Don't leave us like Papa, don't, don't . . ."

Jack's skin was as gray as the cottage. He kissed Tess's forehead. "I'll come back in time," he rasped as he pried his sister's fingers from him. "I will. You'll be safe, I swear."

"What do you mean, 'in time'?" said his mother, her voice eerily thin. "What do you mean, she'll be safe? Jack, what have you done?"

Jack stood. He looked mutely at his mother and sister. And then he turned away from them and ran as fast as Rapunzel had ever seen him move, dodging rocks and jumping fences, careening down the mountainside.

Rapunzel watched him go, dimly aware that she could not follow. She was not really in Dearth. These things had already happened. A memory, that was what this was; the Woodmother was showing her a memory of Jack. Rapunzel suddenly wondered if the Woodmother had *every* memory. Even the ones that Witch had taken from her.

The sky began to move. It drew closer, and its color and texture changed until it looked like stone. She fell to her knees, afraid it would crush her, but it stopped well above her head.

A ceiling. Jack's ramshackle cottage and its gray surroundings had vanished. Now she was inside, standing in a corridor she had never before seen. She put her hand against the stone wall, disoriented.

"Traitor!"

The word was unfamiliar, but the voice . . . the voice was as familiar to her as her own.

"Witch," she mouthed, and her heart swelled. "Witch, where are you?"

"Traitor, traitor . . ."

Witch's voice was thick and broken. Rapunzel turned toward the sound, anxious to help her. The corridor before her was long and lined with many doors. Between the doors, candles flickered on the walls. The marble floor reflected the dancing flames.

"He said he loved me. . . ."

The cry came from somewhere up ahead. Rapunzel ran to the first door on the left and pushed it open.

In a great, dark room lit only by a dying fire, Witch lay on a carpet, sobbing. Her back heaved again and again.

"He was mine . . . ," she managed, her voice muffled in the carpet.

Witch was surrounded by roses. Hundreds of them, all in baskets tied with ribbons. They spilled from the baskets and out onto the carpet, so she appeared to lie weeping in a firelit garden.

"Sit up, girl. Compose yourself."

Now Rapunzel saw the other woman in the room. She looked and sounded like an older version of Witch, except that her face was rigid, like her voice. She sat near the fireplace in a tall chair, her back straight, her eyes hard.

Witch sat up as though pulled by strings. She turned toward the woman and lifted her damp face, and Rapunzel was struck by how beautiful she was — more beautiful and even younger than Rapunzel had ever seen her. There was a softness in her eyes that Rapunzel had never witnessed there. Perhaps it was because they shone with tears. Perhaps it was something else.

"Mother," said Witch, and her voice faltered. "Help me."

"I cannot help you if you behave like common trash. You will exhibit self-control at once."

Witch did not move. "My heart is broken," she whispered.

"Storybook nonsense. Get up from that carpet, Envearia, and do it now."

Witch rose, somewhat clumsily, as though she felt heavy and tired. But when she stood, her posture was graceful, and her back was as straight as her mother's. She wore a long, heavy satin gown, and lavish jewelry hung from her ears and glimmered at her throat. There was even a string of jewels dressing the dark waves of her hair. Rapunzel had never seen her like this. Witch usually dressed quite simply.

"He cannot leave me." Witch's voice was desperate. She swept her eyes over the baskets of roses at her feet. "He *cannot* leave me."

"He can and he has."

"No, it is a mistake. He will return to me. He will realize his folly."

"It is folly — but it is permanent." Witch's mother lifted her nose. "The wedding invitation has arrived."

Witch made an anguished sound and pressed a hand tightly to her mouth, as if to stop herself from vomiting.

"Prince Phillip has made his choice," her mother continued, "and he has sent you his regrets. And so we must begin again."

"You say that as though any prince would do," cried Witch. "As though you would see me married off to anyone wearing a crown, no matter where my heart lies."

"You *will* marry royalty, Envearia. Do you think I have invested twenty years in you for nothing? I trained you for a queen."

Witch fell to her knees and began to sob. "I only want him. I only want *him*. . . ."

"A disgusting outburst," said her mother. "Stop it this instant. I must think. I must plan. I cannot do it with you howling like an animal."

But Witch did not seem to hear her. "I only want him," she said again, swiping at her wet face. "I don't want anything else. I don't care about any of it — not *any* of it, do you hear?"

Witch tore the bright jewels from her throat and flung them into the fire. She pulled the glittering earrings from her ears and ripped the sparkling circlet from her head, yanking some of her dark hair out with it.

"Stupid girl!" cried her mother, rushing forward to pry the jewelry from Witch's clenched hands. "What do you think you are doing?"

"I want nothing he gave me! I want no reminders! I want to remember *nothing*!" And she collapsed upon the carpet again, sobbing violently.

"Great White skies," her mother said. "Do you think you are the first to experience this pain? Count yourself fortunate that you are still young and beautiful and there are still avenues open to you. We will leave the Blue Kingdom and settle in Grey, where my sister has an estate, and where Prince Saras Vesper has not, as yet, courted anyone publicly. He is not Marked, it is his brother, so he will almost certainly inherit the throne. Grey will soon be at war with the Empire, I think, but that is the risk we must take. War will give you a great opportunity to demonstrate loyalty under duress and usefulness in a time of strife, and in this way, you will gain the Vesper family's gratitude and love. We will leave in a fortnight."

Witch remained on her stomach, weeping.

"But first," said her mother, "you will come to your senses. We will attend the wedding of Prince Phillip to —"

"Do not say her name!" Witch screamed into the carpet.

"She will be Her Royal Highness Felicity. Accept it. I will not allow you to embarrass me at the wedding, where Prince Saras Vesper will very likely be. It is your first opportunity to impress him, and believe me, you will not be the only woman there who is trying, nor will you be the most cunning. But do as I tell you and all will go to plan."

"I will not go."

"I beg your pardon?"

"A curse on Phillip and his wife — a curse on their children, and on their children's children! May they suffer heartbreak and humiliation — may their line have no peace!"

"Envearia!"

Witch sat up. Her eyes were different now. There was no softness in them; they were alight, as though a terrible fire had been kindled within her. She reached out to either side of her and clutched handfuls of the roses that littered the carpet, and she gripped them until the thorns broke her skin and lines of blood showed between her fingers. She held the roses up and shook them.

"He thinks that he can send me flowers and ask forgiveness and that it will be over between us," she said. "He thinks there will be no repercussions."

"Repercussions? Envearia, you may be foolish, but even *you* cannot believe it possible to take revenge on the crown prince of the Blue Kingdom. You have no power."

"Not yet." Witch's fingers went white around the rose stems.

"What do you mean, not *yet*?" Her mother gave a brief, cruel laugh. "Do you think you can marry Prince Saras and then turn his army against Prince Phillip? Would you start a war over your own selfish heartbreak?"

"Hang Prince Saras. I will have nothing more to do with princes." Witch was quiet. "There is another way of getting power."

All color drained from her mother's face.

"What do you mean, girl?"

Witch's mother was afraid. It was not only in her voice, but in her eyes.

"I'm not as stupid as you think, Mother."

"No, you are far stupider. Never speak of this again."

But Witch was no longer listening. Rapunzel saw that her eyes were distant, and she was thinking. This expression, Rapunzel knew.

"He will regret his choice," Witch said, and she smiled a smile that made the hairs on Rapunzel's arms stand up.

"Stop." Her mother's voice was sharper than a dagger. "Envearia, I forbid it."

Witch laughed — a light, carefree little laugh — and got to her feet again, throwing the roses to the ground. This time, there was no clumsy heaviness. She moved with the grace and precision Rapunzel was familiar with. Her eyes were dry, and they gleamed. She flashed a wide smile at her mother. The smile was beautiful.

The change was terrible.

"Good-bye, Mother," she said.

"Envearia, *no. Do not do this.*"

Witch walked past Rapunzel and out of the room without looking back. Rapunzel followed her through the door and back into the corridor, but the corridor was gone. In its place stood a dim spiral stairway. Witch was already ahead and out of sight; Rapunzel heard her footfalls on the steps above moving swiftly.

Still clutching her hair in her arms, Rapunzel began to take the stairs two at a time in her eagerness, but she could not catch Witch. She tried to run, but her hair slowed her down, and the climb became steeper with each step.

At the top of the winding stair, she reached a narrow wooden door that stood ajar. From beyond it, she could hear crying — thin, high-pitched crying, unlike any weeping she had heard before. The door was just open enough for her to slide through, and so she did, and when she saw where she was, she gasped.

A tower. With a stone floor and an arching window. Was this her own tower? The light was familiar, but the walls were unadorned and everything seemed too small. Rapunzel took a few steps into the room, and the strange, thin crying grew louder. She looked down to find a basket at her feet, full of blankets that moved and wailed in the blue firelight. A tiny fist poked through the folds of fabric and flailed, and Rapunzel drew a breath of surprise. She had never beheld a baby, but she knew what they were, and she knew that Witch had brought her to the tower as a baby.

So was this . . . her?

Rapunzel knelt before the basket and reached out a hand to move the blankets aside. She wanted to see the tiny creature, and perhaps soothe its pitiful wailing, but her hand passed through the blankets just as it had passed through Jack. She could only watch while the tiny fist waved back and forth, tight and red. She willed the baby to move its arm enough to get the covers out of the way and show its face, but the baby had no such strength.

Rapunzel looked around the tower, wondering why Witch was not there. Maybe she had climbed out through the window. Or maybe the Woodmother had brought Rapunzel into another memory completely. It definitely wasn't her tower, she decided — though the flames were blue, the fireplace was a different shape. There was a rocking chair where the bathtub should have been. There were books on the shelves, but the titles were new to Rapunzel — they were all about witchlife and other kinds of magic. There was no canopied bed either. Just a wooden cradle, standing in the middle of the room.

But there were roses. Roses everywhere. Blooming from the ceiling and the walls, fragrant and beautiful. Whatever this tower was, Witch had been here.

The sounds of horses' hooves pounding the ground and many people shouting made Rapunzel turn her head toward the window. Two grappling hooks gripped the stony windowsill.

"Hurry, Phillip!" she heard a woman's voice cry. "Are they there? Are they alive? Tell me, quickly!"

A large, veined hand gripped the windowsill, and a man of intense masculine beauty hoisted himself up onto the window ledge. Rapunzel thought that she had seen him somewhere before, though she could not place how. He glistened with sweat, and the moisture curled his light hair at his temples and over his forehead. His eyes were green, his nose slightly crooked in a way that somehow only made him more attractive, and his mouth was exquisitely carved; Rapunzel found herself gazing straight at it. In spite of everything she'd been taught about how to treat princes who came to her tower, her heart fluttered and her blood raced. Here was a prince, she thought, whom she might have followed to his lands far, far away.

And this was the Phillip whom Witch had loved.

He swung his legs over the stones and entered the tower. His crown glittered. His cape billowed. When his eyes fell on the baby basket, he knelt before it and pulled apart the blankets. Rapunzel leaned forward to see the baby beneath.

"Valor is here, Felicity!" cried Phillip. "He breathes! He is safe!" He reached into the blankets and picked the baby up. It looked tiny and fragile in his large hands, and Rapunzel stared at its pink, wailing face.

The baby in the basket was not her.

"My son," said Phillip softly, and he touched his broad forehead to the baby's little one.

"Where is Justice?" It was Felicity's voice again, and it was closer now. "She lives? Tell me she is also safe!"

Phillip replaced the baby in his blankets and moved the basket aside. For the first time, Rapunzel saw that it was not the only basket in the room. There was another one behind it, also full of blankets.

Phillip put one strong, shaking hand into this basket and withdrew not a baby but a letter with his name written on it in beautiful script. Rapunzel knew the handwriting at once. It belonged to Witch.

Phillip ripped open the letter and skimmed its contents. As he read it, first rage and then terror contorted his features.

"Envearia," he whispered. "No . . ."

A white hand gripped the windowsill, and a woman with dark red hair, who must have been Felicity, threw herself into the tower. She ran to the first basket and fell to her knees. She seized the baby from his blankets, clutched him to her heart, and began to weep.

"My son," she said brokenly. "My son." As she rocked back and forth, she looked up at Phillip with haunted eyes. "Where is Justice?" she demanded, her voice thick with tears.

Phillip said nothing, but stood as a statue, still staring at the letter.

All at once, Rapunzel knew where she had seen him before — Prince Dash of the Blue Kingdom, who had cut her hair and been turned to stone. Prince Phillip was so like him that they could have been the same person.

Phillip crushed the letter in his fist.

"Answer me!" Felicity pushed the first basket aside and drew the empty one toward her. It came easily. There was no weight in it.

Still clutching her baby in one arm, she began to shake. "She is not here," she whispered. "*She is not here. . . .*"

"A witch . . ."

"A witch took her?" Felicity seized Phillip's sleeve with her free hand. "Why? How do you know this?"

"I knew the woman when she was mortal."

Felicity's expression changed from fearfulness to fury. "Oh, *did* you?" she said, her voice so low that Rapunzel almost could not hear it.

Prince Phillip bowed his head.

"You will hunt her," said Felicity, clutching Valor to her breast as she advanced on him. "You will not rest until my daughter is in my arms and the witch is destroyed."

Light flooded the tower. Rapunzel squinted into the blinding sun, which had risen with force into the sky. Birds sang outside the window, and a pleasant breeze licked through the room and tickled her face, but she turned away from it. An ugly truth had wormed its way into her brain.

She was not the first baby that Witch had brought to a tower.

In fact, Witch had brought two other babies, and apparently she had kept one of them. Prince Phillip's daughter. Justice. Rapunzel wondered what had happened to her.

"I have to get out of here!"

Rapunzel searched the room for the source of the unfamiliar voice.

"Please, just listen to me —"

The second voice was Witch's.

Rapunzel stood. Witch was right there in front of her, looking more like Rapunzel remembered her. Her face was not as young and smooth as Rapunzel was used to seeing it, but she was simply dressed now. They were in a tower, but the fireplace, the furnishings, the shape of the stones in the walls, and the arch of the window were different all over again.

But there were still hundreds of roses; they twisted in vines up the posts of the bed and formed a canopy over it. Beneath the canopy, the mattress was bare. The sheets were gone, and so were the blankets and covers.

"I'm sorry," said the first voice again, and Rapunzel realized that it was coming from the window. She turned toward it.

There, sitting in the window and clutching one of the sheets in her hands, was a girl. She was younger than Rapunzel by a few years at least. Her hair was short, dark, and curly, and her skin was sallow, as though she was sick. Her eyes were bright with tears.

"I don't want to go away from you," said the girl. "You saved me from the Pink soldiers, and nursed me, and you gave me so much to eat, and such nice playthings."

"Then stay with me, Amelia," said Witch. There was desperation in her voice. "I can give you so much more, if you will stay."

"I miss playing in the sun," said the girl, Amelia, still clutching the sheet in her fingers. Rapunzel realized that the sheet was torn — Amelia had made strips from it and tied them together, creating a rope. She had done the same with the blanket and the covers.

The end of her makeshift rope was tied to one of the bedposts. The rest Amelia had piled at her feet, just inside the window. It looked like about as much rope as Rapunzel had hair — enough to get her to the ground if she wanted to leave.

"I can give you sun!" said Witch. "I will take the roof off this tower if you wish it!"

"I want to run," said Amelia. "I've been up here for two years. I can't stand it anymore."

"Where will you live if you go back to the ground?" cried Witch. "How will you eat?"

"Won't you still help me?" said Amelia. "Won't you still love me?"

"The only reason you want to leave," said Witch, ignoring her questions, "is that you remember your freedom. But you don't need to remember — I can help you forget. And then you can stay here and have all the nice things you could ever want."

"Help me forget?" said Amelia, frowning. "What do you mean?"

Rapunzel swallowed the sudden, bitter taste that had risen in her mouth.

"If you will only ask me," said Witch, "I can take away your memories of the war, of the soldiers, of the pain — of everything. You will only remember this place, and me. And then you will be happy here."

Amelia drew back, horrified. "But I wouldn't be me anymore," she said.

"Of course you would!"

"No. I'd be . . ." Amelia shook her curly head. "I'd be empty," she said.

She threw her rope through the window. Gripping the sheet, she swung her legs over the stones and out of the tower. She braced her feet on the outer wall and began to lower herself.

"Don't!" shrieked Witch, leaning out the window.

Behind her, on the bedpost, the end of Amelia's rope strained against her weight as she climbed down. The knot was not secure, Rapunzel realized, feeling queasy. The end of the makeshift rope began to slip through the loops Amelia had made.

Rapunzel ran to the bedpost and tried to hold the knot together, but her hands passed through it. She watched, helpless, as it untied itself.

Witch did not notice. She was shouting after Amelia, "Anything you want! I'll give you anything you want —"

Amelia screamed.

The rope had come undone.

Rapunzel watched it snake rapidly across the floor and out the window. Witch saw it go between her hands, and she snatched for it, but too late.

The next sound was a sickening thud.

And then Witch also screamed. She stared, openmouthed, down at the ground below, and then she sank, shaking, to the floor. She covered her face in her hands and began to rock, moaning.

Her hair turned from dark brown to stark white.

Rapunzel ran to the window and looked down at the ground. Amelia's dark curls gleamed in the sunlight. Her body lay in a heap, her limbs splayed at crazy angles.

The sight was so terrible that it took Rapunzel several minutes to realize that the ground below the tower was not the rich red she was used to seeing. It was rocky and gray. Rapunzel looked out at the horizon and saw that nothing was familiar. Mountains, high and jagged and capped with snow, ran from one end of her view to the other.

Witch had built other towers, in other places.

And Rapunzel was not even the second child that she had tried to keep in one.

Rapunzel backed away from the window, no longer certain of anything in her life. She was not Witch's first child, nor her second. Perhaps she was not the fifteenth or twentieth. Perhaps after her, there would be several others. Hundreds of others. Perhaps Witch had others even now. After all, she was not always with Rapunzel.

Rapunzel looked down at Witch, who still sat rocking, moaning, her face in her hands. The skin on her hands was thin and spotted, as though it had aged many decades. Rapunzel did not need to see Witch's face to know that she had become an old woman in the space of a few seconds.

Of course she had. She had lost her fuel.

The tower shifted subtly, and Rapunzel knew instantly where the Woodmother had taken her now.

Home.

The blue flames in the fireplace made pale shadows in the room. Roses bloomed from the ceiling garden; their petals rained into the bubble bath. Books lined the shelves. The silver bell gleamed on the mantel. The harp played a lullaby Rapunzel had known for as long as she could remember.

"And I f-forgot to wind my b-braid. . . ."

Rapunzel knew her own voice, though it sounded strange in her ears. Perhaps because it was sobbing. Or maybe it was because she had never said those words before. Not that she could remember.

She didn't want to turn. She didn't want to see.

"My poor darling."

Rapunzel winced.

She turned toward the bed, and her heart felt cold. There she lay, the old Rapunzel, collapsed atop her covers, weeping into her pillows. Her slippers and nightgown were clean. Her braid spilled across the floor.

Witch stroked her head and kissed her. "Tell me everything," she said.

"H-he had orange hair," the old Rapunzel wailed. "He grabbed on to my braid and tried to climb up, and I was so frightened!"

Witch gently patted her heaving back. "It must have been awful."

"It was!"

"How dare he come here and give you nightmares?"

"N-nightmares?" The old Rapunzel lifted her head and sniffled.

"Nightmares are very bad dreams," said Witch. "When frightening things happen, nightmares come, and they make you live those things all over again. As long as you remember that prince, he will visit your mind every night and terrorize you."

Rapunzel was amazed. What a cruel thing that was for Witch to tell her. But the old Rapunzel did not see this.

"I *hate* that prince," the old Rapunzel whispered, sitting up in her bed. "I don't want to have awful dreams about him every night."

"I know," said Witch, and she drew her close. "I know. You wish you could forget all about him, don't you?"

"Yes," said the old Rapunzel at once. "I wish I could forget all about him — oh, Witch, I wish I could forget!"

Witch touched her fingertips to the old Rapunzel's temples.

Rapunzel watched her own face as it went slack and the emotion drained out of it. Her pupils grew wide and dark. Her mouth fell open. It took only seconds, and then the old Rapunzel spoke, her voice uncertain.

"Witch?"

She glanced at her nightgown, then at Witch again.

"Was I asleep?"

This part, Rapunzel remembered. She gritted her teeth.

"You were having a bad dream," said Witch, and she embraced the old Rapunzel, who slumped against Witch with a little sigh.

"I was?" asked the old Rapunzel, and she wiped her eyes. She looked at her fingertips, which were wet with tears. "I don't remember it," she said. "It must have been very bad."

"It's all gone now," said Witch. "And I've brought you something lovely for breakfast."

The old Rapunzel gave a little squeal of happiness.

The real Rapunzel turned away from the bed and clenched her fists.

"No more," she said, and for the first time since entering the Woodmother, she could hear her own voice. "No more," she said again, louder. "I've seen enough."

The Woodmother seemed to agree with her. The tower vanished, leaving Rapunzel in a world of dark nothingness, just as when she had first entered the tree. There was nothing above her and nothing below — but this time, she was not alone. The darkness abated slightly, and the Woodmother stood before her, a black silhouette in the shadows. Rapunzel looked up at her slithering branches, no longer surprised that she could be inside the tree and see her at the same time. The Woodmother, it seemed, could show her anything she wanted to.

She did not want to see any more.

"Let me out," she said.

The tree did not respond.

"What do you want from me?"

In the silence, she almost thought she heard the tree reply. She did want something. Rapunzel could feel it.

"What?" she asked. "I won't go back to my tower — is that what you want me to say? You want me to stay away from Witch because she's done terrible things? Because I'm not . . ." Rapunzel's voice failed her momentarily, but she gritted her teeth and found her strength again. "Because I'm not the first girl she's used like this?"

The air whispered and whirled.

"Well, too bad," said Rapunzel, stepping back. "Yes, I've heard the stories — and now I've seen them." She tightened her stomach against the sensation of sickness. "And I believe them. But I'm not afraid of Witch."

The whispers in the air became frantic. The tree's monstrous branches slithered wildly.

"You listen to *me*," Rapunzel commanded, standing as tall as she could and throwing back her head. She pointed a finger at the tree and raised her voice. "I told you to let me out! I'm going back to make her explain, do you hear? I have to make her stop. I'm the only one who can. She can't do this again — not to anyone else. Not ever."

Dawn broke in the darkness, so bright that Rapunzel had to shield her eyes. The black nothingness around her subsided and the sky became golden. Rapunzel found herself standing on a path of stones that led straight to the trunk of the Woodmother.

She caught her breath.

The Woodmother was a creature of incredible beauty. Her trunk was a deep, gleaming bronze that shone like liquid in the dawn light. And her branches, Rapunzel realized in awe and delight, were not slithering at all. They were growing — endlessly growing — reaching infinitely outward and upward, twining and braiding together, blossoming every second with leaves of all colors and flowers of all kinds, stretching as far and as high as Rapunzel's eyes could see and then vanishing into the air.

Rapunzel found that she was kneeling on the path. She didn't remember kneeling. The tree reached for her with one shining branch, and Rapunzel put her hand on it to steady herself as she stood.

The branch was cool and warm together. It grew beneath her fingers, silk and rough, and she was content just to stand there and hold on to it. She could have stayed there forever. But the branch coiled gently around her hand and drew her along the path, toward the great, gleaming trunk.

When Rapunzel reached the Woodmother, the branch withdrew, and she was sorry to feel it gone. She looked down at her empty hand and blinked. There, on her second finger, was a thin bronze ring. It appeared to move in a circle, as though growing and growing forever.

"It's beautiful," Rapunzel whispered, and she closed her fist. "Thank you." She looked up at the tree, who reached for her own trunk with two delicate branches, like hands reaching for a skirt. The Woodmother parted the great, gleaming trunk before Rapunzel, revealing a path that she knew was the way out.

The tree swayed, and her leaves whispered in a language Rapunzel did not understand. But it was comforting.

"Good-bye," she whispered in reply.

Rapunzel stepped into the tree and onto the path.

The Woodmother closed behind her.

CHAPTER TWENTY

*T*HE world outside was just as she had left it, except that dawn had come, pale gray and cold, bringing snowfall with it. Fat white flakes drifted down around Rapunzel, and she shut her eyes and turned up her face to feel them.

When she opened her eyes again, she looked over her shoulder to see if the Woodmother was still there — but she was gone. Where she had gone, and how something so big could move so quickly, Rapunzel had no idea. She supposed she never would.

At the campsite, she saw the fire pit she had made with Jack, and the fairy wheel still abandoned in the snow, and the wagon waiting with their belongings and Prince Frog inside it. But there was no Jack. He must have gone south with Rune, Rapunzel realized, and this knowledge made her feel more alone than she ever had in her life. She didn't blame Jack for going — not at all. She had seen. She understood.

It was time to return to the tower.

Rapunzel grabbed the fairy wheel and fed the end of her braid into it. "Wind up," she said, and when it did, she donned the wheel and drew a deep breath. She had never felt such dread at the thought of her home, but after the things she had seen, there was no other way to feel. She had to journey back; she had to face Witch. What would happen, she did not know. Best to start walking and figure it out when she got there.

She picked up the wagon handle, surprised that Jack had left all of their belongings there for her. He should have taken half for himself.

"I have the money too," she murmured, glancing down at her belt. She wished she could have given him half the coins.

Jack, however, had the compass. Rapunzel squinted at the early morning sun in the east and oriented herself to head south. She started walking. One foot after the other, and then again. And again.

It was going to be a very long journey without Jack to talk to.

She hadn't gone far before she saw a lump of their belongings on the ground off in the distance. Cloaks, it looked like, or blankets and cushions, maybe. It was strange that Jack hadn't left those things near the campsite with the wagon.

She hurried toward the heap. When she reached the pile, she grabbed the top cloak and pulled, but it wouldn't come. Frowning, she tried to dig into the pile of supplies beneath. Her hand struck something solid. She threw back the cloak.

There lay Jack, cold and still, his face as white as snow.

Except that the snow around him was red.

Rapunzel quickly knelt beside him. She touched the red snow and withdrew her fingers to find them slick with blood. Her shivering grew worse, though she no longer felt the cold.

"Jack!" She took his shoulders and shook him. He did not stir. Frightened of the worst, Rapunzel lowered her ear to his mouth, listening for breath. When she heard a slight, shallow exhale, she seized his cold, motionless face in both hands.

"You're not dead," she gasped. "You're not dead, are you? Wake up, Jack, wake up!"

But he didn't wake. And when she lowered her ear to his mouth again, it seemed a long time before she heard a breath — this one slighter and shallower than the last.

He wasn't dead. But he was dying. Rapunzel realized, too late, that he had been right about the lifebreath.

"Help!" Rapunzel cried, getting to her feet and looking around the wide, white, empty world. "Help us, please! Someone!"

No one came, and Rapunzel had no idea what to do. She knew nothing about how to stop dying. Even Rune would have been a welcome sight.

"Rune?" Rapunzel called. "Rune, can you hear me? Woodmother, where are you? Come back! Please, I need your help!"

Nothing answered. Rapunzel knew that she was running out of time. She bent and covered Jack with his cloak.

"I'll get help," she swore. "I'll be back. You are *not allowed* to die. Do you hear me?"

She knew he didn't.

She took off running across the fresh snow, careening into the wind, not sure whom or what she hoped to find, but knowing that she had to find someone.

"Help!" she shouted as she ran. "Help me, please!"

The snow began to fall more quickly, making it difficult to see. Rapunzel stopped and looked back toward where Jack lay. He was already out of sight. Would she be able to find him again? The snow was blotting out the tracks left by her boots.

She stood where she was, afraid to go on, and afraid not to.

"PLEASE!" she cried. "SOMEONE!"

And then it struck her. She had seen the Woodmother — she had performed the task that Glyph had asked. So she was free of the fairies' threat, and she could finally do as all her storybooks had taught her.

Rapunzel cried out from her heart. "WITCH! WITCH, HELP ME! WITCH, I NEED YOU!"

She turned in a circle, staring hard in every direction, searching for a sign that she had been heard. In her storybooks, Witch simply appeared, but that didn't seem to have happened. Rapunzel strained her eyes against the snow. Her breath grew ragged as the seconds passed.

"Witch," she whispered. "Please."

The snow fell so heavily now that at first Rapunzel thought her eyes might be tricking her. But a dark and distant shape appeared on the horizon. As it moved closer, Rapunzel could see that the shape was cloaked and hooded, impossible to recognize. But it could only be one person.

"Witch," Rapunzel cried, sure that it was true, and she raced toward the hooded figure. She pushed the hood back with both hands.

Under the hood stooped a woman — an *old* woman. Her hair was white, her face lined. But her eyes were clear and hazel, and Rapunzel knew them well, even if the rest of the wasted face was foreign to her.

"Witch," she gasped. "You came. You always said that you would come."

Frail, thin arms enveloped Rapunzel. She could feel, as well as see, how much Witch had aged without innocence to fuel her. But that didn't matter now.

Rapunzel took Witch by her hands, which were bony. The skin was loose. There were tears in Witch's eyes.

"Rapunzel," she whispered. "You know me?"

"Of course," said Rapunzel, tears springing into her own eyes in spite of everything she knew. "Witch, help me, please. Jack is dying — there isn't time."

Witch went with Rapunzel through the snow. Rapunzel knelt beside Jack and brushed the fallen snow from his cloak and face. His eyelids and lips were blue.

"His head is bleeding," she said. "And he's barely breathing, and he's so cold. . . ."

Witch braced herself on Rapunzel's shoulder as she lowered herself into the snow. She slid her hands beneath Jack's body. A sizzling noise cut through the muffled, snowy silence, and Witch jerked her hands away, hissing in pain. Smoke rose from her fingertips, which looked charred, as though she'd put them in a fire.

"What happened?" cried Rapunzel.

"Iron," Witch managed, grimacing as she plunged her burned fingertips into the snow. "Where is it?"

Around Jack's neck, Purl's iron chain glinted. Rapunzel shoved her hands under him and rolled him onto his side to find the clasp of the chain. When the back of his head was revealed, she sucked in a sharp breath, and Witch made a low sound.

Behind Jack's left ear, at the base of his skull, his head had been bludgeoned. The wound was a gash, wide and deep. His hair was matted in a glaze of ice and blood.

Rapunzel unfastened the chain. The iron clasp was red and slick. "Get rid of it," said Witch. "Throw it far from here, or I won't be able to help him."

Rapunzel threw the iron chain as far as she could, away into the snow. "Hurry," she begged. "Please, please, hurry . . ."

Witch brushed the hair from Jack's injury and shook her head. "If I can mend him," she said, "you will come home to me?"

"Of course," said Rapunzel. "Just don't let him die. . . ."

Witch was silent as she worked her magic. Her fingers moved over and near Jack's wound, but never touched it. She looked sometimes as though she were playing a harp, and at other times as though she were sewing. Rapunzel watched as Jack's icy blood thawed and his wound began to close, first where it was deep and dark, and then at the surface. His torn skin drew together in a pinched line. He exhaled unevenly.

"Jack!" Rapunzel scrambled to his other side, where she could watch his face. She took his freezing hand in both of hers. "I'm here, it's all right. You'll be all right."

As Witch continued her silent manipulations, Jack became more lifelike. His breathing grew regular. Color was restored to his skin, and the hand Rapunzel was holding grew warmer. He swallowed, and the knot in his throat bobbed up and down.

"My . . . head . . . ," he moaned, and Rapunzel smoothed his hair away from his forehead.

"You were hurt," she said. "But you're all right now. Can you open your eyes?"

Jack's eyelashes fluttered. One eye opened a crack.

"Rapunzel," he said in a thick voice. "The tree . . . are you . . ."

"Shh, don't," she said. "Let Witch finish."

"Let . . ." Jack's eye fell shut again. And then both his eyes opened wide, and he jerked, trying to sit up. "Who's that?" he asked, slapping at Witch's hands. He was too weak to move quickly, but his eyes were panicked. "What's happening? Rapunzel —"

"Jack, don't!" Rapunzel realized her mistake, but it was too late — he would not lie still and let Witch minister to him. He kicked and scratched and tried to roll, and finally he managed to get onto his hands and knees in the snow. He looked up, panting.

Witch sat back on her heels and wiped sweat from her face. She looked drained. "I believe he'll survive," she said. Her voice had changed too, Rapunzel realized. It was older. Thinner. "It's time to go, Rapunzel."

"Go where?" Jack barked. "You're not taking her anywhere."

Witch pushed herself to her feet and held out her frail hand to Rapunzel, who looked at it and realized that she had no choice.

She had made a bargain with a witch.

"Good-bye, Jack," she said as she stood.

"Rapunzel, *don't*."

"I have to," said Rapunzel. "Witch mended you."

"You bargained with her." Jack's expression was anguished. "No . . . *no* . . ."

"Don't worry about me," said Rapunzel. "Go with Rune, save Tess from Geguul, and soon I'll come and visit you. Take care of Prince Frog for me until I get there, all right?"

Before Jack could answer, Rapunzel put her hand into Witch's.

The journey was instantaneous.

Rapunzel breathed in and out, and she was standing in the tower, holding Witch's hand, as though there were no space at all between the First Wood and the Redlands.

"Amazing," she murmured. "How did you do that? You don't seem strong enough."

"When you are with me, I am strong enough for anything."

Rapunzel understood her meaning better than she wished to.

She looked slowly around the tower room. It was exactly the same as when she left. The stones in the walls, the wheel at the window, the books on the shelves, the bathtub, and the bell. There were her toys, her gowns, her curtains. There was her canopy. There, the fireplace. Everything was the same.

But the ceiling was so low compared with the sky, and the walls were so close compared with the world, that Rapunzel felt they were pressing in on her. And though nothing had changed, it looked different to her now. The window wheel — she had used to love to turn its crank and lower her braid for Witch, then wind it up proudly, just as she'd been taught. Now she realized how long she had spent tied to it, with just a few feet of slack hair on which to travel. The bookshelves too — she had gone to them again and again to read about how wonderful she was. Now she saw that the shelves were full of lies, designed to frighten her into choosing her cage over everything else.

She had not even been there for a full minute, and she knew she could not stay. Not forever. Not like before.

"What you must have suffered," said Witch in the strange, thin voice she now had. "My poor Rapunzel — your braid . . ." She let go of Rapunzel's hand and brushed wet hair back from her brow. "I missed you," she said.

Rapunzel knew it was true. What she didn't know was whether Witch had missed her as a person or only as a source of power.

"I missed you too," she said. Whatever else might have changed, that was the truth. "I wanted you so much."

"You never called for me."

"The fairies said they'd kill me if I did, and then they'd kill you too."

"They lied. I warned you about the creatures of the ground. You see how quickly I was able to bring you home — I etched that magic into you when you were an infant, not a week old. At any time, I could have brought you here, if only you had believed in me."

So the fairies *had* tricked her, in the end.

But they had been right too, about many things.

Witch held Rapunzel close. "They even cut your poor hair," she murmured, and stroked the crown of Rapunzel's head. "Let me fix it. Let me make everything comfortable for you, now that you've come back." Witch hugged her tighter. "Welcome home."

But then she broke from Rapunzel and stepped back, holding one hand to her stomach.

"Fairy magic," she murmured, and swept her eyes over Rapunzel. "What's happened to you? What have they done?"

Rapunzel looked down at herself. She had forgotten how many fairy garments and devices she had on.

"The Red fairies made a wheel for my hair to help me carry it," she explained, and she took it off. "Unwind," she said, and her hair came away from the wheel. Rapunzel went to the balcony and put it outside. "Does that help?" she asked when she returned.

Witch glanced at Rapunzel's fairy boots and clothes, and then at the bronze ring that traveled around her finger. "Are you wearing anything else that's fairy-made?" she asked.

"No," Rapunzel lied.

Witch's hazel eyes glinted. "Not your cloak?" she asked. "Are you sure?"

"I bought it at a shop in Cornucopia." This much was true. Rapunzel took off the cloak and laid it over a chair, and Witch touched the little orange-jeweled copper pin.

"Very pretty," she said. "Where . . . ?"

"Princess Daigh of Orange," said Rapunzel. "She gave it to me to help me get home faster."

"Oh?" Witch looked at her. "You planned to come home?"

"Of course. I always planned to come home."

Witch picked up Rapunzel's braid and touched the place where the bandits had cut it.

"Let me fix your hair," she said again.

Rapunzel realized something with a jolt. "How did you know before that my hair had been cut?" she asked.

"Hmmm?" Witch's thin voice was vague.

"When my braid was on the wheel," said Rapunzel. "You couldn't see where the bandits had cut it. How did you know it was cut?"

Witch smiled and patted Rapunzel's braid. "I always know when your braid needs fixing," she said. "Why don't we give your hair a bath and mend it?"

This answer would have satisfied the old Rapunzel. Now, she heard the lie in it.

"No," she said, watching Witch's smile to see when it would falter. "You knew because you saw it when it was unwound. Which means that you followed me, didn't you?"

Witch's smile remained fixed, but her eyes changed, and the look in them was frightening. "You are tired," she said. "Let me draw you a bath."

"No." Rapunzel had no intention of removing her other fairy garments.

"But you're filthy," said Witch, still smiling that awful smile. "Surely you want to change into something clean. And then I'll make you supper, and we can sit and talk, and you can tell me everything that happened."

"And then," said Rapunzel, her heart beating very fast, "you'll ask me if I want to *forget* everything that happened."

The smile cracked. Witch bared her teeth for the briefest moment, then closed her mouth.

"So this is what you think," she whispered. "They've poisoned you against me."

"I've seen for myself," Rapunzel said.

"Seen?" Witch tilted her head. "In the Woodmother, I suppose, you've *seen*. But the Woodmother is a fairy. A very old fairy. After she swallowed you, you saw what she wanted you to see."

"So you *were* there," said Rapunzel. "You *did* see me go into her."

"Of course I was there," said Witch, and now she looked old and feeble, her face framed by white hair, her expression full of sorrow. "I had to find you. I was so frightened for you — oh, my Rapunzel —"

A horrible idea dawned on Rapunzel. "If you were there, then you must have seen what happened to Jack," she said. "Who hurt him?"

"I don't know," said Witch in the same feeble, sorrowful voice. "After the Woodmother took you, I followed that Red fairy — Rune, you called him — as far away as I could before I lost my strength. I didn't see what happened to Jack —"

"No more lies," said Rapunzel hoarsely. "Witch, tell me now. *Who hurt him?*"

Witch gazed at her with her clear hazel eyes, the only feature that remained of the young and beautiful mother that Rapunzel had known and loved.

"I did," said Witch.

Rapunzel stood stricken. She took an uncertain step back and found herself at her bedside. She sat on the bed. Her legs felt weak.

"And so, here we are," said Witch. Her white hair grew thinner on her head, as though she aged with every word she spoke. "You know everything — or think you do — so let's not pretend. Shall I be very plain with you? Do you think you have the stomach for it?"

Rapunzel barely had a voice.

"Witch . . . how could you? Why would you hurt him so badly?"

"To ensure that you would return to me," said Witch. She did not look feeble now. She looked cunning, and her eyes were bright. "I saw how much he cared for you when he tried and failed to pull you from the Woodmother. I assumed your feelings were similar. Nothing so simple as to make you trade your freedom for my help."

Rapunzel was horror-struck.

"And now you are home, as you promised," Witch said, her voice nearly a rasp, "and home you will stay. It can be a comfortable stay, or it can be very unpleasant. That much is up to you."

"I promised. . . ." Rapunzel thought back. What had their bargain been, exactly? "I said that if you mended Jack, I'd come home with you," she said, her voice returning. She stood. "I never agreed to stay once I was here."

"And now that you're here," said Witch, "how will you leave?"

"I'll climb down my hair," Rapunzel said. "I'll cut it off."

"Cut it with what?"

Rapunzel took the dagger from her belt and held it up.

"Oho, I see." Witch gave a croaking laugh. "You have changed indeed. Go ahead. Cut your hair. Roll it on the wheel and climb down. I won't try to stop you."

"Why not?"

"Clever girl." Witch tilted her head and looked fondly at her, but the fondness was a mockery of what it had once been. "I did not raise an imbecile. My mistake."

"I said *why not?* Why won't you stop me?"

"Because I will not have to," said Witch. "You will not choose to go."

"You don't think so?"

"No, I don't." Witch went to the window and looked out. "Because if you go, there is no reason in the world why I should not find your Jack and finish what I started."

Rapunzel trembled. The dagger dropped to the floor. "You mean kill him?"

"Why not? I've killed before," said Witch. "But then, you know that too — or don't you?" She turned from the window and grinned, and the look was so out of place in her withered face that Rapunzel was revolted. "Shall we play a game? I'll tell you terrible stories, and you tell me if you've already heard them."

"Witch, no . . ."

"Let's start with your parents. Natalie and Remoulade — you know about them, I'm sure — I heard you mention your grandmother as you sat by the fire last night. I also saw the book Jack gave you. *Witches: A Master Slayer's Comprehensive Guide*. Written by a bloodthirsty old fool, but very accurate, really. Most other literature about White-hatching is pure fiction."

Rapunzel vomited. She had eaten little recently, and there was not much to come up, so it stayed in her mouth until she swallowed again, shaking.

This was Witch.

"But I know a better game," said Witch, and she crossed the tower to Rapunzel's bedside more swiftly than anyone of her age should have been able to do. "I call it Bargaining. Shall we? No one has beaten me at it, but there is always beginner's luck, so don't despair. You may yet win."

Rapunzel sank onto the bed again and looked up at her, speechless with sickness and fear.

Jack had warned her. They all had.

"Here is my bargain," said Witch, looking down at her with eyes that Rapunzel no longer recognized. "Allow me to take your memories of the time since Glyph first visited this tower. In exchange, I will neither hurt nor kill your Jack." Her grin widened, and Rapunzel could see that her teeth had rotted. They were yellow and black. "Do we have a deal?"

Rapunzel said nothing. She was numb.

"Cat got your tongue?" asked Witch. "Not feeling brave and bold any longer? I can hardly blame you. But I think you'll find, as bargains go, that this one is quite fair. You'll never know what happened. You'll live a happy life. And Jack will go on with his, unhindered."

Rapunzel looked down at the bronze ring that moved on her finger, circling and circling. Why it should have made her feel stronger, she had no idea. But it did. She kept her eyes on it.

"Your turn, Rapunzel," said Witch in a singsong rasp. "Do you have a better bargain to offer me? I'm open to negotiating."

Rapunzel stared at her ring, unmoving. "I need time to think," she said.

"Go ahead," said Witch, and she sat on the bed beside Rapunzel. "Think."

Rapunzel stood and moved to the window. She touched the window wheel.

"Time alone," she said. "I need to think on my own."

"Oh no," said Witch. "I can't be that sporting, I'm afraid. You cannot be trusted on your own. That's been made clear. Now, take your turn and offer me a bargain." She paused. "Or agree to mine, and our lives will return to the easy state we enjoyed before you disobeyed me."

Witch picked up Rapunzel's dagger from where it had fallen and tucked it into the pocket of her cloak. Then she joined her at the window and laid her hand on the wheel, atop Rapunzel's. Her aged fingers bent like claws.

"Will it be so awful?" she asked. "Was I ever unkind to you? Were you ever unhappy?"

Rapunzel watched as Witch's gnarled thumb caressed the back of her hand.

"I don't know," she said. "I don't remember everything, do I?"

Witch patted her hand. "No," she said. "You don't. The bad things are gone. Let me take the memories of your journey — I know it could not have been pleasant. I know there must have been many dangers, many cruelties. If you would give them to me, you would be happy."

Rapunzel looked into Witch's eyes. "But I wouldn't be me anymore," she said, remembering Amelia's words in the Woodmother. "I'd be empty."

Witch's fingers clenched.

"You've heard those words before," Rapunzel whispered.

Witch stared at Rapunzel, her mouth working silently.

"Do you remember Amelia?" Rapunzel thought she saw pain flash in Witch's eyes. "You *do*," she pressed, watching Witch's face as it paled and flushed. "You think about her. You *miss* her. Are you sorry that she died?"

Witch made a noise Rapunzel could not place. Anger, or anguish, or —

"Time to take your turn," Witch snarled, gripping Rapunzel's fingers. "You've had plenty of time to think, haven't you? Take your turn — or accept my bargain."

Rapunzel's mind worked frantically, searching for a way out. If she didn't agree to forget her journey, then Jack would be in danger. He was smart, and he was strong, but Witch had already hurt him once. And if she killed him now, not only would he die, but his sister would be taken to Geguul.

She couldn't let it happen. She wouldn't let it happen.

Witch knew she wouldn't.

Rapunzel closed her eyes. She had to accept the bargain — and then she would know only this tower. This tower, and Witch. Forever.

She began to weep.

"There, there," said Witch, keeping Rapunzel's fingers tight in her grip. "It will all soon be over, when you say yes."

"But . . ." Rapunzel stumbled on an idea. She opened her eyes and spoke through her tears. "Jack will come for me," she said, certain she was right. "I won't remember him, but he'll come."

"Perhaps he will," said Witch, who did not look worried about it.

"Don't you think he'll try to get me to leave again?" asked Rapunzel.

Witch shrugged.

"If he does, you can't touch him. If I agree to your bargain, you can't hurt him —"

"I won't hurt him. I will take extra precautions with *you*," said Witch.

Extra precautions. Rapunzel's insides went cold. What extra precautions could there be? She would already be trapped at the top of a tower, already lashed by her hair to a window wheel — what more would Witch do to her? Chain her up? Tell her that the chains were for her safety? Make her believe she wanted to wear them?

She yanked her hand away from Witch.

"How do I know you'll keep your end of the bargain?" she demanded. "If I don't remember Jack exists, then how can I make sure you aren't lying?"

"A witch's bargain cannot be broken," said Witch, "or the witch forfeits to Geguul."

"And that's where the White Fairy turns you into a giant and keeps you forever," Rapunzel said. "Isn't it?"

Witch's face fell. Rapunzel saw in it, with sudden clarity, the same vulnerable Witch she had seen in the Woodmother, weeping over Prince Phillip.

"Witch — tell me. Is that what will happen to you?"

"You don't care if it does."

"Of course I do."

Witch laughed a harsh and bitter laugh. "No wonder I'm not dead," she said. "Your innocence is indestructible. Now *choose*," she said. "And know this: If you choose your freedom, Jack will be dead within the hour, and I will tell him, as he dies, that it was by your choice."

"He'd understand," Rapunzel said. "He'd be glad I was free."

"Not if it cost him his life."

Rapunzel shook her head. "You don't know him," she said. "And it doesn't matter. I would never choose to let you kill him."

"So you agree?" Witch cried. "Then accept!"

Rapunzel found herself looking again at the Woodmother's bronze ring as it flowed around her finger. She had told the Woodmother that she would return here to stop Witch from doing this again. And she had failed. Witch would go on as she was, perhaps forever, as long as she could trick some father or mother into giving her their baby.

She wondered what had happened to Prince Phillip's other child, Justice. She wondered how Witch had gotten Amelia in the first place. She wondered how many other children there had been. She wondered if Witch had ever eaten anybody. She wondered who Witch had killed.

She wondered a lot of things. She still wondered *why*. Why did Witch do this? Was it to stay young and alive? Was it because Phillip had hurt her? Was there something more she wanted?

"I want answers," Rapunzel said, and looked up from her ring. "I have questions, Witch. I want answers to my questions before you take my memories away."

"What does it matter if I answer your questions? You'll only forget everything I tell you," said Witch impatiently. "Say that you *accept*, Rapunzel. Do it now, or I warn you —"

"No. I want to change the bargain."

Witch's eyes narrowed to hazel slits. "Go on."

"First, you leave Jack out of it — you never touch him, or his sister either. Never."

"And second?"

"Second, you stay with me until tomorrow morning and give me honest answers to all of my questions. And you stop acting horrible — you stop trying to make me feel afraid. I want to sit with you, and listen to you, and hear everything from you. Not from the fairies, not from Purl, not even from Jack — from *you*."

Witch lifted a white eyebrow. "And if I do those things?"

"And if you do those things, then I'll . . ." Rapunzel forced the words out of her mouth. "I'll let you take my memory," she said.

"I *accept*," breathed Witch. Her eyes lit up, her white hair began to thicken, and roses came into her wrinkled cheeks, as though the very idea of Rapunzel's restored innocence had awakened new energy and power within her.

"Tomorrow morning," she said, coming forward to take Rapunzel's face in her hands. "At dawn. I will make your life so beautiful again, Rapunzel. You won't be sorry."

"I won't know to be sorry," said Rapunzel, but Witch did not seem to hear her. She hobbled rapturously around the room, bringing the bath to a bubble, asking the harp to play, and making the fire burn. The tower came to life in the old, familiar ways, and Rapunzel watched it all with a sinking heart. Tomorrow, this would be her world again — her whole world. Forty paces across. One hundred twenty-five and a half paces around. In the morning, when the sun rose, the rest of Tyme would be her enemy again.

"Sit down, Witch," she said. "I'm going to ask my questions now."

"Very well." Witch settled in the rocking chair by the fire and leaned back, smiling. "What do you want to know?"

Rapunzel stayed at the window and looked out at the sunlit

Redlands. What did she want to know? There were so many questions. And there was no time to waste.

"Tell me about the memories you've taken," she said. "What have I already forgotten?"

Witch nodded and began to speak.

The bargain was under way.

CHAPTER TWENTY-ONE

SINCE you were a baby, people have been coming to this tower." Witch took the end of Rapunzel's braid in her hands and began to untie it. "Some to free you, others to thrill themselves . . . It was easy to manage when you were a child. You were so frightened of the people on the ground that you would have nightmares when they came, and you would cry out to me and beg me to take away all the thoughts that made the nightmares. As you grew older, it became more complicated. But you were still fearful. You still preferred to forget."

Her fingers pried at the knotted, dirty ribbon that tied Rapunzel's braid together until she finally worked it loose. She unplaited the first few inches of tangled golden hair upon her lap.

"Don't touch my hair," said Rapunzel.

Witch raised an eyebrow. "Let me bathe it," she said. "I'll mend it."

"No." Rapunzel picked up her braid from the floor at her feet and gave it a sharp yank, pulling it from Witch's reach. "You want to make it pretty so that when my memories are gone, you won't have to explain why it's all dirty and chopped up." She flung it to her feet. "Too bad. I'm not taking off any of my fairy clothes either. That wasn't part of our bargain. You'll just have to deal with my questions about those things later."

"So your clothes *are* fairy-made." Witch sat back again in her chair. "You little liar . . ."

"Keep answering my question. I know that Prince Mick of Orange came, and Prince Dash of the Blue Kingdom."

Witch nodded. "Yes. Both quite recently. You were growing older — a perfect target for romantic idealists."

"And Nexus Keene? He said he tried to kill you, but he couldn't."

"No, he couldn't." Witch looked amused.

"Who else?" asked Rapunzel.

Witch shrugged. "Prince Aydan of Grey. Princess Histria of Crimson. Not long ago, Chieftain Fleet of the Redlands himself came to coax you down. But I had foreseen that you would have persuasive visitors. It is why I wrote your books and trained your mind to despise all those who would come here as rescuers."

"It worked," said Rapunzel, angered by her own gullibility, and angrier knowing that she would soon be gullible again.

Witch placed her hands on the arms of the chair and began to rock. Her hands looked older now, as though she had aged further in the last few minutes. Which, Rapunzel supposed, she had. Every word Witch spoke was another strike against Rapunzel's innocence.

"What did you do to the people who came here?" asked Rapunzel.

"Nothing, usually."

"Nothing? Then how did you make them go away?"

"The power of fear is remarkable," said Witch. "You would ring your bell for me, and before I even arrived, the very threat of my coming would frighten your would-be rescuers so that they fled and never returned." She gave a brief laugh. "Most of them, anyway. Nexus Keene stayed to fight. And Chieftain Fleet returned repeatedly — I had to punish his army to make him surrender. You were getting very difficult to manage."

"Why?"

"Because you liked him better than the others. He is nearer your age."

"Like Jack."

"Ah, *Jack*." Witch's eyes narrowed. "The only one who ever climbed your tower with a rope and hook. The others were afraid, I suppose, that you would unhook them and let them fall. You did threaten to do it on several occasions."

"Is that why *you* climb my hair?" asked Rapunzel. "And not a rope?"

"Yes," said Witch. "I expected that a time would come when you knew too much and would not agree to unknow it. Under such circumstances, I would not want to climb a rope that you could easily detach. Your hair, on the other hand . . . You can't get rid of me without getting rid of yourself in the bargain, can you?"

"I'd never detach a rope with you on it," said Rapunzel.

"So you say. But people do unthinkable things when they are angry."

Rapunzel considered this for a moment. "You said you didn't usually do anything to the people who came here," she said. "But you turned Prince Dash to stone."

Witch paused in her rocking. "So I did," she said. "So I did."

"Why did you hurt him and not the others?" asked Rapunzel, and when Witch didn't answer at once, she said, "Was it because he looked like Prince Phillip?"

Witch's faint gasp was enough. Rapunzel knew she had struck truth.

"I suppose it was," Witch said. "I didn't think . . . But he looked so much . . ."

"They could be the same person," Rapunzel finished.

"Phillip's hair was more golden," said Witch softly.

"Why did he leave you for that other woman?" Rapunzel asked. "What was wrong with you? Did he leave you because he could tell what you were really like?"

Witch flinched. "I . . ." Her eyes darted to the fire, and then to Rapunzel. "I don't know."

"Answer the question."

"That *is* the answer," said Witch. "Maybe he could tell. I don't know."

"Did you really love Phillip?"

"Yes."

"Then why did you take his babies?"

Witch jerked. She wrung her withered hands. "The Woodmother showed you a great deal," she said. "A very great deal."

"Answer my question."

"I took his children to punish him. To make him feel the helpless grief I felt."

"You gave Valor back. But you kept the girl baby. Why?"

"Justice?" Witch shook her head. "I didn't keep her for long."

"Did you kill her? Did you eat her?"

Witch cried out in dismay. "No, I didn't *eat* her," she said. "I cared for her."

"Because she gave you power?"

"Only my first taste of power. It was very brief. Phillip's wife would not rest until the baby was returned. I was cornered when

Justice was a few months old, and I had to let her go. But still that woman hunted me." Witch's eyes grew dark. "She pursued me like no other has pursued me since, and she had all the resources of the Blue Kingdom to help her do it. I spent nearly five decades in hiding after that foolish kidnapping. I paid the price — but so did she. So have her children, and her children's children."

"What do you mean?"

"I cursed that family," said Witch. "Phillip's sons, and the sons of his sons, have all been just like him."

"Oh." Rapunzel wasn't sure she understood, but she had more pressing questions. "Who have you killed?" she demanded.

Witch gave a croak of amazement. "You ask so casually," she said. "Doesn't it hurt you to hear these things? Or has the world so hardened you already?"

"Of course it hurts me," said Rapunzel. "You know it does. You're growing weaker with every word you say to me. I can see it happening."

And then it struck her that the bargain she'd made was a good one.

A remarkably good one.

If she asked Witch enough difficult questions and received enough terrible answers, then her innocence would be destroyed, and Witch would have no more power at all. Witch would wither away, and their bargain would die with her. This possibility seemed to occur to Witch at the same moment. A look of horror froze upon her face.

"No," she said, meeting Rapunzel's eyes. "No, don't try it."

"Who have you *killed*?" Rapunzel repeated. "Answer me now."

Witch's hands tightened on the arms of the rocking chair. "Chieftain Fleet's parents — the old chieftain and chieftainess of the Redlands."

"Why?"

"To create a distraction."

"From what?"

"I needed the government and fairies of the Redlands preoccupied," said Witch, "so that they would not notice when I planted my roses around the Red Glade and began to sink my magic into their clay."

"How did you kill them — the old chieftain and chieftainess?"

"I sent their carriage over the edge of a deep quarry."

"Who else was hurt?"

"The driver was killed. The chieftain's son was also with them, and the boy's legs were ruined. They had to be cut off."

Rapunzel gasped, horrified, and Witch's wrinkled mouth grew more wizened as she spoke.

"Rapunzel, this won't work," she said. "No matter what I tell you, there is too much you haven't seen and felt. I cannot destroy your innocence by talking."

Rapunzel ignored her. "Who else did you kill?"

"Warriors of the Redlands."

"Why?"

"I already told you why. To stop Chieftain Fleet from persuading you to trust him. Unlike your other visitors, I believe the chieftain understood that I posed a great threat to his nation. He was so persistent. The Red fairies must have warned him that if he did not separate you from me, then his fortress would be vulnerable. So he acted, and

I killed his warriors to frighten him into a full retreat. His conscience will not let him send more of his people to reckon with me."

Rapunzel's stomach hurt. But as Witch spoke of the terrible things she had done, her skin grew more translucent, and her hair grew visibly thinner. Chunks of it fell out upon her shoulders.

Rapunzel continued the assault.

"What about Amelia?"

"I didn't kill Amelia," said Witch instantly. "That was an accident."

"Who else have you killed, then?"

"Rapunzel, you may as well relent. This interrogation will not serve you."

"Who *else?*"

"I haven't killed anyone else."

"But I thought you were old. How old are you really?"

"I am one hundred and seventy-one."

"Didn't you have to eat a lot of babies to get that old? Aren't the babies all dead?"

"I have *never*," said Witch, her voice so strong that it was almost youthful again, "*ever* eaten *anyone*. How absolutely vile."

"But I thought that witches —"

"Inelegant witches. Beastly witches." Witch looked proud. "I have *imagination*. I found methods no other witch had discovered. I had regular sources of innocence at every time, except during the life of Phillip's wife. And she lived a long life." Witch's expression turned sour. "I hid myself in the caves of Violet, and I aged."

"And then what?"

"When I was sixty-seven years old, that miserable woman finally died," said Witch. "I was free to explore my power. I had had a great deal of time to plan. I went to Crimson, which was being reclaimed by the Pink Empire. The entire Crimson Realm was in chaos — armies were slaughtered, children were orphaned. Some of those children were injured and sick. I opened a home for those who were mortally afflicted, and I cared for them as they died."

Rapunzel was aghast. "You used dying children to get power?"

"Yes. Would you rather I had eaten them?"

"No, but —"

"But? These children were orphans of war, starving and thirsty and suffering. I gave them peace. They died in comfort, in security. None of them was the worse for helping me."

"Is that where you got Amelia? You rescued her from soldiers."

Witch rubbed her head. "The Woodmother was generous with details," she said. "Yes, Amelia lived in the sick house with the other children. Unlike the others, she made a full recovery. She shouldn't have. She was close to death. But I nursed her with . . . particular care, perhaps. When she returned to health, I asked her if she wanted to come to live with me in a tower, high up and far away from everything terrible, and have every lovely thing that she could think of. She said yes. So I built a tower for her, and we went to it."

"What happened then?"

"You already know."

"Describe it. Tell me everything you remember."

Witch closed her eyes with a pained look, as though she had a strong headache. And then she spoke about the two years she had spent with Amelia in another tower, in the Violet Peaks, caring for her and trying to cultivate what remained of her innocence.

"It was during this time that I learned how powerful I might become with a child who truly belonged to me. Amelia was grateful to me for saving me, and she loved the way I spoiled her. But her first love was for the parents she remembered. She was never fully mine.

"Still, with her as my constant companion, I was strengthened. Even though she was not a pure innocent by any means, as she attached herself to me, I became more powerful than I had yet been. How much stronger I would be, I realized, if I could only convince her to forget the evils she had experienced. Then she would be not only innocent, but able to bond with me fully — she would remember no one else — and she would no longer feel trapped. I knew then that I had found the perfect method, not only for sustaining my power but for discovering its deepest potential."

"Did you like Amelia?" Rapunzel asked grimly. "As a person?"

"Yes."

"Why?"

"She had spirit. She had the intelligence of a child of the streets, yet a gentleness, even after all she had seen and suffered."

"But you were willing to get rid of her mind to make yourself more powerful."

"I thought Amelia would want to forget," said Witch. "She had terrible memories. Monstrous things had happened in her life, atrocities that you cannot imagine. It seemed a solution that allowed us both to thrive. But I was wrong."

"She died rather than give her memories to you."

"She didn't mean to die."

"And were you sorry? Do you still think of her?"

"Yes." Witch leaned back in the rocking chair. She closed her eyes and yawned, again revealing her rotten teeth. A few were now missing. "I'm tired," she said.

"Stay awake," said Rapunzel, who herself was weary. But there was no time for sleep now. They could sleep after Witch had erased her memories. She planted herself in front of Witch and spoke loudly. "How many other children were there?"

"What do you mean?"

"There was Justice, and then Amelia. After Amelia, how many more children did you put in towers?"

"Just you."

"You're lying."

"I cannot lie. After Amelia, there was only one tower."

"What did you do with all those years between her and me?"

"I moved from place to place, opening homes for children of war. Until recently, there was no shortage of war in Tyme. But the innocence I gained from them was impure. Those children had seen too much violence and felt too much grief and pain to be of significant use to me from a magical perspective."

"So what did you do? How did you get me?"

"Don't you know the tale?"

"You tell it."

Witch did so as she rocked. "Your mother was pregnant with you," she said. "Very pregnant, and not in good condition — she could barely sit up. Your parents had just moved down to Yellow Country from Green. It was a long journey that a woman in late pregnancy should never have undertaken. She arrived weak and feverish and could not leave her bed — which made my part easy. Your father felt responsible for your mother's discomfort. I knew he would want to satisfy her every wish. I waited until I heard her say that she craved rampion, and then I moved that plant up onto the little hill at the back of my garden, where your father would see it over the top of the fence."

"And then he stole it."

Witch nodded. "When I caught him, I offered him a choice. He could die, or he could give you to me."

Rapunzel knew what her father had chosen. "And he didn't tell my mother?"

"No." Witch opened her eyes. "Remoulade was a coward. I knew it the moment I met him. The perfect tenant for my bait house."

"Bait house?"

"After Amelia, I built houses in several places and rented them only to couples who were pregnant. I kept the rent low to attract them. And then I tempted them with whatever I thought might cause them to steal from me, to get them into a bargain."

"To get an infant?"

"To get an infant. It could not be a kidnapping — I had made that mistake. It would have to be a solid bargain. It took great patience, but in the end, it paid off. I got you."

"And what happens when I die?"

"I will get another infant."

"Do you have bait houses right now, in case I die or run away?"

"Yes."

"Is anybody living in them?"

"Yes."

"Pregnant women?" Rapunzel asked shrilly. "Mothers with children inside them? Didn't my mother scream when you took me away from her?"

"Yes."

"Didn't you feel sorry?"

"No."

"Why? How could you do it? She looked so happy in the picture where I was inside her — she wanted me, Witch. Why didn't you let her keep me?"

"I needed you. And Natalie was a fool — you were better off with me."

"But my mother would have let me run outside, and learn to swim, and read real books, and have a pet frog, and meet new people, and so many other things that you've never let me do."

Witch closed her eyes again. She rocked in the chair.

"She was going to name me Charlotte," said Rapunzel. "Did you know that?"

Witch snorted. "No."

"Your mother named you Envearia?"

"Yes."

"Why did she name you that?"

"Because it was her name."

"Why didn't you tell me to call you Envearia?"

"I never liked my mother's name," said Witch. "I didn't care to hear it anymore."

"Then why not have me call you Mother? Why tell me to call you Witch?"

"Because that is what I am."

Rapunzel stopped. Every answer Witch gave her led to more questions she had not known existed. She studied Witch, who now looked dangerously frail in her chair by the dying blue fire. The light made shadows in her gash-like wrinkles and illuminated the deep circles beneath her sunken eyes and cheeks. Bits of hair drifted from her head like white feathers.

The bargain was killing her.

Rapunzel looked into the fire. It was one thing to know that Witch *ought* to die, to feel that it was only fair to kill her. Taking memories, Rapunzel thought, was a kind of killing too. But to bring death down on Witch deliberately . . .

She glanced back at Witch's ruined face again, then closed her eyes and tried to call to mind the Witch she remembered, the Witch she had left behind, whom she had so completely trusted, and who had betrayed her. She pictured their last night together in this tower, the night before her birthday. Witch's face swam into view in Rapunzel's memory. Her hazel eyes sparkled, her hair fell in lovely dark waves, her cheeks glowed as she told Rapunzel what a wonderful present she was going to give her — not a toy, she had said, and ever so much better than a snack. . . .

"You were going to give me something wonderful for my birthday," Rapunzel said abruptly. "You said it was more wonderful than I could guess. What was it?"

Witch stopped rocking and gazed up at her. "The Redlands," she said.

Rapunzel's mouth dropped open. "The Redlands? The whole Redlands?"

"That's right."

"I don't understand. How?"

"I planned to seize the Fortress of Bole." Witch closed one bony fist as though crushing something within it. "What you don't realize, Rapunzel, is that until you ran away, I was the most powerful witch who ever lived. No witch in history has ever had a source of innocence like you, constant and perfect. You allowed my power to grow unmitigated. Chieftain Fleet has done everything he can to fortify his position, but it would not have been enough to keep me from getting through. I was unstoppable."

"Then why hadn't you already seized the fortress?"

"Glyph."

"So you poisoned her with your roses," said Rapunzel, remembering how they had cracked through the very sky of the fairy glade, darkening that world.

"She had to be dealt with, and so did her clan. Even *I* could not easily wipe out an entire race of fairies. I have been working to crush the Red Glade for over a decade."

"Is that what you were doing whenever you weren't with me?"

"Mostly."

"And then Glyph came here to ask for my help, but she broke her wing. Why didn't she come before? If you were hurting them for so long, why didn't she visit me earlier?"

"For a long time, the Red fairies did not know what I was doing. When they discovered it, they thought that they could fight me without assistance. By the time they realized they were wrong, their magic had been all but strangled, while, thanks to you, my powers had grown to unprecedented heights. I buried their glade, and there was nothing they could do."

"Why didn't they move somewhere else?"

"They abide near the Fortress of Bole. They have a duty to guard it."

It made sense now that Rune had been desperate to protect his mate, and his clan, and their home. Rapunzel understood why the fairies hated her.

"Glyph fought me until her own powers were nearly decimated," Witch continued. "She came to this tower out of desperation and threw herself away in the attempt, clearing the road for me at last. I was ready to take the fortress that night. But before I could begin, you climbed down from the tower, and with your departure, my power ebbed. Not completely, but enough. I was forced to wait."

"Then Glyph didn't throw herself away," Rapunzel said. "Her plan worked. I left the tower. I found the Woodmother, and she showed me the truth about you. Everyone else tried to tell me — they tried and tried, but I wouldn't listen. Glyph knew I wouldn't. She knew I had to see it for myself, so she made me go with Jack to the First Wood, and I'm glad she did."

Witch did not comment.

"Are the Red fairies powerful again, now that you're weak?"

"No," said Witch. "It will be a long time before they fully recover."

"So once you've taken my memories, you'll attack them again?"

"I did not toil for so long to be defeated on the doorstep of success."

Rapunzel wished that she had thought to include something about the safety of the Red fairies in her bargain, but it was too late. The Redlands would be seized. The Red fairies would be defeated. Glyph would probably be killed. And it was Rapunzel's fault, for coming back to the tower.

She put her head in her hands.

She was a fool.

"Why do you even *want* the Redlands?" she asked, her voice muffled. "Is it really a gift for me? Am I going to be allowed to run around outside?"

"No."

"So it's for you. What are you going to do with it?"

"I want the ground on which the Fortress of Bole is built."

"Why?"

"I cannot fully explain. There is some power hidden beneath the castle there. I don't pretend to understand it yet, but I will discover what it is, and I will use it."

"But Witch" — Rapunzel lifted her head, bewildered — "why?"

"Why what?"

"Why do you want power at all? What do you do with it?"

"I keep myself alive," said Witch. "Beyond that, I do whatever I wish. Power is power. Without power, others make your choices for you. *With* power, your life is your own. I will not suffer myself to be controlled by anyone. Never again."

Rapunzel thought of the disturbing way Witch had sat up when her mother had told her to. Like she'd been pulled by strings. Her life hadn't been her own then — and it wasn't now either. Not really.

"You're still controlled," Rapunzel said. "The White Fairy gets you when you die."

Witch shrank back. "Then I will not die," she said, but her eyes darted toward the ceiling.

"What if I went to Geguul and White-hatched?" Rapunzel asked. "I bet I could get out of this bargain if I did. I bet the White Fairy could help me. How do I get there?"

Witch looked petrified. "Rapunzel, listen to me." She reached out and gripped Rapunzel's wrist. "Don't go to Geguul. *I forbid it.*"

"You sound like your mother," said Rapunzel, and Witch snatched her hand away. Rapunzel rubbed her wrist where Witch's fingers had dug into it.

"I can tell you how to go to the White," Witch said, trembling. "But Rapunzel, if you trade your mortality to her, you cannot ever take it back."

"Do *you* want to take it back?"

Witch keened softly and leaned over her knees, hiding her face in her thin, wrinkled hands. Rapunzel crouched before her chair.

"Witch? If you could be mortal again, would you?"

Witch nodded.

"Are you afraid of Geguul?"

"Yes." The word was barely a whisper.

The sunlight in the tower was the rich orange of sunset. It fell in long, broad beams through the window and the balcony doors, lighting the fleecy carpets beneath Rapunzel's feet as she regarded Witch. For the first time since they had arrived at the tower, she felt compassion. Witch had White-hatched to punish Phillip, and now she was trapped. She didn't want to belong to Geguul. Just like Jack's giantess. Rapunzel wondered how many witches felt the same.

The wind rustled in the woods. It passed through the tower windows, lifted the curtains, and blew across the ceiling garden. No petals fell. Rapunzel looked up and realized that there were no roses left.

The fire had gone out too.

"Light," Rapunzel said, knowing that it wouldn't. The fireplace stayed dark. Witch's powers were so depleted that she could not even make a simple flame. "Is there any wood here?" she asked. "I know how to make a fire. It'll be dark soon; we should have one."

"No, there isn't any wood."

"There's paper, though, and there's my furniture."

"Rapunzel . . ."

Witch was too weak to stop her. Rapunzel took rolls of parchment from her little desk and ripped them up. She crinkled them into balls and stuffed them under the grate. Then she looked around for furniture she could break and decided that the desk chair was her best option. She held it sideways against the ground and stomped on one leg with her booted foot. When the chair was entirely in pieces, she brought her wood to the fireplace and dug into the pouch in her belt where she kept flint and tinder.

She lit the fire. As the sun went down, the flames caught hold of the broken bits of chair and a healthy fire roared up. The tower looked very different than Rapunzel had ever seen it; orange flames were cozier than blue ones. She stifled a yawn and sat down beside the fire, in front of Witch's chair. She propped up one knee and leaned an arm on it. It was then that she noticed Witch's expression.

"What is it?" she asked. "Why are you looking at me like that?"

"You have become very capable."

"I made a lot of fires on the journey," said Rapunzel. "I did a lot of things."

"Tell me."

Rapunzel shook her head. "I'm the one asking the questions."

Witch looked disappointed, but said nothing, and Rapunzel tried to decide whether the disappointment was real or whether Witch was only faking it to trick her. Then she remembered that she could ask anything and Witch would have to give an honest answer.

"Do you actually *care* what I did on the journey?" she asked. "Or do you just want to distract me from asking more questions?"

"Both," said Witch.

"You know everything already, don't you?" she demanded. "I thought you followed me."

"No. I met you at the end." Witch looked smaller now, and her cloak hung more loosely from her frame. "I could not risk following closely."

"Why not?"

"As long as you intended to return to me, you were still mine. And once you were out of the Red Glade, I could still do magic — I was significantly weakened, but not ruined. But I did not know what had passed in the Red Glade. I did not know how much the Red fairies had told you of your history, or how much you believed. If I had approached you and asked you to come home and you had said no, then I would have lost my power completely. I had to be certain that you would say yes."

"How did you know where I was going?"

"I learned your destination from a royal guard of Yellow Country."

"I won a jacks competition there," Rapunzel said, and she realized that she would never play in the championship match at the ATC. She wouldn't know she was supposed to go.

"So the guard told me," said Witch. "I always said that your skill at that game was great."

"I wish you could have been there."

"I wish so too."

"Do you really mean that?"

"Yes."

Rapunzel didn't understand why this meant so much to her. Everything Witch had done and planned to do should have made Rapunzel care nothing about her opinion. But she did care.

"Are you proud of me?" she asked.

"In many ways, yes."

"Then why don't you want me to stay as I am?"

"I need you innocent if I am to survive and regain my power quickly."

More of Witch's hair had fallen from her head. Her scalp was visible in the firelight, and it was covered in dark spots.

"On the journey," said Rapunzel, "Jack answered all my questions. He wanted me to know things. I'll miss him."

"You won't know to miss him."

Rapunzel shook her head. "I don't think that's true," she said. "I won't know him, I won't remember him, but I'll miss him. I just won't know what the feeling is, or why I'm feeling it."

"Perhaps that is the case."

They fell silent. Rapunzel wondered what else there was to ask, and her stomach gave a ravenous growl.

"I'm hungry," she said. She hadn't eaten in a long time. "And thirsty."

"I have nothing for us to eat or drink."

Rapunzel reached for her belt and grabbed her water skin. At least she had that much. She uncorked the skin and drank from it, then held it out to Witch.

Witch stared at her. "You are offering it to me?"

"Of course. Are you thirsty?"

Witch looked torn. "Yes," she said reluctantly.

"Have a drink, then."

"No."

Rapunzel looked down at the skin, bemused. "It's fine, it's clean. I washed it out the other day," she said, corking the skin and setting it down where Witch could reach it if she changed her mind. "Why don't you want to drink from it, if you're thirsty?"

Again, Witch looked as though she would rather not have answered. "I do not want to take from you," she said.

Rapunzel wondered why, when Witch was about to steal so much from her, she would hesitate to accept a little water. And then she knew in a flash what the answer was.

"It's a bad feeling, isn't it?" she asked, remembering how Jack had described guilt. "Heavy. And it sits right here. . . ." She rested a fist under her rib cage and closed the other hand over the back of her neck.

Witch had stopped rocking. "Yes."

"Then don't do it," said Rapunzel, looking up at her. "Don't hurt me, Witch. Please."

They looked steadily at each other through another long silence.

"Rapunzel, if you wish to tell me about your journey, then now is your chance," Witch said at last. "Or, if you still have questions, I will answer them."

Rapunzel had only one important question left. But she was not sure she could bear the honest answer.

"Have you ever been inside the Red Glade?" she asked Witch instead.

"No."

"Do you want to hear what it looks like?"

Witch was quiet for a moment. "Yes," she said.

Rapunzel described it. And then she described what it had been like to walk for days in slippers and a nightgown, carrying her hair. She told Witch of the Stalker and of climbing out of the river, of making a canopy with her hair in the rain, of Cornucopia and Governor Calabaza, and of the Blue fairy Serge. She told her of being robbed by bandits, Prince Frog's near death, the lifebreath, and Prince Mick and Nexus Keene and Princess Daigh. She told her of the Ubiquitous dogsled, and camping in the snow, and the beauty of the Woodmother.

She did not mention Purl or anything that had occurred at her house. And she told Witch nothing of Jack's home or his bargain with Geguul — Jack would not have wanted Witch to know his business.

She talked for hours about everything else. Sometimes she stood, to show Witch a thing she meant or to pace from one thing in the tower to another as she grew more excited by the telling. Witch's quiet attention was fixed on Rapunzel. She asked questions, but more often she only smiled, or looked frightened or angry at something Rapunzel would say.

The story was a long one, and Rapunzel was exhilarated and exhausted together when she had finished telling it. The world was dark, although the sky outside was bright with stars. Rapunzel went out onto the balcony to look at them.

"Come out here with me," she said. "I want to see the world before I forget it."

"I cannot go that far."

"I'll help you."

Rapunzel took a chair to the balcony. She helped Witch to stand and hobble into the night, and she settled her in the chair, covering her knees with a blanket. She sat on the stones beside her and rested her head on Witch's knee, looking up at the sky.

Witch's hand touched her hair. "You could kill me now, you realize." Her voice was paper-thin, and her breath rattled. "You could throw me from this tower."

Rapunzel shuddered. She knew that she should kill Witch, for the sake of the Redlands, if not for her own life. To push her from the tower would have been so easy — Witch was so light.

"No," she said. "I couldn't."

They were quiet together for a long time, perhaps even hours, until the darkness began to change. The stars were not so visible. Dawn was near.

"Was your mother always unkind to you?" asked Rapunzel,

gazing at the disappearing stars. "She was cruel when I saw her in the Woodmother."

"Is that your final question?" Witch's voice was unreadable.

"No. I have one more."

"Very well. Yes, my mother was always unkind. I don't know what you saw, but I imagine it was a fair sample of the rest."

"I saw the time when your heart was broken," said Rapunzel. "When Phillip sent you roses and you decided to go to Geguul. You wouldn't have gone if your mother had been kinder. Would you?"

"I don't know. Perhaps not."

"She should have sat with you like this. Comforted you."

"She was not that kind of mother."

"Did she love you?"

"No, I don't believe she ever did."

Rapunzel drew a deep breath and exhaled. The last question. Though she feared the answer, this was her only chance to ask.

"Do you love me?"

The wind blew softly across the balcony. The sky lightened. If the answer was no, she would not have to know it long.

"Yes," Witch said.

Rapunzel buried her face in Witch's cloak and stayed there, still and silent, her blood coursing with relief and fear. She heard the morning birds begin to sing, but she did not move.

"Dawn," said Witch in her rattling voice.

Rapunzel raised her head.

The end of the bargain had come. She wondered if she would ever leave the tower again. She supposed that she would not.

"Close your eyes," Witch said softly. "It will soon be over."

Rapunzel pulled away from Witch and looked up at her. She tried to be still, but her body was shaking, shivering, and it wouldn't stop.

"Don't do this," she whispered through chattering teeth. "Don't kill me."

"I'm not going to kill you."

"I'll be gone," said Rapunzel. "It's the same as being dead."

Witch gazed at her.

"Witch, if you love me . . . if you love me . . ."

"Close your eyes."

It was no use. Tears came to Rapunzel's eyes, and she looked through them at Witch, who swam in her vision, unrecognizable.

"Good-bye," she said, her voice quaking as she shook.

"It isn't good-bye," said Witch. "I'll be here with you still."

"But I won't — know you —" The awful shaking worsened. Rapunzel hugged herself to stop it, but it was beyond her control. "I won't — love you — anymore —"

Witch looked as though Rapunzel had struck her. She cringed, and her already shrunken form grew smaller yet.

"You will love me better," she said, "when you know me less."

"That's not — the way it is." Rapunzel shook her head. "You're not good — I know it — you've done terrible things, and you're going to do another." She reached out for Witch's hands and took them. "But I see you — and I love you. It means more now. It's real now. It wasn't real — before."

Witch's thin chest rose and fell rapidly.

"It is time," she said.

"Wait! Take these first —"

Rapunzel released Witch's hands and dug jittering fingers into the belt pouch where she kept her jacks. She laid them in Witch's lap. "To remember me by," she managed. "I won't remember — this Rapunzel. You will. Don't — forget me — when I'm gone. Please."

The sun rose over the mountains in the east. The Violet Peaks. Rapunzel thought of Jack and his sister, Tess, and how they would be safe. It was the best last thought she could give herself. Jack would be safe. Jack would finish his journey. She had failed in the rest of it, but at least she had done one good thing.

Witch raised her hands to either side of Rapunzel's head.

"Close your eyes," she rasped again.

Rapunzel closed her eyes.

Through her mind went a thousand memories at once. The first time she cracked a Ubiquitous acorn — the first time she felt the falling snow — the smell of the campfire — Prince Frog's clammy skin — Purl's hair — Glyph's wing — Jack's laugh —

Witch's fingertips touched her temples.

Chapter Twenty-Two

IT was like being underwater in the river again, only this time, she would never surface. Rapunzel kept her mind fixed on Jack. As long as she could remember him, it had not happened yet. In a moment, she would not remember. In a moment . . . any moment . . .

Rapunzel's shaking redoubled, and a low sound escaped her lips. Why was Witch waiting? It was agony to know that it was coming. . . .

Something warm and papery pressed Rapunzel's forehead. Then it ended. Rapunzel dimly realized that it had been a kiss. She heard Witch's rattling voice.

"I release you."

Witch's fingertips slipped from her temples. Rapunzel opened her eyes. Witch had fallen back in the chair. Pale dawn light touched the crags of her shriveled face and lit the sparse white tufts of hair that remained on her head. Her eyes were closed, and her hands lay curled in her lap.

"Witch?" Rapunzel said uncertainly.

"Go" was all she said.

"Go?" Rapunzel repeated. In the pink light of dawn, everything seemed to be moving. Spinning. "Go? You're letting me . . ."

Witch's eyes fluttered open. They shone in the light.

"Do not forget me," she managed, and then her eyes fell shut again, and she drew a shallow, rasping breath.

"Oh, *Witch* —"

With a cry of joy, Rapunzel flung herself at Witch and held her tight, half speaking, half sobbing. "Witch — Witch, I knew — I told them —"

"You must go." Witch's hand touched her hair, then fell away.

"No, I won't leave you!" said Rapunzel, wiping her eyes on Witch's shoulder. "I'll stay with you — I'll stay because I want to stay. I don't want you to die. I don't want you to go to Geguul. I won't let you."

"Your ring," Witch said weakly. "Your clothes. They hurt me."

Rapunzel drew back — she had forgotten how cloaked she was in fairy magic. She untangled her arms from Witch and stood up.

"I must eat something," said Witch. She winced and appeared to age yet another degree; her eyes were bleary now. "In the woods, just west of here, blueberries grow wild. Will you go and pick some for me?"

"No, I can't. I'm afraid you'll die."

One corner of Witch's sunken mouth twitched. "I will not die," she said. "That I can promise. But you must hurry. . . . I am hungry. Please, Rapunzel. If you love me."

Rapunzel hesitated. "Can I at least give you water before I go?"

"Water," Witch said. "Yes."

She ran into the tower for her water skin. Her trembling fingers slipped as she uncorked it, and she nearly dropped the cork. She could scarcely focus. Witch loved her, and her memories still belonged to her — Jack was safe, and so was the Redlands. Relief made her dizzy. She returned to the balcony, and though the sight of Witch's patchy, spotted scalp disturbed her, she kissed it gently before bringing the water to Witch's lips. Witch took the pouch from her hand and drank.

"Do I really have to leave you?" asked Rapunzel, distressed. "Are you sure you'll be all right? You look so frail —"

"Find me food," Witch wheezed, "quickly."

Rapunzel glanced through the open balcony door and across the tower room, toward her window wheel. It was empty.

"I'll have to cut my hair to climb down," she said. "Won't I?"

"Yes." Witch slipped a hand into the pocket of her cloak and withdrew Rapunzel's dagger. Rapunzel took it and pulled her braid over her shoulder. She held the hair out in front of her chest and braced herself. She had faced worse than this. Far worse. But she felt a stab of regret as she raised the knife.

"A little longer, please," Witch said hoarsely. "Your beautiful hair . . ."

Rapunzel took a few feet of it into her hand and then laid what would soon be the end on the balcony railing. She placed the dagger's blade to the golden cord.

One — two — three — she sawed through it. She looked down at the shorn, blunt end of the rope she had created.

"That's it, then," she murmured to herself. She sheathed the dagger and reached out to touch Witch's face with gentle fingertips. "I'll wind it on the wheel," she said. "Don't move — just rest. Get better."

Rapunzel went to her window wheel. With fingers that still shook, but now for very different reasons, she wound her severed braid several times around the wheel, tucking it in as she went to be sure it was secure. She tossed the rest through the window and looked down. She would have to jump about ten feet at the bottom, but that was all right.

"Witch, I'm going," she called out, and was startled when she felt a touch at the back of her shoulder. She spun to find Witch standing there, more aged and fragile than ever, yet somehow erect.

"I want to make sure that the braid remains secure," Witch said in a voice that was thin and cracked. "I will be here watching as you descend."

Rapunzel didn't argue. As she had seen Witch do thousands of times, she straddled the window, took the braid in her hands, swung her other leg through, and braced herself on the tower wall.

She hung there for a moment, looking up at Witch. It had always been her standing in the window and Witch climbing down. It was strange and wonderful to see things from this angle.

"I'll be right back," Rapunzel said. "I love you, Witch."

Witch's eyes glistened.

Rapunzel climbed down. It was so easy. She shook her head as she descended and felt the near weightlessness of her remaining hair. Her braid came loose at the back of her neck — it had unplaited itself with nothing to tie it off. Wind caught at the strands, and Rapunzel laughed when she saw a golden wisp float up beside her.

When she came to the end of her braid, she jumped. She landed badly and stumbled to the ground in a heap, breathing hard.

She looked up at the window. She could no longer see Witch clearly, but the tail of her severed braid was being hauled up the side of the tower. She would have to call out for it when she returned, just as Witch had always done.

Rapunzel waved at the window as the tail of her braid vanished through it. "I'm all right!" she shouted. "See you in a minute!"

And then she turned and ran — ran like she had never before

run — westward across the beautiful red ground on which the tower stood and headlong into the Redwoods.

She had never felt such freedom. No braid, no wheel, no wagon . . . She ran and jumped over stones and streams — she laughed, and tears coursed down her face. When she tripped and fell, she dropped down among the wild blueberry bushes and onto the beautiful dirt. She rolled over and looked up at the distant treetops, her lungs burning, her legs buzzing, her heart as light as her hair — lighter, even. She thought it would rise straight out of her and fly.

"Rapunzel!"

She gasped with joy and scrambled to her feet.

"Jack!"

She raced toward him. He was running too, leaping over things, looking safe and sound except for the bandage wrapped around his head.

They met in a crash and hugged tightly, panting. Neither seemed willing to let go. Rapunzel pulled back at last to look at him, but held on to his hands.

"Tess," she said immediately. "Did you get to see Glyph? Did she give you what the giantess wants?"

But Jack only stared at her.

"Rapunzel," he said. He looked stupefied. "Your *hair*."

She looked down to see waves of it winding around her waist, brushing the tops of her legs, getting caught on all the pouches of her belt and in the fastening of her cloak. She pulled her hands from Jack's, gathered her hair at the nape of her neck, and swung it back behind herself. It was like nothing. She grinned.

"You were right," she said. "I should have cut it off. When are you going to the Peaks to save Tess?"

Jack gave a dazed laugh. "Now sounds good," he said.

"And where's Prince Frog?"

"He's safe, he's fine — we'll go and get him."

"What about your head?" she asked. "Who bandaged it?"

"Rune," said Jack, and he jabbed a thumb over his shoulder. "He's coming. We were all coming to . . . uh. Save you, I guess." He laughed again. "Guess you were right too. You climbed down just fine." His expression grew serious. "But Rapunzel, how did you get free? The witch — did you kill her?"

"She's alive," said Rapunzel. "She let me go."

"Let you *go?*"

"Yes, and I need to go back. She's hungry, and I —"

"Go *back?*" Jack said in dismay. "Rapunzel, that witch almost killed me."

"I know."

"And you want to go back." He looked furious. "There's nothing that'll teach you, is there?"

"Jack." Rapunzel put a hand on his shoulder. "It's finished. She's alive, but it's finished."

"She tricked you."

"Not this time, I promise. If you'd been there, you'd know."

"Why? What happened?"

"It's a long story," said Rapunzel, who wasn't sure she ever wanted to tell it. Not even to him. "I'm asking you to believe me. Can you do that? Witch is so weak, Jack. If I don't take care of her, I'm afraid she'll die and go to Geguul, and I don't want her to go there."

Jack seemed to be debating his reply when the woods were

suddenly full of shimmering red trails of light and the noise of many wings.

"Where is Envearia?"

The voice was Rune's. He flew straight to Rapunzel, while the many fairies who were with him hung back, hovering among the trees.

"She's alive," said Jack. "She let Rapunzel go."

"Is this true, prisoner child?" Rune's voice was desperate with hope.

"My name is Rapunzel."

"Then answer me now, Rapunzel — *Did she set you free?*"

"Yes."

Rune exhaled. "Thank the clay beneath us," he murmured. "We can finish it." He turned in the air and addressed the other fairies. "Go! Now, while she is weak! Kill her!"

"NO!" Rapunzel shouted, and she turned back toward the tower. "WITCH! THE FAIRIES ARE COMING! WITCH, CLIMB DOWN! GET OUT!"

But though she had not run for long, the tower was too far away for Witch to hear her, and the fairies were already gone, speeding toward the tower, leaving nothing behind them but trails of angry red light. Rapunzel took off running after them. "Witch!" she shouted. "Witch!"

Jack called her name, but she could not wait for him. Rune flew rapidly alongside her. She ran faster until she came to the trees at the edge of the forest. In a flash, Rune stood before Rapunzel, human-size. She slammed into him, and he seized her and pinned her arms to her sides. She fought, kicking to get free.

"LET ME GO!"

"I cannot."

"You don't understand! She won't hurt you — you're safe, I swear —"

"We will be safe when she is dead."

Rapunzel tried to bite him, but Rune got one of his arms around her neck.

"You do not understand what is at stake."

"Yes I do, and she won't hurt the Redlands anymore. Please don't kill her!"

Rune's grip tightened. "It will be over soon," he said.

"Please —"

A white light, brighter than the sun, burst through the morning sky above the tower. Rapunzel winced, and Rune threw up his hands to shield himself, letting her go. Though she could barely see the ground in front of her, she ran toward her tower, its stones glaring beneath the terrible white light.

"WITCH!"

"Do not go to her, Rapunzel!" Rune caught her again and dragged her back. "It is the White — it is Geguul."

"But I can't let the White Fairy take Witch away! She's so frightened —"

"Envearia knew what she bargained for," said Rune. "And she knew what it meant to let you go. Once she surrendered you, she knew very well that she would age beyond human limits. Severing her bond with you has drained her of all remaining power and brought her quickly to the point of death. But witches cannot die. They can only be collected by the White."

I will not die. That I can promise you. Rapunzel realized that Witch had tricked her one last time. She had made Rapunzel leave the tower so she could be collected. Rapunzel still fought Rune, squinting against the light.

In the center of the clearing, the tower glowed like white fire. At the top, from the circling balcony, something was rising into the air — something dark and cloaked and limp, rising toward the hole of white light that broke the sky.

"Witch," Rapunzel whispered, her hands jerking toward the light as though there were something she could do to pull Witch down, to make it stop.

Thunder cracked. The ground shook beneath Rapunzel's feet. Dark lightning erupted from the ground at the center of the clearing, shattering the tower like glass and striking Witch's limp body where it had almost disappeared into the light.

The white light vanished with a piercing howl, and the sky closed behind it. The tower crumbled in a cloud of smoke. Witch's body fell like a stone into the rubble.

"NO!" Rapunzel screamed, and she tore herself free from Rune. She ran toward the wreckage, where Witch lay askew atop a heap of jagged and broken stones. Rapunzel struggled to climb up the heap, but it was high and treacherous, and it shifted where she stepped. Among the broken stones, she saw fragments of her old mirror. The glint of her silver bell. The torn sleeve of an old gown. Everything smashed and gone. Everything.

Witch. ·

"Envearia is dead." Rune's voice was dazed behind her. Uncertain. "Dead," he repeated. "Like any human. The White did not take her — her remains are here in Tyme. So she has passed into the Beyond, but how?"

The Red fairies gathered around Rune's shoulders in a mass of small, shimmering wings.

"A witch has passed into the Beyond," said one.

"It is unprecedented," said another.

"It is finished!" cried a third. "She is gone!" The fairies burst into a frenzy of triumphant cheers.

"But what happened?" said Jack. "What was that black lightning?"

Rune shook his head. "Envearia is not in Geguul," he said. "That is all I can tell you. Perhaps Eldest Glyph can explain it. . . . Perhaps no one can."

Rapunzel crumpled against the heap of rubble that had once been her tower, and she wept there, not caring that the rocks cut into her, not caring that the fairies were jubilant. Witch was gone. She was not in Geguul with the White Fairy, but that was cold comfort. She was dead and gone forever, in the Beyond, where Rapunzel could not reach her.

Chapter Twenty-Three

*R*APUNZEL looked into the mirror.

It was a large mirror, framed in wood that had been intricately carved to look like flowers, leaves, and branches. It reflected a low-ceilinged room that was furnished with more carved wooden fixtures. The bed frame appeared to be made of twisting roots; the bureau looked as though it were covered all over in tree bark. Everything Rapunzel had seen so far in the Fortress of Bole gave her the impression that many hands had built the place, and with much care.

"You poor dear thing," said Nan for the hundredth time, tucking a wisp of hair into the braided crown she had fashioned on Rapunzel's head. She was an aged woman, but stout and healthy, with skin that was faintly lavender in color. "Up there in that tower for so long, with no one to help you. What a brave girl you are."

Rapunzel studied herself to keep her mind off the woman's words. She hadn't looked in a mirror for so long that it hadn't occurred to her how much the journey might have changed her. She was thinner now. Browner. Freckles stood out on her nose and cheeks. And of course, there was her hair.

But her eyes had changed the most. They went deeper, when Rapunzel looked into them. They knew things.

"When I think of what that witch did to our poor warriors," Nan said, "killed them where they stood with a stroke of her magic, and left Chieftain Fleet there in the wreckage. Heartless beast. She deserved a worse death, if you ask me."

Rapunzel flinched.

Nan unpinned a golden curl. It fell over Rapunzel's shoulder and touched the waist of her red gown. Nan had found the gown for her, for the feast that Chieftain Fleet was giving tonight in her honor. It used to be his mother's, Nan had said, and she had taken down the hem to make it long enough. She had been very kind.

She didn't know how much it hurt Rapunzel to hear her rejoice in Witch's death. And she had good reasons to rejoice, so Rapunzel stayed quiet and let her. She alone grieved Witch, so she would have to do it within herself.

A ceramic vase stood at one side of the mirror. Out of it bloomed a rose, red and perfect. Rapunzel reached out a fingertip and gently touched the edge of one velvet petal.

"I do grow a nice garden," said Nan. "Fleet always likes my roses."

"I like roses too."

"Then I'll pin it in your hair," said Nan, and she clipped the rose short and tucked it into the back of the braided crown on Rapunzel's head. "There now!" she said. "Stand up and let me see."

Rapunzel stood.

"Aren't you a picture!" said Nan, and she gathered up her workbag. She paused in the doorway and gave Rapunzel a look of mingled pity and gratitude. "Brave girl," she said again.

She left the room, and Rapunzel sank onto the bed in silence, trying to brace herself for the evening ahead. Rune had delivered her and Jack to the Fortress last night, and she had stayed alone in this room ever since, too exhausted in body and heart to want even Jack's company. In a moment, she would be downstairs among many people who wanted to celebrate that Witch was dead, and, worse, who wanted to give her the credit for it. When the door opened, Rapunzel thought about telling whoever it was that she wasn't ready to go down yet. But when she saw her visitor, she was too surprised to protest.

"Glyph!"

Glyph smiled. She was human-size, and she walked with a limp toward Rapunzel. Her face was a brighter, healthier-looking red than it had been the last time Rapunzel had seen her, and she looked beautiful in her pale blue shift, with her good wing shining behind her. The broken wing was gone.

"Where is your wing?" Rapunzel asked, afraid of the answer.

Glyph's one wing fluttered gently. "I will not fly," she said, "but I will live. The Redlands is safe, Rapunzel, so do not grieve my wing. I gave it willingly and would have given more."

"I'm sorry." Rapunzel wished there were something more useful to say.

Glyph smiled at her. "I wished to see you and thank you privately."

"Don't thank me," said Rapunzel. "Please don't. Everyone's thanking me, but I wish they wouldn't. I didn't kill Witch."

"No. You did something more."

"What, finding the Woodmother?"

"You passed the Woodmother's gift to Envearia," said Glyph. "You taught her to see the past and present clearly. It is a deed no one, not even myself, thought possible — and it saved Envearia's life."

"But I didn't save her life," said Rapunzel. "She's dead. I saw her bones."

It had been so strange. The sand-colored, dry, brittle objects had been all that was left of Witch. Rapunzel had wrapped them in her severed hair and buried them where the tower once stood.

"Her mortal life," said Glyph. "The White was unable to claim her for Geguul."

"What is the White?"

Glyph sat beside her on the bed. "Have you never heard the story of the Shattering, or, as scholars call it, the Dissolution?"

"No."

"It is the story of how all of us were born. There were fourteen Great Fairies, each one a keeper of life. They agreed to shatter, becoming the fairies, the beasts, the trees, the very countries of Tyme."

"Fourteen Great Fairies — but there are only thirteen countries, aren't there?"

"The Black has no country. The Black shattered first and became humanity, giving shape to Tyme and bringing the spark of mortality to all its lands."

Rapunzel thought of the black lightning that had struck Witch's body, sending the White light howling back.

"The others shattered afterward, one by one," said Glyph. "First the Great Red Fairy, then all the rest. Even Violet, in the end. Only the White refused to shatter. She is still All, and she sits in Geguul alone."

"Is that why she makes giants? To keep her company?"

"In part, perhaps."

"Does she ever come down from the sky?"

"She cannot. Those who wish for a piece of the White Fairy's power, or who are lured by the promise of immortality, must travel to Geguul and make the terrible bargain that Envearia did."

"Immortality — living forever?"

"Yes."

"Then Witch could have lived forever?"

"She gave up her power when she set you free. Without that power, she could not survive — she should have been long dead. That is why all you found of her were bones."

Rapunzel was quiet as she processed these ideas.

"Do fairies live forever, then?" she asked.

"Yes and no," said Glyph. "We fade, but we return. And we live long lives, many of us, before we fade. I am nearly five hundred years old."

Rapunzel's eyebrows went up. Five hundred. It made Witch sound suddenly young.

"Why," she asked, "did the Black want to become mortality? Why make humans who die if you can make fairies? What's the point?"

Glyph smiled a little. "You have joined the great search," she said.

"For what?"

"The answer."

Rapunzel didn't know what to say to this, so she looked down at her hands. On her finger, the Woodmother's bronze ring flowed endlessly. She rubbed it with her thumb.

"Do you know what that is?" asked Glyph. "Did the Woodmother tell you?"

"What, the ring?" Rapunzel looked up at her. "It's a ring."

"It marks you as a daughter of the First Wood," said Glyph. "A sister to the very trees of Tyme themselves."

Rapunzel was flummoxed. "Sister to the trees?" she repeated. "I don't understand."

"Every fairywood in Tyme has been opened to you," said Glyph. "And to those who travel with you."

"What? Really?" She looked at the ring in awe. "I can travel fairy-woods?" she asked. "I can go wherever I want — as fast as I want?"

"As fast as the trees can take you," said Glyph. "You will have to learn where all the fairywoods begin and how to find them. The trees will teach you."

"Then I can take Jack back to Dearth, instead of Rune doing it?"

"Rune will accompany you this once to show you the way so that no time is lost."

"Oh," said Rapunzel, who still found Rune's company unpleasant. But Jack could not afford to be late, or Tess was the one who would suffer. "Did you give Jack what the giantess asked for?" she asked.

"I cannot make her mortal," said Glyph with a shake of her head. "No one has the power to interfere in Geguul. But I gave Jack a gift that I believe will satisfy her — a magic mirror. It will allow her to glimpse Tyme again while she waits to be free."

"Free?" asked Rapunzel. "I thought the giants had to stay in Geguul forever."

"Nothing stays the same forever," said Glyph quietly. "Not even Geguul."

Rapunzel was relieved. The suffering of the giants had bothered her from the moment she had heard about it. Even if they had done terrible things, it was wrong to torment them forever. Forever was too long. Some witches were sorry. Some witches deserved to be set free.

She curbed these thoughts at once when she felt tears beginning to threaten. If she started to cry, she thought she might not stop for a long time, and she wanted to be alone to cry like that. She wished she could hide in her tower just for that purpose.

"I have one more question," she said instead.

"Ask."

"Witch said there was some kind of power under this castle. What is it?"

Glyph considered her for a long moment. "You are one of very few who have ever known even that much," she said. "Most fairies do not know, and I myself understand it little. It would be a great favor to the Redlands if you never spoke of this again to anyone. Not even Jack."

"Oh," said Rapunzel, startled. "Well — all right."

"Now, steady yourself for the night ahead. Tomorrow morning, you will leave with Jack and Rune. And one day, I hope that you will return to the Red Glade." Glyph touched her fingertips to the center of her chest and bowed her head. "Under happier circumstances."

✦ ✦ ✦

Downstairs, in the great dining hall of the Castle of Bole, Rapunzel was welcomed with joy so intense that it unnerved her. She wanted to sit with Jack, but she was beckoned to sit several seats away from him instead, beside Chieftain Fleet himself, who looked barely older than she. He had brown skin and long dark hair, and he wore a robe that draped over his wheelchair all the way to the ground. It was like a quilt, only all the squares were covered with embroidered designs that seemed to tell stories. The chieftain was kind, and solemn, and seemed to understand better than the others that Rapunzel did not want to celebrate. Perhaps that was because he had felt grief too; after all, he had survived the carriage accident that had crushed his legs and killed his parents.

Witch had done that awful thing. Yet Rapunzel missed her. She wondered if she would ever understand why.

The feast commenced. Rapunzel ate more than she had expected to be able to, and her appetite made her feel guilty. She should not have been hungry, with Witch gone. She should not have wanted seconds on dessert.

When she had pushed back her plate, she turned to Chieftain Fleet.

"Thank you for trying to get me to come down from the tower," she said under the din of everyone else's conversations. "I'm so sorry for everything Witch did — to your warriors and your parents and your legs."

The chieftain said nothing for a moment. His dark eyes seemed to empty. When he spoke, his voice was careful.

"There's nothing for you to be sorry for," he said. "Now, tell me all about the perils you escaped on your journey. I heard you met with a Stalker — is it true?"

Rapunzel worried that she had upset him, but if the chieftain was pained, he did not show it. He seemed to delight in listening to her, becoming livelier with each tale she told. Eventually he sat back in his wheelchair, wearing an expression of deep satisfaction, and he raised his goblet high into the air.

"A toast," Chieftain Fleet called out, and the great hall went quiet as the goblets went up. "To Rapunzel, who has come through many perils, and to Jack, brave and true. May they live long, and may their adventures guide them often back to us. We will welcome them always."

This was met with warm approval, especially from Prince Frog, who croaked avidly from his perch on Jack's shoulder. When everyone had drunk, the feast dispersed and the diners left their places to mingle in groups all over the dining hall and its adjoining rooms. Many of them kept their eyes on Rapunzel, and she heard her name float up from their circles.

"Let them speak with you," said the chieftain. "They want to honor you."

She didn't want any honor, but that didn't matter. She was pulled from her seat by earnest guests who wanted to thank her, kiss her hands, cry on her neck, touch her hair, and tell her of the grief that Witch had caused them. Many of them had sons and daughters who had been among the warriors slain by Witch, and they were fierce in their gratitude. All of them believed Rapunzel responsible for bravely ending the life of the witch who had so grieved them. None of them saw the pain they caused her.

After enduring several of these upsetting conversations, Rapunzel attempted to slip out of the crowd, but was stopped by a small, plump woman who called herself a scribe and said she wrote for the *Town Criers*. She had a kind, persuasive voice, and she rapidly asked a series of questions that Rapunzel barely knew how to answer.

When she had escaped the scribe, she hurried into another room to look for Jack. Instead, she saw a tall, pale man in a dark leather coat, with silver threads of hair at his temples and a lustrous amulet resting against his chest.

Nexus Keene. Prince Mick had called him a witch slayer, and he himself had spoken of planning to kill Witch. Rapunzel didn't want to talk to him, but he had already seen her.

"Rapunzel," Nexus Keene said warmly, and the people he had been speaking with bowed low at his departure as he came forward to meet her. "How is your frog?"

The question gratified Rapunzel, but not quite enough.

"Prince Frog is fine," she said. "How did you get to the Redlands so fast? You were near Independence just a few days ago."

"Being among the Exalted has its benefits," said Nexus Keene, smiling. His eyes were kind, but there was something active in them. He watched her for a moment.

"What is it?" asked Rapunzel. "Do you want your book back? The one about witches?"

"No. I have a question," the Nexus admitted. "But I hesitate to ask it. You've been through an ordeal, and your grief must be overwhelming. Perhaps most people cannot imagine Envearia as a loving mother with a human heart. But I can."

His words took Rapunzel by such surprise that tears sprang into her eyes. She looked away from him, not wishing to cry. She was not ready.

The Nexus's voice was gentle. "I have slain many witches, and I know how they begin. Desperate. Panicked into evil. When I met you at the camp in Commonwealth Green, I saw that you were thriving — intelligent, healthy, and full of feeling. Envearia could not be wholly wicked and raise such a daughter."

Rapunzel looked at him, grateful.

"What did you want to ask me?" she said.

"How did Envearia escape her bargain with Geguul?"

"Why do you want to know that?"

"Because perhaps I can help other witches do the same." Nexus Keene pushed a gloved hand through his hair, and Rapunzel saw that his forehead was deeply lined. "Duty compels me to kill witches; they cannot be allowed to prey on children. But I don't want to give them to the White. I hope to find another way."

"I don't know how she escaped," said Rapunzel honestly. "Glyph said I saved Witch's life."

"How?"

"By teaching her to see the past and present clearly. I don't really know what that means."

Nexus Keene nodded. He appeared to be deep in thought. "I thank you," he said after a moment. "Should you ever think of anything else, I would be happy to hear from you, Rapunzel."

He bowed to her, and Rapunzel returned the gesture, hoping she was doing it right. Nexus Keene withdrew, and in half a second, Jack was at her elbow. He looked rugged and elegant at once in a kilt and tunic similar to what the chieftain's warriors wore. And there was something else different about him too, she thought — something beyond the fact that his hair and nails were clean. Something that made her stomach jump funnily.

"What were you and the Nexus talking about?" he asked.

"Where have you *been*?" Rapunzel replied, moving Prince Frog from Jack's shoulder to her own. "I was looking for you, and then I couldn't get away from all the people."

"I was with the warriors," he said, looking delighted with himself. "Smoking a cigar."

"You smell horrible."

"Yeah, well. Look, you've got correspondence — these came for you by Relay."

Rapunzel accepted the slips of paper he handed to her. "Relay?"

"I'll explain later. Read the messages. There's one from Prince Mick and Princess Daigh."

"And one from Prince Dash," said Rapunzel, delighted. She had forgotten all about him.

To Rapunzel of the Tower in the Redlands:

You have broken the witch's curse upon me and my family. Thank you.

Should you ever visit Quintessential, you are welcome to Charming Palace.

Most sincerely,

His Royal Highness Prince Dash of the Blue Kingdom

"Look, Jack, I'm invited to Charming Palace!"

"Great." Jack did not sound quite like he meant it.

"And there's one from Purl!" Rapunzel read the message quickly, devouring the words with her eyes.

Rapunzel ~ I knew you were your own woman. Visit me again soon and tell me how it happened. I'm proud of you, my granddaughter. ~ Purl Tattersby

When she looked up from Purl's note, Rapunzel found many stares fixed on her as guests spoke to one another in low voices. A few of them began to approach her, looking anxious to tell their tales, and she took a step back toward the door. She did not want to hear any more about how much they hated Witch.

"I have something for you too," Jack was saying.

"Do you know how to get outside?" she asked him in a low voice.

"Sure, come on."

She followed him quickly through massive wooden doors, all carved to look like beasts of the woods. When they came out onto the wide, torchlit steps, Rapunzel took a deep breath of the night air and sat down.

Jack walked down a few steps and turned to look at Rapunzel. "You okay?" he asked.

"I wish we could leave for Violet right now."

"I know," said Jack. "I just want to see the giantess and get it done."

"Wait until your mother sees you come back," she said, turning her mind away from Witch and toward something happier. "Wait until she hears all you've done! She was so scared you'd disappear like your father — and Tess will be so happy to see you too."

"Yeah, she will," said Jack. He gave Rapunzel an appreciative glance and cleared his throat. And then the two of them spoke at the same time.

"You know, you look really —"

"You said you had some —"

Rapunzel stopped. She leaned forward over her knees. "I look really?" she prompted. "Yes, go on."

Jack shoved his hair back from his forehead, and it fell down again at once. "Pretty," he finished, and Rapunzel went hot from head to toe. It was nice, the way he was looking at her.

Really nice.

"Well, you look handsome," she returned, feeling for the first time a sense of shyness as she looked at Jack, with whom she had never before been shy. "I like the clothes they gave you."

"Thanks," he said. "So, uh — what were you saying?"

"Oh!" Rapunzel forgot her shyness. "You said you had something for me."

Jack dug into the pocket of his jacket. "Here," he said, and he held out Rapunzel's jacks to her. "Rune gave me these when . . . you know. When the fairies were sorting through what was left of the tower."

Rapunzel took the jacks and held them tightly.

"They found a lot of money in the rubble too," said Jack. "A great chest of coins, Rune said. I guess Envearia must have hidden her fortune there, so now it's yours."

But there he stopped. He peered at Rapunzel. "I never told you about what my mother said when I left Dearth," he said, "that she thought I'd disappear like my father. Did I?"

Rapunzel shook her head, smiling a little.

"Then how do you know?"

"The Woodmother."

"How? What happened in that tree, anyway?"

"It's a good story," Rapunzel said. "Let's save it for the journey."

EPILOGUE

*T*HE beanstalk had all but withered. Jack climbed it, but it was terrifying to watch him go. Rapunzel wanted to follow, but Rune had strictly forbidden it, and so she watched almost without breathing as Jack made his way from one sagging leaf to the next. He climbed ever higher and became smaller and smaller until he was out of sight beyond the clouds.

Whether an hour or two or ten passed, she did not know. The light changed over the gray landscape, and Rapunzel held Tess tightly by the hand. On Tess's other side stood Jack's mother, who had barely spoken a word since he had returned to Dearth and told her the whole truth about his reason for departing. She waited in rigid silence.

It was difficult to tell at first, but it seemed that something at the very top of the beanstalk was moving. Rapunzel and Tess gripped each other more tightly. Jack's mother began to rock.

Jack came unmistakably into view. He climbed down much too slowly and carefully for Rapunzel and Tess, who were both bouncing on their toes by the time he came to the bottom of the stalk and leapt the rest of the way to the gray ground.

"Which one of you belongs to Geguul now?" his mother demanded. "Which one?"

"Neither of us," said Jack. A grin split his face. "The giantess released me from the bargain — she accepted Glyph's gift. She said she understood."

Jack's mother made a strangled sound and threw her thin arms around his neck. She held him, crying bitterly.

"It's all right," he said, looking rather bashfully toward Rapunzel as his mother wept all over him. "Shh. We're safe. It's over."

Tess flung herself at them and was enveloped in their embrace, and Rapunzel watched their joy with a glad heart.

Jack's mother let go of her children and wiped her eyes. "Thank the skies," she managed. "If anything had happened to you while you were away looking for those fairies . . . If you hadn't come back —"

"Jack *always* comes back," said Rapunzel with feeling, and Jack's mother looked at her in some surprise. She didn't seem to know what to make of Rapunzel. "He came to my tower three times, and he's the only one who ever climbed it with a rope, so he's the bravest. He stayed with me all the way from the Redlands to Commonwealth Green. And even though Witch hit him in the head, he *still* came back to my tower to find me. You can trust him."

Jack gazed at Rapunzel, light glinting in his black eyes.

"*I* knew you'd come back, Jackie," said Tess, leaning against him. "I carved notches in the wall for every day you were gone, and I knew you'd be home soon."

"Good old Tessie," said Jack, rumpling her dark hair.

"Want to see the notches?"

"Course I do."

They had a simple supper of eggs and bread that night. The money from the golden goose had not been much, but it had been enough.

"You know the great chest of coins, from my tower?" said Rapunzel as she and Jack left the little gray cottage together and walked out into the purple evening light.

"Yeah?"

"Well, Chieftain Fleet told me that his treasurer sorted through it, and it's an enormous fortune."

Jack lifted an eyebrow. "Just bragging, or do you have something in mind?"

"I still want to travel together," Rapunzel replied. "Like we talked about before. With the money Witch left, we can go anywhere, and I want to visit every single country. You'll come with me, won't you?"

"Obviously."

"Good. Then I have one more idea," she said, unable to contain it any longer. It was something that had occurred to her on the journey from the Redlands to the Violet Peaks. "I was thinking, what if we use the money to move your family out of Dearth? What if we find them a house in Maple Valley, near Purl? Then our families would be near each other, and Tess could grow up with all those pretty leaves around, and it would be perfect. Wouldn't it?"

Jack said nothing for a moment. He looked away from Rapunzel, up into the barren, jagged mountains that loomed over the village.

"You'd do that?" he asked. His voice sounded different. Lower.

"Of course I would."

He dragged the knuckles of one hand under his left eye, and then his right. It was several moments before he looked at her.

"It's a great idea," he said. "If my mother goes for it."

"Let's go and ask her."

They went inside, and Jack did ask. And though his mother protested that she would not take such a gift, Rapunzel was undeterred. She begged to be allowed to spend a portion of her inheritance in this way, which, she pointed out, would make her as happy as it would make anybody else. Jack chimed in, arguing that it would make their lives far easier, as they traveled, to have both families close together, and Tess coaxed and cajoled and pleaded with her wide blue eyes. Jack's mother's pride could not withstand this combined attack, and so she accepted, looking dazed, and the next hour was spent in merry planning.

It was a happy ending, Rapunzel thought. If she'd been in her tower reading one of her books, it would have said *and Rapunzel lived happily ever after, with Witch to love and protect her always.* Every one of her stories had ended that way.

But Witch was gone.

"Rapunzel, show Tess," said Jack, and Rapunzel realized she had not been listening.

"Show her what?"

"Fifteensies. Seriously, she's amazing. Watch this."

Rapunzel pulled her jacks out of her belt. As she poured them into her hand, she felt a sudden certainty that Witch was with her.

"The trick is to do it outside," she said. "Come on."

They went out into the darkening night, where Rapunzel demonstrated fifteensies and taught Tess how to catch jacks backhanded. When it was time to go to sleep, she pitched a tent beside Jack's cottage and lay down with Witch's jacks closed in her fist. Happy endings were no good anyway, she thought, yawning. Happy endings were still endings. Instead, tomorrow was coming, and there would be more adventures when it came.

TYME

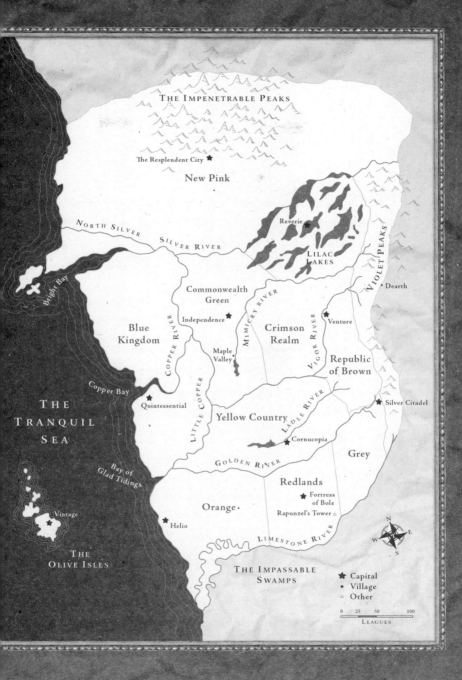

THE IMPENETRABLE PEAKS

The Resplendent City ★

New Pink

NORTH SILVER

SILVER RIVER

Reverie ★

Bright Bay

Lilac Lakes

VIOLET PEAKS

Dearth •

Commonwealth
Green

MIMICRY RIVER

Blue
Kingdom

COPPER RIVER

Independence ★

Crimson
Realm

VIGOR RIVER

Venture ★

Copper Bay

Maple
Valley •

Republic
of Brown

THE
TRANQUIL
SEA

Quintessential ★

LITTLE COPPER

Yellow Country

LADLE RIVER

Silver Citadel ★

Cornucopia ★

Grey

GOLDEN RIVER

Bay of
Glad Tidings

Redlands

Vintage ★

Orange •

Helio ★

Fortress
of Bole ★

Rapunzel's Tower △

THE
OLIVE ISLES

LIMESTONE RIVER

N

THE IMPASSABLE
SWAMPS

W   E

S

★ Capital
• Village
△ Other

0   25   50   100

LEAGUES

ACKNOWLEDGMENTS

THIS book exists because I had help. Everyone who ever encouraged me is responsible for putting a little fuel in the tank. Many thanks to all the Morrisons and Flynns, as well as to my friends, my colleagues, my in-laws, my teachers, and my students.

My deep gratitude belongs to the following people:

Ruth Virkus, kindred spirit and cocreator of Tyme, whose heart and imagination are equally extraordinary;

Cheryl Klein, editor and friend, who is both luminous and a conductor of light;

Kristin Brown, whose beautiful cartography has made Tyme a realer place;

Ammi-Joan Paquette, whose gentle guidance came at just the right moment;

The family members and friends who for years have read drafts (of this and many other stories), given feedback, offered resources, and generally kept the faith, especially: Melissa Anelli, Polly Beam, Maureen Berberian, Kristin Brown, Lisa Campos, David Carpman, B. K. DeLong, Maggie Dier, Marie Flanigan, Mary Flynn, Lindsey King,

Ben Layne, Jennie Levine Knies, Maureen Lipsett, Kathy MacMillan, Heather Mbaye, Erin McCormack, Gerry Morrison, Mick Morrison, Mike Morrison, and Devin Smither;

My parents, Gerry and Mike, who always believed;

Devin, whose patient, unflagging support makes everything possible; and Malcolm, who makes it all worth the while.

Finally, thanks to the SQ family. If you were part of that, then you are part of this.

This book was edited by Cheryl Klein and designed by Sharismar Rodriguez and Carol Ly. The production was supervised by Elizabeth Starr Baer and Elizabeth Krych. The text was set in Adobe Jenson, with display type set in Arrus BT. The title page was hand-lettered by Iacopo Bruno. This book was printed and bound by Command Web in Jefferson City, Missouri. The manufacturing was supervised by Shannon Rice.

Doris Fürk

Pretty in Paris

PINK · Ein Imprint von Oetinger Taschenbuch

2. Auflage 2017

© Oetinger Taschenbuch in der
Verlag Friedrich Oetinger GmbH, Imprint PINK,
Poppenbütteler Chaussee 53, 22397 Hamburg
Dezember 2015

Originalausgabe

Alle Rechte vorbehalten
Umschlaggestaltung: ZERO Werbeagentur
Umschlagmotiv: Mädchen: © Getty Images/Westend61
Hintergrund: FinePic®, München
Druck und Bindung: Livonia Print SIA,
Ventspils iela 50, LV-1002, Riga, Lettland
ISBN 978-3-86430-048-6

www.oetinger-taschenbuch.de

»MISTDING! MERDE!« Dieser blöde Ausziehgriff am Koffer hakt wieder einmal. Ich hätte einen neuen kaufen sollen. Aber jetzt ist es zu spät. Mein Schüleraustausch beginnt miserabel. Da stehe ich nun, mit einem Gepäckstück in Kleinwagengröße, und weit und breit ist kein Kofferwagen zu sehen. Zurück fliege ich auf keinen Fall mit diesem Folterinstrument. Ob es hier vielleicht Geschäfte gibt, die noch geöffnet haben?

Warum hab ich nur so ein Pech gehabt? Monique ist in München gelandet, Frederic in Berlin. Lilly und Michelle sitzen wahrscheinlich gerade in einem Kaffeehaus in Wien. Nur mich hat es in die Provinz verschlagen. Nach Salzburg. Wer verbringt denn seinen Schüleraustausch in Salzburg? Und da nicht einmal im Zentrum, sondern in einem reizenden dörflichen Vorort. So hat es jedenfalls die Agentur beschrieben. Ich will wenigstens in der Stadt wohnen!

Was ist, wenn die Vororte hier genauso schlimm sind wie die von Paris? Voller Straßengangs, Kleinkrimineller und Drogendealer?

Wenn ich daran denke, wie ich vor einem halben Jahr

durch die Banlieues gestreift bin, nur um André bei einem seiner Konzerte zu sehen. Und dann hat er mir bloß ein paar freundschaftliche Küsschen auf die Wangen gehaucht und mich seinen Kumpels als » eine Schulfreundin « vorgestellt. Dafür habe ich das Risiko auf mich genommen, in einer der miesesten Gegenden von Paris ausgeraubt zu werden.

Doch was soll ich sagen? Liebe macht blind. Im Nachhinein betrachtet, hat sich mein Einsatz gelohnt – hoffentlich. Gestern in der Schule hat er mir gestanden, dass er mich vermissen wird, und mir einen Kuss auf die Lippen gedrückt. Einen richtigen. Der dauerte zwar nur ganz kurz, weil dann Marc und Marie-Claire kamen, aber man küsst doch niemanden einfach nur so, oder?

Dummerweise bin ich nicht die Einzige, die auf André steht. Mit seinen eisblauen Augen, den schwarzen Haaren und der rauchigen Stimme ist er der Schwarm aller Mädchen. Keine Ahnung, was er machen wird, wenn wir uns drei Wochen lang nicht sehen. Hoffentlich trifft er keine anderen Mädchen ... Merde. Ich will nach Hause! Zurück zu André, zurück nach Paris. Dort gehöre ich, Fabienne Henry, hin. Hätte ich bei der Anmeldung zum Schüleraustausch schon gewusst, dass André und ich ... aber jetzt kann ich es nicht mehr ändern.

Ich habe die Flughafenhalle erreicht und sehe mich um. Doch außer meinem eigenen Spiegelbild in der Glasscheibe der Ausgangstür entdecke ich kein bekanntes Gesicht. Und selbst ich komme mir fremd vor. Abgerackert. Müde vom Flug und vom Kofferschleppen. Meine Schultern hängen runter. Meine langen honigblonden Locken sehen zerzaust aus. Ich seufze leise. Dieser Schüleraustausch ist die schlechteste Entscheidung meines Lebens.

Und überhaupt! Wo sind nur meine Gasteltern? So groß ist der Flughafen nun wirklich nicht, dass ich sie übersehen könnte. Mon Dieu, ist dieser Koffer schwer. Ich kugle mir gleich den Arm aus.

»Fabienne? Fabienne Henry?«

Ich wirbele herum, und da steht der Schwarzenegger und grinst. Er hat zwar graumelierte Haare, einen Bierbauch und einen Oberlippenbart, aber mit der breiten Nase und dem kantigen Kinn erinnert er mich stark an den Terminator.

»Oui«, rutscht es mir heraus. Mehr fällt mir nicht mehr ein, und das nach fünf Jahren Schuldeutsch.

»Prima! Ich bin der Peter Gruber, dein Gastvater. Komm, gib mir das Ding.«

Er schnappt sich meinen Koffer, als wäre er aus Pappmaché, und wendet sich zum Ausgang. Jetzt erst sehe ich die weiß gesockten Füße, die in braunen Sandalen stecken. Dazu passend trägt er eine kurze Trekkinghose und ein grün kariertes Hemd. Jetzt bin ich doch froh, den großen Koffer mitgenommen zu haben, trotz kaputtem Ausziehgriff. An Kleidung mangelt es mir nicht. Und drei Wochen überlebe ich auch in Salzburg.

Das verrostete Auto wirkt wenig vertrauenserweckend. Ich schätze, es ist mindestens doppelt so alt wie ich. Peter verstaut mein Gepäck im Kofferraum und deutet auf den Beifahrersitz. Als ich einsteige, schlägt mir ein merkwürdiger

Geruch entgegen. Es riecht irgendwie nach Schweinestall. Ob meine Gastfamilie auf einem Bauernhof lebt? Davon hat die Agentur gar nichts gesagt.

Auf der Rückbank herrscht ein ziemliches Durcheinander. Ich kann einen recht beachtlichen Baumsetzling, jede Menge Gartenzeugs, eine große Decke und einige Blumentöpfe ausmachen. Zum Glück ist der Beifahrersitz relativ sauber.

Eigentlich fände ich es ganz schön, wenn meine Gasteltern einen Bauernhof hätten. Ich liebe Tiere und Katzen ganz besonders. Zu Hause habe ich selbst eine. Sie heißt »Bastet«, weil sie aussieht wie die ägyptische Katzengöttin. Ihre fast nackte Haut bedeckt nur ein ganz weicher, zarter Flaum, und ihre Ohren sind riesig. Bastet ist eine Sphynx-Katze, und sie schreitet wie eine Prinzessin durch unsere Wohnung. Wenn ich Bastet streichle, dann schnurrt sie und stupst mit ihrer warmen Nase so lange gegen mein Bein, bis ich sie auf den Schoß nehme. Hoffentlich sorgt mein Austausch gut für sie.

Wir lassen die rot-weiße Schranke des Flughafenparkplatzes hinter uns und kommen an einem riesigen Shoppingcenter vorbei. Große Tafeln werben für bekannte Kleidungsmarken. Ich richte mich auf, um besser erkennen zu können, um welche Geschäfte es sich handelt.

»Das ist relativ neu hier. Ein Outlet-Center. Unsere Tochter Helene liebt es, dort nach Schnäppchen zu stöbern. Vielleicht möchtest du auch einmal einen Samstag hier verbringen. Ihr Mädels liebt doch shoppen, oder?«, fragt mein Gastvater.

»Oh ja, das wäre prima!« Ein Stein fällt mir vom Herzen. Salzburg ist vielleicht doch nicht so schlecht.

Wir fahren auf die Autobahn. Ich lehne mich viel entspannter als noch vor fünfzehn Minuten zurück und schließe einen Moment die Augen. Ein Fehler, denn Peter macht eine Vollbremsung. Automatisch reiße ich die Hände hoch. Hinten rumpelt es. Der Sicherheitsgurt schnürt mir die Luft ab. Herr Gruber flucht laut und unverständlich. Anscheinend hat ihn ein anderes Auto geschnitten. Vom Rücksitz dringt plötzlich lautes Gekreische nach vorn.

»So ein Blödmann! Tut mir leid, Fabienne. Alles in Ordnung mit dir?«, fragt mein Gastvater.

Ich nicke wortlos, während ich mich besorgt nach hinten umdrehe. Nun, da das Gartenwerkzeug am Boden verteilt liegt und die Decke verrutscht ist, sehe ich eine graue Transportbox. Genauso eine haben wir auch für Bastet, nur in Blau. Ich will gerade Herrn Gruber nach der Katze fragen, da ertönt ein ohrenbetäubendes Quieken, wie ich es noch nie zuvor bei einer Katze gehört habe. Ob sie sich verletzt hat?

Ich schaue noch einmal nach hinten – und glaube meinen Augen nicht zu trauen.

Im Katzenkorb liegt ein Schwein!

»Oh, unsere Susi ist wieder wach«, bemerkt Herr Gruber ungerührt.

Mit offenem Mund starre ich die Sau an, die nun zufrieden zu schmatzen beginnt.

»Mon Dieu!«, rufe ich überrascht.

»Darf ich vorstellen?«, fährt mein Gastvater fröhlich fort. »Das ist Susi, unser Hausferkel. Und das ist Fabienne, unsere Austauschschülerin.«

Die kleine Sau drückt ihre rosa Schnauze gegen die Gitterstäbe und grunzt vergnügt.

»Ein Hausferkel?«, frage ich erstaunt.

»Ja, Susi gehört Helene. Sie ist ganz zahm, wie ein Hund, und schläft gewöhnlich bei Helene im Zimmer.«

»Ähm ...« BEI MIR SCHLÄFT EIN SCHWEIN IM ZIMMER?

»Aber jetzt, wo Helene in Paris ist, kann Susi natürlich auch woanders schlafen.«

Ich mag alle Tiere, wirklich. Aber ein Schwein als Haustier?

»Du wirst Susi sicher schnell ins Herz schließen. Die Arme hatte heute Mittag eine Zahn-OP in Salzburg.«

Skeptisch mustere ich die Box und kann kaum glauben, wie sich meine Welt in der letzten halben Stunde verändert hat. Ein Schwarzenegger-Gastvater, ein Zimmerferkel mit Zahnschmerzen und ein Auto, dessen Verfallsdatum im letzten Jahrtausend liegt. Das ist wirklich nicht das, was ich mir vorgestellt habe.

Ich klappe den Kosmetikspiegel herunter und blicke hinein. Eigentlich sehe ich aus wie immer, nur etwas müder als sonst. Mein Teint ist blass, meine grünen Augen sind rot gerändert und die blonden Locken leicht zerzaust. Plötzlich muss ich kichern. Meine Situation erinnert an einen traurigen Abklatsch dieser Uralt-Doku-Serie: Paris Hilton auf dem Bauernhof.

Die Fahrt dauert eine halbe Ewigkeit. Susi will anscheinend mit mir Freundschaft schließen. Sie wimmert wie ein Baby, nur viel höher. Doch sobald ich mich umdrehe und in die Box gucke, hört sie auf. Also schaue ich immer wieder zu ihr nach hinten, während mich Gastvater Peter ausfragt.

Ob ich oft auf den Eiffelturm gehe, gerne Crêpes esse, schon mal Froschschenkel probiert habe, nur Haute Couture trage und meine Familie einen Renault oder Citroën fährt. Schon seltsam, welches Bild die Welt von uns Franzosen hat. Dabei fühle ich mich nicht besonders französisch, sondern ganz normal ... Meine Gedanken kreisen meistens um André, die Schule, meine Freunde, Klamotten, Ausgehen, Musik, meine Zukunft – und nicht um den Eiffelturm oder die Beine von irgendwelchen armen Tieren. Ich esse überhaupt nichts, was Augen hat.

»Und stimmt es, dass die Österreicher am liebsten Wiener Schnitzel essen?«, kontere ich.

Peter grinst mich an. »Also ich schon, aber keine Sorge, wir wissen von der Austauschorganisation, dass du Vegetarierin bist. Erika, meine Frau, hat sich die letzten Tage stundenlang den Kopf zerbrochen, was sie für dich kochen kann. Du wirst uns ganz bestimmt nicht verhungern.«

War das ein Versprechen, mich zu mästen?

»Nein, sicher nicht«, sage ich versöhnlich.

»Wir Österreicher lieben auch Nachspeisen, Süßigkeiten, Aufläufe und Kuchen ...« Genießerisch klopft Peter sich mit einer Hand auf den Bauch. »Ich mag besonders gern Marillenknödel. Hast du die schon mal probiert?«

Mit halbem Ohr höre ich noch, was Peter sagt, doch der

Blick aus dem Fenster lenkt mich ab. Inzwischen haben wir die Stadt endgültig hinter uns gelassen. Es wird grüner und grüner. Wald, Wiesen, Felder.

»Ähm, Herr Gruber?«

»Ja, Fabienne?«

»Wie weit ist Ihr Dorf eigentlich von Salzburg entfernt?«

»Ach, so an die fünfunddreißig Kilometer, aber ich verspreche dir, du wirst das Leben auf dem Land lieben. Kein Großstadtstress, keine Hektik, keine …«

»… Zivilisation?«, frage ich und umklammere mein Smartphone.

Peter lacht. Schweinchen Susi grunzt. KANN ES NOCH SCHLIMMER KOMMEN?

Zwanzig Minuten später kenne ich die Antwort. Schlimmer geht immer. Wir erreichen die Dorfeinfahrt.

»Willkommen daheim, liebe Fabienne«, sagt Peter und hält am Ortsschild. Ich lese den Namen darauf und kann es kaum glauben.

»Ich dachte, Helene würde in einem Ort namens Tarsdorf wohnen?«

»Ja, ja. Wir gehören zur Gemeinde Tarsdorf! Aber unser Ort heißt …«

»FUCKING?!«

»Na ja, so sprechen es nur die Engländer aus. Wir sagen Fuuuucking«, erklärt Peter und zieht das U in die Länge, wie bei Toulouse. »Ich weiß, viele finden unseren Ortsnamen komisch. Und ehrlich gesagt, wir eigentlich auch. Aber soll ich dir was sagen? In Fucking lebt sich's fucking good! Du wirst schon sehen.« Grinsend legt er den ersten Gang wieder ein. Mit einem Ruck fährt die Uraltkiste weiter, mitten in das winzige Dorf hinein. Ich entdecke eine Kirche, ein Wirtshaus, mehrere Bauernhöfe und Wohnhäuser, ansonsten nur Natur pur.

PARIS! ICH WILL ZURÜCK NACH PARIS!

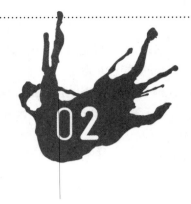

DAS IST MEIN ERSTER FLUG. Wie schön die
Wolken aussehen, wie Zuckerwatte. Wenn Mama recht hat,
dann werden die nächsten drei Wochen die besten meines
Lebens. Paris, die Stadt der Liebe, der Kunst, der Mode.
Wie ich mich freue. Helene Gruber erobert die große, weite
Welt.

Pling! Meine Sitznachbarin sieht mich skeptisch an.
»Soll man Handys nicht ausschalten?«, fragt die magere,
ältere Frau, und ihre silberblauen Löckchen wippen wie
Sprungfedern.

»Nur beim Start und bei der Landung«, erwidere ich
und krame in meinem Täschchen nach dem Smartphone.

Eine SMS. Wahrscheinlich hat mir meine Freundin Lena
gesimst, die leider zu Hause bleiben musste. Ich wische über
das Display, lese die Nachricht und erstarre.

»Alles in Ordnung, Kindchen? Brauchst du eine Tüte?«
Die hagere Dame drückt mir einen Papierbeutel in die Hand.

Ich schüttle den Kopf. »Nein danke. Ich brauche wohl
eher ein Navigationsgerät.«

»In der Luft?«, erwidert die Frau lächelnd. »Keine Angst,

Schätzchen. Der Pilot verfliegt sich schon nicht. Du kommst ganz bestimmt in Paris an.«

»Das befürchte ich auch«, sage ich und lese erneut die Nachricht.

Liebe Helene, leider müssen wir noch etwas Dringendes erledigen und können dich nicht vom Flughafen abholen. Bitte fahr mit der Métro …

Die Schrift verschwimmt vor meinen Augen. Da versetzen mich meine Gasteltern eine halbe Stunde vor der Landung in einer Millionenstadt. Ob man den Piloten noch bestechen kann, zurückzufliegen?

Doch es leuchtet schon das Anschnallzeichen auf, und die Stewardess kontrolliert, ob die Gurte bei allen geschlossen sind. Ich atme tief durch und rede mir selbst Mut zu. Warum sollte ich es nicht schaffen, mit der Métro zu meiner Gastfamilie zu fahren? Immerhin bin ich Klassenbeste in Französisch … aber wie viel bringt mir ein knappes Jahr Schulfranzösisch wirklich? Oje, ich darf jetzt nur nicht in Panik geraten.

Das Flugzeug ruckelt. »Leichte Turbulenzen«, informiert uns der Kapitän. Ich werde gegen die Flugzeugwand gedrückt, und mir kommen die Tränen.

Die ältere Dame sieht mich besorgt an. »Keine Sorge, Kindchen. Wir stürzen schon nicht ab.« Sie zieht ein Stofftaschentuch hervor und gibt es mir.

»Danke. Tut mir leid, ich bin nur so nervös«, flüstere ich und wische mir über die Augen.

»Kein Problem. Ist wohl dein erster Flug, hm?«

Ich nicke. »Ich mache einen dreiwöchigen Schüleraustausch. Und meine Gasteltern holen mich nicht einmal ab. Ich soll … mit der Métro fahren!« Tränen kullern mir über die Wangen. Ich kann gar nichts dagegen tun.

»Ach, Kindchen. Das ist doch nicht so schlimm. Du hast doch bestimmt die Adresse.«

Ich lege den Kopf zurück und schließe die Augen. Es mag schon sein, dass andere in meinem Alter kein Problem damit haben, sich allein in einer Großstadt durchzuschlagen. Doch bislang war ich noch nicht mal allein in Salzburg, und nun soll ich mich in einer Millionenmetropole zurechtfinden?

Ich balle die Fäuste. »Ich schaff das, ich schaff das, ich schaff das«, flüstere ich mir Mut zu.

Mein persönliches Mantra, und als ich nach der Landung durch die Halle gehe, glaube ich es sogar … zumindest für eine Minute.

Die Menschen am Flughafen laufen wie die Ameisen wild durcheinander. Es herrscht ein lautes Gewirr aus Stimmen und Sprachen. Küsse werden verteilt, Tränen weggewischt, Umarmungen verschenkt, es wird gelacht und geredet, eine Ansammlung glücklicher Pärchen und Familien … nur ich stehe hier ganz allein inmitten der Menschenmassen. Niemand, der auf mich wartet. Keiner, der mich empfängt. Hilflos sehe ich mich um.

Plötzlich steht die alte Dame wieder neben mir. Sie zeigt nach rechts. »Zur Métro geht es da entlang. Aber wenn du dir unsicher bist, dann nimm dir doch ein Taxi.« Lächelnd winkt sie einem älteren Herrn im Nadelstreifenanzug zu, der aussieht, als wäre er direkt einem Schwarz-Weiß-Film entsprungen. »Ich wünsche dir eine schöne Zeit in Paris. Du wirst sehen, wer einmal hier war, kommt immer wieder.«

»Da... da... danke«, stammele ich leise.

Doch sie hört mich nicht mehr, weil sie sich schon dem Mann zugewandt hat. Die beiden fallen sich in die Arme. Ich komme mir dumm vor, sie länger anzustarren, und mache mich auf die Suche nach dem Taxistand. Eigentlich wollte ich nicht schon am Ankunftstag mein ganzes Taschengeld ausgeben. Gern hätte ich für meine Familie ein paar Souvenirs mitgebracht, zum Beispiel ein cooles Mousepad für meinen Bruder. Er ist ein echter Computerfreak, was ganz gut ist. Schließlich können ältere Brüder ziemlich ätzend sein. Florian hockt aber die meiste Zeit vor dem Bildschirm und stört niemanden.

Ich schlängle mich zum Ausgang durch und entdecke direkt vor der Tür einen Taxistand. Was für ein Glück!

Nun müsste ich nur noch wissen, was das Licht oben am Dach bedeutet. Ist weiß frei und orange besetzt, oder war es genau umgekehrt?

Vorsichtig klopfe ich an die Fensterscheibe eines Taxis. Der Fahrer lässt die Scheibe ein Stück hinunter und brummt: »Non, Mademoiselle, vous ...« Ich verstehe ihn nicht, so schnell quasselt er. Dann fährt er plötzlich, ohne ein weiteres Wort zu verlieren, die Scheibe wieder hoch und starrt nach vorne, als wäre ich gar nicht mehr da.

Unschlüssig stehe ich da, mit meinem rosaroten Trolley, und weiß nicht, was ich tun soll. Wenn doch Lena hier wäre, oder wenigstens Florian. Der könnte mit seinem iPad die schnellste Verbindung in die Innenstadt herbeizaubern und mich wie ein lebendiges Navigationsgerät durch Paris lotsen.

»Mademoiselle? Mademoiselle?«

Ich dreh mich um. »Meinen Sie mich?«, frage ich den jungen, dunkelhäutigen Mann mit der bunten Mütze und dem Punkt auf der Stirn.

»Oh, Allemande, du suchst ein Taxi? Meins ist frei!«, antwortet er lächelnd und entblößt eine Zahnlücke zwischen den Vorderzähnen.

Ich muss wohl automatisch Deutsch gesprochen haben. »Österreich – Autriche«, sage ich und halte ihm den Zettel mit der Adresse hin.

Er nickt und nimmt den Zettel. »Schön. Wien. Ich habe Familie dort. Meinen Bruder. Komm, gib mir deinen Koffer.« Die Fahrt dauert ziemlich lange, und Jai, so heißt der Taxifahrer, erzählt mir in gebrochenem Deutsch seine halbe Lebensgeschichte, dass er eigentlich studiert und acht Sprachen spricht … Ich brauche gar nicht viel zu sagen. Er schwärmt begeistert von Indien und seiner Familie, seinem großen Bruder in Wien und dem Kaiserschmarrn seiner Schwägerin. Allerdings kann ich ihm nur schwer zuhören, so schnell saust er um die Kurven, überholt und hupt, wenn ihm jemand im Weg steht. Mir wird richtig schwindelig bei dieser Irrfahrt durch Paris.

»Das ist doch der Triumphbogen!«, rufe ich aufgeregt.

»Ja, wir sind gleich da«, sagt Jai und grinst mich durch den Rückspiegel an.

»Gleich da«, murmele ich und kann meinen Blick nicht von der Prachtstraße lösen.

Als wir den Triumphbogen fast erreicht haben, biegt Jai ab und hält keine fünfhundert Meter weiter am Bordsteinrand.

»So, da sind wir auch schon. Das macht 47,70 Euro.« Stirnrunzelnd betrachte ich den Zettel mit der Adresse meiner Gastfamilie. »Sind Sie sich sicher, dass es hier ist? Nummer fünfzehn? Ich wollte eigentlich zu meiner Gastfamilie und nicht zu irgendeiner Sehenswürdigkeit.«

»Das ist die richtige Adresse. Eine gute Adresse, die deine Familie da hat.«

»Aha«, erwidere ich ungläubig.

Das Haus Nummer fünfzehn sieht aus wie ein Museum. Alt, klotzig und pompös. Und hier soll ich wohnen?

Ich krame in meinem Portemonnaie und gebe Jai fünfzig Euro. »Stimmt so«, sage ich und steige aus.

»Warte, ich helfe dir mit dem Koffer.« Jai springt aus dem Auto, lädt den Koffer aus und drückt ihn mir in die Hand. »Und falls du mal wieder ein Taxi brauchst, ruf an, okay?« Er gibt mir seine Karte und zwinkert mir mit seinen großen schwarzen Augen zu.

»Mach ich, danke.«

Staunend gehe ich auf das Eingangsportal zu. Die große Tür öffnet sich automatisch, und ich betrete eine Halle mit glänzenden Marmorfliesen und stuckverzierter Decke. Hinter einem Empfangstresen sitzt ein bulliger Pförtner, der müde von seiner Zeitung hochblickt. Ich schüttle den Kopf und will schnell wieder hinaus. Vielleicht ist Jai noch da. Er hat sich bestimmt in der Straße geirrt.

»Mademoiselle Gruber? Willkommen. Bienvenue. Madame Henry erwartet Sie schon. Oben im Penthouse.« Der Portier nickt mir erwartungsvoll zu.

Verunsichert sehe ich ihn an. Kann es sein, dass ich direkt in einem Hollywoodfilm gelandet bin? Auf jeden Fall fühle ich mich im Moment so.

»Ähm. Merci, Monsieur. Ganz oben?«, frage ich nach.

»Oui, Mademoiselle. Oben. Im Penthouse«, erklärt er freundlich und zeigt auf den Fahrstuhl.

Ich hole tief Luft, straffe meine Schultern und gehe zum Lift. Die auf Hochglanz polierten Türen schweben zur Seite. Langsam drücke ich auf die Acht und beobachte, wie sich die gläsernen Türen geräuschlos schließen. Es ist wie in diesem einen Film, den Mama so liebt: *Pretty Woman*. Zugegeben, der Vergleich hinkt etwas, aber ich komme mir vor wie Aschenputtel in dieser Glitzerwelt. Fehlt nur noch der Märchenprinz. Übermütig dreh ich mich im Fahrstuhl. Wenn das kein Grund zu tanzen ist, dann weiß ich auch nicht. Ich fühl mich richtig *Pretty in Paris*.

Wenn meine beste Freundin Lena erfährt, wo ich gelandet bin, wird sie sich bestimmt in den Hintern beißen, dass sie nicht beim Schüleraustausch mitgemacht hat. Es ist unglaublich: Ich, Helene Gruber, werde nur ein paar Hundert Meter von den Champs-Élysées entfernt in einem Penthouse wohnen!

MEINE GASTFAMILIE wohnt tatsächlich in einem Bauernhaus. Eigentlich ist es sogar ein richtiger Hof, bestehend aus vier großen Gebäuden, die durch Tore miteinander verbunden sind. Peter Gruber lenkt den Wagen durch eines der riesigen Scheunentore in den Innenhof.

Vor dem Wohnhaus trippelt eine brünette, etwas rundliche Bäuerin auf und ab, die hektisch mit zwei kleinen französischen Fähnchen wedelt und über das ganze Gesicht strahlt. Neben ihr steht ein in sich zusammengesunkener Junge, vermutlich mein Gastbruder. Er starrt auf den Boden, und ich kann mir gut vorstellen, dass er sich für seine begeistert herumhüpfende Mutter schämt. Mir würde es wahrscheinlich genauso gehen.

»Das sind Florian, mein Sohn, und Erika, meine Frau. Die beiden freuen sich schon sehr, dich kennenzulernen«, erklärt Herr Gruber und stellt den Motor ab.

Während mein Gastvater Susi aus ihrer Box befreit und den Koffer auslädt, stürmt Frau Gruber auf mich zu und schließt mich in die Arme. Ein süßer Vanilleduft steigt mir in die Nase.

»Fabienne, schön, dass du da bist. Hattest du eine gute Reise?«

»Ja, danke, Frau Gruber«, murmele ich, etwas überrumpelt von so viel Herzlichkeit.

»Erika. Nenn mich bitte Erika. Du bist bestimmt müde vom Flug. Komm herein in die gute Stube, ich hab eine kleine Mahlzeit für dich gekocht.«

Sie schiebt mich in Richtung Haustür. »Ach, und das hier ist Florian«, stellt sie mir den Jungen im Vorbeigehen vor.

»Hallo, Fabienne, schön, dass du da bist«, sagt dieser gelangweilt und sieht mir kurz in die Augen. Im nächsten Moment ist er knallrot im Gesicht, und ich muss ein Kichern unterdrücken. Wie es aussieht, ist Florian etwas schüchtern.

»Hallo, Florian«, sage ich, und er wird noch eine Spur röter.

Wir gehen hinein. Herr Gruber und Susi folgen mit etwas Abstand. Im Inneren des Gebäudes ist es dunkel, was an den ziemlich kleinen Fenstern liegt. Die Decken sind niedrig, und schwarze Holzbalken verlaufen über den ganzen Plafond.

»Unser Vierseithof ist zweihundert Jahre alt. Damals hat man so gebaut, und wir haben das Haus unverändert gelassen. Das ist sicher ungewohnt für dich«, meint Erika lächelnd.

Ich blicke mich um und erwidere: »Wir wohnen auch in einem sehr alten Haus. Aber bei uns sind die Räume ganz hoch, die Decken voller Stuck und die Fenster riesig.«

»Komm, lass uns in die Stube gehen. Ich hab eine Kleinigkeit für dich vorbereitet«, wiederholt meine Gastmutter.

Sie führt mich in ein großes Esszimmer. Auf dem Tisch türmen sich Mehlspeisen, Käselaibe, verschiedene Brotsorten, Obst und Gemüse. An den Deckenbalken hängen Girlanden in den französischen Nationalfarben, und auch die weißen Stoffservietten sind mit blau-roten Schriftzügen bestickt. Ich bin gerührt, dass die Familie so einen Aufwand für mich betrieben hat.

»Schau. Dort sitzt du, wo das T-Shirt mit deinem Namen liegt.« Erika zeigt auf einen gedeckten Platz.

Ich trete näher und muss schrecklich lachen. Es ist keine Stoffserviette, die neben meinem Teller liegt, sondern ein zusammengefaltetes T-Shirt. Ich halte es vor mir hoch. WILLKOMMEN IN FUCKING, FABIENNE, steht da in geschwungenen Buchstaben.

»Das hab ich für dich gemacht. Ich hoffe, die Größe passt.« Erwartungsvoll blickt mich meine Gastmutter an.

»Ganz bestimmt. Das ist sehr nett von Ihnen. Mir hat noch nie jemand etwas selbst gestickt«, sage ich.

»Erika, nenn mich bitte Erika.« Sie strahlt und sieht dabei ganz jung und vergnügt aus, gar nicht mehr so bäuerlich und altmodisch wie vorhin auf dem Hof.

Plötzlich stürmt Susi zur Tür herein und macht es sich unter dem Tisch gemütlich. Es ist zwar niedlich, aber auch irgendwie komisch, dass Susi wie ein Hund behandelt wird. Vielleicht fühlt sich die kleine Sau schon wie ein Dackel und hat inzwischen ganz vergessen, dass sie ein Schwein ist.

»Komm, setz dich und greif zu. Nach dem Essen zeige ich dir dein Zimmer und den Rest des Hauses«, sagt Erika.

»Gern«, entgegne ich. »Könnte ich nur vorher kurz ins Badezimmer, mich frisch machen?«

»Aber selbstverständlich!« Meine Gastmutter zeigt mir den Weg.

Ich bleibe ein paar Minuten länger als nötig vor dem Waschbecken stehen. »Fabienne Henry, da hast du aber eine ganz außergewöhnliche Gastfamilie erwischt«, sage ich zu meinem Spiegelbild. Es lächelt mir aufmunternd entgegen. Na ja, auch wenn meine Schulfreunde in größeren Städten gelandet sind, bezweifle ich, dass sie nach ihrem Austausch mehr zu erzählen haben als ich. Wer hat schon ein echtes Schwein am Esstisch sitzen?

Die ganze Familie hat am Tisch Platz genommen, und das kleine Ferkel hockt grunzend unter dem Tisch. Zum Glück hat sie es sich bei Peters Füßen bequem gemacht, sodass ich wohl keine Angst haben muss, dass sie mir zwischen die Beine läuft. Dennoch nehme ich vorsichtig Platz, um das Tier nicht auf dumme Gedanken zu bringen.

»Flo, pack dein Handy weg. Das gehört sich nicht«, ermahnt Peter seinen Sohn.

Florian guckt ihn groß an. »Ich dachte, ich soll den Fucking-Blog auf dem neuesten Stand halten? Wäre doch gut, ein paar Fotos von unserem Willkommenstisch hochzuladen.«

Peter seufzt.

Siegessicher grinst Florian mich an. »Ich zeig dir später meinen Blog. Ich hab 'ne echt coole Homepage für unseren Ort gebastelt. Da kommt alles rein, was gerade aktuell ist. Ich poste jedes Fest, jeden Klatsch und Tratsch und natürlich auch dich – unsere exklusive Austauschschülerin. Wir haben übrigens auch einen Fucking-Chat für die Fuckinger Jugend.«

Er spricht den Ortsnamen einmal Englisch und einmal Deutsch aus, während er weiter ungeniert auf seinem Smartphone herumtippt. Ich muss kichern. Flo ist ein waschechter Nerd, es fehlen nur noch die Hornbrille und eine Zahnspange.

»Weißt du, Fabienne, seit wir den neuen Handymast haben, ist das Internet bei uns echt schnell. Ich bin jetzt daueron und kann fast alles mit dem Handy machen.«

Ich ziehe mein Smartphone aus der Tasche und prüfe die Internetverbindung. Tatsächlich ist sie überraschend schnell. »Komm, ich mache mal ein Foto«, sage ich.

»Oh ja, aber mit der versammelten Mannschaft!« Florian legt sein Handy weg und schnappt sich Susi.

Ich knipse meine Gastfamilie, und dann fotografiert Florian mich. Das Hochladen der Fotos dauert dann leider doch eine Weile. Ich nutze die Zeit und schreibe André eine kurze SMS.

Wie geht's dir? Rate mal, wie der Ort heißt, in dem ich wohne!

Meiner Mutter schreibe ich, dass ich gut angekommen bin. Dann macht das Handy endlich *Pling*. Die Fotos sind online, die SMS verschickt.

»Aber jetzt weg mit den strahlenverseuchten Dingern und guten Appetit!«, sagt Erika.

Florian und ich lassen unsere Smartphones verschwinden und stürzen uns aufs Essen. Wenn man davon absieht, dass der Ort Fucking heißt, der Bruder ein Nerd und das Haustier ein Ferkel ist, sind sie eigentlich ganz nett, die Grubers.

Sie bemühen sich auf jeden Fall, und diese mit Konfitüre gefüllten und im Rohr gebackenen Hefeklöße sind ein Traum. Da sage ich nicht Nein, als mir meine Gastmutter noch eine zweite Ofennudel anbietet. Selbst an das bettelnde Gequieke unter dem Tisch kann man sich gewöhnen, solange das Ferkel nicht zu nahe kommt. Ich werfe Susi sogar ein paar Krümel auf den Boden.

»Du verwöhnst unsere kleine Sau genauso wie Helene«, bemerkt Erika lächelnd.

Ich zucke mit den Schultern. »Ich bin eben eine Tierfreundin.«

»Dann bist du bei uns genau richtig. Außer Kühen, Pferden und anderem Viehzeug gibt es hier nämlich nicht viel zu sehen«, sagt mein Gastbruder mit vollem Mund.

Florians Bemerkung holt mich auf den Boden der Tatsachen zurück. Es stimmt. Ich sitze hier in der Pampa, zwar mit netten Leuten, aber dennoch im Nirgendwo.

NACH DEM ESSEN zeigt mir meine Gastmutter den Rest des Hauses und schließlich Helenes Zimmer, in dem ich schlafe. Es befindet sich im Obergeschoss und liegt gegenüber von Florians Zimmer, aus dem laute Musik herausschallt. Der Raum ist recht einfach eingerichtet: ein Bett, ein Schrank und ein Schreibtisch. Mitten im Zimmer steht mein Koffer, groß und klobig wie ein Ufo. Durch die vielen Starposter und Fotos von Helene, ihrer Familie und ihren Freundinnen wirkt das Zimmer dennoch nett und gemütlich, wie die ganze Familie.

Erika drückt mir einen kleinen Zettel in die Hand. »Das ist der Code fürs Internet. Also pack in Ruhe aus, richte dich ein, und wenn du was brauchst, dann komm einfach runter in die Stube. Wir sind immer für dich da.«

»Ähm. Danke. Aber ich denke, ein wenig Ruhe wird mir jetzt guttun«, antworte ich.

»Bestimmt«, sagt Erika und drückt sanft meine Hand. »Es ist wirklich schön, dass du da bist, und du sollst dich bei uns wohlfühlen.«

Ich nicke unsicher. Meine Gastmutter dreht sich um und

schließt leise die Tür. So viel Aufmerksamkeit ist ungewohnt für mich. In Paris bin ich meistens allein zu Hause oder hänge bei meinen Freunden herum. Meine Eltern sind nur selten daheim. Doch hier scheint es anders zu sein.

Ziemlich erledigt vom heutigen Tag packe ich meinen Koffer aus. Als ich fertig bin, beschließe ich, noch einmal nach unten zu gehen und mir eine Flasche Mineralwasser zu holen. Nach all dem süßen Essen ist mein Mund ganz trocken. Unbemerkt will ich noch mal in die Küche schleichen, aber das knarrende alte Holz verrät mich.

»Fabienne, brauchst du etwas?«

Erika streckt ihren Kopf zur Wohnzimmertür hinaus. Auf ihrer Nasenspitze thront eine Brille, in der Hand hält sie Nadel und Faden.

»Ich wollte mir nur etwas Wasser holen. Stickst du wieder ein Shirt?«, erkundige ich mich.

Erika hustet verlegen und verbirgt schnell ihre Handarbeit hinterm Rücken. »Nein«, sagt sie schließlich und wird genauso rot wie Florian vorhin.

Wie lustig. Die ganze Familie scheint zum Erröten zu neigen. Durch ihre Heimlichtuerei macht sie mich aber erst recht neugierig. Geduldig bleibe ich stehen und mustere Erika fragend.

»Das Shirt, das ich dir gestickt hab …«

»Ja?« Warum macht sie es denn so spannend?

»… ist eigentlich nur ein schwacher Ersatz für die original Fuckinger Unterhöschen!« Erika strahlt mich an und holt ihre Stickerei wieder hervor.

»Mon Dieu!«, keuche ich beim Anblick des zarten Damenslips, auf dem in geschwungener Stickerei Fucking An steht.

»Den bekommt eine Andrea. Aber es ist jeder Name möglich«, erklärt Erika ernst.

»Du stickt da im Ernst Fucking Andrea drauf?«

»Ja. Willst du meine Kollektion sehen? Florian hat mir auch einen Onlineshop installiert. Meine Wäsche verkauft sich sehr gut im Netz.«

Noch immer etwas verdattert, nicke ich. Ich bin ja einiges gewöhnt, aber dass meine Gastmutter sogar Unterwäsche mit dem schweinischen Ortsnamen bestickt, hätte ich nicht gedacht. Da heißt es immer, wir Franzosen seien so hemmungslos, und dann kommt man in die Pampa, und da werden solche Slips bestickt!

»Ich zeig dir mal mein Sortiment«, sagt Erika, und ich folge ihr ins Wohnzimmer.

Während Erika in dem großen Eichenschrank kramt, lasse ich mich auf dem durchgesessenen Ledersofa nieder. Voller Stolz breitet meine Gastmutter ihre Wäschestücke auf dem Wohnzimmertisch aus. Es sind unterschiedliche Modelle dabei: zarte Seidenhemdchen und große, altmodische Schlüpfer.

»Eigentlich laufen alle Modelle gut, aber der klassische Slip ist der Dauerbrenner im Shop«, erklärt Erika. »Leider hat Florian mir verboten, dir ein Original Fuckinger Unterhöschen als Willkommensgeschenk zu überreichen. Aber wenn du möchtest, sticke ich dir noch eine Garnitur – oder deinen Eltern?«

»Wow«, sage ich und danke Florian im Stillen. Ich wäre

wohl wirklich aus allen Wolken gefallen, wenn ein Slip neben meinem Teller gelegen hätte. Inzwischen wundere ich mich allerdings über gar nichts mehr. Ich bin in der wohl außergewöhnlichsten Gastfamilie der Welt gelandet.

»Und, möchtest du eine Garnitur?«, fragt Erika mit glänzenden Augen.

Es wäre herzlos von mir, ihr Angebot abzulehnen und ihre Freude zunichtezumachen.

»Unbedingt. Kann ich ein rosa Höschen haben?«, frage ich und deute auf den schmalen Slip.

»Natürlich. Und möchtest du lieber lila oder dunkelrosa Garn für die Schrift? Wenn ich genug Zeit hab und nicht zu viele Bestellungen hereinbekomme, nähe ich deiner Mutter auch noch eins.«

Ich nicke automatisch, und Erika klatscht begeistert in die Hände. In dem Moment tritt mein Gastbruder ins Wohnzimmer.

»Mama, du hast doch nicht wirklich … die arme Fabienne. Was wird sie jetzt nur von uns denken!«, schimpft Florian und läuft puterrot an, als er die ausgebreitete Wäsche sieht.

»Keine Sorge! Ich finde Erikas Kollektion toll und freue mich schon auf meinen Slip«, erwidere ich.

Florian schüttelt den Kopf. Ich kann mich nur zu gut in ihn hineinversetzen. Wenn ich daran denke, dass meine Mutter … mon Dieu! Ich würde im Erdboden versinken.

»Könnte ich vielleicht eine Flasche Mineralwasser haben? Ich würde mir gern eine mit hochnehmen«, lenke ich von der leicht angespannten Situation ab.

»Hm«, brummt Florian und dreht sich um.

Ich steh auf. »Danke, ich bin schon sehr gespannt auf meinen Slip. Gute Nacht, Erika.«

»Gute Nacht, Fabienne. Schlaf gut!«

Florian schlurft in die Küche, und ich folge ihm. Schweigend drückt er mir eine Flasche Wasser in die Hand.

»Danke«, sage ich.

»Denkst du jetzt, dass wir alle voll durchgeknallt sind?«, fragt Florian.

Ich zucke mit den Schultern. »Ein bisschen vielleicht«, gebe ich zu und muss bei seinem entsetzten Blick laut lachen.

Es dauert einen Moment, dann grinst Florian. »Ich fürchte, du hast recht. Aber wir sind nett, ehrlich.«

»Das glaub ich dir«, beruhige ich ihn. »Ich bin ziemlich müde und geh mal wieder in mein Zimmer.«

»Wenn du was brauchst und nicht mit der Unterhosenstickerin reden willst, weißt du ja, wo du mich findest.«

»Prima. Bis dann. Gute Nacht.«

Die Treppe ächzt auch diesmal wieder schrecklich. In diesem Haus muss ich mich wohl an einige Besonderheiten gewöhnen. Hoffentlich sind meine Klassenkameradinnen wenigstens etwas normaler.

Zurück im Zimmer lasse ich mich müde auf mein Bett fallen. Ob André online ist? Immer wieder gucke ich auf mein Handy, aber es hängt sich dauernd auf, wenn ich ins Netz will. Keine SMS von André. Ob er gerade mit der Band probt? Oder irgendwie zu beschäftigt ist, um seine Nachrichten zu checken? Seltsam, er hat mich doch gestern erst geküsst. Müsste er da nicht genau wie ich dauernd auf sein Smartphone gucken? Ach, Jungs …

Schließlich habe ich keine Lust mehr, auf das kleine Display zu starren, und fahre meinen Laptop hoch. Ich gebe den Code ein und bin innerhalb einer Minute online. Das Hochladen der Fotos hat funktioniert, und sie haben bereits vierzehn Likes und zwei Kommentare.

»Ist das ein Gremlin *gg*?«, fragt Valérie.

»Dussel, das ist ein Ferkel! Du hast wohl Tomaten auf den Augen«, antwortet Denise.

Ich muss lachen und setze meinen Kommentar unters Bild:

»Meine Lieben, hier bin ich, mitten in Fucking in Österreich, und ja, das ist ein Ferkel. Es heißt Susi und ist so was wie der Haushund.« Ich schließe das Foto.

Dann schreib ich Valérie noch etwas genauer, in welcher unglaublichen Situation ich mich befinde. Bevor ich mich auslogge, gebe ich noch den Namen Helene Gruber ins Suchfeld ein. Bestimmt fünfzig Suchergebnisse. Neugierig scrolle ich nach unten, und gleich an vierter Stelle lacht mir ein hübsches blondes Mädchen entgegen. Ein Blick auf eines der Wandfotos genügt. Das ist die richtige Helene. Ich schicke ihr eine Freundschaftsanfrage und gleich noch eine Nachricht.

DIE FAHRSTUHLTÜR öffnet sich, und ich trete in einen Flur mit dunkelrotem Teppich am Boden. Mit den wertvoll aussehenden Gemälden an den Wänden sieht es hier aus wie in einem Fünfsternehotel. Da komme ich mir mit meiner Jeans, meiner weißen Shirt-Bluse und dem kleinen rosa Trolley irgendwie fehl am Platz vor. In einem solchen Gebäude erwartet man rauschende Kleider, wie sie die Königinnen früher trugen. Ich drücke auf den Klingelknopf neben der Wohnungstür.

Die Tür schwingt auf, und vor mir steht, das Handy fest ans Ohr gedrückt, eine top gestylte, schlanke Frau. Sie trägt einen recht kurzen Pagenkopf, und ihre akkurat geschnittenen Haare glänzen im tiefsten Blauschwarz.

Ohne das Telefonat zu beenden, nickt sie mir lächelnd zu und winkt mich herein. Unsicher folge ich Madame Henry in ein offenes, modern eingerichtetes Wohnzimmer. Meine Gastmutter deutet auf eine große naturweiße Ledercouch, und ich setze mich.

Schweigend lasse ich meinen Blick durch den Raum schweifen. Die dunklen Holzmöbel mit den cremefarbenen Fronten, auf denen nur eine Vase oder ein Bilderrahmen steht, lassen das Wohnzimmer seltsam unbewohnt erscheinen. Fast habe ich das Gefühl, mich in einem Möbelhaus zu befinden.

Nach ein paar Minuten ist Madame Henry fertig mit ihrem Gespräch. Als sie zu mir kommt, springe ich schnell auf. Lächelnd haucht sie mir, ohne mich zu berühren, Begrüßungsküsschen auf die Wangen.

»Hallo, Helene. Ich muss mich nochmals bei dir entschuldigen, dass ich dich nicht abholen konnte. Aber mir wäre beinahe ein großer Immobiliendeal geplatzt. Ein ganz wichtiger Kunde war sehr unzufrieden mit der Beratung meiner Kollegin. Es tut mir leid.«

»Schon in Ordnung, Madame Henry.«

»Du darfst mich gerne Brigitte nennen. Hast du gut hergefunden?«

»Ja, also, es hat alles gut geklappt mit dem Taxi«, erwidere ich und spüre, wie mir das Blut in die Wangen schießt. Schon dumm, wenn man so leicht errötet wie ich. Florian macht immer Scherze darüber, obwohl es ihm selbst auch nicht viel besser geht. Dennoch nennt er mich Rotköpfchen oder lebendige Ampel.

»Wie viel musstest du ausgeben? Fünfzig, sechzig Euro?« Brigitte hastet zum Esstisch, auf dem ihre Handtasche steht. Einen Moment später hält sie mir einen Hunderteuroschein hin. »Hier hast du eine kleine Entschädigung. In Paris kannst du ein bisschen Taschengeld gut gebrauchen.«

»Ähm, danke«, sage ich schüchtern und nehme den Schein. Plötzlich höre ich ein leises Mauzen hinter mir, und mit einem Satz landet eine merkwürdig aussehende Katze auf der Couch und sieht mich auffordernd an. Sie hat riesige Ohren, noch größere Augen und ist am ganzen Körper nackt. So eine seltsame Mieze hab ich noch nie gesehen, außer auf Bildern oder im Fernsehen.

»Oh, Ihre königliche Hoheit Bastet möchte dich kennenlernen«, meint Brigitte lachend.

»Das ist aber eine ganz besondere Katze«, sage ich und strecke meine Hand nach dem Tier aus.

»Sie gehört Fabienne. Die beiden sind ein Herz und eine Seele, und ich weiß manchmal gar nicht, wer die größere Prinzessin ist, unsere Tochter oder unsere Sphynx-Katze.«

»Oh, ist die weich und warm«, bemerke ich verwundert.

Bastet schmiegt sich an meine Hand und schnurrt zufrieden. Brigittes Telefon klingelt erneut. Sie wirft einen Blick aufs Display und drückt seufzend den Anrufer weg. »Die Arbeit. Tut mir leid, aber ich muss zurückrufen. Dein Zimmer ist ganz hinten rechts, gegenüber ist dein Bad. Fabienne hat alles für dich vorbereitet.«

»Vielen Dank, ich – «

Schon wieder schrillt das Handy. Meine Gastmutter meldet sich, bittet um einen Moment Geduld und hält den Hörer zu, sodass der Anrufer nicht mithören kann. »Helene, meine Liebe. Sieh dich ruhig um. Ich muss wirklich telefonieren. Wenn Richard zu Hause ist, dann gehen wir schön essen. Ich habe für uns einen Tisch reserviert.« Sie wendet sich wieder ihrem Telefon zu und läuft dabei hektisch im Wohnzimmer auf und ab.

Es hat wohl keinen Sinn, dass ich auf sie warte. Also

nehme ich meinen Trolley und gehe in mein Zimmer. Bastet schreitet elegant neben mir her. Mit der Selbstverständlichkeit einer heimlichen Herrscherin macht sie es sich auf dem Bett gemütlich. Ich schaue mich in Fabiennes Reich um. Ihr Zimmer ist mindestens dreimal so groß wie meins. Auch das Bett ist riesig, und darüber hängt ein gerahmtes Twilight-Poster mit – ich kann es kaum glauben! – den Unterschriften der Hauptdarsteller. Wow! Nicht, dass ich jetzt der absolute Fan wäre, aber schließlich ist es nicht leicht, an Autogramme der Stars zu kommen.

Am anderen Ende des Zimmers stehen eine kleine Couch, ein dazu passender Tisch und ein Schreibtisch mit Fabiennes iMac. Daneben befindet sich eine weitere Tür. Als ich sie öffne, stehe ich inmitten eines begehbaren Kleiderschranks, der voll von schicken Blusen, Röcken und Schuhen ist. Ganz vorne klebt ein Zettel an einer Schublade: Hallo, Helene, bedien dich ruhig, wenn dir etwas gefällt. Aber Louisa soll es dann reinigen lassen. Merci.

Ich bin geschockt. Was für ein Luxus. Fabienne überlässt mir hier ein halbes Schloss samt ihrer Party-Outfits und Mini-Königstiger, und in meiner Familie erwartet sie … na ja, ein Bauernhof mit Hausschwein. Da beschleicht mich doch gleich das schlechte Gewissen. Hoffentlich sind meine Eltern und Florian nett zu ihr. Ich atme tief ein. Bastet schleicht um meine Beine und mauzt leise. Ich nehme sie auf den Arm, und sie schmiegt sich zufrieden an meine Brust.

Es klopft an der Tür, und Brigitte schaut herein. »Helene, leider hab ich schlechte Nachrichten. Unser gemeinsames

Essen fällt aus. Ich muss noch einmal zurück in die Firma und weiß nicht, wie lange es dauern wird. Mein Mann kommt gegen acht Uhr abends heim. Kommst du bis dahin allein zurecht?«

»Ja, das werde ich schon«, flüstere ich, obwohl mir bei dem Gedanken, ganz alleine in der riesigen Wohnung zu sein, flau im Magen wird.

»Gut. Hier hast du ein paar Restaurant-Flyer. Bestell dir einfach, was du gerne möchtest. Auf dem Küchentisch liegen dreißig Euro. Ich mache, so schnell ich kann. Fühl dich einfach wie zu Hause. In Ordnung?«

»In Ordnung«, wiederhole ich.

Madame Henry stöckelt davon, und ich bleibe mit Bastet allein zurück. Meine Familie sitzt jetzt bestimmt mit Fabienne um den großen Tisch. Alleine essen macht traurig, erst recht am allerersten Abend in Paris. Doch der heutige Abend ist bestimmt eine Ausnahme. Morgen haben meine Gasteltern sicher Zeit, mir die Stadt zu zeigen. Dann begnüge ich mich heute eben damit, mein riesiges Zimmer zu erkunden.

Als ich aufstehen will, klammert sich Bastet an mich – anscheinend will sie weiter gestreichelt werden. Ganz einsam bin ich also doch nicht.

»Na, Kätzchen, dann wollen wir uns mal einrichten. Ich verspreche dir auch, dass ich mich gut um dich kümmere, während deine Fabienne weg ist.«

Miau, macht Bastet und sieht mich mit klugen Katzenaugen an, als hätte sie jedes Wort verstanden.

DIE ZEIT ZIEHT SICH wie ein ausgelutschter Kaugummi. Obwohl ich mir fest vorgenommen habe, mein neues Territorium zu erkunden, warte ich insgeheim doch auf meine Gasteltern. Langsam weiß ich nicht mehr, was ich machen soll. Lena hab ich schon eine SMS geschrieben, dass ich gut angekommen bin, und der Koffer ist ausgepackt. Schließlich halte ich es nicht mehr aus und rufe zu Hause an.

»Alles okay bei dir?«, fragt Mama besorgt.

»Hm. Alles bestens.« Ich schwärme ihr von der Wohnung vor und versuche, glücklich zu klingen, obwohl ich beim Klang von Mamas Stimme irre Sehnsucht bekomme. Sie erzählt mir, dass Fabienne sich auch schon ins Zimmer zurückgezogen hat und dass sie noch ein wenig sticken will. Mir wird ganz schwer ums Herz. Vielleicht war dieser Austausch doch keine so gute Idee. Da ich Mama aber nicht beunruhigen will, versichere ich ihr euphorisch, dass es toll hier ist.

Als ich auflege, ist es gerade einmal kurz nach sieben. Mein Magen brummt, aber auf Lieferessen hab ich keine

Lust. Wer weiß, ob mir die Pizzen hier schmecken. Außerdem traue ich mich nicht, Essen am Telefon zu bestellen. So gut ist mein Französisch nicht, dass ich mir sicher sein kann, verstanden zu werden. Hat Brigitte nicht gesagt, ich solle mich wie zu Hause fühlen?

Ich gehe zum Kühlschrank und öffne die Tür. Du meine Güte! Warum haben die einen überlebensgroßen Kühlschrank, wenn er so gut wie leer ist? Karotten, Pilze und Schnittlauch sind im Gemüsefach. Milch, drei Eier, etwas Magerschinken, zwei fettarme Joghurts, das war's. Kein Wunder, dass Madame Henry so schlank ist.

Zum Glück entdecke ich noch eine Packung Toast und ein paar Tomaten. Also gibt es Eieromelette mit Kräutern, Schinkenstückchen und Tomatensalat.

Nach dem Essen geh ich mit dem Handy ins Netz und checke meine Facebook-Seite. Meine Schulfreundinnen wünschen mir viel Spaß beim Austausch, außerdem habe ich eine Freundschaftsanfrage und eine Nachricht bekommen. Als ich sie öffnen will, drängelt sich Bastet dazwischen. Sie mag es wohl nicht, wenn man mit dem Handy beschäftigt ist.

»Du bist ja schlimmer als Papa«, sage ich lachend und setze die Katze zur Seite. Sofort dreht sie beleidigt den Kopf weg und beginnt sich zu putzen. Eine echte Diva.

Fabienne Henry hat mir geschrieben.

Hallo, Helene,
hier ist Fabienne, deine Austauschschülerin. Ich hoffe, du fühlst dich wohl in meinem Zimmer. Gern

kannst du meinen iMac benutzen. Ich hab dir einen
eigenen Zugang angelegt. Klick einfach auf Gast,
der Code lautet »bastet_henry«. Ach ja, und bitte,
kümmere dich gut um die lebende Bastet. Sie
ist sehr empfindsam und eine absolute Kuschel-
tigerin. Ich freu mich, wenn du meine Freundschaftsanfrage annimmst. Wir haben uns sicher
viel zu erzählen. Deine Familie ist ja sehr witzig,
besonders Susi.
LG Fabienne

Ich nehme ihre Freundschaftsanfrage sofort an.

Hallo, Fabienne,
danke für deine Anfrage und dass du so großzügig
bist. Du hast ja tolle Kleider und ein tolles Zimmer.
Bastet geht es prima, sie will dauergekrault werden. Danke auch, dass ich deinen Mac benutzen darf.
LG Helene

Keine Minute vergeht, schon öffnet sich das Chatfenster.

Hallo, Helene,
schön, dich kennenzulernen. Wie geht's dir? Seid
ihr gar nicht essen? Mama hatte doch extra einen
Tisch reserviert! Bei deiner Mutter hat es auf jeden Fall ganz phantastisch geschmeckt.

Ich erzähle Fabienne, dass ihrer Mutter etwas dazwischen-gekommen ist. Wie es scheint, kennt sie das. Sofort tröstet sie mich und schickt mir einen Ich-umarme-dich-Smiley. Doch mir macht auch noch ein anderes Thema Sorgen.

Du, Fabienne?

Ja?

Wegen Montag, Schule und so … ich bin echt nervös. ☹

Musst du nicht. Es sind alle ganz nett. Du hast nichts zu befürchten. Wirst sehen, meine Klasse ist echt entspannt.

Ich hoffe, Fabienne hat recht. Bisher war nämlich noch gar nichts entspannt. In dem Moment höre ich die Wohnungstür. Meine Gasteltern sind zurück. Ich schaue auf die Uhr. Inzwischen ist es halb zehn. Schnell verabschiede ich mich von Fabienne.

Brigitte und ihr Mann Richard wirken erschöpft. Monsieur Henry ist kleiner als seine Frau, etwas rundlich und hat einen lichten blonden Haarkranz. Erneut beteuern die beiden, wie leid es ihnen tut, dass sie keine Zeit für mich hatten. Dann entschuldigen sich die beiden. Sie müssen noch reden … beruflich. Tja, dann werde ich mich wohl in mein Zimmer zurückziehen und versuchen zu schlafen. Vielleicht knipse ich auch noch ein paar Fotos, damit Lena mir glaubt, dass ich tatsächlich in einem Schloss lebe …

DER SONNTAG VERGEHT SCHNELL. Ich schlafe lange, frühstücke kurz, probiere die Schuluniform, höre Musik und klicke mich ein wenig durchs Netz.

Zum Mittagessen führen mich meine Gasteltern in ein nobles Restaurant aus. Danach gehen sie mit mir ein Stück die Champs-Élysées entlang und erklären mir, wie ich zur Schule komme.

Den Nachmittag verbringen wir wieder in der Wohnung. Brigitte schreibt ein Immobilienangebot, Richard bereitet ein Meeting vor, und ich surfe im Internet. Schließlich wird es Abend, und der gefürchtete Montag rückt näher.

Hallo, Fabienne,
wünsch mir Glück für morgen. Ich hab echt Bammel vor dem ersten Schultag. Deine Eltern waren heute übrigens ziemlich cool und haben sich ein wenig Zeit genommen. Wir waren essen, und es war echt lecker. Bastet geht's gut. Sie hat die erste Nacht bei mir im Bett geschlafen. Ich hoffe mal, sie darf das.
Tschüss Helene

Hallo, Helene,

nur keine Panik, es sind alle ganz locker bei mir im Lycée. Freut mich, dass meine Eltern für dich Zeit hatten. Sie sind leider oft gestresst. Dein Papa hat mich heute zum Nachbarhof geführt und mir die Pferde gezeigt. ☺ Ist ja toll, dass ihr direkt neben einem Reiterhof wohnt. Vielleicht trau ich mich auch mal, eine Stunde zu nehmen. Bastet schläft bei mir übrigens auch immer im Bett. Susi geht es auch gut. Sie schläft derzeit bei deinem Bruder. Ein Schwein unterm Bett, das war mir irgendwie etwas unheimlich.

Adieu und relax – morgen wird schon.

LG F.

G L Ü C K L I C H E R W E I S E hat mich Brigitte heute Morgen mit dem Auto zum Lycée gefahren. »Dort drüben ist deine Schule«, sagt sie und deutet auf ein großes Gebäude, das sich in einer riesigen Parkanlage befindet. Unsicher steige ich aus dem Wagen. »Viel Erfolg«, wünscht mir meine Gastmutter und braust davon.

Ich zupfe meine Schuluniform zurecht. Bei mir zu Hause gibt es so etwas nicht, und ich fühle mich unwohl in dem kurzen Faltenrock, der weißen Bluse und dem Jackett. Eigentlich ist es in Frankreich nicht mehr üblich, eine Schuluniform zu tragen, aber Fabienne besucht eine Privatschule, in der andere Regeln gelten.

Eine Gruppe lachender Mädchen steuert auf den Schuleingang zu. Unauffällig schließe ich mich an und lausche dem aufgeregten Geplapper.

In der Schule herrscht ein lautes Durcheinander. Die Gänge sind voller Schüler, die ihre Sachen aus dem Schließfach holen und in ihre Klassenräume strömen. Verzweifelt versuche ich mich zu orientieren. Gibt es denn hier keine Hinweisschilder für Neuankömmlinge? Am besten eins, auf dem in Großbuchstaben steht: HELENE GRUBER, BITTE DEN ROTEN PFEILEN FOLGEN!

Ratlos blicke ich mich um. Die Situation kommt mir seltsam vertraut vor. Nur dass dieses Mal kein Jai in Sicht ist. In dem Moment rempelt mich ein Junge an. Meine Tasche fällt mir aus der Hand, und meine Bücher purzeln auf den Gang.

»Oh, das tut mir leid. Warte, ich helfe dir«, entschuldigt er sich.

Wir greifen gleichzeitig nach der Mappe, sehen uns an … und Wum! Das sind die blauesten Augen, die ich je gesehen habe. Noch dazu hat er schwarze Haare, eine olivbraune Haut und ein Lächeln, das selbst einen Eisklotz schmelzen lassen würde.

»Sorry«, sagt er nochmals und gibt mir meine Mappe zurück. »Du bist nicht von hier, oder? Bist du eine der Austauschschülerinnen?«

»Ja genau, ich bin Fabienne Henrys Austauschschülerin«, erwidere ich. Schon wieder kriecht mir warmes Blut den Hals empor, wie Schnecken an einem Salat. Ich sehe bestimmt schon aus wie eine Tomate auf zwei Beinen.

»Na dann, herzlich willkommen! Ich bin André. Wenn du Fabiennes Austauschschülerin bist, sind wir in derselben Klasse. Willst du gleich mitkommen?«

»Helene«, sage ich, obwohl er mich nicht nach meinem Namen gefragt hat, »Danke, ich wär echt froh, wenn du mir den Weg zeigen würdest. Eure Schule ist ja riesig.«

»Große Geister brauchen eine große Schule«, verkündet André theatralisch und tippt sich dabei gegen die Stirn.

»Du bist wohl ein großer Denker, hm?«

»Aber sicher, hast das du nicht gemerkt? Schließlich habe ich durch meine herausragenden Fähigkeiten gleich erkannt, dass du die Austauschschülerin bist ... und weil du kein Namensschild an der Jacke trägst.« Grinsend deutet er auf sein eigenes.

Nun muss ich auch lachen. Wenn alle hier so nett sind wie André, dann waren meine Sorgen wirklich unbegründet.

Das Klassenzimmer befindet sich im ersten Stock. Pünktlich zum Stundenklingeln treten wir ein. Mindestens fünfzehn neugierige Augenpaare mustern mich, wodurch meine Gesichtsdurchblutung gleich wieder in Schwung kommt. Es ist ungewohnt für mich, so viele Jungs in der Klasse zu haben. Bei mir zu Hause sind viel mehr Mädchen in der Schule.

Obwohl alle die gleiche dunkelblaue Uniform tragen, erkenne ich kleine Unterschiede. Wie sich die Mädchen ihr Halstuch umgebunden, die Strümpfe angezogen oder auch eine Brosche angesteckt haben. Einige tragen auch Ohrringe, Halsketten oder Ringe an den Fingern, und auch ihre Brillen sehen mehr nach Schmuck als nach Sehhilfen aus. Die Jungs haben sich vor allem ihre Haare gestylt und den Krawattenknoten mal streng, mal lässig gebunden.

»Ich an deiner Stelle würde mich auf Fabiennes Platz setzen«, meint André und deutet auf einen freien Stuhl in der hintersten Reihe.

»Aha. Und warum?«

»Weil du da in allerbester Gesellschaft bist«, erklärt er augenzwinkernd, »da sitzen nämlich mein Kumpel Marc, Marie-Claire und ich.«

Schon stehen die beiden eben Genannten neben mir und

hauchen mir Küsschen auf die Wangen. André übernimmt es, mich vorzustellen. Gerade als ich etwas zu Marie-Claire und Marc sagen will, fällt die Klassentür ins Schloss. Eine kleine, hagere Professorin trippelt auf hohen Absätzen zum Lehrerpult.

»Das ist Madame Nain, unsere Deutschlehrerin. Setz dich lieber schnell hin. Sie kann ziemlich sauer werden«, zischt André mir zu.

Madame Nain? Die Professorin heißt tatsächlich Zwerg und ist auch noch klein und dünn? Ich muss grinsen.

»Auf die Plätze, aber flott! Warum sitzen Sie noch nicht? Beim Läuten haben Sie auf Ihren Plätzen zu sein«, schimpft Madame Nain mit hoher Stimme. Ihr Blick fällt auf mich. Sie zieht die Augenbrauen hoch und schenkt mir ein perlweißes Lächeln. »Oh unsere Austauschschülerin ist da, darum die Aufregung«, ruft sie erfreut. »Ruhe, Mesdemoiselles, Messieurs! Mademoiselle Gruber, kommen Sie bitte zu mir nach vorne und stellen Sie sich vor.«

Na toll. Ich liebe Vorstellrunden, besonders, wenn ich an der Reihe bin – denn dann herrscht Rotköpfchen-Ampelalarm! Schüchtern erhebe mich. Alle starren mich an, als ich durch den Mittelgang gehe. Ich stottere meinen Namen und Wohnort.

»Fu... Fugg... Bitte schreiben Sie es doch an die Tafel«, fordert mich Frau Zwerg auf, und brav schreibe ich Helene Gruber/Fucking auf das dunkle Grün der Tafel.

Das ganze Klassenzimmer hält den Atem an, dann beginnt jemand zu kichern, und schließlich bricht die ganze Klasse in tosendes Gelächter aus, sogar Madame Nain.

Auf einmal ist meine Nervosität weg. Ich erzähle vom Leben auf dem Land, bis es zur Pause klingelt. Schnell knipst Madame Nain noch ein paar Fotos für die Schulhomepage. André und sein Freund Marc nehmen mich in die Mitte. Im Nachhinein frage ich mich, warum ich eigentlich so viel Angst vor dem ersten Schultag hatte.

09

DIE CAFETERIA ist groß und unpersönlich. Da ich jedoch in Begleitung von Marc, Marie-Claire und André hier bin, fühle ich mich dennoch wohl. Ich blicke mich um. An der einen Seite befindet sich eine riesige Essensausgabe, genau wie man es aus den amerikanischen Fernsehserien kennt. Man lädt sich auf ein Tablett, was man gerne essen möchte. Auf der anderen Seite stehen die Tische mit den Bänken. Marc, André und Marie-Claire schleppen mich einfach durch die Cafeteria. Im Nu sitze ich mit einem Salat, einem Brötchen und einer kleinen Flasche Mineralwasser an einem Tisch direkt am Fenster.

»Und, Helene? Wie gefällt es dir bisher bei uns?«, fragt Marie-Claire.

»Na, wie wohl? Großartig. Immerhin hat sie uns kennengelernt und noch dazu Frau Professor Deutschzwerg«, erwidert André lachend.

Ich kichere. »Ja, die ist ein echtes Original, diese Madame Nain.«

»Du musst sie mal erleben, wenn sie zum Giftzwerg mutiert. Doch zum Glück sind nicht alle Deutsch sprechenden

Frauen klein und giftig, wie man sieht. Du bist jedenfalls das genaue Gegenteil: witzig und hübsch.« André lächelt mich an, und mir wird ganz heiß im Gesicht.

»Es ist wirklich nett bei euch. Heute Morgen war mir noch ganz flau im Magen, aber jetzt geht's mir schon viel besser.«

»Wahrscheinlich warst du einfach nur hungrig«, bemerkt Marc. »Mit uns kann es schließlich nichts zu tun haben, denn wir sind ganz nett.«

Viel zu nett, denke ich und wage es nicht, in Andrés Richtung zu schauen. Er hat es innerhalb kürzester Zeit geschafft, mich wie eine Verkehrsampel rot blinken zu lassen. André sieht einfach verdammt gut aus. Dieses Lächeln. Diese Augen. In denen könnte ich mich glatt verlieren. Ob er zu allen Mädchen so nett ist? Auf jeden Fall wird er ziemlich umschwärmt. Als wir vorhin zur Cafeteria gelaufen sind, haben ihn mindestens zehn Mädels kichernd mit Küsschen begrüßt. Und dennoch hat er mich nicht aus den Augen gelassen und ist auf keinen Flirtversuch eingegangen. Ob das etwas zu bedeuten hat?

»Helene?«, fragt Marc.

»Wa... was?«, stottere ich.

Marc zeigt erneut auf mein Tablett.

Ich kichere. »Stimmt. Wahrscheinlich bin ich nur hungrig. Mein Magen knurrt auch schon.«

»Meiner auch ... grrr!«, scherzt André und nimmt sein Baguette in die Hand. Dabei zwinkert er mir zu.

Mein Puls rast, aber ich versuche, mir nichts anmerken zu lassen. Stattdessen konzentriere ich mich auf Marie-

Claire, die von einem Film erzählt, den sie am Wochenende gesehen hat. Sie spricht extra langsam, damit ich auch alles verstehe, und Marc erklärt mir immer mal wieder ein Wort. Die Clique gibt sich richtig Mühe mit mir. Was für ein Glück, dass ich die drei gleich kennengelernt habe! Ich kann es kaum erwarten, nach Hause zu kommen und Fabienne von meinem ersten Schultag zu berichten!

Hallo, Fabienne,
mein erster Schultag war prima, und deiner? Du hattest übrigens recht. Deine Klassenkameraden sind wirklich nett. Im ersten Moment war ich zwar schockiert, weil euer Lycée so groß ist, aber dann hab ich André kennengelernt, und er hat mir euren Klassenraum gezeigt. Er war ziemlich nett, genau wie Marc und Marie-Claire. Eure Madame Nain ist ja eine witzige Gestalt. Da passt der Name voll! ☺ Meld dich mal. Ich hock bestimmt noch eine Weile mit Bastet vorm PC und surfe.
Tschüssi
Helene

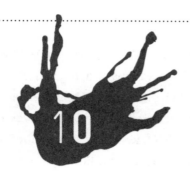

ICH HABE NOCH NIE so eine alte, kleine Schule gesehen, außer vielleicht in dem Dorf, wo meine Urgroßmutter wohnt. Die Wände sind grau und rissig, die hohen Fenster von dünnen grünen Alu-Rahmen eingefasst. »Höhere Bundeslehranstalt für wirtschaftliche Berufe« steht über der Eingangstür. Das soll meine Schule sein?

Es ist zehn Uhr. Laut der Agentur sollte ich am ersten Schultag erst zur dritten Stunde da sein, damit alles für mich vorbereitet werden kann – was immer das auch bedeuten mag. Zögernd gehe ich in das Gebäude. Ein ungewohnter Geruch schlägt mir entgegen. Es riecht gar nicht nach Schule, sondern eher wie in einem Restaurant. Ein Mädchen mit einer Kochmütze und einer Schürze tritt auf den Gang. In den Händen hält sie einen großen Kochtopf samt Deckel.

»Oh, du bist sicher Fabienne. An unserer kleinen Schule spricht es sich herum, wenn eine Austauschschülerin kommt. Alle sind schon ganz aufgeregt, aber du bist ganz schön früh dran. Wir sind noch gar nicht fertig mit Kochen. Am besten, du gehst erst mal in die Schulküche«, sagt sie und setzt sich in Bewegung. »Ach ja! Ich bin übrigens Sophie. Schön, dass du da bist«, ruft sie noch über die Schulter und schleppt den Topf keuchend die Treppe hoch.

Laut einem Hinweisschild an der Wand befinden sich dort oben das Direktorat und das Lehrerzimmer. Müssen die Schüler hier etwa ihre Lehrer bekochen? Unser Geschichtslehrer hat uns mal erzählt, dass es früher üblich war, im Winter ein Holzscheit mit in die Schule zu nehmen – zum Heizen des Schulgebäudes. Andernfalls hätte gar kein Unterricht stattfinden können. Ich stelle mir vor, dass die österreichischen Schüler ihre Lehrer bekochen müssen, damit diese überhaupt arbeiten. Bei der Vorstellung muss ich grinsen.

In der Schulküche dampft und raucht, zischt und brutzelt es. Mädchen mit Schürzen und Kochmützen wuseln in der großen Edelstahlküche herum, schnippeln Gemüse, braten Zwiebeln an und unterhalten sich dabei in voller Lautstärke. Plötzlich steht eine ebenfalls weiß beschürzte Frau vor mir. Ihre grau-braunen Haare sind streng nach hinten gekämmt und zu einem Knoten gefasst.

»Fabienne, richtig?« Sie lächelt mich an. »Herzlich willkommen bei uns! Ich bin Frau Professor Pfeifer. Eigentlich sollte das Essen schon fertig sein, wenn du kommst. Bei uns ist es nämlich üblich, dass wir unseren Gästen ein kleines Menü kochen, bevor sie selbst an den Herd dürfen. Eine kulinarische Begrüßung sozusagen.«

»Selbst an den Herd? Heißt das etwa, ich werde hier auch kochen?«

»Ja, natürlich. Kochen, Servieren und Handarbeiten sind drei unserer Hauptfächer. Du bist schließlich an einer Höheren Bundeslehranstalt und nicht an einem Gymnasium.«

Irgendwie hab ich plötzlich zu viel Spucke im Mund, ich schlucke hektisch wie ein Ertrinkender. Ich und kochen? Außer Crêpes und Käseplatten hab ich noch nie etwas selbst zubereitet. Wo bin ich hier bloß gelandet?

»Frau Professor Kronbichler bedankt sich für die Suppe!«, ruft Sophie atemlos, die gerade zurück in die Küche gekommen ist.

»Aha, sehr gut. Da hat die 3b eine ziemliche Aufgabe zu bewältigen.« Frau Professor Pfeifer gibt einem blonden Mädchen ein Zeichen, das auf den ersten Blick fast wie Helene aussieht. »Lena, nimm doch bitte Fabienne mit an deinen Kochplatz und zeig ihr alles. In einer halben Stunde essen wir.« Mit diesen Worten macht sie auf dem Absatz kehrt und wendet sich einem kurzhaarigen Mädchen zu, das schimpfend eine schwarz rauchende Pfanne in die Luft hält. Ich bin vielleicht kein Kochgenie, aber angebrannte Zwiebeln erkenne selbst ich.

»Hallo, ich bin Lena, Helenes beste Freundin«, begrüßt mich das blonde Mädchen. »Da drüben ist mein Kochplatz.«

»Fabienne Henry«, stelle ich mich vor und folge ihr.

Lena stellt sich an eins der großen Spülbecken und beginnt, Erdbeeren zu waschen. Unschlüssig schaue ich ihr zu.

»Wieso hat Sophie eigentlich für Frau Professor Kronbichler gekocht?«, frage ich schließlich.

»Ach, da gibt's so einen kleinen Konkurrenzkampf zwischen Frau Professor Kronbichlers Klasse und uns. Wir kochen immer abwechselnd ein Gericht, und die andere Klasse muss raten, welche Zutaten verwendet wurden. Diesmal wird es schwierig. Wir haben in unsere Kartoffelsuppe nicht nur die normalen Gewürze, sondern auch etwas Safran und Kreuzkümmel getan. Daran werden sie einige Zeit knabbern. Wahrscheinlich geht dieser Punkt an unsere Klasse. Wir liegen drei Punkte zurück, und wenn wir nicht aufholen, dann müssen wir das Büfett fürs Abschlussfest vorbereiten!«

Lena legt die gewaschenen Erdbeeren in eine weiße Schüssel. »Willst du mir vielleicht beim Nachtisch helfen?«

»Ich, ich … kann nur Crêpes«, stottere ich verlegen.

»Perfekt. Ich mache Erdbeersahne und du ein paar Crêpes. Das wird ein leckeres Dessert, viel besser als immer nur Apfelstrudel. Du musst wissen, dass wir die Pfeifer schon insgeheim Frau Strudelpeter nennen, weil es bei ihr immer Strudel gibt«, flüstert mir Lena zu. »Na ja, und außerdem sieht sie aus wie der Struwwelpeter, wenn sie ihre Haare nicht zusammengeknotet hat. Die stehen ab, als hätte sie in eine Steckdose gegriffen.«

Ich muss grinsen und erzähle ihr von unserer Madame Nain und wie wir sie sonst so nennen: die Zwergenkönigin, Baronin der Gnome, Deutschwichtel. Lena lacht und stellt mir eine Schüssel, eine Packung Eier und eine Milchtüte hin. Während ich den Crêpeteig anrühre, erklärt Lena mir, dass die Schüler in dieser Schule nicht nur Abitur, sondern auch gleichzeitig eine Ausbildung zum Koch und Kellner machen. Da dieser Schultyp mehr Mädchen anspricht, gibt es in der Klasse auch nur einen einzigen Jungen. Er heißt Sebastian, ist blond und zart und sieht selbst fast aus wie ein Mädchen. Ich muss an André denken und frage mich, ob er ein klein wenig Sehnsucht nach mir hat. Mir fehlt er jetzt schon, besonders weil ich in einer Mädchenschule gelandet bin.

Als Frau Professor Pfeifer uns auffordert, die Schüsseln und Platten in den Speisesaal zu bringen, wundere ich mich über den erstaunlichen Berg hauchzarter Crêpes, den ich ganz nebenbei gezaubert habe.

Das gemeinsame Essen macht Spaß, nicht zuletzt weil die Lehrerin so von meinen Crêpes schwärmt und mich über die Maßen lobt. »Einfach lecker«, finden auch meine neuen Klassenkameradinnen. Sebastian, der dünne Junge, nimmt sich glatt einen zweiten Crêpe. Ich bin direkt ein bisschen stolz auf mich. Damit habe ich den ersten Schreck, gleich an den Herd zu müssen, ganz gut überwunden. Die nächsten Unterrichtsstunden, Deutsch, Mathematik, Biologie und Sport, verlaufen weit weniger überraschend. Mit Lena verstehe ich mich gut, aber auch Sophie ist nett. Die Schule ist wahrscheinlich ganz okay, trotz Kochen und Kellnern.

DIE BUSFAHRT ZURÜCK NACH FUCKING
ist die Hölle. Sie führt quer durch die Pampa und dauert
eine gute halbe Stunde. In Paris fahre ich immer mit der
Métro oder nehme mir ein Taxi. Mit einem Bus durchs
Land zu schaukeln, ist nicht so mein Ding. Ich schnappe
mir mein Smartphone und sehe nach, ob André sich auf
meine letzte SMS gemeldet hat. Oh, mon Dieu, ich habe
tatsächlich eine Nachricht von ihm bekommen.

> Haben diese Woche einen Gig im Jay Jays! Geile
> Sache, nicht wahr? Da versäumst du einen echt coo-
> len Auftritt!
> Bis dann
> André

Was soll das denn? Ich hab ihn in der letzten SMS gefragt,
wie es ihm geht, und ihm sogar gestanden, dass ich an ihn
denke. Und was macht er? Er schreibt irgendwas von seiner
Band, als wäre ich ein x-beliebiges Groupie. Er hat mich geküsst, verdammt noch mal! Mir ist zum Heulen zumute.

Der Bus tuckert durch die grüne Landschaft, und passend zu meiner Stimmung setzt ein Sommerregen ein.

Als wir in Fucking ankommen, gießt es in Strömen. Natürlich hab ich keinen Schirm dabei. Meine Laune ist im Eimer. Appetit hab ich nach dem Schulessen und dieser SMS auch keinen mehr, trotz der köstlichen Duftwolken, die durch das Bauernhaus wabern. Erika runzelt die Stirn, als sie meinen unberührten Teller sieht. Zum Glück hat sie so viel Feingefühl, nicht lange nachzufragen, was los ist. Meine Portion landet in Susis Napf, die freudig grunzt.

»Entschuldigt, es war einfach anstrengend heute. Darf ich schon in mein Zimmer gehen?«, frage ich meine Gasteltern.

»Natürlich. Ruh dich aus«, erwidert Peter.

Ich flüchte nach oben und werfe den Computer an.

Eine Nachricht von Helene, aber nichts Neues von André. War ja klar. Ich öffne Helenes Nachricht.

Aha, André war also nett. Zu nett vielleicht? Ich will gerade zurückschreiben, als *Pling!*, eine neue Facebook-Nachricht von Helene eintrudelt.

Hallo, Fabienne, bist du da? Wie lief es? Haben sie dich bekocht? Ich durfte ja nichts verraten! ;-)

Hi! Es war superlecker. Deine Schule ist ja seltsam. Kochen, Kellnern, Stricken – und ich dachte, so was gibt's nicht mehr.

Bei uns schon! ☺ Hast du gleich Anschluss gefunden?

Ja, ich hab zusammen mit Lena gekocht. War echt nett mit ihr. Und du hast gleich André kennengelernt?

Ja, André, Marc und Marie-Claire. Wenn ich André nicht getroffen hätte, würde ich wohl jetzt noch durch die Schule irren und meine Klasse suchen.

Übertreib nicht! Du hättest es auch ohne André geschafft.

War schon gut, dass er da war. Wir haben auch die Pause zusammen verbracht. Er ist echt witzig, da ging es mir dann gleich viel besser. Neu zu sein ist ja nicht einfach. Er war sogar so nett, mir den Weg zur U-Bahn zu zeigen, und zum Abschied hat er gesagt, dass er sich schon freut, wenn wir uns morgen wiedersehen. Du hast echt tolle Freunde!

Hab ich dir doch gesagt. Freut mich, dass es dir gut geht.

Wir chatten eine Weile. Helene klingt euphorisch, wenn sie von der Schule berichtet, und traurig, wenn sie von daheim erzählt. Ja, es stimmt schon, meine Eltern haben wenig Zeit. Mich ärgert das auch manchmal.

Nachdem Helene sich ausgeloggt hat, poste ich ein Foto von Schweinchen Susi und schreibe als Kommentar dazu, dass in Fucking alle saumäßig nett sind. Dann klicke ich auf Andrés Seite. Vielleicht ist er ja on oder hat etwas gepostet.

Mon Dieu! Was ist das denn? Auf Andrés Pinnwand prangt ein neues Foto: Helene inmitten meiner Klassenkameraden. Neben ihr Marc, der wie immer schüchtern auf den Boden blickt, und André, der ihr überhaupt nicht schüchtern ein Küsschen auf die Wange haucht. Glückselig grinst Helene in die Kamera. IST ANDRÉ ETWA SOOOO NETT ZU IHR? So nett, wie er nur zu mir sein sollte? Er hat mich doch geküsst! Ich dachte, es wäre ihm ernst mit uns. Oder macht er das nur für die Kamera? Er ist ein ziemlicher Selbstdarsteller. Ich schnappe nach Luft, bemühe mich ruhig zu bleiben, aber mir kommen die Tränen. Andrés unpersönliche SMS, sein Schweigen und jetzt das! So ein Mist!

ICH BIN STOLZ AUF MICH, denn heute bin ich das erste Mal mit der U-Bahn zur Schule gefahren. Brigitte hätte mich auch wieder mit dem Auto gebracht, aber ich wollte es unbedingt allein schaffen.

In der Schulgarderobe treffe ich auf Marie-Claire. »Na, hast du gut geschlafen? Oder hast du vom Deutschwichtel geträumt?«

Ich schüttle den Kopf. »Nein, alles okay. Ich hab gestern Abend noch mit Fabienne gechattet. Sie muss sich total verloren vorkommen. Im Vergleich zu Paris ist Fucking wirklich die totale Einöde.«

»Ach, ich glaube, es gefällt ihr ganz gut bei euch. Sie hat ein Bild von eurem Ferkel bei FB gepostet. Susi ist echt witzig.«

»Wer ist witzig?« André steht auf einmal neben uns.

»Susi, das Hausschwein von Helene. Hast du Fabiennes Posting nicht gesehen?«, fragt Marie-Claire.

André zuckt mit den Schultern. »Gibt Wichtigeres als FB. Unseren Gig am Donnerstag zum Beispiel.«

»André und Marc sind angehende Rockstars, musst

du wissen«, erklärt Marie-Claire. »Manchmal glaube ich, André interessiert sich für nichts anderes mehr als seine Gitarrenriffs.«

»Wenn ich erst berühmt bin, machst du keine Witze mehr darüber. Und ich hab sehr wohl auch noch etwas anderes im Kopf«, sagt er und lächelt mich so süß an, dass mir fast die Luft wegbleibt.

Langsam glaube ich wirklich, er flirtet mit mir.

»Oh, dann sollten wir uns vielleicht gleich ein Autogramm geben lassen«, überspiele ich lachend meine Verlegenheit.

»Klar, aber dann musst du auch zu einem meiner Konzerte ko–«

Die Schulglocke läutet, und Marie-Claire unterbricht André. »Jetzt kannst du mal zeigen, was du als Künstler so draufhast.« Grinsend wendet sie sich mir zu: »Wir haben jetzt nämlich eine Doppelstunde Kunst. Da machen wir echt coole Sachen, du wirst schon sehen.«

Es ist schon seltsam. Abgesehen von der Sprache ist es anscheinend überall gleich: Die Hauptfächer heißen so, weil sie hauptsächlich anstrengend und langweilig sind, und die Nebenfächer, weil es ganz nebenbei Spaß macht, dem Unterricht zu folgen.

Im Kunstraum riecht es nach Farbe und Terpentin. Ich setze mich gleich zu meinen neuen Freunden an den Tisch. Unsere Aufgabe ist alles andere als leicht: Wir sollen eine kleine Tonfigur modellieren – nach dem Vorbild der Venus von Milo!

Ich knete den Ton so lange, bis er weich ist, dann versuche ich eine Figur zu formen. Nach einer Stunde sieht meine Venus schon ganz annehmbar aus, aber Marcs Venus kippt dauernd nach vorne.

»Ich würde zu einer Brustverkleinerung raten«, sagt Marie-Claire lachend und deutet auf die ziemlich beachtliche Oberweite der Statue.

»Was meint ihr?«, fragt Marc und blickt in die Runde.

André pappt ihm einen neuen Tonklumpen auf die Tischplatte. »Ja, Mann. Oder du verpasst deiner armen Venus ein Stützkorsett, bevor ihr das Kreuz bricht.«

»Stützkorsett. Pah! Ich bekomm das schon hin.« Marc kratzt etwas Ton von der Vorderseite seiner Venus und klebt ihn hinten ran, direkt auf den Po der Statue.

»Das nennt man dann wohl Gewichtsverlagerung«, bemerkt Marie-Claire grinsend.

»Was sagt ihr zu meinem Prachtexemplar?«, will André wissen.

Ich schaue mir seine Tonfigur an, die mit ihrer Turmfrisur eher an Marge Simpson als an die Venus von Milo erinnert, und sage lieber nichts.

»Und Helene? Was meinst du?«, fragt André erwartungsvoll.

»Na ja. Ungewöhnlich. Modern?«, weiche ich aus.

»Siehst du nicht, dass meine Venus eine Mini-E-Gitarre hält? Sie ist die rockigste Venus aller Zeiten!«

»Stimmt, jetzt erkenne ich es auch. Sie ist der Jimi Hendrix unter den Venussen, oder wie sagt man?«, entgegne ich und merke, wie ich erröte.

»Venen natürlich«, kommentiert Marc trocken.

»Dummie«, sagt Marie-Claire kichernd.

»RUHE!«, ruft Herr Bertram. »Mehr Konzentration, Herrschaften, wenigstens die letzten zehn Minuten.«

»Na, das reicht doch. Schönheitsoperation erfolgreich beendet«, meint Marc zufrieden.

Ich staune, denn jetzt steht Marcs Tonfigur nicht nur gut, sondern hat echt Ähnlichkeit mit der Venus von Milo. Er scheint wirklich Talent zu haben. Nachdem wir unsere kleinen Statuen ins Regal gestellt haben, räumen wir den Ton weg und wischen den Tisch sauber. Dabei lehnt sich André zu mir herüber, und ich spüre, wie allein durch seine Anwesenheit meine Wangen zu glühen beginnen.

»Auf was für Musik stehst du?«, erkundigt er sich ganz beiläufig.

»Weiß nicht. So ziemlich alles«, erwidere ich. Meine Haut kribbelt. Wahrscheinlich bin ich schon wieder knallrot wie eine Ampel.

»Vielleicht magst du ja wirklich mal zu einem meiner Konzerte kommen. Oder zu einer Probe? Ist immer cool, vor Publikum zu spielen.«

»Ja, warum nicht«, antworte ich leise.

»Am Donnerstag haben wir einen Auftritt im Jay Jays. Es würde mich total freuen, wenn du kämst«, sagt er und legt eine Hand auf meine Schulter.

Ich blicke zu ihm auf, direkt in seine eisblauen Augen. Mein Herz rast. Bestimmt werde ich gleich ohnmächtig.

»Ähm ...«

»Sie kennt sich in Paris nicht aus, Mann«, unterbricht Marie-Claire mein hilfloses Gestotter.

André dreht sich zu ihr um und nimmt seine Hand von

meiner Schulter. Ein heißer, kribbelnder Fleck bleibt zurück, aber mein Kreislauf beruhigt sich wieder.

»Ach ja, stimmt. Marie-Claire, könntest du Helene nicht einfach abholen und mitbringen?«, fragt André und setzt einen Dackelblick auf.

»Sag schön bitte, dann mach ich's«, antwortet Marie-Claire lachend.

»Büüüddddeeee«, scherzt André und klimpert mit den Wimpern.

»Gut. Ich hätte es auch so getan«, sagt Marie-Claire, »sofern Helene überhaupt Lust hat. Wie sieht's aus?« Sie schaut mich fragend an. »Die beiden Möchtegern-Rockstars sind gar nicht mal so schlecht.«

»Wir sind gut! Extrem gut sogar«, mischt sich Marc ein, der als Letzter seinen Platz sauber gemacht hat.

»Klar, ich komme gern«, antworte ich.

»Prima. Das wird sicher ein cooler Abend. Jetzt, wo du dabei bist ...« André lächelt mich an und berührt – rein zufällig? – meinen Arm.

»Komm, ich zeige dir, wo die Schürzen hingehören«, sagt Marie-Claire, und ich folge ihr zu einem großen Schrank. Als wir außer Hörweite sind, raunt sie mir zu: »Erwarte nicht zu viel. Das Jay Jays ist nur ein zweitklassiger Pub, und die Jungs, na ja, sie sind ganz okay, aber ein zweiter Jimi Hendrix ist nicht dabei. Den gibt's nur als Tonfigur.«

»Ach, es wird bestimmt toll. Ich war noch nie auf einem Konzert – von einer richtigen Band, meine ich. Bisher hab ich nur Dorf-Kapellen und Bierzelt-Bands gesehen.«

»Ehrlich? Na dann ...«

»… kann ich gar nicht enttäuscht sein«, beende ich ihren Satz. »Ich weiß nur nicht, was ich anziehen soll. Hast du vielleicht einen Tipp für mich?«

»Hm, ich würde sagen, am besten was Stylisches, aber bleib leger.«

NACH DER SCHULE bringt André mich wieder zur U-Bahn, diesmal gemeinsam mit Marc und einem ganz in Schwarz gekleideten, stillen Jungen aus der Parallelklasse. Er heißt Luca und ist der Schlagzeuger der Band. Die drei wollen noch in den Proberaum, sich auf das Konzert vorbereiten, und – welch ein Zufall – meine U-Bahn-Station liegt auf dem Weg.

Beim Abschied drückt mir André als Einziger drei Küsschen auf die Wangen. Eine Mischung aus Pfefferminz-Kaugummi und herbem Jungs-Geruch steigt mir in die Nase.

»Bis morgen«, sagt er mit seiner rauchigen Stimme.

Meine Beine zittern, als ich die Stufen zum Bahnsteig hinuntergehe. Die ganze Fahrt über schwirrt mir der Kopf. Wahrscheinlich bilde ich mir nur ein, dass André an mir interessiert ist. Da hab ich so ein Talent dafür, wie vorigen Sommer bei Levin. Meine erste große Liebe. Bei ihm war ich mir auch so sicher, dass er mehr von mir will. Und dann …

Ich muss unbedingt mit Fabienne chatten und ihr erzählen, wie wahnsinnig aufmerksam und nett alle zu mir sind, besonders André. Vielleicht erfahre ich dann mehr über ihn. Nicht dass ich wieder auf die Schnauze falle, wie damals.

Hallo, Fabienne! Bist du da?

Klar, wo sonst. Fucking ist ja keine Metropole. ;-)

Super. Dass du on bist, meine ich. Nicht dass Fucking ein Kaff ist. ☹ Wie läuft's bei dir?

Ganz okay. Heute gab's 'ne Stichflamme in der Schulküche, weil Sebastian die Pfanne mit dem Fett auf dem Herd vergessen hatte. Die Pfeifer ist gehüpft wie ein Karnickel auf Möhrendoping und hat immerzu »Feuer, Feuer« geschrien. Ziemlich hysterisch. Lena hat dann ganz cool einen Deckel auf die Pfanne geschleudert und war danach die große Heldin.

Wahnsinn. Da bin ich mal ein paar Tage weg, und schon passiert was. Sonst ist Kochen nämlich oft langweilig. Euer Kunstunterricht ist da viel cooler. Und überhaupt, Paris ist so eine tolle Stadt! Außerdem sind alle so freundlich zu mir. Stell dir vor, André hat mich zu seinem Konzert eingeladen! Marie-Claire will mich abholen, und dann fahren wir gemeinsam hin. Cool, oder?

Hm. Cool.

Du, wegen André …

Was ist mit ihm?

Wie ist er eigentlich so? Er hat ja einige Verehrerinnen … Kann es sein, dass er ein richtiger Mäd-
chenmagnet ist?

Ja, das trifft es ganz gut …

Ich hab irgendwie den Eindruck, dass er zu mir besonders nett ist. Er hat mich wieder zur U-Bahn gebracht und mir drei Küsschen auf die Wangen gegeben. Glaubst du …?

WAS???

Na ja, du weißt schon. Ob er mich mag und so …

André mag alle Mädchen. Wie du schon sagtest.
Ein Mädchenschwarm eben. Ich würde mir an deiner Stelle nicht den Kopf darüber zerbrechen.
Wahrscheinlich will er einfach nur nett sein. Weil
du ja vom Land kommst. So tickt André eben.

Ach. Na gut. Ich dachte nur. Danke. Du bist echt eine
liebe Freundin. ♥ Schließlich will ich mich nicht
zum Affen machen.

Verstehe ich. Erzählst du mir dann, wie es beim Konzert war? Ich würde auch gern mal ausgehen. Aber hier gibt es ja nur Wald und Wiesen.

Sag das nicht. Nächste Woche findet bei uns das traditionelle Maifest mit Tanz, Bierzelt und Musik statt. Das ist immer der Höhepunkt des Jahres! Wird dir sicher gefallen. Vielleicht wirst du sogar zur Maikönigin gewählt. So hübsch, wie du bist.

Ja, mal sehen. Ich geh jetzt off. Deine Mum hat gesagt, heute ist Familienspieleabend.

Lass dich von meinem Bruder nicht übers Ohr hauen. Florian schummelt immer. Ich häng noch ein bisschen mit Bastet auf dem Schoß im Netz ab. Deine Eltern sind schon wieder beruflich unterwegs. ☹ Sag mal, ist das nicht auch schlimm für dich, wenn deine Eltern nie daheim sind?

Sie sind eben viel beschäftigt. Das hat aber auch seine guten Seiten. Ich kann tun und lassen, was ich will, solange ich mich an ein paar Grundregeln halte. Meist finde ich es ziemlich cool, immer sturmfrei zu haben. So, ich muss jetzt los. Ich werde aufpassen wie ein Luchs, wenn dein Bruder an der Reihe ist. Schummeln ist wirklich das Allerletzte. Thx für die Warnung. CU.

WAS SOLL ICH NUR ANZIEHEN? Marie-Claire hat stylisch, aber leger gesagt. Ich habe nicht einmal ein schwarzes T-Shirt dabei. Überhaupt finde ich meine Sachen viel zu gewöhnlich für Andrés Konzert. Lena hat schon recht, wenn sie sagt, dass meine Klamotten brav und langweilig sind. Mist! Ich hab kein passendes Outfit und bin außerdem spät dran. Langsam werde ich echt nervös. Bestimmt steht Marie-Claire gleich vor der Tür.

Ob ich vielleicht mal in Fabiennes Kleiderschrank schaue? Schließlich hat sie mir angeboten, etwas zu leihen. Ich werfe nur mal einen kurzen Blick in ihren Schrank.

Wow! Fabienne ist besser ausgestattet als so manche Boutique in Salzburg. Lena würde vor Begeisterung einen Schreikrampf bekommen.

Miau! Miau! Bastet streicht an meinen Beinen entlang und springt elegant auf einen Stapel Angorapullis. Ob sie das darf? Nicht dass sie mit ihren Krallen Fäden zieht. Ich versuche sie zu verscheuchen, doch keine Chance. Madame wirft mir nur ganz majestätisch einen abschätzigen Blick zu, als würde sie sagen wollen: Ich bin hier der Boss!

Seufzend streichle ich der Katzenpharaonin über die weiche Haut, und Bastet beginnt zu schnurren. Da entdecke ich, genau einen Regalboden über ihr, ein schwarz glänzendes Shirt mit Nieten auf den Schultern. Das ist genau das Richtige für heute Abend. Schnell schnappe ich es mir.

Bastet schmiegt ihren Kopf an meinen Bauch und verlangt nach weiteren Schmuseeinheiten.

»Sorry, Prinzessin. Ich muss mich fertig machen. Wenn du lieber im Schrank bleiben willst, meinetwegen.«

Fabiennes Shirt ist meine Rettung. Meine alte Jeans passt perfekt dazu. Zum Glück habe ich mir meine schwarzen Stiefeletten mitgenommen, obwohl es draußen schon recht warm ist. Ich trage etwas schwarzen Kajal rund um die Augen auf und föhne meine Haare etwas wilder als sonst.

Es klingelt. Das wird Marie-Claire sein. Auf dem Weg zur Tür stolpere ich fast über Bastet.

»Na, Mieze? War dir doch langweilig, ganz allein im Schrank?« Ich streichle ihr sanft über den Rücken. Die arme Katze teilt mein Schicksal. Sie ist hier genauso viel alleine wie ich, denn Brigitte und Richard sind ja so gut wie nie zu Hause. Bestimmt vermisst Bastet ihre Fabienne. Und heute lasse ich sie ebenfalls allein, wenn auch nur für einen Abend.

Ich öffne die Wohnungstür.

»Hi. Coole Klamotten! Das Shirt ist von Fabienne, oder?«, begrüßt mich Marie-Claire und schließt die Tür hinter sich. Sie sieht auch ziemlich gut aus in ihrem schwarzen Lederrock, den kniehohen Stiefeln, dem knallroten Top und der schwarzen Lederjacke.

»Ja. Fabienne hat gemeint, ich dürfte mir was ausleihen.«

»Echt? Das ist ja voll nett von ihr. Wollen wir gleich los?«

»Ich hole nur noch schnell meine Jeansjacke und die Handtasche«, sage ich.

»Alles klar.« Marie-Claire bückt sich und krault Bastet.

»Tschüss, Mieze. Bis später«, verabschiede ich mich von unserem Haustiger.

Wir laufen durch die kühle Abendluft, und mit jedem Schritt verschwindet meine Nervosität etwas mehr. Es wird bestimmt ein toller Abend.

Die Fahrt mit der U-Bahn dauert ziemlich lange. Wir müssen zweimal umsteigen, und ich bin froh, dass Marie-Claire sich so gut auskennt. Noch dazu macht es richtig viel Spaß mit ihr, da sie außerhalb der Schule noch viel witziger ist.

»Guck mal, dort. Popeye mit Olivia!« Sie zeigt auf ein Pärchen, das tatsächlich große Ähnlichkeit mit den Zeichentrickfiguren hat. »Wetten, deren Einkaufstüten sind voller Spinat?«

»Und Olivia muss alles schleppen, das ist ja mal wieder typisch«, witzele ich.

»Du weißt doch, wie die Jungs sind. Immer den großen Macker markieren, aber wenn's drauf ankommt, die Mädels die ganze Arbeit machen lassen. Ist in der Schule auch nicht anders. Wenn ich an das letzte Bio-Referat denke, das ich mit André halten musste ... da hab ich alles recherchiert, und er hat es nur noch abgelesen, der faule Kerl.«

Ich nicke mitfühlend. Das ging mir früher in der Mittelschule auch nicht anders.

Mit Marie-Claire vergeht die Zeit wie im Fluge, obwohl wir eine gute halbe Stunde durch die Unterwelt fahren.

Das *Jay Jays* entpuppt sich als kleine Spelunke in einer düsteren Seitengasse. Zum Glück sieht es im Pub selbst viel freundlicher aus. In der Mitte des Raums stehen dicht gedrängt viele kleine Tische mit Bänken und Stühlen. Ganz hinten befindet sich die Bühne, auf der schon die Instrumente aufgebaut sind, rechts davon verläuft ein L-förmiger Tresen.

Die anderen Gäste scheinen auch Schüler zu sein. Mir fällt sofort auf, wie viele Mädchen da sind, wahrscheinlich Andrés Fanklub. Ich bin mir nicht sicher, ob sie auch bei uns auf die Schule gehen. Abgesehen von den Schülern aus meiner Klasse erkenne ich niemanden.

»Und?«, fragt Marie-Claire. »Wie gefällt's dir?«

»Gut«, antworte ich, »wo wollen wir sitzen?«

Marie-Claire zeigt auf einen freien Tisch ganz nahe bei der Bühne. »Den haben uns die Jungs reserviert.«

Als der Kellner kommt, bestelle ich eine Cola, Marie-Claire nimmt einen Red Bull.

»Bin schon gespannt, wie du die Musik findest«, sagt meine neue Freundin.

»Sie muss super sein, sonst wären nicht so viele Groupies da, oder?«, antworte ich und nicke in Richtung eines Mädchens, das ein Shirt mit I♥André trägt. Wie peinlich!

»Ach, das ist Denise. Die ist in der Parallelklasse und steht voll auf André. Ich glaub, die ist schon seit der Grundschule in ihn verknallt«, erzählt Marie-Claire kichernd.

»Echt? Eine Sandkastenliebe?«

»Ja, aber einseitig, glaub mir. André geht ihr aus dem Weg, so gut er kann. Und ehrlich gesagt, nervt sie mich auch ein wenig. Dieses ewige Schmachten, André hier, André da – das ist auf die Dauer echt anstrengend!«

Der Kellner bringt unsere Getränke. Gleichzeitig betreten André, Marc und Luca die Bühne, und das Publikum beginnt zu johlen.

Ein älterer Mann, Mitte fünfzig, schiebt sich nach vorn und ergreift das Mikrofon. »Heute zum zweiten Mal hier, die *Rock Rockets*. Freut euch auf Luca, Marc und André!«, moderiert er die Band an.

Als er Andrés Namen nennt, kreischen ein paar Mädchen wie verrückt. Ich finde das ehrlich gesagt etwas peinlich. Schließlich steht da oben nicht *Coldplay*, sondern eine Schulband. Kein Grund also, sich wie ein Groupie zu benehmen.

»Das war Jay Jay. Ihm gehört der Laden. Eigentlich heißt er Charles«, schreit mir Marie-Claire ins Ohr.

Luca gibt mit seinem Schlagzeug den Takt vor. Das Publikum verstummt, André setzt mit der Gitarre ein, und Marc übernimmt den Bass.

Ich lehne mich zurück. Zuerst spielen die drei einfach wild darauflos. André schmettert ein irre schnelles Gitarrensolo. Danach beginnt er den ersten Song zu singen, und ich bin wirklich verblüfft, wie toll seine Stimme klingt. Richtig erwachsen, fast wie ein echter Rockstar.

»Ganz okay, nicht wahr?«, zischt Marie-Claire mir zu.

Ich kann nur nicken, denn ich bin wie gebannt von Andrés Auftritt. In dem Moment tritt Marc neben André ans Mikro, und gemeinsam singen sie den Refrain. Die beiden harmonieren perfekt: André hört sich tief und rauchig an, Marc, der eine Tonlage höher singt, klar und warm. Ich kann gar nicht sagen, wer mich mehr beeindruckt.

Als die Menge zu klatschen beginnt, hält auch mich nichts mehr auf dem Stuhl. Begeistert springe ich auf und kreische genauso laut wie alle anderen. So viel zum Thema Groupies und Schulband. In dem Moment fängt André meinen Blick auf und zwinkert mir hinter dem Mikrofon zu.

Nachdem die Band vier englische Songs gespielt hat, folgt ein französischer Song. Außer mir scheinen alle das Lied zu kennen, denn sie grölen so laut mit, dass ich nicht einmal im Ansatz verstehe, um was es geht.

Nach dem Lied wird es still. André nimmt das Mikro und steigt von der Bühne. Er kommt direkt auf mich zu, und der Scheinwerfer folgt ihm, bis wir beide im Lichtkegel stehen. Der ganze Pub starrt mich an. Marie-Claire kichert, und mir wird heiß.

»Das schönste Mädchen des Abends darf sich aussuchen, ob wir vor der Pause noch *Bed of Blooms* oder *Rain of Roses* für euch spielen.« André nimmt meine Hand und deutet einen Handkuss an.

Mein Herz rast, und ich merke, wie ich knallrot werde.

»Schöne Helene, bei welchem Lied willst du mich auf die Bühne begleiten?«

Abwehrend schüttle ich den Kopf. Aber die Gäste im *Jay Jays* brüllen schon laut ihren Musikwunsch und meinen Namen.

»Du kannst dich nicht davor drücken«, sagt André und grinst mich an.

»*Be... bed of Blooms*«, stottere ich.

»Ihr habt es gehört! Ein Bett voller Blüten für meine Helene und einen Applaus!«

Das Publikum klatscht und pfeift laut, während André mich auf die Bühne schleppt. Von hier oben aus sehe ich die Menge kaum, so stark blenden mich die Scheinwerfer. Ich will wieder die Treppe hinuntergehen, doch André hält meine Hand fest. Voller Leidenschaft beginnt er zu singen und blickt mir dabei die ganze Zeit in die Augen.

Ich versuche tief durchzuatmen, aber mein Herz will sich einfach nicht beruhigen. Es hämmert erbarmungslos gegen meine Rippen. Als das Lied zu Ende ist, legt André seine Gitarre zur Seite und trägt mich von der Bühne, als wäre ich leicht wie eine Feder. Ich sehe Fotoapparate aufblitzen.

»Danke. Du warst atemberaubend!«, sagt Andre und küsst meine Wange, nachdem er mich an meinem Platz abgesetzt hat. »Und schön, dass du gekommen bist!«, bemerkt er noch, bevor er zu seiner Band zurückgeht.

»In 'ner halben Stunde geht's weiter«, verkünden die *Rock Rockets*, bevor sie hinter der Bühne verschwinden.

»Komm, wir schauen mal nach den Jungs«, sagt Marie-Claire.

»Backstage?«, frage ich und bin noch immer ganz durcheinander.

»Klar. Wir dürfen das.«

DIE ROCK ROCKETS werden schon von ihren Fans belagert. Denise sitzt beinahe auf Andrés Schoß, so dicht quetscht sie sich an ihn ran. Doch André scheint es nicht zu stören. In dem Moment steht Marc auf und stemmt die Hände in die Hüften. Auf einmal sieht er richtig selbstbewusst aus.

»Mädels! Jetzt aber raus mit euch. Gönnt uns ein paar Minuten Pause, sonst haben wir nachher gar keine Energie mehr.«

Denise murrt beim Hinausgehen. Ich will auch kehrtmachen, da spüre ich, wie mich jemand festhält.

»Ihr könnt natürlich bleiben«, sagt Marc. »Nur die aufdringlichen Girlies sollten verschwinden.«

Er wirkt irgendwie verändert. So, als hätte der Auftritt ihm eine ordentliche Portion Selbstbewusstsein gegeben.

»Setz dich zu uns, Helene.« André klopft auf den Platz neben sich. »Wir haben Apfelschorle, Cola und Red Bull. Nimm dir, was du magst.«

»Danke«, sage ich und greife nach einer Apfelschorle. Ich bin so aufgewühlt, dass ich André gar nicht in die Augen schauen kann. Mit meinem erzwungenen Auftritt hat er mich völlig aus dem Gleichgewicht gebracht. Normalerweise mag ich es nämlich überhaupt nicht, im Mittelpunkt zu stehen. Hilfe suchend blicke ich zu Marie-Claire, doch die ist schon in ein Gespräch mit Luca vertieft.

»Ich hoffe, du nimmst es mir nicht übel, dass ich dich auf die Bühne geschleppt habe. Aber ich wollte nicht wieder Denise da oben haben. Da hab ich jedes Mal Angst, dass sie mich zu Boden wirft und abknutscht.«

»Hm«, brumme ich.

»Davon träumst du wohl«, meint Marc grinsend und boxt André in die Seite.

»Eure Musik ist echt super«, versuche ich das Thema zu wechseln.

»Ja, aber so richtig gut sind wir erst, seit Marc bei uns mitmacht«, erklärt André.

Marc zuckt mit den Schultern und blickt auf einmal wieder schüchtern zu Boden. »Ich bin halt nicht so der Typ für große Auftritte. Das hat mich schon Überwindung gekostet. Außerdem bin ich mir nie sicher, ob ich gut genug bin.«

»Bist du. Auf alle Fälle«, sage ich.

Marc lächelt mich an und wird rot, genau wie ich, wenn ich mich unsicher fühle. Schnell macht er eine wegwischende Handbewegung und versteckt sich hinter seinem Colaglas.

»Ach, die Mädchen interessieren sich sowieso nur für André. Wir könnten den größten Mist spielen, die würden immer noch kreischen, solange unser Sonnyboy auf der Bühne steht«, meldet sich Luca zu Wort.

»Fans sind wichtig. Aber wirklich bedeuten tun mir andere Menschen etwas«, behauptet André.

Ist es Zufall, dass sein Knie einen kurzen Wimpernschlag lang meins berührt und er mich dabei anblinzelt? Mein Puls beginnt schon wieder zu rasen wie ein Pferd auf der Trabrennbahn, und ich weiß genau, dass meine Wangen mindestens so rosig schimmern wie die von Marc. Mir fällt nichts anderes ein, als mich ebenfalls hinter meinem Glas zu verkriechen. Die kühle Apfelschorle tut meinem trockenen Hals gut.

Inzwischen diskutieren die Jungs darüber, welche Songs sie als Zugabe spielen sollen.

»Hey, nach dem Konzert bleibt ihr aber schon noch ein bisschen, oder?«, fragt Marc.

Marie-Claire grinst. »Keine Sorge, ihr drei sollt nicht die Einzigen sein, denen morgen im Unterricht die Augen zufallen.«

Nach der dritten Zugabe bauen die Jungs ihre Instrumente ab, und die Bühne wird zur Tanzfläche. Mit Brigitte habe ich vereinbart, dass ich vor Mitternacht zu Hause bin, also bleibt mir noch eine knappe Stunde. Als der DJ die erste Platte auflegt, stürmen Marie-Claire und ich nach vorn und mischen uns unter die Tanzenden. Es dauert nicht lange, bis André, Marc und Luca zu uns stoßen. Während Marie-Claire mit Marc und Luca in der Menge verschwindet, bleibt André ganz dicht an meiner Seite. Obwohl sich Denise und ihre Freundinnen dauernd zwischen uns drängen, tanzt er nur mit mir. Ich bin froh, dass es auf der Bühne so dunkel ist und niemand meine roten Ohren sehen kann.

Kurz nach elf verlassen Marie-Claire und ich den Pub, die drei Rockstars bleiben noch.

»Morgen werden sie direkt vor dem Giftzwerg einschlafen«, meint Marie-Claire.

»Oje, dann gibt es sicher einen Zwergenaufstand«, erwidere ich grinsend.

Müde, aber glücklich verabschieden wir uns voneinander.

Als ich nach Hause komme, sind Richard und Brigitte ausnahmsweise schon daheim und sitzen mit einem Glas Rotwein vorm Fernseher. Es ist das erste Mal, dass ich die beiden so entspannt erlebe. Brigitte dreht den Ton ab, als ich mich zu ihnen setze.

»Und wie war es?«, will Richard wissen.

»Großartig. Wenn ich darf, würde ich gern öfter mal mit meinen Klassenkameraden weggehen.«

»Ich wüsste nicht, was dagegensprechen sollte. Es ist fünf vor zwölf. Wie es aussieht, kann man sich auf dich verlassen.« Brigitte lächelt. »Du sollst die Zeit hier ja genießen. Man ist nur einmal jung.«

»Danke, das ist prima«, antworte ich und erhebe mich gähnend. »Gute Nacht.«

»Gute Nacht. Schlaf schön«, antwortet Brigitte und stellt den Ton wieder an.

Ich geh ins Bad und falle anschließend ins Bett. Mein Puls rattert noch immer wie eine Eisenbahn. So einen aufregenden Abend hatte ich schon lange nicht mehr. Eigentlich wollte ich Fabienne noch schreiben. Aber das muss bis morgen warten. Ich schließe meine Augen, und es kommt mir so vor, als würde immer noch Andrés Pfefferminz-Jungsgeruch in der Luft liegen. Meine Gedanken wirbeln wild durcheinander, und ich fühle mich wie im Märchen. Ob André mein Prinz ist?

WARUM MELDET SICH ANDRÉ NICHT? Es kann doch nicht so schwer sein, einen kurzen Gruß über WhatsApp, eine SMS oder meinetwegen auch eine Chat-Nachricht zu schicken. Auf FB habe ich gesehen, dass die halbe Klasse zu Andrés Konzert gehen wollte. Langsam quält mich die Sehnsucht nach meinen Freunden. Ja, es ist ganz nett hier. Doch selbst wenn ich am tollsten Strand der Welt liegen würde – ohne André würde mir das Herz wehtun.

Es ist Freitagnachmittag, und das Wochenende steht vor der Tür. Partytime. Aber ich hocke hier in der Einöde und starre abwechselnd auf die grasenden Pferde und mein Smartphone. Bei den Pferden ist mehr los als in meinem Posteingang. Langsam bereue ich es, dass ich Lena abgesagt habe, die heute Abend ins Open-Air-Kino gehen wollte.

Florian kommt aus dem Haus und setzt sich zu mir in die Sonne. Susi läuft im Schweinsgalopp hinter ihm her und legt sich zu seinen Füßen.

»Na, Schwester auf Zeit, was geht?«

Ich zucke mit den Schultern.

Flo lehnt sich zurück. »Die Landjugend hängt Freitagabend immer in Thomas' Partyhütte ab. Das ist der Junge, dem die Pferde gehören, die du die ganze Zeit anstarrst, als würden sie gleich Gold kacken.« Florian lacht über seinen eigenen Witz.

Ich ziehe eine Augenbraue hoch, worauf er verlegen zu hüsteln beginnt und seine Wangen eine rosa Farbe annehmen. Er räuspert sich. »Wir planen heute das Maifest. Tom hat gefragt, ob du dabei bist.«

»Ich weiß nicht«, sage ich und werfe erneut einen Blick auf das Display.

»Wie du meinst. Du kannst es dir ja noch überlegen. Ich geh dann mal wieder runter. Papa braut gerade ein paar neue Fässer *Fucking Helles* fürs Maifest.«

»Was macht er?«, frage ich erstaunt.

»Papa hat eine Mini-Brauerei im Keller, nur leider hat er es noch nicht geschafft, ein Gewerbe anzumelden. Dabei wäre *Fucking Helles* und *Fucking Dunkles* bestimmt ein richtiger Verkaufsschlager. Papa ist der beste Schwarzbierbrauer der ganzen Gegend!«, erklärt Florian mit stolzgeschwellter Brust. »Willst du zusehen?«

Ich schüttle den Kopf. Für eine Lehrstunde in Bierbrauen hab ich jetzt ehrlich keinen Kopf. Da schwirrt mir André zu sehr in den Gehirnwindungen herum.

»Dann ein anderes Mal«, schlägt Flo vor. »Ich will ein paar Bilder knipsen. Vielleicht schafft Paps es bald, die Brauerei offiziell zu machen. Dann könnte ich sein Bier auf unserer Fucking-Homepage bewerben. Ich hab mir auch schon einen Slogan überlegt: *Trink dein Bier, egal ob lang-*

sam oder schnell. Hauptsache, Fucking dunkel oder hell. Was
meinst du?«

»Klingt lustig«, sage ich lächelnd.

Florian schlägt sich auf die Oberschenkel und steht auf.

»Susi, komm!«, ruft er, aber die kleine Sau rührt sich
nicht von der Stelle. Freundlich grunzt sie mich an.

»Sie kann ruhig bleiben«, sage ich.

»Auch gut«, meint Florian und trottet davon.

Susi quiekt vergnügt und rutscht näher an meine Beine
ran. Anfassen will ich das Ferkel noch immer nicht, aber
es stört mich schon nicht mehr, dass Susi fünf Zentimeter
von meinen Zehen entfernt hockt.

»Na, Susi, wer ist wohl die ärmere Sau von uns beiden? Du, weil du ein Ferkel bist? Oder ich, weil ich so
saudumm bin, dauernd aufs Smartphone zu gucken, ob
sich ein gewisser Kerl vielleicht dazu herablässt, mir zu
schreiben?«

Seufzend öffne ich Facebook. André ist nicht on, aber er
hat ein paar neue Bilder auf seiner Seite gepostet. Im *Jay
Jays* war offenbar die Hölle los. Mein Herz sticht vor Kummer. Ob man an Sehnsucht sterben kann?

Langsam scrolle ich die Fotos durch. Tanzende Leute auf
der Bühne. Ich erkenne Marie-Claire und Marc. Auf einem
Bild ist auch Helene. Sie tanzt mit André. Viel zu eng für
meinen Geschmack. Ich schlucke schwer und zoome den
Bildausschnitt näher heran. Er hat seine Arme um ihre Hüften gelegt, und die Hände fast schon an ihrem Po! Und wie
sie ihn anhimmelt. Merde! Trägt sie etwa auch noch mein
Nieten-T-Shirt? Gut, ich hab ihr ausdrücklich erlaubt, dass

sie sich in meinem Kleiderschrank bedienen kann – aber doch nicht, um mit André zu flirten!

Ich blinzle die bitteren Tränen weg, die sich in meine Augenwinkel stehlen. Ruhig, Fabienne. Denk nach! Vielleicht ist das nur eine blöde Momentaufnahme. So etwas kommt vor. Der Auslöser wird genau in dem Augenblick gedrückt, in dem eine Situation eindeutig erscheint, aber in Wirklichkeit ist alles ganz anders. Warum sollte sich André auch an Helene heranmachen, wo er doch genau weiß, dass sie meine Austauschschülerin ist?

Ich straffe die Schultern und schiebe das Smartphone zurück in meine Hosentasche.

»Los, Susi, wir gehen die Pferde besuchen.«

Wie ein wohlerzogener Hund erhebt sich das Schweinchen und trottet hinter mir her zur Weide. Die Pferde kommen neugierig an den Zaun getrabt. Vorsichtig strecke ich meine Hand aus und streichle den braunen Haflinger, der sich besonders weit zu uns herüberbeugt. Warme Luft schlägt mir aus seinen Nüstern entgegen. Es ist schön, so ein großes Pferd mal ganz aus der Nähe zu sehen.

»Das ist Fallabella. Sie ist schon ziemlich alt, aber genau das richtige Pferd, um mit dem Reiten anzufangen.« Neben mir ist plötzlich ein Junge in meinem Alter aufgetaucht. Er geht in die Knie und krault Susi, die sich auf dem Rücken wälzt und die Streicheleinheiten genießt.

»Ich bin Tom, eigentlich Thomas. Florian hat mir schon gesagt, dass du vielleicht ein paar Reitstunden nehmen willst. Du bist doch Fabienne, oder?«

»Ja, bin ich«, antworte ich überrascht.

»Hätte mich auch gewundert, wenn Florian auf einmal Damenbesuch bekommen würde.« Tom erhebt sich und zwinkert mir zu. »Ich muss dann los. Es gibt noch eine Menge vorzubereiten für heute Abend.«

»Ah. Die Partyhütte.«

»Du kennst dich ja schon bestens aus, wie eine echte Fuckingerin!« Er grinst. »Dann bis später. Du bist doch dabei, oder?«

»Mal sehen«, gebe ich unentschieden zurück.

Tom winkt beim Weggehen. Ich bleibe noch eine Weile bei Fallabella stehen und streichle ihr Fell. Ich sollte wirklich die Gelegenheit nutzen und Reitstunden nehmen. In Paris ist das nicht so einfach wie hier.

NACH DEM ABENDESSEN mache ich mich in meinem Zimmer zurecht. Im Laufe des Nachmittags bin ich zu dem Entschluss gekommen, dass ein paar Stunden in Toms Partyhütte allemal besser sind, als daheim die ganze Zeit aufs Handy zu starren.

Geübt ziehe ich mit dem Eyeliner den Lidrand nach. Noch etwas Mascara und Lipgloss, und voilà, ich bin fertig!

Pling! Eine Chatnachricht. Ausgerechnet jetzt, wo ich mir vorübergehend eine Handy-Pause verordnet habe. Mein Herz flattert, ohne dass ich etwas dagegen tun kann. Schon schießt mir der hoffnungsvolle Gedanke durch den Kopf: André?

Ich gucke aufs Display, und welche Überraschung, er ist es natürlich nicht. Jungs! Wieso kann man nicht mit ihnen, aber auch nicht ohne sie? Dafür ist Helene im Chat, verlässlich wie der Hahn auf dem Misthaufen.

Fabienne? Bist du da?

Hallo, Helene. Ja. Bin on. Wie war das Konzert?

Wow! Ich hatte schon lange nicht mehr so einen phantastischen Abend! Marc und André waren der Hammer. Wieso hast du mir nicht erzählt, wie genial André singen kann? Später hat er sogar noch mit mir getanzt. Mir ist jetzt noch ganz schwindlig davon, und ich konnte mich den ganzen Schultag nicht konzentrieren. Er ist so … ich weiß gar nicht, wie ich ihn beschreiben soll.

Aha. Also war es schön für dich.

Ja!!! ☺ Ich bin so froh, dass ich beim Austausch mitmache. Auf die Stadtführung morgen freu ich mich auch schon total. Anfangs hatte ich ja noch Angst, wie du weißt, aber jetzt finde ich Paris einfach nur super. Übrigens, vielen Dank, dass ich mir deine Klamotten ausleihen darf! Du bist echt eine tolle Freundin.

Freut mich. Bis später. Ich mach Schluss für heute. Tschüss.

Schnell schließe ich das Chatfenster. Verdammt! Ich hatte so gehofft, dass die Bilder auf Facebook einfach nur blöde Schnappschüsse waren. Doch da habe ich mich getäuscht. Helene steht auf André! Auf meinen André! Sie weiß vielleicht nicht, dass er mein André ist, aber wieso macht sie sich sofort an ihn ran? Ich würde mich hier in Fucking – bei Helenes Freunden – niemals einem Jungen an den Hals werfen. Aber sie scheint da überhaupt keine Hemmungen zu haben. Das ist so gemein!

Ich gehe ins Bad und schaue in den Spiegel. Die ganze Wimperntusche ist verlaufen. So kann ich auf keinen Fall zur Party gehen. Besser, ich leg mich gleich ins Bett und heule mich in den Schlaf. Ach, André, ich hatte so gehofft, du würdest mich auch ein kleines bisschen vermissen!

ICH SCHLAGE DIE AUGEN AUF und bin einfach nur glücklich. Es ist Saaamstaaag! Heute wollen mir meine neuen Freunde Paris zeigen! Voller Tatendrang setze ich mich im Bett auf. Bastet liegt zusammengerollt neben meinen Füßen und hebt müde den Kopf.

»Guten Morgen, Eure Hoheit. Leider hab ich keine Zeit für ein Schmusestündchen. Ich muss mich jetzt herausputzen, und dann wird die Stadt unsicher gemacht!« Voller Vorfreude schwinge ich die Beine aus dem Bett.

Irritiert erhebt sich Bastet und streckt sich ausgiebig. Was ist sie doch für ein edles Geschöpf! Nur ihr Gähnen passt nicht zu ihrer majestätischen Erscheinung.

André, Marc und Marie-Claire stehen um Punkt neun vor der Tür.

»Salut, Helene. Super, dass du schon fertig bist«, begrüßt mich Marie-Claire. »Wenn man in den Louvre will, sollte man nicht zu spät dran sein, denn sonst ist es brechend voll dort.«

»Oh, wir gehen ins Museum?«, frage ich enttäuscht.

»Erst die Arbeit, dann das Vergnügen!«, verkündet André und seufzt theatralisch.

»Hey, ihr Kunstbanausen! Die Mona Lisa ist Weltklasse«, mischt sich Marc ein. »Und die Arbeit hatte wohl vor allem Leonardo, nicht wir. Der arme Kerl hat gut drei Jahre für das Bild gebraucht. Und ob die Dame eine angenehme Gesellschaft war, weiß ich nicht. Vermutlich fehlten ihr nämlich die Schneidezähne. Darum lächelt sie so verstohlen.«

André legt eine Hand auf Marcs Schulter. »Da hat ja jemand besonders gut aufgepasst. Du machst doch nur einen auf Kunstexperte, um Helene zu beeindrucken!«

Marc schüttelt Andrés Hand ab und verpasst ihm einen Stoß in die Seite.

»Lasst uns gehen, bevor ein Hahnenkampf ausbricht«, sagt Marie-Claire.

»Ja. Ich bin schon ganz gespannt auf die Stadt! Ich will alles sehen!«

»Alles kannst du in Paris nicht sehen, noch nicht mal, wenn du zweihundert Jahre alt werden würdest. Aber wir zeigen dir heute die Highlights. Nicht wahr, Jungs?«

Kaum zu glauben, aber das Museum kostet keinen Eintritt. Jugendliche unter achtzehn Jahren dürfen die Mona Lisa kostenlos bestaunen. Das ist bei uns in Österreich ganz anders, da ist spätestens mit sechs Jahren überall Schluss mit gratis.

Meine neuen Freunde führen mich durch den Louvre. Wir wandern an ägyptischen Skulpturen vorbei und an Gemälden, die ich bislang nur im Fernsehen oder in Kunstbüchern gesehen habe. Schließlich stehen wir vor dem berühmtesten Bild des Museums: der Mona Lisa. Zentimeterdickes Panzerglas schützt das wertvolle Gemälde. Eine Gruppe Japaner schiebt sich nach vorn und knipst mindestens hundert Bilder. Wir stellen uns brav in die Warteschlange, bis wir an der Reihe sind.

»Da lob ich mir doch die moderne Zahnmedizin. Stellt euch vor, ich müsste immer so gucken«, witzelt Marie-Claire und imitiert das berühmteste Lächeln der Welt.

»Stimmt. Mona kann einem echt leidtun, zumal sie auch sonst nicht besonders attraktiv war«, meint André. »Wenn Leonardo da Vinci die Wahl gehabt hätte, dann hätte er bestimmt lieber dich gemalt, Helene. Du bist hundertmal schöner.«

So rot, wie ich werde, schlage ich in Sachen Farbintensität locker Leonardos Meisterwerk.

»Und ich?«, gibt sich Marie-Claire gespielt empört.

»Du bist zigmal schöner«, antwortet André grinsend.

»Da soll man nicht beleidigt sein. Kommt, gehen wir lieber zur Venus von Milo. Mal sehen, ob sie im Original auch so eine tolle Figur hat.« Marie-Claire deutet mit den Händen zwei melonengroße Brüste an.

»Na super, diese Kunststunde verfolgt mich bestimmt noch bis zum Abi!« Marc seufzt.

»Wolltest du nicht sogar Kunst studieren?«, entgegnet André lachend.

Vor dem Louvre steht ein kleiner Crêpe-Wagen, und wir reihen uns in die Warteschlange ein. Gemälde machen hungrig, auch wenn man sie nur betrachtet und nicht selbst malen muss.

Als André seinen Crêpe bestellt, flirtet er mit der jungen Verkäuferin, die vor Verlegenheit ganz rot wird. Offenbar hat André nicht nur auf mich diese Wirkung. Das Mädchen ist vielleicht zwei, drei Jahre älter als wir, und im Handumdrehen hat André herausgefunden, dass sie diesen Job nur am Wochenende macht.

Nachdem er in seine Teigrolle gebissen hat, seufzt er zufrieden. » So eine gute Crêpe habe ich noch nie gegessen! In Zukunft kaufe ich meine Crêpes nur noch bei dir.«

Das Mädchen kichert und macht eine wegwischende Handbewegung. Dann wendet sie sich schnell dem nächsten Gast zu, der schon ungeduldig wartet.

Mit den Crêpes in der Hand schlendern wir Richtung Seine.

» Du alter Charmebolzen! Du hast das arme Crêpe-Mädchen total durcheinandergebracht«, meint Marc, als wir außer Hörweite sind.

» Neidisch?«, fragt André, aber Marc verdreht nur die Augen. Dann fragt er mich, ob ich lieber erst eine Bootsfahrt auf der Seine machen möchte oder zu Fuß den Eiffelturm besteigen will.

» Die Bootsfahrt, bitte!«, erwidere ich. » Nach dieser Wanderung durch die Kunstgeschichte würde ich gern erst mal eine Weile sitzen.«

» Danke, Helene! Du rettest mich und meine Füße«, sagt Marie-Claire. Ihre hochhackigen Schuhe hätten mich schon längst zu Fall gebracht.

Unsere Bootsfahrt startet direkt vor dem Eiffelturm. Während wir darauf warten, an Bord zu gehen, kauft Marie-Claire schon online die Tickets für den Eiffelturm. »Dann können wir gemütlich eine Stunde durch die Gegend tuckern und uns berieseln lassen. Danach sind wir direkt wieder am Eiffelturm, sparen uns die Warterei und stürmen die 704 Stufen in Windeseile hoch!«, verkündet sie und lässt ihr Smartphone wieder in der Tasche verschwinden.

Insgeheim bewundere ich Marie-Claire, die sich so gut in der Stadt auskennt. Obwohl sie genauso alt ist wie ich, scheint sie schon viel selbstständiger zu sein.

Wir haben wahnsinniges Glück und ergattern die besten Plätze auf dem Oberdeck. Die Fahrt beginnt, und die Touristeninformationen werden sowohl auf Englisch als auch auf Französisch abgespielt.

»Oh. Notre-Dame!«, schwärme ich, als wir an der mächtigen Kathedrale vorbeifahren.

»Der Glöckner und seine Esmeralda, was?« André grinst mich schelmisch an.

Schon schießt mir das Blut in die Wangen. Es kann doch nicht sein, dass dieser Junge eine schlimmere Wirkung auf mich hat als eine Achterbahnfahrt auf dem Oktoberfest!

Ob André seine Komplimente überhaupt ernst meint? Oder ist das alles nur ein Spiel für ihn? Und wie er mich andauernd ansieht. So, als wäre ich etwas Besonderes. Genauso war es mit Levin. Die bittere Erinnerung an meine erste Liebe kommt wieder hoch, und ich versuche, sie zu verdrängen. Irgendwie erinnert mich André an ihn. Levin hatte auch eine geradezu magnetische Anziehungskraft auf

Mädchen. Sie flogen auf ihn wie Motten auf eine Straßenlaterne. Ich beobachte André aus den Augenwinkeln. Es ist nicht leicht, hinter seine Fassade zu schauen.

»Vielleicht interessiert sich Helene für das Bauwerk und nicht für den Glöckner«, unterbricht Marc meine Überlegungen. »Wenn du willst, können wir die Kirche in den nächsten Tagen mal besichtigen.«

Ich bin überrascht, dass der Vorschlag von Marc kommt, und muss die Information erst mal verarbeiten.

»Oh, jetzt hab ich dich verschreckt«, sagt Marc und klingt ein wenig enttäuscht.

»Nein. Das wäre nett«, beeile ich mich zu antworten.

»Unser Marc kommt aus der Reserve«, bemerkt André grinsend und kassiert dafür böse Blicke von allen Seiten.

Marc und Marie-Claire zeigen mir alle Sehenswürdigkeiten entlang der Seine, und André klopft weiter fröhlich Sprüche. Die Sonne scheint warm auf meine Haut, und ich wundere mich nicht länger, dass mein Herz dauernd Purzelbäume schlägt und ich rot werde. Das liegt bestimmt an Paris und am Frühling. Schließlich sind wir in der Stadt der Liebe, und da muss man einfach Schmetterlinge im Bauch haben.

»Und was willst du einmal werden?«, fragt mich André, nachdem er lang und breit erklärt hat, wie er sich seine große Musikerkarriere vorstellt.

»Tierärztin. Ich liebe Tiere«, antworte ich.

»Echt? Noch so eine Tierfreundin«, wundert sich André.

»Kennst du noch jemanden, der Tierarzt werden will?«

»Ja, direkt neben dir«, wirft Marc schüchtern ein.

»Wirklich? Das ist ja toll. Auf was willst du dich spezialisieren? Ich glaube, ich würde mich für die klassische Kleintierpraxis entscheiden, obwohl ich auch Pferde und Kühe mag.«

»Wenn ich es mir aussuchen könnte, dann würde ich im Zoo arbeiten. Dort jobbe ich jedes Jahr in den Ferien.«

»Toll! Das würde ich auch gerne machen, aber unser nächster Zoo ist in Salzburg und, na ja … eher klein. Ferialstellen bieten die gar nicht an. Zum Glück haben wir ein paar Tiere auf unserem Hof. Unser Schweinchen Susi ist echt herzig. Du müsstest einmal sehen, wie sie um Leckerlis bettelt. Herzzerreißender als jeder Dackel.«

»Mann. Tierverrückte unter sich. Ich hol mir noch eine Cola, bevor wir wieder anlegen. Marie-Claire, willst du auch was?«, fragt André und steht auf. Marie-Claire schüttelt den Kopf, und André verschwindet in Richtung Restaurant.

»Was hat er denn?«, frage ich.

»Nicht die ungeteilte Aufmerksamkeit«, entgegnet Marie-Claire. »Auf jeden Fall finde ich es toll, dass ihr beide den gleichen Berufswunsch habt.«

»Wenn du willst, zeige ich dir den Pariser Zoo«, bietet Marc an.

»Vor oder nach Notre-Dame?«, frage ich lächelnd.

»An zwei verschiedenen Tagen, wenn du magst. Damit wir wirklich Zeit haben. Ich werde sehen, dass mein Freund Claude arbeitet. Er ist Tierpfleger bei den Manatis. Claude lässt uns bestimmt einen Blick hinter die Kulissen werfen.« Marc schaut mir in die Augen, und mir wird heiß. Meine Güte, jetzt geht es mir mit Marc schon genauso wie mit André! Daran muss wirklich diese verhexte Stadt schuld sein.

»Oh, das wäre wunderbar! Ich habe noch nie im Leben echte Seekühe gesehen«, schwärme ich.

»Dann wird es aber Zeit!«

»Ja, find ich auch«, sagt André, der plötzlich mit einem Glas Cola in der Hand wieder neben uns steht. »Ich freu mich jedenfalls schon aufs Treppensteigen. In fünf Minuten sind wir wieder beim Eiffelturm, und dann werden wir sehen, wer hier die beste Kondition hat.«

»Ich bring dich nach Hause«, sagt André bestimmt, als wir wieder unten sind.

»Wir können dich alle gern begleiten«, wirft Marie-Claire ein.

»Das ist wirklich nicht nötig. Inzwischen weiß ich, wo ich umsteigen muss«, entgegne ich.

»Ach was. Das ist kein großer Umweg für mich«, beharrt André.

»Musst du aber echt nicht. Der Tag war so toll, und ich will dich nicht aufhalten.«

»Du kannst mich nicht daran hindern, dieselbe Métro zu nehmen wie du!« André setzt eine eingeschnappte Miene auf.

»Also gut. Überredet«, gebe ich mich geschlagen und verabschiede mich mit Wangenküsschen von Marie-Claire und Marc. Sein Duft steigt mir in die Nase, als seine Lippen meine Wangen berühren, und ein angenehmer Schauer läuft mir über den Rücken. »Danke für heute«, sage ich und folge André zur U-Bahn.

Ich weiß nicht genau warum, aber irgendwie kommt unsere Unterhaltung nicht richtig in Schwung. Irgendwann höre ich André auch nur noch mit halbem Ohr zu. Vielleicht, weil ich zu müde bin, vielleicht auch, weil ich mir unsicher bin, ob er es ernst meint mit mir. Ich bin froh, als wir endlich da sind.

»Es war ein schöner Tag mit dir«, haucht André mir beim Abschied ins Ohr.

»Finde ich auch. Es ist wundervoll, wie ihr mich aufnehmt und mir alles zeigt. Danke noch mal!«

»Gern geschehen. Mit dir ist jede Minute ein Vergnügen.« Er küsst mich auf die Wangen und geht zurück zur Métro.

Ich bin erleichtert, als ich wieder allein bin.

BASTET BLICKT ZU MIR HOCH und miaut herzzerreißend.

»Komm her, Prinzessin«, sage ich und nehme die Katze auf den Arm.

Schnurrend schmiegt sie sich an mich, und ich kraule ihr den Hals. Es ist so einfach mit Tieren. Ich muss nur auf mein Gefühl hören, und dann weiß ich, was Bastet von mir will. Warum ist bei uns Menschen alles so viel komplizierter? Eigentlich müsste ich glücklich sein, denn ich hatte einen tollen Tag mit der Clique. Stattdessen starre ich Löcher in die Luft.

»Na, Bastet. Kannst du mir vielleicht sagen, was ich will? Heute Morgen dachte ich noch, ich wäre in André verliebt, aber jetzt bin ich mir nicht mehr sicher.«

Bastet beginnt sich das Fell zu lecken. In Gedanken sehe ich Andrés Gesicht vor mir. Sein Lachen, seine eisblauen Augen. Natürlich finde ich es schön, dass er mir Komplimente macht und mir das Gefühl gibt, etwas ganz Besonderes zu sein. Plötzlich schiebt sich Levins Bild davor. Levin war auch immer charmant. Wochenlang hat er mich umschwärmt und meine Knie bei jeder Begegnung in Butter verwandelt.

Er war in den Sommerferien bei seiner Tante in Fucking zu Besuch, weil seine Eltern arbeiten mussten. Erst konnte ich es gar nicht glauben, dass sich ein gut aussehender siebzehnjähriger Junge aus der Stadt für mich interessiert. Doch Levin hat nicht lockergelassen. »Am liebsten würde ich die Schule in Wien schmeißen und bei Thomas im Reitstall anfangen, nur damit ich immer bei dir sein kann. Und das, obwohl du nichts essen möchtest, was ich gekocht habe. Du bist einfach meine Helene. Ohne dich … das halte ich nicht aus!«

Schließlich hab ich ihm geglaubt, wahrscheinlich, weil ich auch endlich einen Freund haben wollte. Damals war ich die Einzige in meinem Freundeskreis gewesen, die noch keinen Jungen geküsst hatte. Im Vergleich zu Lena war ich ein echter Spätzünder. Ich glaube, Levin hat das gespürt. Er hat gemerkt, wie sehr ich mir insgeheim einen Freund gewünscht habe. Als er mich dann das erste Mal geküsst hat, haben sich seine Lippen wie Samt angefühlt. So weich, so warm. Ich war sofort bis über beide Ohren in ihn verliebt.

Die nächsten Wochen bin ich wie auf Wolken durch Fucking geschwebt und hab alle angestrahlt wie ein Glühwürmchen überm Waldsee. Ich dachte, Levin würde es genauso gehen. Wie hätte ich auch ahnen können, dass er keine ernsthaften Gefühle für mich hegt? So, wie er mich umgarnt hat? Ich war so verliebt in ihn, dass ich fast alles für ihn getan hätte.

Doch dann hab ich ein Telefonat zwischen ihm und seinem Wiener Kumpel belauscht. Obwohl Levin noch am Tag zuvor lachend mit dem Traktor übers Feld gefahren war, hat er plötzlich nur gelästert über das Landleben – und am schlimmsten über mich. Er hat geprahlt, dass er die dumme Landpomeranze jetzt endlich rumgekriegt hat und er mich noch vor Ferienende ganz knacken würde. Sein Kumpel könne schon mal die Kohle lockermachen, weil er die unnahbare Helene erobert hätte.

Als ich das gehört habe, ist mir richtig schlecht geworden, und am liebsten hätte ich ihm direkt vor die Füße gekotzt. Aber ich hab mich bloß geräuspert, und Levin ist alle Farbe aus dem Gesicht gewichen. Wie ein Geist sah er aus und hat sofort einen auf lieb gemacht. Dass ich etwas falsch verstanden hätte. Doch ich hab ihm gesagt, dass ich ihn ziemlich gut verstanden hätte und dass es nun mit uns vorbei wäre.

Damit war die Sache gegessen und mein Herz für den Rest des Sommers gebrochen. Nächtelang hab ich geweint. So sehr, dass sich sogar Florian Sorgen gemacht hat. Irgendwann hab ich ihm dann die ganze Geschichte erzählt, und Flo hat ein total peinliches Foto von Levin auf der Fucking-Homepage gepostet: Levin, wie er völlig betrunken aus einer Blumenvase trinkt, in der noch die Blumen stecken. Einen kurzen Moment hab ich Flos Aktion lustig gefunden, aber dann war der Schmerz doch größer als der kleine Funken Schadenfreude. So eine Enttäuschung will ich nie wieder erleben. Lieber bleibe ich für den Rest meines Lebens allein.

Die Erinnerung treibt mir die Tränen in die Augen. Bastet schaut mich irritiert an. »Vielleicht täusche ich mich ja in André«, flüstere ich heiser und kraule Bastet weiter.

Die Mieze schnurrt beruhigend. Seufzend wische ich mir die Tränen aus den Augenwinkeln. Vielleicht meint André es ja tatsächlich ernst. Immerhin hat er mich heute nach Hause gebracht, obwohl das nicht nötig gewesen wäre. Jungs sind echt schwierig. Eigentlich müsste man bei der Geburt eine Gebrauchsanweisung für das andere Geschlecht mitgeliefert bekommen. Woher soll ich denn wissen, ob André wirklich an mir interessiert ist oder nur eine schnelle Eroberung machen will?

Da ist Marc ganz anders. Bei ihm hab ich nicht das Gefühl, dass er mich um jeden Preis beeindrucken will. Er ist zwar eher schüchtern, aber dafür scheint er alles ehrlich zu meinen, was er sagt. André ist ein Selbstdarsteller, was aber nicht heißen muss, dass er es nicht ernst mit mir meint.

Miau, klagt Bastet, die ich durch meine Grübelei schon wieder vernachlässigt habe. Schnell streiche ich ihr über das Fell, und zufrieden schmiegt sie sich wieder an mich. Mein Blick streift den Laptop, und mir kommt eine Idee.

»Weißt du was, Bastet? Ich könnte doch einfach mal Fabienne fragen, was sie denkt. Sie kennt André schon viel länger als ich und kann mir vielleicht weiterhelfen. Das ewige Nachdenken bringt mich jedenfalls nicht weiter, und Fabienne scheint mir eine gute Ratgeberin zu sein. Wer, wenn nicht sie, weiß, wie die Jungs hier ticken?« Ich stehe auf, und Bastet sieht mir verwirrt nach. »Wir schmusen später wieder«, verspreche ich ihr und setz mich an den Schreibtisch.

ES IST SAMSTAG. Inzwischen habe ich mich beruhigt. Natürlich darf ich nicht darüber nachdenken, was André momentan tut, aber das schaffe ich irgendwie.

»Sicher kommst du mit! Oma Amalia will dich unbedingt kennenlernen. Außerdem ist Petting total schön. Es liegt direkt am See, und wir können nach dem Mittagessen baden gehen«, sagt Florian und grinst mich breit an.

»Der Waginger See ist der wärmste Badesee Bayerns. Da kann man sogar im Mai schon schwimmen«, fügt Erika hinzu.

»Und Oma Amalia kocht herrlich«, mischt sich nun auch Peter ein.

»Na gut. Überredet. Obwohl es von Fucking nach Petting schon ein Rückschritt ist«, erwidere ich kichernd.

Meine Gasteltern sehen sich einen Moment lang verwirrt an, nur Florian bricht sofort in lautes Gelächter aus.

Dann schmunzelt auch Erika. »Die Jugendlichen von heute, nix als schmutzige Gedanken im Kopf!«

»… sagt die Mutter mit den Fucking-Unterhöschen«, kommentiert Florian trocken.

Jetzt prusten alle endgültig los, und selbst Schweinchen Susi hüpft quietschend auf und ab. Sie freut sich, dass sie mitdarf, wenn auch im Katzenkörbchen.

Kaum haben wir Susi aus ihrer Transportbox befreit, stürmt sie auf einen Apfelbaum im Garten zu und wühlt in der Erde. Ich sehe mich um. Oma Amalia wohnt genau wie meine Gastfamilie in einem Bauernhaus. Allerdings ist ihr Hof winzig klein, und im Stall stehen keine Kühe, sondern drei blitzblank polierte Traktoren.

»Opa Bruno sammelt und restauriert alte Traktoren. Das ist sein Hobby«, erklärt mir Florian, »ich glaub, er verbringt mindestens so viel Zeit mit den Treckern wie ich im Netz. Der blaue dort ist angeblich besonders wertvoll.«

»Aha«, antworte ich. Viel mehr als die alten Gefährte interessiert mich die phantastische Aussicht. Der kleine Hof liegt direkt am See, auf dem einige Enten und Schwäne schwimmen.

»Oma und Opa haben einen eigenen Badesteg, der hinaus auf den See führt. Wenn du willst, kannst du später baden gehen«, sagt Peter und deutet in Richtung Wasser.

»Ich glaube, ich geh nur mal gucken«, sage ich. Obwohl ich vorsorglich einen Bikini in meine Handtasche gepackt habe, möchte ich eigentlich nicht, dass mich meine Gastfamilie beim Schwimmen sieht. Ich bin nicht prüde, doch ich will nicht riskieren, mich morgen halb nackt auf der Fuckinger Homepage wiederzufinden. Florian ist nett – aber er hat auch einen an der Waffel. Dauernd postet und kommentiert er alles im Internet. Das ist sogar mir zu viel des Guten.

»Ihr Lieben! Huhu!« Eine alte Frau, die erstaunlich modern gekleidet ist, kommt aus dem Haus gestürmt.

»Oma Amalia«, sagt Florian.

»Ich hab sie mir ganz anders vorgestellt. In Kleid und Schürze oder so«, flüstere ich.

»Nein, meine Oma trägt nur Jeans oder Petticoats. Meine Großeltern sind im Boogie-Woogie-Verein und die größten Elvis-Fans weit und breit. Oma ist modisch irgendwann in den Jahren der Jeansrevolution hängen geblieben. Aber abgesehen davon ist sie eine ganz typische Omama. Du wirst schon sehen.«

Und wie ich das sehe. Oma Amalia hat weiße Locken, ein rundes Gesicht und eine mit Fingerabdrücken verschmierte Brille auf der Nase. Freudestrahlend drückt sie die ganze Familie zur Begrüßung an ihren Busen und verteilt großzügig feuchte Schmatzer auf die Wangen. Bei mir ist sie glücklicherweise etwas zurückhaltender.

Lächelnd nimmt sie meine Hand und tätschelt sie sanft. »Fabienne. Wie schön, dass du mitgekommen bist. Ich habe extra für dich ein vegetarisches Mittagessen gekocht. Es gibt Kartoffelsuppe mit selbst gebackenem Weißbrot und als Nachtisch warmen Apfelstrudel mit Vanilleeis.«

»Hm. Klingt lecker«, bemerke ich ehrlich erfreut.

Nur Peter macht ein unglückliches Gesicht und seufzt.

»Für Florian und dich hab ich natürlich zwei Schnitzel in die Pfanne geworfen. Nicht sauer sein, Susi. Männer sind nun mal Fleischtiger«, erklärt Oma Amalia und streichelt das kleine Schweinchen, das einen ganz erdigen Rüssel hat. »Für dich hab ich auch einen Kübel Reste zur

Seite gestellt. Aber so schmutzig, wie du bist, isst du besser im Garten.«

Wir folgen Oma Amalia in das alte Bauernhaus. Ein köstlicher Duft zieht durch den Flur, und mir läuft das Wasser im Mund zusammen. In der Stube treffen wir auf Opa Bruno, der die Servietten faltet.

»Gerade rechtzeitig fertig geworden«, begrüßt er uns strahlend.

Helenes Opa ist mir auf Anhieb sympathisch. Er trägt auch Jeans, eine, die über den Bauch geht, und darüber ein gestreiftes Hemd. Sein Gesicht ist von Falten durchzogen, freundlichen Falten, die vom Lachen kommen. Mit seiner spiegelblanken Glatze und dem weißen Haarkranz sieht er genauso aus, wie ich mir Helenes Opa vorgestellt habe.

»Du bist also Fabienne. Schön, dich kennenzulernen. Ich hoffe, es gefällt dir bei uns«, sagt er und schüttelt mir die Hand.

»Bisher schon. Es ist natürlich ganz anders als in Paris, aber die Menschen hier sind sehr nett.«

»Und das Essen ist gut. Zumindest das von Amalia und Erika«, sagt er und grinst.

»Stimmt. Wenn ich noch länger bleiben würde, müsste ich mir sicher bald eine neue Garderobe zulegen.«

Das ist noch nicht mal gelogen. Die Kartoffelsuppe schmeckt so lecker, dass ich mir noch einen großen Nachschlag geben lasse. Das selbst gebackene Brot ist sogar noch warm. Als Oma Amalia den Nachtisch hereinbringt, platze ich schon fast. Doch der Apfelstrudel mit Vanilleeis duftet so gut, dass ich ihn einfach probieren muss.

»Wie wird denn ein Strudel gemacht?«, frage ich Oma Amalia.

»Ach Kindchen. Strudel machen ist eine Kunst. Die ersten Teige musste ich alle wegschmeißen. Der Teig muss nämlich sehr geschmeidig sein. Man muss ihn ganz dünn ausziehen können, bis er durchsichtig wie Glas ist. Wenn du willst, kann ich es dir gern mal zeigen.«

»Oje, das klingt kompliziert. Ich glaub nicht, dass ich es so schnell lerne.«

»Außerdem wäre es eine Schande, bei dem herrlichen Mai-Wetter den ganzen Tag in der Küche zu hocken und zu backen. Traktorfahren lernt man auf jeden Fall schneller als Strudelbacken. Was ist, Kinder? Kann ich euch zu einer Rundfahrt überreden?« Bruno lächelt mich warm an.

»Ich bin dabei«, sagt Florian.

»Ich auch. Traktor bin ich noch nie gefahren.«

»Dann wird es aber Zeit. Direkt neben unserer Wiese gibt es einen Privatweg, wo ihr Kinder mal ans Steuer dürft.«

»Ehrlich?«, frage ich verblüfft. »Ich dachte, Ihre Traktoren seien besonders wertvoll?«

»Und genau deshalb müssen sie gefahren werden. Alte Modelle halten wesentlich mehr aus. Und nur wenn sie benutzt werden, verrosten sie nicht. Auch für unsere Trecker gilt: Wer rastet, der rostet. Also los!«, ruft Opa Bruno und klopft sich auf die Oberschenkel.

»Bis später, Liebling«, sagt Oma Amalia lächelnd.

Bruno beugt sich vor und küsst seine Frau sanft auf die Wange. Mir wird warm ums Herz. Liebe kann so schön sein, und wie man hier sieht, auch lange anhalten. Meine

Eltern gehen nur selten so liebevoll miteinander um wie Bruno und Amalia oder Peter und Erika. Dafür sind sie viel zu gestresst. Ich seufze leise.

»Alles in Ordnung?«, erkundigt sich Bruno. »Du willst doch mitkommen, oder hast du Angst vorm Traktorfahren?«

»Nein, ich will mit. Hab nur gerade an etwas anderes gedacht«, antworte ich schnell.

Bruno sieht mich einen Moment zweifelnd an, dann nickt er wissend. »Ja, ja. Du hast wohl eher an jemand anderen gedacht.«

Draußen vor der Haustür liegt Susi satt und zufrieden in der Sonne und macht ein Mittagsschläfchen. Opa Bruno fährt den blauen Traktor aus dem Stall. Florian und ich klettern zu ihm auf die Fahrerbank.

Traktorfahren ist laut, holprig und lustig. Wir fahren ein Stück am See entlang. Dann biegen wir auf einen Feldweg ab, und ich muss mich festhalten, um nicht vom Sitz zu purzeln.

»Das ist ein ganz neues Fahrgefühl, was?«, ruft Bruno über den Lärm hinweg.

»Klasse. Fast wie Achterbahn fahren«, schreie ich zurück.

»So, jetzt bist du an der Reihe, Florian. Gib aber nicht zu viel Gas. Und erklär Fabienne gleich mal die wichtigsten Schritte.«

Florian strahlt bis über beide Ohren. Kaum zu glauben, aber Opa Bruno hat es geschafft, dass mein Gastbruder mal offline ist. Ich rücke dichter an ihn ran und lasse mir erklären, wie der Traktor funktioniert. Gas, Kupplung, Bremse, gar nicht so anders als bei unserem Auto.

»Wichtig ist, dass du die Kupplung ganz durchdrückst. Sonst bekommst du den Gang nicht rein. Ältere Modelle haken schon mal ein wenig«, sagt Florian.

Er dreht eine Runde auf der Wiese. Dann bin ich dran.

»Keine Sorge. Der Motor lässt sich nicht so leicht abwürgen. Das ist ein Traktor, und der läuft mit Diesel. Traktorfahren ist wirklich leicht. Auf den Privatwegen fahren bei uns schon Kinder Trecker.«

»Aha. Also kann Helene auch Traktorfahren?«

»Sicher. Und jetzt gib Gas«, fordert Florian mich auf.

Ich blicke mich nach Opa Bruno um. Er nickt mir aufmunternd zu. Mit zitternden Händen lege ich den Gang ein. Langsam geh ich von der Kupplung und gebe Gas. Der Traktor bewegt sich.

»Ich fahre! Schaut doch, ich fahre!«

»Lenken nicht vergessen!«, erinnert mich Opa Bruno.

Schnell steuere ich den Traktor zurück auf den Weg. Ich war schon im Gras gelandet, aber mit einem Traktor ist das kein Problem. Sein Einsatzgebiet sind Wiesen und Felder.

»Toll!«, rufe ich lachend.

»Dann schalt mal einen Gang höher, Mädchen«, meint Bruno.

Das lasse ich mir nicht zweimal sagen. Ich wusste gar nicht, dass ich so mutig bin und Traktorfahren so viel Spaß bringt!

»Unsere Fabienne ist ein Naturtalent. Kaum zu glauben, dass sie aus Paris kommt und noch nie einen Traktor gefahren hat«, lobt mich Bruno, als wir wieder auf dem Hof angekommen sind. »Schade, dass du nicht länger bei uns bleibst. Im Juni findet unser Traktorrennen um den See statt. Da würde ich dich gleich anmelden.«

»Wäre ich dafür nicht zu jung?«

»Nein, nein. Den Traktorschein kann man schon mit sechzehn machen, und in Ausnahmefällen sogar mit vierzehn.« Ich schüttle den Kopf. »Nein, ehrlich. Es hat total Spaß gemacht, aber bei einem Rennen würde ich sowieso nie mitfahren. Da hätte ich zu viel Angst.«

»Auf jeden Fall darfst du, wann immer du bei uns im Land bist, eine Runde mit mir drehen«, bietet Opa Bruno an.

»Danke, das ist sehr nett von Ihnen.«

Nachdem wir den Traktor zurück in den Stall gebracht haben, setzen wir uns zu Erika und Amalia auf die Terrasse. Ich genieße den tollen Ausblick auf den See und die warme Sonne auf der Haut. Die Erwachsenen reden übers Maifest und wie viel Bier wohl gebraucht wird. Florian verwandelt sich wieder zurück in den Nerd und wischt auf seinem Handy herum. Ich lasse meins absichtlich in der Tasche. Der Tag war bislang ziemlich gut, und ich will ihn mir nicht durch André, Helene oder beide zusammen vermiesen lassen.

»Darf ich mit ein paar Brotresten die Schwäne füttern gehen?«, frage ich, als mir das Kaffeetrinken zu langweilig wird.

Oma Amalia steht auf und holt aus der Küche eine Tüte mit Brot. »Eigentlich soll man die Wildvögel nicht füttern. Aber heute machen wir mal eine Ausnahme. Außerdem kann Susi ja nicht alles alleine fressen.«

»Stimmt. Nicht dass sie ein fettes Schwein wird«, meint Florian, der kurz von seinem Smartphone aufblickt.

Ich gehe zum Steg hinunter. Die Enten und Schwäne kommen sofort herbeigeschwommen. Ich lasse mir Zeit beim Füttern. Die Sonne scheint herrlich warm vom Himmel. Anmutig fischen die Schwäne die Brotstücke aus dem Wasser.

Ein richtig romantischer Augenblick. Fehlt eigentlich nur André. Womit ich wieder bei dem Thema angelangt bin, das ich bisher so erfolgreich verdrängt habe. »Liebe ist eine Krankheit. Und ich bin ein unheilbarer Fall«, sage ich leise.

»Fabienne! In fünf Minuten fahren wir! Wir müssen heute noch mit den Vorbereitungen fürs Maifest beginnen«, ruft mir Erika vom Ufer entgegen.

DAHEIM ANGEKOMMEN, machen sich meine Gasteltern gleich daran, Bierfässer zu zählen und irgendwelche Fahnen vom Dachboden herunterzuholen. Florian klärt mich auf, dass es hier Tradition ist, den Frühling zu feiern. Zu diesem Anlass wird der ganze Ort in Tracht aufmarschieren, es wird Musik gespielt und getanzt werden. Ich nicke, aber in Gedanken bin ich woanders. Schließlich halte ich es nicht länger aus. Ich entschuldige mich und gehe in mein Zimmer. Dort setze ich mich an den Laptop und schaue, wer im Chat ist. Natürlich ist André nicht on, dafür aber Helene.

Fabienne? Bist du on? Unsere Sightseeingtour heute war super! Nur leider bin ich total durch den Wind. Hast du schon die Fotos auf FB gesehen? Ich weiß echt nicht, wie ich mich jetzt verhalten soll ...

Ja, ich bin gerade on gegangen. War heute bei deiner Oma und deinem Opa. Essen und Traktorfahren. War sehr nett. Warte, ich guck gleich wegen der Fotos. Und dann erzählst du mir in Ruhe, warum du so durch den Wind bist.

Du bist ein Schatz, Fabienne. Ich bin so froh, dass du on bist. Ehrlich. Die Sache ist … André war heute wieder so nett zu mir. Wenn ich mit ihm zusammen bin, hab ich immer das Gefühl, na ja … etwas Besonderes zu sein. Ich glaub, er mag mich wirklich. Auf jeden Fall war der Tag heute echt schön.

Ich schlucke und klicke auf Helenes FB-Seite. Da sind etliche Fotos. Vom Louvre, der Seine, Notre-Dame vom Boot aus, der Clique und dem Eiffelturm. Auf einem Bild steht Helene zwischen Marc und André. André hat seinen Arm um Helenes Taille gelegt und lächelt sie ganz verliebt an. Der Schuft! Kein Wunder, dass sie total durch den Wind ist, wenn er sie die ganze Zeit umgarnt. Aber warum lässt sie das überhaupt zu? Wenn es ihr unangenehm wäre, dann würde sie doch die Finger von ihm lassen. Aber nein, sie himmelt André an und bittet mich auch noch um Hilfe! Sie ist doch nur noch ein paar Tage in Paris. Sucht sie etwa ein Abenteuer? Pah, Freundin! Ich gucke zurück auf das Chatfenster. Helene schwärmt, wie phänomenal der Tag war. Ob er ohne André genauso schön gewesen wäre? Ich balle die Hände zu Fäusten und beiße die Zähne aufeinander.

Marc hat echt Ahnung von Kunst, glaube ich. Und bei der Bootsfahrt habe ich dann festgestellt, dass Marc und ich denselben Berufswunsch haben. Lustig,

was? Auf jeden Fall hatte ich das Gefühl, dass André richtig eifersüchtig war, weil ich mich eine Weile nicht ausschließlich mit ihm unterhalten habe. *gg* Ich finde deine Freunde echt cool und Paris auch. Eure Stadt hat so viel zu bieten. Der Blick vom Eiffelturm war echt der Hammer. Weißt du was? Ich würde mich gern bei deinen Freunden dafür revanchieren, dass sie dieses ganze Touri-Programm für mich veranstaltet haben. Hast du vielleicht eine Idee, was ich mit ihnen machen könnte?

Eine Idee??? Merkt Helene denn gar nichts? Sie zieht mit meinen Freunden durch die Stadt, flirtet mit meinem André und ... Merde! Die beiden werden bestimmt ein Paar. Und ich hocke hier in der Pampa und sehe vor lauter Tränen den Bildschirm nicht mehr. Ich will zurück nach Hause! Auf der Stelle! André, wieso tust du mir das an? Ich liebe dich doch! Das musst du doch wissen! Verdammt! Was mach ich nur?

Hey, Fabienne, bist du noch da? Hast du einen Tipp für mich? Ich würde André und die anderen gern überraschen.

André steht total auf Burger, also eigentlich auf alles, was mit Amerika zu tun hat. Lade ihn zum Bowlen ein und am besten danach noch ins Hard Rock Cafe. Das gefällt ihm bestimmt.

Toll! Oh danke, Fabienne. Marie-Claire und Marc

essen aber auch gern Burger, oder? Ich würde die beiden nämlich auch gern einladen.

Sicher. Wer liebt Bowlen und Burger nicht, hm?

Ich weiß, wer nicht. André. Er hat mal gesagt, er würde lieber Sägespäne essen als einen Burger.

Danke. Du bist die beste Austauschpartnerin der Welt! Wenn ich etwas für dich tun kann, sag Bescheid. Bussi ♥♥♥

Mon Dieu! Was hab ich getan? Ich starre ungläubig auf den Bildschirm. Helene wird sich blamieren. Dieser Abend wird bestimmt schrecklich für sie. Entsetzt über mich selbst schüttle ich den Kopf. Da geht die angelehnte Zimmertür auf, und Susi trottet herein. Ganz selbstverständlich kuschelt sie sich an meine Füße. Ich bücke mich und streichle das erste Mal das kleine Ferkel.

»Ach, Susi! Ich habe den schlimmsten Fehler meines Lebens gemacht. Dein Frauchen vertraut mir, und ich verhalte mich wie ein Miststück. Dabei bin ich normalerweise nicht so. Glaubst du mir?«

Susi hebt den Kopf und grunzt. Mit ihren kleinen Schweinsaugen guckt sie mich verständnisvoll an.

»Ich kann jetzt nicht mehr zurück«, flüstere ich traurig.

MARIE-CLAIRE IST SOFORT BEGEISTERT
von der Idee, erst Bowlen und dann ins Hard Rock Cafe
zu gehen. Die beiden Jungs reagieren eher etwas zögerlich.
Vielleicht, weil ich einmal erwähnt habe, dass ich nicht besonders viel Taschengeld bekomme. Doch ich erkläre ihnen,
dass ich einfach darauf bestehe, sie einzuladen. Nach allem,
was sie für mich getan haben, ist das das Mindeste. Schließlich geben sich André und Marc geschlagen.

»Natürlich gehen wir bowlen, wenn du das gerne möchtest«, sagt Marc und wirft André einen kurzen Blick zu, den
ich nicht deuten kann.

Im Internet habe ich sogar ein Bowlingcenter gefunden,
das ganz in der Nähe des Hard Rock Cafes ist. Langsam
werde ich großstadttauglich. Wenn ich wieder zurück in Fucking bin, dann mache ich in Zukunft auch Salzburg unsicher. Lena wird sich freuen, dass ihre sonst so schüchterne
und unsichere Freundin endlich aus der Reserve kommt.

Wie verabredet, warten die drei vor der Tür des Bowlingcenters.

»Hallo, schön, dass ihr alle da seid«, begrüße ich sie freudig. Wangenküsschen werden ausgetauscht. Andrés Duft steigt mir in die Nase, und ich werde rot. Zum Glück habe ich etwas Make-up aufgetragen.

Wir betreten das Bowlingcenter, und ich hab sofort das Gefühl, in einem alten amerikanischen Film gelandet zu sein. Es gibt kleine Sitzecken mit roten Lederbänken, eine Jukebox an der Wand, und Elvis singt seinen Jailhouse Rock.

»Cooler Laden!«, sagt Marc leise.

»Ja, so etwas hab ich noch nie gesehen«, stimme ich ihm zu.

André zuckt mit den Schultern. »Ja. Ganz okay. Du hast eine gute Wahl getroffen.«

»Google sei Dank«, sage ich, und alle lachen.

Ein Mitarbeiter des Centers heißt uns willkommen und händigt uns rot-weiße Bowlingschuhe aus. Dann zeigt er uns die Bahn und nimmt unsere Getränkebestellung entgegen.

Nachdem er uns die Limos gebracht hat, geht's an die Mannschaftseinteilung.

»Helene und ich sind ein Team. Gemeinsam werden wir euch plattwalzen«, verkündet André.

»Na, hoffentlich enttäusche ich dich nicht«, sage ich schüchtern.

»Ich kann mir nicht vorstellen, dass du mich jemals enttäuschen könntest.«

Ich schlucke. Ist das wieder nur so ein Spruch, oder meint André es ernst? Lässig streicht er sich die schwarzen Haare aus dem Gesicht. Wie seine Augen leuchten, und dazu dieses charmante Lächeln. Bin ich etwa tatsächlich verliebt? Nein, dafür kenne ich ihn doch viel zu wenig. Außerdem sollte ich mir nicht zu viel auf seine Worte einbilden, denn André flirtet mit jedem Mädchen. Ich sollte besser vorsichtig sein, damit ich nicht wieder so eine Enttäuschung wie mit Levin erlebe.

»Ich schlage vor, wir spielen erst einmal eine Runde, und dann tauschen wir die Partner. Ich will auch mal gewinnen«, sagt Marc und kassiert einen freundschaftlichen Boxer von Marie-Claire.

»Willst du etwa behaupten, ich könnte nicht ein paar läppische Pins umwerfen?«, fragt sie empört.

»Na ja, ich dachte da nur an unser letztes Fußballspiel, bei dem du über den Ball gestolpert und platt wie ein Rochen auf dem Bauch gelandet bist«, mischt sich jetzt André ein und rudert grinsend mit den Armen in der Luft.

»Das war Fabiennes Schuld. Sie hat den Pass versaut.« Marie-Claire zieht eine Schnute, dass Daisy Duck eifersüchtig werden könnte.

»Nicht sauer sein, Süße«, sagt André und wirft ihr einen Kuss zu.

»Charmeur«, meint Marie-Claire.

I'm the great pretender, schmettert der King aus den Lautsprecherboxen.

»Oder bist du eher ein great pretender?«, fragt Marc unschuldig, und wir Mädels lachen lauthals.

Wir beschließen, erst mal drei Spieldurchgänge zu machen. Die erste Runde gewinnen André und ich ganz knapp. Partnertausch.

»Sind eigentlich alle Mädchen bei euch so fucking hübsch?«, flüstert mir André ins Ohr.

So ein gemeiner Kerl! Den Wurf hab ich ordentlich verhauen. Ich funkle ihn böse an. Er grinst über beide Ohren, und schon bekomme ich wieder weiche Knie. Ich bin mir sicher, dass André weiß, wie er auf Mädchen wirkt – und er spielt diesen Vorteil gnadenlos aus. Ohne auch nur den winzigsten Anflug von Schuldbewusstsein wendet er sich Marie-Claire zu und feuert sie an. Da liegen die beiden auch schon eine Nasenlänge vorn.

»André ist ein Meister der Ablenkungsmanöver, also mach dir nichts draus«, tröstet mich Marc.

Ich sehe ihn zweifelnd an. Schüchtern lächelt er mir zu und wird ganz rot dabei. Irgendwie süß. Sollte es noch jemanden mit dem Rotköpfchen-Gen geben?

»Wir Tierretter müssen einfach gewinnen«, sagt er und wendet schnell den Blick ab.

»Genau, Marc, beim nächsten Wurf holen wir den Rückstand auf«, sage ich selbstbewusst.

»André, gib alles!«, feuert Marie-Claire ihn an.

André zwinkert siegessicher und vergeigt den Wurf.

Marc und ich schlagen ein.

»Ja, ja. Freut euch nur. Das ist nur passiert, weil ihr zwei mich nervös macht!«, behauptet André und deutet auf Marie-Claire und mich.

»Als ob dich Mädchen nervös machen könnten«, antwortet Marie-Claire locker und stemmt die Hände in die Hüften.

Am Ende gewinnen André und Marie-Claire dann doch um einen Punkt.

»So, jetzt aber, Jungs gegen Mädchen! Wir Mädels werden euch zum Heulen bringen!«, rufe ich.

Marie-Claire lacht. »Genau, wir werden haushoch gewinnen!« Tatsächlich ist meine Spielpartnerin erstaunlich gut und schafft mehrere Strikes. Am Ende haben wir die Jungs um Längen geschlagen.

»Girlpower!«, jubeln wir.

»Glück gehabt«, behaupten die Jungs.

»Können!«, kontern wir und klatschen uns ab. Ausgelassen tanzen wir ein paar Schritte zum schnellen Rock 'n' Roll des King, und ich amüsiere mich königlich. Ich bin Fabienne echt dankbar für ihren tollen Tipp – sonst säße ich jetzt wahrscheinlich allein zu Hause mit Bastet vorm PC.

André legt den Arm um seinen Kumpel Marc. »Was meinst du? Die beiden spielen mit unfairen Mitteln. Wie sollen wir uns konzentrieren, wenn die zwei so verführerisch tanzen?«

»Das ist eine ganz schlechte Ausrede«, erwidert Marie-Claire. »Verloren hattet ihr nämlich schon vorher.«

»Hast du am Wochenende eigentlich schon etwas vor?«, fragt Marc plötzlich. »Wegen dem Zoo, meine ich. Mein Kumpel Claude hat Wochenendschicht. Also wenn du Lust hast, mein Angebot steht noch.«

»Au ja, da würde ich gern mitkommen!«, rufe ich begeistert.

»Worum geht's?«, fragt André neugierig.

»Veterinärtermine«, erwidert Marc grinsend.

»WILLKOMMEN IN DER BURGERHÖLLE«,
bemerkt André und verzieht das Gesicht.

Wir haben das Hard Rock Cafe erreicht, und Marc hält uns die Tür auf. Andrés Spruch soll wohl ein Scherz sein, aber ganz sicher bin ich mir nicht. Mir gefällt das Lokal gut. Es passt zum heutigen Abend: erst Bowlen mit Elvis, dann Burgeressen mit den Rockstars der letzten Jahrzehnte. Die Wände sind mit Musikinstrumenten und Autogrammen geschmückt. Ich will mir auf jeden Fall ein T-Shirt kaufen, und Florian bringe ich auch eins mit.

»Setzen wir uns an den Tisch dort in der Ecke? Von da aus können wir fast das ganze Lokal überblicken«, sage ich, und die anderen folgen mir nach hinten.

»Ist cool hier«, meint Marie-Claire und angelt sich eine Karte.

»Wer will sich mit mir die große Hard-Rock-Platte teilen?«, frage ich in die Runde. »Da sind Burger, Chickenwings, Maiskolben, Ofenkartoffeln und Salat dabei.«

»Für eine Million Euro nicht«, antwortet André. Er sieht richtig angeekelt aus.

Seine Reaktion erschreckt mich ein bisschen. So patzig kenne ich ihn gar nicht.

»Sorry. Ich nehme ein Steak«, sagt Marc schulterzuckend.

»Ich teile aber wirklich gerne«, wiederhole ich noch mal. Der Kellner kommt und fragt nach unseren Wünschen. Marie-Claire, Marc und ich geben unsere Bestellung auf, nur André sitzt mit verschränkten Armen am Tisch und presst die Lippen aufeinander. Mir wird ganz mulmig zumute, wenn ich ihn ansehe. Irgendetwas läuft gerade richtig verkehrt. Ob ich ihn verärgert habe? Manchmal sage oder tue ich Dinge, ohne zu merken, dass ich damit jemanden beleidige.

»Was ist denn los? Hab ich was falsch gemacht?«, traue ich mich schließlich zu fragen.

»Ach nichts. Du hast gar nichts verkehrt gemacht, ehrlich. Ich steh nur nicht auf dieses amerikanische Zeug. Bowlen okay, wenn es sein muss, dann mach ich da mit. Aber Burger essen – nein, danke. Ich nehm einfach eine Cola und klaue mir vielleicht ein paar Fritten von euren Tellern«, erwidert André cool und öffnet die verschränkten Arme.

Sein Lächeln wirkt echt, aber mir wird heiß und kalt zugleich. Nicht, weil er mich nervös macht, sondern weil wir nur wegen ihm hier sind. Hab ich Fabienne etwa falsch verstanden? Habe ich ein NICHT überlesen? So nach dem Motto, alle stehen auf Bowlen und das Hard Rock Cafe außer André. Was für ein Reinfall!

Ich schlucke schwer. »Es tut mir leid, dass du keine Burger magst«, flüstere ich.

»Wieso? Das konntest du doch nicht wissen. Schließlich

mögen fast alle Burger und Chickenwings. Ich bin da wohl die einzige Ausnahme«, sagt André und ist schon wieder ganz der Alte. »Das liegt vielleicht daran, dass ich mal eine sehr unangenehme Erfahrung gemacht habe.«

»Oje, jetzt kommt gleich die eklige McDonald's-Geschichte!« Marie-Claire stöhnt und verdreht die Augen.

»Nur die tischverträgliche Kurzvariante«, beruhigt sie André. »Um es in einem Satz zu sagen: Als Siebenjähriger hab ich mich bei McDonald's so schrecklich übergessen, dass ich mich auf der ganzen Heimfahrt übergeben musste, und das ausgerechnet an meinem ...«

»... Geburtstag«, beendet Marc grinsend den Satz. »Und dann durften alle Kinder leckeren Kuchen essen, nur der arme André nicht. Seitdem ist er Burganer, oder besser gesagt, Fast-Foodarier. Armer Kerl! Er weiß gar nicht, was ihm entgeht.«

André zuckt gleichgültig mit den Schultern. »Na ja, du konntest das ja nicht wissen, Helene. Ich verzichte einfach auf das Essen und trink nur was!«

Die Stimmung am Tisch ist wieder gut, doch meine Laune ist im Keller – denn ich hätte es wissen müssen! Schließlich habe ich extra Fabienne gefragt. Als Freundin von Marc und André müsste sie doch die McDonald's-Geschichte kennen, oder? So ein Mist! Hat sie mir etwa absichtlich einen falschen Tipp gegeben? Aber warum sollte sie das tun?

Der Kellner bringt unser Essen an den Tisch, und wir greifen gierig zu, sogar André angelt sich hin und wieder ein paar Pommes. Doch mir bleiben die Chickenwings im

Hals stecken. Meine Gedanken schwirren durcheinander wie ein ganzer Schwarm Stechmücken im August.

Ich entschuldige mich und flüchte mit meinem Smartphone auf die Toilette. Hastig überfliege ich meinen letzten Chat mit Fabienne. Nein, ich habe nichts überlesen oder falsch verstanden. Fabienne hat mir tatsächlich das Hard Rock Cafe vorgeschlagen. Aber warum? Ich dachte, sie wäre meine Freundin. Ich dachte, ich könnte ihr vertrauen. Am liebsten würde ich auf der Stelle losheulen. Doch ich muss mich zusammenreißen. Im Restaurant sitzen meine neuen Freunde und haben keine Ahnung, was mit mir los ist. Schnell wische ich mir die Augen trocken und wasche mein Gesicht. Ich muss wenigstens so tun, als wäre alles in Ordnung, sonst verderbe ich den anderen noch den Abend.

Marc kommt mir entgegen und hält mich sanft auf. »Hallo, Helene. Alles okay bei dir? Du warst auf einmal so still. Da dachte ich mir, ich frag mal unter vier Augen. Geht es dir nicht gut?«

»Ähm, na ja …«, stammele ich.

Marc lächelt mich an, und da bricht die ganze Geschichte aus mir heraus. »Es ist wegen dem Hard Rock Cafe. Fabienne hat mir den Tipp gegeben, dass ihr alle auf Bowling, Burger und dieses Lokal stehen würdet.« Ich hole tief Luft. »Und jetzt stellt sich heraus, dass André es überhaupt nicht mag. Nein, dass er Burger sogar hasst! Was ich gut verstehen kann, denn ich würde auch keine Burger mehr anrühren, wenn sie mir meinen Geburtstag verdorben hätten. Es ist nur … ich komme mir so unendlich dämlich vor!«

»Ach was. Mach dir keine Sorgen. André verhungert

nicht, nur weil er sich heute Abend mal nicht pappsatt essen kann, und Marie-Claire und ich finden es doch toll. Dass André nach all den Jahren noch immer einen kleinen Vogel hat, was American Food betrifft, ist nun wirklich nicht deine Schuld.«

»Aber warum hat mir Fabienne diesen Tipp gegeben? Sie müsste doch wissen, dass André keine Burger mag und Bowlen auch nicht so klasse findet. Ihr wisst das doch auch, oder? Die Geburtstagsstory scheint ja allgemein bekannt zu sein.«

»Klar. Hm. Schwierige Frage. Eigentlich ist Fabienne gar nicht der Typ dafür, dass sie dumme Scherze mit anderen treibt. Das macht eher André. Entweder sie hat es doch nicht gewusst, oder sie hat in dem Moment nicht dran gedacht – oder sie ist eifersüchtig auf dich.«

»Auf mich? Um Himmels willen. Weshalb das denn?«

Marcs Gesicht verzieht sich zu einem Grinsen. »Na, weil du total hübsch bist und nett und überhaupt …« Schnell blickt er zu Boden, aber er kann es nicht aufhalten. Schon wieder kriecht ihm diese gemeine Röte, die ich so gut kenne, den Hals hoch. »Ich glaube, sie ist verknallt in André. So wie fast alle Mädchen«, flüstert er.

Ungläubig schaue ich ihn an. Daran hatte ich gar nicht gedacht. »Das könnte natürlich sein«, überlege ich laut. »Aber warum hat sie denn nie etwas gesagt? Sie hätte mir doch erzählen können, dass sie in André verliebt ist.«

»Vielleicht ist es ihr peinlich?«

Ich nicke nachdenklich. Das könnte ich verstehen. Immerhin ist André der Schwarm aller Mädchen. Mir war es damals auch peinlich zuzugeben, dass ich in Levin verliebt bin. Und nachdem ich auch noch herausgefunden hatte, dass er es nicht ernst mit mir meint, hätte ich mich am liebsten unter der Bettdecke verkrochen. Dennoch war es gemein von Fabienne, mich mit André ins Hard Rock Cafe zu schicken. Offenbar hatte sie gehofft, dass er mich nach der Aktion keines Blickes mehr würdigt. Ich atme tief durch und lasse die Schultern sinken.

»Komm, gehen wir lieber zurück, bevor die anderen sich wundern. Ich reiß mich zusammen und bin wieder besser drauf, versprochen. Danke fürs Zuhören«, sage ich und lege Marc eine Hand auf den Arm.

Er lächelt mich an, und seine Augen leuchten warm. Marc hat sich wirklich Sorgen um mich gemacht. Ich bin froh, ihn ihm einen echt guten Freund gefunden zu haben.

Hallo, Helene, bist du da? Ich muss dringend mit dir reden … Hallo??? Bitte, wenn du on bist, dann schreib mir, okay?

Nichts. Keine Antwort. Ob meine Lüge aufgeflogen ist? Ob Helene jetzt nichts mehr von mir wissen will? Merde. Was mache ich jetzt nur? Seit dem Wochenende herrscht Funkstille bei uns. Liegt es vielleicht daran, dass Helene inzwischen mit André zusammen ist und keine Zeit mehr zum Chatten hat? Hat er vielleicht sogar sein Burgertrauma überwunden und aus Liebe zu Helene den Doppelwhopper mit extra viel Käse bestellt?

Ich bekomme Bauchweh, wenn ich nur daran denke. Mein dummes verliebtes Herz hat mich in ein eifersüchtiges Biest verwandelt. Dabei habe ich immer gelacht, wenn meine Freundinnen von ihren Intrigen und Spionage-Aktionen erzählt haben. Und jetzt sitze ich selbst wie ein liebeskranker Dackel vorm Computer und hoffe, irgendeinen Hinweis auf Andrés Beziehungsstatus bei Facebook zu entdecken. Ich habe, mon Dieu, wie peinlich, André sogar eine mitleiderregende WhatsApp-Nachricht geschickt. Was soll ich sagen? Er hat mir nicht geantwortet.

»He, Fabienne, kannst du uns bitte mit dem Festzelt helfen?«

Florian steckt seinen Kopf zur Tür herein. Offenbar hab ich vor lauter Grübeln ganz die Zeit vergessen.

»Was soll ich tun? Das Zelt aufbauen?«, frage ich wenig begeistert.

»Nein, es steht natürlich schon. Das haben wir Jungs gemacht. Aber die Mädchen sind jetzt mit Schmücken dran. Girlanden aufhängen, Blumen hinstellen und so Zeug. Es wäre prima, wenn du mithilfst.« Florian lächelt mich an.

»Noch fünf Minuten. Dann bin ich da, okay?«

»Prima. Je mehr Hände mithelfen, desto schneller geht es.«

Ein letztes Mal checke ich alle Seiten und Chats. Seit drei Tagen ist nichts mehr passiert auf FB. Helene schweigt. André schweigt. Mein schlechtes Gewissen und meine Angst, André endgültig verloren zu haben, fressen sich unaufhaltsam durch meine Eingeweide, wie rotierende Rasenmählermesser. Helene, bitte melde dich! Ich brauche Gewissheit! Und ich brauche deine Hilfe wegen diesem dummen Fest.

Alle sind im Maifieber, und niemand hat Zeit für mich. Ich habe keine Ahnung, was ich morgen anziehen soll. Dieser dumme Feiertag! Mir ist überhaupt nicht nach Feiern zumute. Ich möchte nur noch heulen.

Mitten auf der Dorfwiese steht ein riesiges Festzelt. Erika, Peter und Florian stellen gerade die Biertische auf.

»Hallo, Fabienne. Magst du gleich mal unsere Fuckinger Tischdecken auflegen?«, fragt mich Erika und deutet auf einen großen Korb neben ihr.

»Ich helfe gern mit.« Plötzlich steht Thomas neben uns und zwinkert mir fröhlich zu.

Gemeinsam schmücken wir die Tische.

»Freust du dich schon auf morgen?«, fragt Thomas. »Du hast ja echt Glück, beim größten Fest weit und breit dabei zu sein.« Mit geschickten Handgriffen breitet er ein riesiges Tischtuch aus.

»Ja, doch«, erwidere ich und gebe mir Mühe, fröhlich zu klingen. »Ich weiß nur nicht, was ich anziehen soll. Auf ein Dorffest bin ich, ehrlich gesagt, nicht vorbereitet.«

Thomas mustert mich kritisch von oben bis unten. »Dir müsste doch bestimmt eins von Helenes Dirndln passen. Schau doch mal in ihren Schrank, da findest du sicher was Schönes. Oder du kommst so, wie du bist. Das ist auch okay, irgendwie …«

»Das klingt nicht überzeugt«, entgegne ich.

Thomas zuckt mit den Schultern und grinst entschuldigend.

»Ich werde Helene fragen, ob sie mir ein Kleid leiht«, erkläre ich.

»Das macht sie sicher. Und ich wette, du siehst genial aus im Dirndl.«

»He, Thomas. Hilf uns mal mit dem Tresenaufbau und überlass das Serviettenfalten den Mädels, bevor du die Deko noch ganz ruinierst«, ruft einer der Jungs hinten im Zelt.

»So blöd stell ich mich beim Dekorieren aber nicht an, oder?«, fragt mich Thomas.

»Das machst du ganz okay, irgendwie ...«, kontere ich lächelnd.

Lachend geht er zurück zu den anderen. Ich decke gemeinsam mit Erika die restlichen Tische, während hinten der Tresen aufgebaut und zig Fässer Fucking Bier herbeigeschleppt werden.

»Glaubst du, dass mir Helene eins ihrer Trachtenkleider borgen würde? Ich will sie später noch selbst fragen, aber wenn ich sie im Chat nicht erreiche ...«, frage ich Erika in einem passenden Moment.

»Aber natürlich. In ihrem Schrank hängen einige wirklich schöne Dirndl. Nimm dir einfach eins. Ich wasche es danach«, bietet meine Gastmutter an.

Ich nicke dankbar. Es erleichtert mich, dass ich zumindest das Kleiderproblem gelöst habe. Später werde ich noch mal versuchen, Helene anzuchatten. Schließlich möchte ich auch wissen, was nun mit ihr und André ist.

Peter kommt zu uns und klatscht in die Hände. »So, Mädels, ich glaub, ihr seid auch fertig. Ich werde heute noch etwas Bier brauen. Meine ganzen Vorräte, abgesehen von einem kleinen Fass, sind im Zelt. Und wenn ich nicht schleunigst zu brauen beginne, dann sitzen wir nach dem Maifest alle auf dem Trockenen. Fabienne, willst du diesmal zugucken?«

Ich nicke ergeben. Etwas Besseres habe ich nicht vor, und vielleicht bringt mich die Braukunst ja auf andere Gedanken.

Bestens gelaunt schließt Peter den Keller auf. Bisher war ich noch nie hier unten, aber heute bin ich in der richtigen Stimmung, um in diese Gruft hinabzusteigen.

Erwartungsgemäß ist es feucht und kühl unter dem Haus. Doch dank der langen Neonröhren ist es wenigstens hell im Keller. Florian ist auch mitgekommen, und er hat seine ganze Fotoausrüstung dabei. Ich erinnere mich daran, dass er meinen Brauversuch unbedingt posten wollte.

»Muss ich mich vorher noch stylen, oder bin ich schick genug für eure Homepage?«, frage ich ihn und grinse frech.

»Du ... du bist immer hübsch«, stottert er und wird wieder einmal rot.

Ich kichere. »Aber deinen Paps könnte man noch etwas aufhübschen, findest du nicht?«

Das hat Peter gehört und dreht sich gespielt empört um.

»Was stimmt denn nicht mit meiner Kleidung?«, fragt er und zupft an seinem rot-grünen Karohemd herum.

Plötzlich leuchten Florians Augen auf. »Ich hab's!« Er strahlt und drückt mir seine Ausrüstung in die Hände. »Bin gleich wieder da. Fangt nicht ohne mich an.«

Wie ein geölter Blitz rast er die Treppe hoch.

»Oh mein Gott. Mir schwant Schlimmes«, sagt Peter und verdreht die Augen.

»Was? Mon Dieu? Was holt er?«, will ich wissen.

»Ich tippe mal auf Erikas Stickereien«, prophezeit Peter.

»Non! Auf keinen Fall. Ich braue nicht in Unterwäsche!«, rufe ich entsetzt.

»Aber nicht doch, Erika hat einmal ...«

Doch da ist Florian schon wieder zurück, vollgepackt

mit bestickten Kochschürzen und Hauben. Ich atme erleichtert auf. Damit kann ich leben.

Nur Peter schüttelt vehement den Kopf. »Nein, Florian. Ich trage weder eine rosa noch eine lila Schürze! Ich bin ein Mann!«

»Ich finde, Lila würde dir ausgezeichnet stehen«, behaupte ich kichernd.

Peter verzieht den Mund. »Nein! Niemals!«

»Dann stimmen wir eben ab«, sagt Florian ungerührt, »wer dafür ist, dass Papa sich die wunderschöne lila Schürze mit der tollen Fucking Helles-Stickerei umbindet, hebe die Hand.«

Mein Arm schießt hoch, und Flo zeigt natürlich auch auf.

»Überstimmt. Laut Familiengesetz wird getan, was die Mehrheit für richtig befindet. Das heißt, du musst die Schürze anziehen, Papa!«, verkündet Florian und gibt Peter die Schürze und die Kochmütze.

»Verräterin!« Peter zwinkert mir zu. »Helene war immer auf meiner Seite! Ich will meine Tochter zurück!«

Er kann seine Beschwerde aber nicht so ernst meinen, dazu glitzern seine Augen zu vergnügt.

Ich lache und nehme die rosa Kochgarnitur. Fucking Dunkles steht bei mir drauf. Peter sieht urkomisch aus mit seiner Schürze und der Haube, und ich muss einen Lachanfall unterdrücken. Gemeinsam posieren wir fürs erste Foto.

Dann zeigt mir Peter den großen Braukessel, die Fässer, die Flaschen und das ganze Werkzeug, das er zum Brauen verwendet.

»Am wichtigsten ist, dass alle Geräte schön sauber sind«, erklärt er.

»Ja, beim Bierbrauen kann Papa sogar abwaschen und putzen«, witzelt Florian herum und kassiert dafür einen bösen Blick von Peter.

»Wenn ich mir den Zustand von deinem Zimmer gerade vorstelle, würde dir ein kleiner Putzfimmel auch guttun, Flo.«

Florian presst die Lippen zusammen. »Ich bin ein pubertierender Jugendlicher. Ich habe ein natürliches Recht auf Schmutz und Unordnung.«

»Akzeptiert«, gibt Peter sich geschlagen, »dein Zimmer sieht sogar noch recht ordentlich aus, wenn ich an meins damals zurückdenke.«

Grinsend verfolge ich das Wortduell der beiden. Bisher war ich immer der Meinung, dass es solche Familien nur im Fernsehen gibt. Bei uns zu Hause ist es nie so lustig. Erstens haben meine Eltern beruflich zu viel am Hals, und zweitens sind auch unsere Gespräche wesentlich sachlicher.

»Zurück zum Thema. Bierbrauen ist eigentlich ganz einfach. Man braucht nur Gerstenmalz, Hopfen, Hefe und Wasser.« Peter verfällt in einen richtigen Lehrertonfall. Er erklärt mir ganz genau, wie viel Wasser ich in dem Kessel erhitzen und wann ich das Malz hineingeben soll. Ich halte mich exakt an seine Vorgaben. Während Peter alle naselang die Temperatur des Gebräus misst, knipst Florian wild drauflos.

Bierbrauen ist ganz schön anstrengend. Besonders das Abseihen des Getreides. Maische nennt sich das und ist irgendwie eklig. Kaum zu glauben, dass aus dem Gebräu später einmal echtes Bier werden soll. Aber Peter schwört, dass alles mit rechten Dingen zugeht. Ich komme bei der Arbeit richtig ins Schwitzen.

»Frau Strudelpeter ist nicht so streng wie du«, klage ich.

»Die macht auch nur Strudel, Schnitzel und Knödel. Bierbrauen ist eine Kunst«, erwidert Peter grinsend.

Die Brühe wird aufgekocht und blubbert bedrohlich vor sich hin. Sie sieht aus wie die Ursuppe, direkt aus der Hölle, und schäumt vor sich hin, als wolle sie den ganzen Keller überfluten.

»Das wird ein herrliches Bier. Du kannst stolz auf dich sein«, lobt mich mein Gastvater.

Nach guten drei Stunden lustiger Schufterei und derber Scherze ist das Bier so gut wie fertig. Probieren kann man es jedoch nicht.

»Die blödeste Arbeit ist das Warten«, sagt Peter.

»Ich druck dann Etiketten für die neue Charge »Fabiennes Fucking Bier« aus«, meint Florian, »das darf ich doch, oder?«

»Sicher. Nimmst du dafür die Fotos von heute?«

Florian nickt.

»Super, dann bin ich eine Dorfberühmtheit und gerate nicht in Vergessenheit, wenn mich die Großstadt wiederhat.«

Florian freut sich, und auch Peter lächelt zufrieden. »So ein Glück. Ich hatte schon Angst, Flo würde mich lila-beschürzt auf die Flaschen drucken«, sagt er.

»Nein. Ich will das Bier ja verkaufen. Da eignet sich Fabienne besser als Model, findest du nicht?«

»Willst du etwa sagen, ich bin nicht fotogen?«, ruft Peter empört und dreht sich wie Austria's Next Topmodel um die eigene Achse.

»Doch, Paps. Du kommst aufs Plakat, direkt vors Haus.«

Peter bleibt der Mund offen stehen. Damit hat er wohl nicht gerechnet.

Es ist schön zu sehen, wie viel Spaß die beiden zusammen haben.

Vielleicht könnten Mama und ich auch mal was gemeinsam unternehmen, einen ganzen Tag lang, nur wir zwei. Dann würden wir vielleicht auch mal wieder zusammen lachen. Über andere Dinge, aber das wäre auch gut.

ICH SCHAFFE ES NICHT. So einfach ist das. Natürlich sollte ich anders reagieren, aber ich kann es nicht.
Ich fühle mich gekränkt. Es macht mich traurig, dass Fabienne mir falsche Tipps gegeben hat.

Das Chatfenster blinkt mich verzweifelt an.

Hallo, Helene, bist du da? Hallo?

Fabienne will wissen, ob sie sich ein Dirndl von mir leihen
kann. Ich klicke den Chatroom weg, obwohl mich sofort
das schlechte Gewissen plagt. Eigentlich möchte ich mit
Fabienne chatten, schon alleine, weil ich wissen will, warum sie mir diese Tipps gegeben hat. Außerdem hab ich so
viel zu erzählen, und ich bin auch neugierig, was zu Hause
los ist. Lena hab ich die letzten Tage nicht erreicht, und mit
Mama will ich nicht telefonieren. Sie würde bestimmt sofort merken, dass mich etwas beschäftigt, und dann müsste
ich ihr von Marc und André erzählen. Das will ich nicht.
Also bleibt nur Fabienne. Sie wäre genau die richtige Person, um über mein Dilemma zu reden. Aber ich kann nicht.

Wenn ich meine Finger auf die Tastatur lege, spüre ich einen Knoten in meiner Kehle, der mir die Luft abschnürt. Ich merke, wie weh mir Fabiennes falsches Spiel tut. Vielleicht schaffe ich es ja morgen. Wahrscheinlich brauche ich einfach ein wenig Abstand. Ganz bestimmt aber brauche ich selbst jemanden, der mir hilft.

Das Wochenende, das gemeinsame Bowlen, das Essen im Hard Rock Cafe, all das hat mich nur noch mehr verwirrt. André ist nach wie vor sehr charmant und sogar ein wenig eifersüchtig, wenn ich mit Marc über unsere Tierarztträume plaudere. Marc aber hat sich auf einmal geöffnet und sich als wahnsinnig intelligent, einfühlsam und witzig gezeigt. Seitdem ertappe ich mich dabei, wie ich mir uns zwei als Paar vorstelle. Er ist mir einfach so ähnlich. Wir lachen über die gleichen Dinge, haben den gleichen Berufswunsch und nehmen unsere Tierliebe sehr ernst. Ich freu mich schon wahnsinnig auf unseren Besuch im Zoo.

Der neu eröffnete Pariser Zoo ist an sich schon eine Sensation, denn jetzt kann man in die Lebensräume der Tiere eintauchen, ohne sie zu stören. Ich bin schon so gespannt. Marc hat mir versprochen, dass wir gemeinsam mit seinem Kumpel Claude einige Tiere füttern dürfen.

Als würde Bastet ahnen, dass ich gerade von anderen Vierbeinern träume, springt sie schnurrend auf meinen Schoß. In dem Moment klopft es an der Tür.

»Helene, bist du da?«, ruft Brigitte.

Ich wundere mich, dass meine Gastmutter schon zu Hause ist.

»Sicher. Komm herein.«

Brigitte streckt ihren Kopf zur Tür herein. Sie lächelt breit. »Du hast doch vorgeschlagen, dass wir mal zusammen kochen könnten. Steht dein Angebot noch? Mein Kunde hat mich spontan versetzt, und ich habe keine Lust mehr, auszugehen. Wie wäre es? Wollen wir Richard mit einer selbst gemachten Köstlichkeit aus meiner fast unberührten Küche überraschen? Ich hab auch schon eingekauft.«

»Diese Küche fleht danach, endlich bekocht zu werden«, antworte ich lächelnd und steh auf. Ein gemeinsamer Kochabend mit Brigitte wird mich bestimmt ablenken und mein schlechtes Gewissen für ein paar Stunden beruhigen.

Meine Gastmutter hat Lebensmittel für eine ganze Fußballmannschaft gekauft. Ich muss lachen, als ich die proppenvollen Tüten sehe. Zum Glück ist reichlich Gemüse dabei und nichts, was nach Schnecken oder Muscheln aussieht.

»An welches Gericht dachtest du denn?«, frage ich.

»Eine Art Gemüselasagne vielleicht. Ich hab Teigblätter und eine Packung Béchamelsoße besorgt.« Stolz zieht sie eine Fertigsoße aus dem Einkaufsbeutel.

»Wir wollen kochen, nicht Tüten aufreißen«, sage ich.

Brigitte lacht. »Gut. Dann warte ich auf deine Befehle. Wenn ich Regie führe, gibt es nach zwei Stunden Schwerstarbeit Gemüse und Teigplatten – gewaschen, geschnippelt und roh.«

Ich kichere. Bis jetzt wusste ich nicht, dass Brigitte so lustig sein kann. Wir machen uns an die Arbeit. Zuerst werden die Tomaten gehäutet und geschnitten, dann bereiten wir die Karotten, Zucchini, Erbsen und Pilze vor. Daraus kochen wir eine kräftig gewürzte Tomaten-Gemüsesoße.

»Gebe ich zuerst das Mehl und die Butter in den Topf oder die Milch? Helene? Wo bist du mit deinen Gedanken?«

Oje. Hilfe suchend hält mir Brigitte einen großen Topf unter die Nase.

»Tut mir leid. Ich musste gerade …«, stottere ich und werde natürlich rot dabei.

»… an einen Jungen denken. Stimmt's?«

Ich nicke verlegen. Brigitte kann vielleicht nicht so gut kochen, dafür aber umso besser Gedanken lesen.

»Fabienne starrt auch immer Löcher in die Luft, wenn sie mit Jungsgeschichten beschäftigt ist«, sagt Brigitte und stellt ächzend den Topf ab.

»Mein Problem ist, dass ich keine Ahnung habe, wer der Richtige für mich ist. Außerdem will ich nicht noch mal so eine Enttäuschung erleben wie damals bei Levin«, platzt es plötzlich aus mir heraus. Offenbar hat sich bei mir so viel angestaut, dass mein Gefühlschaos trotz meiner Schüchternheit einfach übergeschwappt ist.

»Oh! Gleich mehrere. Das ist immer schwierig. Verlass dich auf dein Gefühl. Wenn es einer der Jungs schafft, dass du mit ihm die Zeit vergisst und du keine Sekunde mehr an den oder die anderen denkst, dann ist er der Richtige.« Brigitte zwinkert verschwörerisch. »Und die Enttäuschung gehört zur Liebe dazu. Daran wächst man. Du brauchst dir aber wahrscheinlich keine Sorgen zu machen, den gleichen Fehler zweimal zu begehen. Dafür bist du zu intelligent. Hör auf dein Herz, Helene«, sagt sie ruhig und sieht mir dabei tief in die Augen.

Es ist gerade so, als könnte sie meine Gefühle voll und

ganz verstehen. Vielleicht befand sie sich früher mal in einer ähnlichen Zwickmühle. Ich schlucke schwer und ringe mir ein Lächeln ab. Mein Herz hatte bei Levin immer leise Zweifel angemeldet. Diesmal sollte ich wirklich genau hinhören, für wen es schlägt.

Nachdem die Béchamelsoße fertig ist, schichten wir abwechselnd Nudelblätter und Gemüse auf, bis die Form voll ist. Dann schiebt Brigitte sie in den vorgeheizten Ofen.

Während wir den Salat zubereiten, erzählt meine Gastmutter mir von ihrem Job und wie sie Richard kennengelernt hat. Ich spüre, dass sie sich nach mehr Familienleben sehnt.

»Vielleicht könnt ihr ja einen festen Kochabend einführen? Fabienne, Richard und du? Dann steht diese Traumküche auch nicht länger nur zur Zierde in der Wohnung«, schlage ich vor.

Brigitte lächelt. »Das ist eine gute Idee. Fabienne gefällt sie sicher auch. Manchmal hab ich ein schlechtes Gewissen. Sie bekommt zwar alles, aber wirklich Zeit für sie und ihre Sorgen haben wir beide nicht. Dabei weiß ich, dass sie auch mit einem Jungen zu kämpfen hat. Alex, Adam oder so.«

»André«, flüstere ich so leise, dass Brigitte mich nicht hört. Langsam bin ich mir sicher, dass Fabienne tatsächlich aus purer Eifersucht das Hard Rock Cafe vorgeschlagen hat.

Die Wohnungstür geht auf. Richard kommt nach Hause.

»Hm. Was duftet denn hier so köstlich? Brigitte, hast du etwa die arme Helene zum Küchendienst verdonnert?«

»Ich hab selbst gekocht. Mit ein klein wenig Unterstützung«, erwidert Brigitte schmunzelnd.

»Meine Frau. Da dachte ich, ich kenne dich. Und dann so etwas!«, bemerkt Richard erfreut.

Wir decken gemeinsam den Tisch und essen zu Abend. Fabiennes Eltern tauen richtig auf. Richard ist ein klasse Witzeerzähler.

»Was heißt Schwiegermutter auf Französisch?«, fragt er schelmisch grinsend. Ich schüttle ahnungslos den Kopf.

»Grand Malheur«, antwortet er lachend.

Kaum zu glauben. Ich bin schon zwei Wochen hier, und erst heute habe ich das Gefühl, bei meinen Gasteltern angekommen zu sein. Manche Menschen brauchen etwas mehr Zeit, wie Brigitte, wie Richard. Vielleicht auch Marc?

HELENE HAT SICH NICHT MEHR GEMEL-DET. Ich schätze, es geschieht mir recht. Sie hat bestimmt herausgefunden, dass ich sie absichtlich zum Bowlen und ins Hard Rock Cafe geschickt habe. Nach dem Maifest muss ich endlich mit offenen Karten spielen und ihr alles erzählen: von André und von meiner dummen Eifersucht. Hoffentlich verzeiht sie mir. Der Liebeskummer macht mich schon richtig krank. Bisher habe ich das immer für ein Gerücht gehalten, aber es stimmt leider wirklich. Vor lauter Eifersucht habe ich mich total verändert. Mein Bauch rumort und sticht vor Sorge und schlechtem Gewissen. Ist ein Junge diesen Kummer überhaupt wert?

Ich seufze und denke an André. Trotz allem, was passiert ist, fehlt er mir. Doch außer ein paar nichtssagender SMS und WhatsApp-Gruppennachrichten hab ich seit Wochen nichts mehr von ihm gehört. Dafür hatte sich Helene immer treu und brav gemeldet. Traurig öffne ich ihren Schrank. Ich habe bislang noch nicht einmal einen Blick hineingeworfen.

Auf den Einlegeböden stapeln sich jede Menge bunte T-

Shirts und Jeans. Ganz vorne auf der Kleiderstange hängt ein kurzes Dirndl. Unten im Schrank entdecke ich ein Paar High-Heels-Sandalen, die perfekt dazu passen.

So etwas trägt man hier? Puh, das hätte ich den Landmädchen gar nicht zugetraut. Das Kleid ist beinahe neonpink und sehr figurbetont. Am Haken hängen auch noch Strümpfe mit Strumpfhaltern. Ich überlege kurz, ob ich nicht doch lieber in meinen Klamotten zum Fest gehen sollte. Aber ich meine mich zu erinnern, dass ich im Fernsehen schon öfter deutsche und österreichische Frauen in derartigen Kleidern gesehen habe, zum Beispiel auf dem Oktoberfest in München. Und das Letzte, was ich will, ist unangenehm auffallen. Wenn alle hier ein Minidirndl tragen, dann mache ich das auch.

Ich schlüpfe in das Trachtenkleid. Es passt wie angegossen. Offenbar haben Helene und ich die gleiche Größe. Die Strümpfe ziehe ich aber auf keinen Fall an. Das ist mir zu viel. Eine falsche Bewegung, und jeder kann die Strapse sehen. Da müsste ich den ganzen Tag steif wie ein Stock in der Ecke stehen und hätte dennoch dauernd Angst, dass der Rock hochrutscht. Zum Glück habe ich eine ganz normale Strumpfhose eingepackt. Ich probiere Helenes Schuhe, und da sie vorne offen sind, passen sie mir ganz gut. Noch ein wenig Make-up, Lipgloss und Mascara, und ich bin fertig. Gut, so kann ich gehen, beschließe ich und stake die Treppe hinunter. Die Sandalen sind wirklich extrem hoch.

Nun würde ich mir doch wünschen, ich hätte nicht ausgeschlafen und wäre schon vor zwei Stunden mit den anderen zum Fest gegangen. Es wäre sicher lustig gewesen, wenn wir gemeinsam in unseren bunten Trachten durchs Dorf gelaufen wären. Doch der Weg ist nicht weit, und es ist gut zu wissen, dass heute alle verkleidet sind.

Bestimmt haben sich schon alle auf der Dorfwiese versammelt. Ich biege auf die Hauptstraße ein und höre Blasmusik. Als ich den Platz erreiche, erstarre ich. Da stehen die ganzen Dorfleute, die Männer in Lederhosen, Hemden und Trachtenjacken und die Frauen in knöchellangen dunkelblauen und roten Dirndlkleidern. Nichts wie weg hier! Nur schnell umziehen und in Jeans und T-Shirt wiederkommen!

Doch ich habe die Rechnung ohne meine High Heels gemacht. Eine unachtsame Bewegung, ein Stein – und schon liege ich mit meinem quietschrosa Minikleid auf der Straße.

»Fabienne!« Erika stürmt auf mich zu und streckt ihre Hände aus, um mir aufzuhelfen.

»Was – um Himmels willen – hast du denn da an?«, fragt sie verblüfft, als ich wieder auf den Beinen bin. »Das ist ja Helenes Faschingskostüm.«

Ich schaffe es nicht, zu antworten. Stattdessen schlüpfe ich aus diesen verdammten Schuhen und laufe so schnell wie möglich weg.

»Fabienne! Warte doch! Fabienne!«

Vor lauter Tränen sehe ich nichts mehr. Im Heuschober ist es dunkel, obwohl draußen die Sonne scheint. Ich setze mich auf einen Strohballen und weine. Wie hat das nur passieren können? Ich hatte gleich so ein komisches Gefühl, als ich das Kleid angezogen habe. Und dann auch noch dieser peinliche Sturz! Jetzt halten mich sicher alle für eine überdrehte, tollpatschige und hysterische Gans. Wie schrecklich!

Das ist die gerechte Strafe dafür, dass ich Helene so schlecht behandelt habe. MON DIEU, WAS SOLL ICH NUR MACHEN? Im Ort kann ich mich nicht mehr blicken lassen.

»Fabienne? Bist du da drin?« Erika, Thomas und zwei Mädchen aus dem Dorf spähen vorsichtig zum Scheunentor herein. Ich verhalte mich ganz still. Hoffentlich gehen sie wieder und lassen mich in meinem Elend allein.

Quiek, quiek! Susi galoppiert erbarmungslos auf mich zu und verrät mein Versteck. Grunzend stupst sie ihren feuchten Rüssel gegen mein Bein. Erika und die anderen folgen dem Verräter-Schwein.

»Hier steckst du, Schätzchen. Warum bist du denn einfach weggelaufen?«

»Weil, weil ... ach, welche Blamage! Dieses Kleid ... und mein Sturz. Ihr haltet mich bestimmt alle für total dumm.«

»Ach was! Ist doch nur halb so schlimm.« Erika setzt sich neben mich und legt ihren Arm tröstend um meine Schultern.

»Wir holen dir schnell ein richtiges Dirndl. Nicht wahr, Vero?« Die Mädchen nicken einander zu und schwirren davon. Zurück bleiben Erika, der Nachbarjunge Thomas, Susi und ich.

»Meine beiden Schwestern Vero und Nicki werden dich im Handumdrehen in ein fades Landei verwandeln«, verspricht Thomas. »Obwohl du mir als Katze noch besser gefällst, glaub ich.«

»Als Katze?«, frage ich leise.

Thomas lacht. »Ja, ja. Unser ganzer Ort ist beim Faschingsumzug als Daniela Katzenberger und Lucas Cordalis gegangen. Das war im Februar.«

»Aha«, sage ich. »Und ich hab ausgerechnet dieses Kleid erwischt. Ein Faschingskostüm.« Erneut schießen mir Tränen in die Augen.

»Das war meine Schuld. Ich hätte dir sagen sollen, dass unsere Trachten im großen Kleiderschrank im Flur hängen. Es tut mir leid, Fabienne«, gesteht Erika kleinlaut. »Ich hab es einfach vergessen in all dem ganzen Vorbereitungsstress.«

»Verges... sen?«, stottere ich.

Erika nickt schuldbewusst.

Thomas' Schwestern kommen mit einem ganzen Arm voller Dirndl herein.

»So, jetzt wollen wir dich mal ordentlich aufbrezeln«, verkündet Vero. »Und du, Thomas, zisch ab. Das ist Mädchensache!«

Erika nickt Thomas ernst zu. »Komm, lass deine Schwestern machen. Und dich – Fabienne – will ich ohne verheulte Augen wiedersehen. In Ordnung?«

»Kann ich mich wirklich noch im Dorf blicken lassen, ohne dass sich alle über mich lustig machen?«, frage ich.

»Natürlich. Wenn jemand schuld an deinem Versehen ist, dann bin das wohl ich. Und außerdem hat Fucking schon Schlimmeres gesehen als ein hübsches Mädchen in einem Minidirndl.«

»Ja? Was denn?«

»Herrn Pfarrer Berschl zum Beispiel, splitterfasernackt,

nur eingewickelt in ein Altartuch. Weil ihm ein paar Lausbuben den Haustürschlüssel und die Kleider versteckt haben, als er gerade in seiner Saunahütte war«, meint Thomas lachend.

»Als ob nicht alle wüssten, wer diese Lausbuben waren«, sagt meine Gastmutter und gibt Thomas einen Klaps. »Florian und du, ihr zwei Schlingel.«

Lachend gehen Thomas und Erika hinaus, während Vero und Nicki mir helfen, in ein rot-grünes, knielanges Dirndl zu schlüpfen. Nebenbei erzählen sie mir die ganze Geschichte von Pfarrer Berschl, seiner neuen Saunahütte hinter dem Pfarrhaus und dem Altartuchdesaster.

Die beiden sind so nett, dass ich mich nach einer Weile wieder wie ein normales Mädchen fühle.

Nicki steckt mir die Haare hoch. Zufrieden betrachtet sie ihr Werk. »Ja, so siehst du klasse aus.«

»Es lacht mich auch keiner aus, wenn ich jetzt zurück ins Dorf gehe? Bei uns in Paris ist ein falsches Outfit ein echter Fauxpas. Ich könnte mich monatelang nicht mehr bei meinen Freunden blicken lassen.«

Die beiden schütteln den Kopf. »Bei uns zählt nicht die Kleidung, sondern der Mensch. Und du bist nett. Das ist die Hauptsache.«

Ich schlucke schwer. »Ihr seid unglaublich nett zu mir. Leiht mir einfach eure Kleider und kümmert euch um mich, obwohl draußen das Fest in vollem Gange ist.«

Nicki und Vero lächeln. »Das ist doch selbstverständlich. Wir Mädels müssen zusammenhalten«, meint Vero. »Das Wichtigste im Leben sind doch gute Freunde!«

Ich muss an Helene denken, und mein Herz zieht sich schmerzhaft zusammen. Wir gehen zurück zum Dorfplatz. Die Musikkapelle spielt, und einige Pärchen tanzen.

Ich setze mich zu meiner Gastfamilie auf die Bierbank.

»Alles in Ordnung?«, fragt mich Erika.

Ich nicke und sehe dem lustigen Treiben zu. Es dauert nicht lange, bis Thomas vor mir steht und mich um einen Tanz bittet. Meine Ausrede, dass ich nicht tanzen kann, lässt er nicht gelten. Thomas zieht mich einfach auf die Tanzfläche und wirbelt mich im Kreis herum. Ich lache und vergesse doch glatt meinen kleinen Fauxpas.

»Darf ich dir die nächsten Tage mal unsere Gegend zeigen? Hoch zu Ross vielleicht?«, flüstert mir Thomas ins Ohr, als wir wieder zum Platz gehen. Mir wird heiß, vielleicht vom Tanzen, vielleicht aber auch von der Vorstellung, auf einem Pferd zu reiten. Schüchtern zucke ich mit den Schultern.

»Also abgemacht! Ich hole dich morgen um elf Uhr ab, und dann reiten wir zum kleinen Waldsee«, sagt Thomas erfreut.

Ich kann gar nichts antworten, schon hat mich Florian zu sich gezogen. »Selfie-Foto mit unserer Austausch-Maikönigin«, sagt er und hält sein Handy vor unser Gesicht. Er drückt sich ganz nah an mich heran und knipst ein Bild.

»Das kommt bestimmt gut auf unserer Homepage«, sagt er.

Ich kann es kaum glauben, aber ich bin glücklich. Ein wenig zumindest. Die Menschen hier sind alle so herzlich und fröhlich, dass ich gar nicht anders kann, als mitzufeiern.

Hallo, Helene!
Ich muss dringend mit dir reden. Heute ist mir etwas total Peinliches passiert. Ich bin versehentlich in deinem Faschingskostüm zum Maifest gegangen. Zum Glück waren deine Familie und deine Freundinnen total nett und haben mir schnell ein anderes Dirndl geholt. Ich glaube, du bist genauso nett wie sie. Bitte gib mir die Chance, dir alles zu erklären. Okay?

Einen Augenblick zögere ich. Meine Hände zittern, und eine Mischung aus Angst und Scham schnürt mir die Luft ab. Doch ich atme tief durch und tippe auf Senden.

Flupp, die Internetverbindung ist weg. Ausgerechnet jetzt. Merde!

»GEHT'S DIR NICHT GUT, Helene?« Brigitte sieht mich mit großen Augen an.

»Doch, doch«, wiegele ich ab. Seit einer halben Stunde versuche ich durch zwanghaftes Dauerstreicheln von Bastet meine Nerven zu beruhigen. Ich bin viel zu früh aufgestanden. Habe mich viel zu schnell fertig gemacht, und jetzt warte ich, nervös wie ein Wespenschwarm, auf Marc, der mich zu unserem gemeinsamen Zoobesuch abholt.

Brigitte sitzt mir gegenüber am Küchentisch und runzelt die Stirn. »Sprich dich aus. Es hilft, glaub mir«, sagt sie lächelnd.

»Ach, es ist wegen Marc. Ich weiß nicht, ob er mich genauso gern hat wie ich ihn. Wir haben so viel gemeinsam, aber er ist so wahnsinnig schüchtern.«

»Also ist der zweite Junge aus dem Rennen?«

Ich zucke mit den Schultern. »Ich glaub schon. Er ist ein echter Mädchenschwarm. Total nett und charmant, aber solche Jungs hat man nie für sich allein. Jedes Mädchen flirtet mit ihm. Sicher bin ich mir trotzdem nicht, und jetzt weiß ich nicht, was ich tun soll.«

»Vertrau auf dein Gefühl. Wenn es dir sagt, dass Marc der Richtige ist, dann musst du vielleicht die Initiative ergreifen. Wenn ich damals nichts unternommen hätte, wären Richard und ich nie ein Paar geworden.«

In dem Moment klingelt es an der Tür, und ich springe wie von der Hornisse gestochen auf. Draußen steht Marc und starrt wie immer schüchtern auf den Boden.

»Hallo, Marc«, begrüße ich ihn freudig.

Er blickt auf und wird leicht rot dabei. »Hallo, Helene.«

»Ich freu mich so auf die Manatis«, sage ich strahlend.

»Ich mich auch ...«

So wie er mich ansieht, habe ich das Gefühl, er würde mich meinen und nicht den Zoobesuch.

Nun schießt mir auch das Blut in die Wangen. »Bis später, Brigitte«, rufe ich schnell über die Schulter zurück. Dann gehen wir.

Der Zoo liegt am Rande eines größeren Waldgebiets, des Bois de Vincennes. Nachdem er sechs Jahre lang umgebaut wurde, leben die Tiere nun in verschiedenen Zonen, die ihrer ursprünglichen Heimat nachempfunden wurden. Wir gehen als Erstes in die Zone Guayana, denn dort arbeitet Marcs Freund.

»Da vorne ist Claude!« Marc deutet auf einen schlanken, langhaarigen Tierpfleger.

Lächelnd kommt Claude auf uns zu. »Hallo, ihr zwei. Schön, dass ihr da seid.« Der Tierpfleger ist vielleicht dreißig und sieht wie ein alternativer Biolehrer aus: hippiemäßig, lässig und cool.

»Und du bist also Helene? Freut mich, dich kennenzulernen! Kaum zu glauben, dass Marc endlich jemanden gefunden hat, der genauso verrückt nach Tieren ist wie er selbst. In den Ferien musste ich ihn abends regelrecht aus dem Zoo schleifen, sonst hätte er glatt bei den Affen übernachtet.« Er reicht mir die Hand und drückt sie kaum spürbar.

Lachend schüttele ich ihm die Hand. »Ich kann Marcs Tierliebe gut verstehen. Mir geht es da genauso.«

Marc sieht mir in die Augen, und ein angenehm warmes Gefühl kribbelt durch meinen Bauch.

»Prima. Dann wollen wir den Manatis einen Besuch abstatten. Marlene wartet schon auf ihre Streicheleinheiten«, sagt Claude.

»Man kann sie streicheln?«

»Marlene schon. Sie wurde von Hand aufgezogen und ist total auf Menschen fixiert. Wusstest du, dass man mit Seekühen genauso schwimmen kann wie mit Delphinen?« Claude grinst. »Dein Freund hat das schon mal gemacht.«

»Aber unfreiwillig«, erklärt Marc, »ich bin ausgerutscht und mitten in den Manati-Sumpf gefallen.«

»Zum Glück bist du nicht in einem Haifischbecken gelandet. Ich hab dich lieber in einem Stück«, sage ich ernst.

Marc weicht meinem Blick aus. »Du ... du bist nett«, stottert er schüchtern.

Schon wieder werden meine Wangen heiß. Meine Güte, ist das alles kompliziert. Warum müssen ausgerechnet zwei Menschen, die gleich schüchtern sind, aufeinandertreffen?

Schweigend folgen wir Claude zu den Becken. Marcs

Blicke streifen mich ununterbrochen. Ich spüre es regelrecht, wenn er mich ansieht. Es fühlt sich an, als würde er mir jedes Mal einen Mini-Elektrostoß verpassen. Keinen, der wehtut, sondern einen, der mein Herz ein klein wenig schneller schlagen lässt.

Beim Füttern der Manatis komme ich nicht nur den Tieren nah. Marc kniet ganz dicht neben mir am Rand des Stegs, und immer, wenn ich mich zu weit nach vorne beuge, greift er nach mir. »Nicht dass du mit Marlene auf Tauchkurs gehst«, meint er lachend.

Marlene ist eine dicke, träge und freundliche Seekuh. Genüsslich frisst sie die Wasserpflanzen aus meiner Hand und lässt sich dabei ausgiebig kraulen. Ihre Haut ist fast wie die von Susi, nur in Grau. Doch plötzlich schlägt sie mit dem Schwanz ins Wasser, und ein ganzer Schwall landet direkt in meinem Gesicht. Ich kreische erschrocken auf. Noch einmal blickt Marlene hoch, als würde sie mich spitzbübisch angrinsen, dann taucht sie unter.

»Oh Mann, du Arme. Warte, ich habe ein Taschentuch«, sagt Marc und beginnt, die Wassertropfen von meinen Wangen zu tupfen. Unter seiner Berührung wird mir heiß und kalt zugleich. Er kommt immer näher. Seine Lippen sind leicht geöffnet. Gleich ist es so weit. Ich spüre es. Mein Puls rast, meine Haut glüht. Bitte, lass mich nicht länger warten. KÜSS MICH ENDLICH!

»Hier, damit kannst du dich abtrocknen.« Claude reicht mir lächelnd ein Handtuch.

Mist! Ich wäre lieber noch einen Moment nass geblieben. »Sorry. Ich hätte dich vorwarnen müssen. Marlene ist ziemlich verspielt. Sie glaubt, sie kann mit jedem eine Wasserschlacht veranstalten«, erklärt Claude.

»Halb so schlimm«, murmele ich und trockne mich ab. Das Wasser stört mich nicht. Nur der verpasste Kuss, der tut weh.

Marc ist wieder ganz verschlossen und räumt die Eimer mit den Futterpflanzen zusammen. So eine Gelegenheit ergibt sich so schnell nicht wieder. Doch was hat Brigitte mir geraten? Wenn er der Richtige ist, dann soll ich die Initiative ergreifen. Ich beobachte Marc, und mein Gefühl sagt mir, dass er es wert ist. Alle meine Zweifel sind verschwunden. Wenn ich mit ihm zusammen bin, dann fühle ich mich wohl und sicher. Marc ist zwar leider genauso schüchtern wie ich, aber dafür eben kein Draufgänger und Mädchenschwarm. Ich muss einfach Mut beweisen und den ersten Schritt tun … Wenn das nur so einfach wäre. Blödes Rotköpfchen-Schüchternheits-Gen!

»Tiere pflegen macht hungrig. Findest du nicht?«, frage ich Marc, nachdem wir gemeinsam mit Claude noch einen Rundgang durch die anderen vier Zonen gemacht haben und er uns zu jedem Zoobewohner eine Geschichte erzählt hat. Der Tag ist rasend schnell vergangen. Dummerweise hat Marc keinen weiteren Versuch mehr gestartet, mich zu küssen.

»Darf ich dich auf einen Imbiss einladen?«, fragt er mich.

»Gern. Wo gehen wir hin?«

»Willst du vor einer typisch kitschigen Touristenkulisse essen oder schnöde bei McDonald's?«

»Da lass ich mich lieber Touri nennen«, antworte ich.

Marc lacht. Wir gehen zur U-Bahn, und wie selbstverständlich nehme ich seine Hand. Einen Moment lang wirkt er irritiert, dann aber strahlt er mich an. Sein Daumen streichelt meine Finger, wodurch mein Herz ein paar Extraschläge macht. Hand in Hand spazieren wir durch das frühlingshafte Paris. Die Sonne wirft warme Strahlen vom Himmel. Es ist beinahe perfekt.

Marc führt mich in ein Bistro vor dem Eiffelturm, in dem es nur so wimmelt vor Touristen. Sprachen vermischen sich wie Smarties auf einem Eisbecher. Mein Croque Monsieur schmeckt zwar nur nach Käse, aber die Aussicht und Marc an meiner Seite machen das Essen zu einem besonderen Erlebnis.

»Bald bist du wieder zu Hause. Wirst du Paris vermissen ... und ... vielleicht auch uns?« Marc hustet nervös.

Ich unterdrücke ein Kichern. »Bestimmt sogar. Du wirst mir sehr fehlen.«

»I-ich?« Marc schluckt. »Ich dachte, André wird dir fehlen.«

»Auch ein bisschen. Aber du noch mehr.«

Unsere Fingerspitzen berühren sich, und wir verschränken die Hände. In meinem Bauch kribbelt es, genau wie vorhin am Becken bei Marlene. Nur dass sich diesmal kein Claude zwischen uns drängen kann. Marc beugt sich vor. Langsam. Zaghaft. Dann endlich spüre ich seine Lippen auf meinen. Ganz zart. Ich schmelze dahin wie ein Apfelstrudel mit Vanilleeis in der Mittagssonne. Nun ist es perfekt.

28

»DAS DARF DOCH WOHL NICHT WAHR SEIN!« Es ist halb zehn Uhr morgens, und das halbe Dorf hat sich ungläubig vor dem umgesägten Mast versammelt. Und nicht nur die Fuckinger sind da, auch die Leute aus dem Nachbarort Hucking stehen unschlüssig herum.

Peter schüttelt den Kopf. »Was habt ihr euch bloß dabei gedacht, unseren Funkmast umzusägen?«

Ein etwa siebzehnjähriger Junge tritt vor. »Der Franz, der Dennis und ich haben wohl zu viel Bier getankt gestern. Wir dachten, das wäre euer Maibaum.«

»Maibaum? Ich glaub es nicht. Da hattet ihr aber einen ziemlichen Knick in der Optik! In eurem Alter sollte man noch nicht so viel trinken, dass man komplett die Orientierung verliert.« Peter schüttelt den Kopf.

Ich halte mich im Hintergrund und beobachte das Schauspiel. Neben mir schmatzt Susi. Ich hab das kleine Ferkelchen richtig lieb gewonnen. Peter redet den jungen Männern weiter ins Gewissen. Wenigstens ist jetzt klar, warum ich gestern plötzlich kein Netz mehr hatte. Ob meine Nachricht noch bei Helene angekommen ist?

»Jetzt stehen wir da wie im Mittelalter. Abgeschnitten vom Rest der Welt. Das dauert sicher eine Weile, bis wir einen neuen Mast bekommen.«

Thomas lächelt mich an. »Was meinst du, sollen wir die Zwangspause nutzen und einen Ausritt wagen? Wir reiten auch ganz langsam.«

»Warum nicht?«, antworte ich. Ohne Internet und Handyempfang muss ich weder auf eine Nachricht von André noch von Helene hoffen.

»Prima. Wollen wir uns um drei Uhr bei dir treffen? Ich nehme einen Picknickkorb mit.«

»Abgemacht.« Susi grunzt vorwurfsvoll, gerade so, als hätte sie verstanden, dass ich ohne sie wegwill. »Ich kann nicht jedes Mal eine Sau mitschleppen«, erkläre ich ihr und kraule sie hinter dem Ohr.

Wir kehren der aufgebrachten Dorfjugend und dem umgesägten Mast den Rücken. Ich freue mich auf den Ausflug. Inzwischen ist mir klar geworden, dass ich nicht länger auf ein Wunder hoffen kann. André wird sich nicht melden. Ich werde erst in Paris wissen, ob aus uns noch etwas wird.

Die Menschen hier sind so nett und warmherzig. Thomas' Schwestern haben sich gestern so lieb um mich gekümmert, und es ist ein toller Tag geworden. Nur wegen André vergrabe ich mich in Frust, Angst und Eifersucht. Dabei gibt es hier so viel zu erleben: Traktorrennen, Ausritte, Hausschweine, Dorffeste mit Tanz und Musik, coole Jungs wie Thomas und witzige Freaks wie Florian. Ich will mehr aus Fucking mitnehmen als ein Unterhöschen! Ich will tolle Erinnerungen haben an meinen ersten Schüleraustausch!

Darum werde ich die letzten Tage genießen, die ich hier bin. »Jawohl«, sage ich laut, und Susi schaut mich erstaunt an.

Thomas steht mit Fallabella und einem zweiten gesattelten Pferd vor der Tür. »Das ist Plattfuß. Er ist Fallabellas bester Freund, und sie folgt ihm auf Schritt und Tritt.«

»Plattfuß ist aber kein besonders schöner Name für ein so edles Tier.« Vorsichtig streichle ich das schwarze Ross an der Seite.

»Er heißt so, weil er gleich nach seiner Ankunft meinem Vater auf den Fuß getreten ist. Der Name war mein Vorschlag. Ich war damals aber auch noch etwas jünger. Es hätte aber noch schlimmer kommen können. Stell dir mal vor, Plattfuß hätte meinem Vater einen Tritt in den Hintern verpasst«, sagt Thomas todernst.

Wir prusten beide los. Als ich wieder atmen kann, sage ich zu dem Pferd: »Dann bin ich ja froh, dass du nur Plattfuß heißt.«

»Kommst du alleine hoch, oder soll ich dir helfen?« Thomas deutet eine Räuberleiter an.

»Es geht schon«, erwidere ich und schwinge mich auf das Pferd. Fallabella macht einen Schritt vorwärts, und ich kralle mich am Sattelknauf fest.

»Ich führe dich das erste Stück. Dann bekommst du ein Gefühl fürs Reiten«, erklärt Thomas. »Plattfuß, komm, es geht los.«

Er nimmt Fallabellas Zügel, und sie setzt sich in Bewegung. Das schwarze Pferd trottet gemächlich hinterher.

»Wahnsinn. Der gehorcht dir ja aufs Wort«, bemerke ich staunend.

»Wenn man mit den Tieren zusammen aufwächst, ist das ein Selbstläufer. Außerdem hab ich mit Absicht Plattfuß genommen. Fallabella und er sind ein eingeschworenes Team und beide perfekte Anfängerpferde. Gutmütig wie eine Deutsche Dogge.«

»Du vergleichst das Pferd, auf dem ich gerade sitze, mit einer Dogge und glaubst, mich damit zu beruhigen? Mon Dieu, an deinem Umgang mit Mädchen musst du noch arbeiten.«

»Du läufst aber jetzt nicht kreischend davon, oder?«, fragt Thomas mit gespieltem Entsetzen.

Ich kichere. »Nein. Dafür macht es mir viel zu viel Spaß, auf Fallabella zu reiten.«

Er nickt erleichtert. »Gut. Dann gebe ich dir jetzt die Zügel. Ich reite vor. Fallabella folgt ihrem Pferdefreund ganz automatisch. Wenn du stehen bleiben willst, ziehst du an den Zügeln. Sonst brauchst du nichts zu machen. Fallabella weiß schon, was sie zu tun hat.«

Wir verlassen den Ort und reiten über eine Wiese bis zu einem kleinen Wäldchen. Ich muss wohl zu fest an den Zügeln gezogen haben, denn Fallabella bleibt stehen.

Thomas dreht sich um. »Keine Angst, ich entführ dich schon nicht in den tiefen dunklen Wald. Ich will dir nur unseren sagenumwobenen See zeigen. Es sieht dort aus wie im Urwald. Total cool. Und eine Seejungfrau wohnt auch unten auf dem Grund, außerdem jede Menge Kröten, Frösche und Molche.«

»Mon Dieu! Du weißt echt, was Mädchen wollen. Ich hab immer schon von einem Picknick in einem Sumpf voller Kröten geträumt.«

»Entschuldigung. Ich dachte, es würde dir gefallen. Wir ... wir können auch kehrtmachen.« Thomas sieht ehrlich besorgt aus.

»Das war doch nur ein Scherz! Ich bin zwar eher an den Großstadtdschungel gewöhnt, hab aber auch nichts gegen ein bisschen echte Wildnis. Los, reite du voraus, du Fröschebezwinger!«, erwidere ich grinsend.

Der See hat seinen Namen nicht verdient. Es ist eher ein großer Teich oder ein Sumpfloch mit Wasserpflanzen. Wurzeln und Stämme von versunkenen Bäumen ragen heraus, Schilfgras wächst in hohen Büscheln um das ganze Ufer herum. Wir steigen ab und binden die beiden Pferde an einem Baum fest. Fallabella und Plattfuß beginnen sofort damit, Grashalme zu fressen.

»Hier ist es tatsächlich wie im Dschungel«, stelle ich überrascht fest.

»Cool, nicht? So geheimnisvolle Orte gibt es in Paris bestimmt nicht!«

»Nö. Wir haben nur so etwas Ödes wie den Glöckner von Notre-Dame«, kontere ich.

Gemeinsam breiten wir die Picknickdecke aus. Thomas hat einen ganzen Korb voller Proviant mitgebracht, mit Limo, Brot, Butter und Käse, Weintrauben und sogar Erdbeeren.

»Du hast dir ja echt Mühe gegeben. Toll.«

Thomas zuckt mit den Schultern. »Na ja, ich dachte, wenn

ich schon mal die Gelegenheit bekomme, dich allein zu treffen, dann muss ich dir auch etwas bieten. Du hast dich ja leider etwas rargemacht. Ich hätte dich gerne bei unseren Abenden in der Partyhütte dabeigehabt.«

Plötzlich habe ich ein schlechtes Gewissen, denn er hat recht. Ich habe viel zu viel Zeit mit meinen Gedanken an André und Paris verschwendet, statt die Menschen hier etwas besser kennenzulernen.

»Es ist halt alles so anders hier als daheim«, entschuldige ich mich.

»Das versteh ich gut. Es muss schwierig für dich gewesen sein. Du hast geglaubt, du wohnst in der Nähe von Salzburg, und dann landest du in Fucking.«

Ich nehme mir ein paar Weintrauben und lasse sie im Mund zerplatzen. »In Salzburg gibt es dafür bestimmt keine Geisterseen mit Moorjungfrauen.«

»Moorjungfrau«, wiederholt Thomas grinsend, »das ist ein cooler Name. Du bist ganz schön kreativ.«

Während wir essen, erzählt Thomas mir mit düsterer Stimme die alte Sage von der Jungfrau und dem bösen Riesen. »Einst kehrte der grausame und riesige Ritter Veit zu früh von der Jagd heim und fand die Jungfrau Mechthilde betend vorm Altar seiner Burgkapelle vor. Als Mechthilde merkte, dass der böse Kerl ihr Gewalt antun wollte, verfluchte sie ihn und wünschte sich auf den Grund des Huckinger Sees. Ihr Gebet wurde erhört, und sie lebt seither in den Tiefen des Moorsees. Die Burg des boshaften Veits aber versank mit ihr im Morast. Nur der grausame Ritter wandert seither als Waldgeist umher und sucht sein Heim. Und immer wenn ein Kind verschwindet, munkeln die Leute, der Riese hätte es geschnappt und als Opfer im See versenkt.«

»Wahnsinn, du kannst ja gruselig erzählen«, sage ich und reibe mir über meine Unterarme, wo sich schon eine Gänsehaut gebildet hat.

Thomas hustet verlegen. »Na ja, ich hoffe, ich hab dir keine Angst eingejagt. Wahrscheinlich wollte ich dich nur ein wenig beeindrucken. Paris bietet dir so viel mehr, als ich es hier könnte, aber im Schauergeschichtenerzählen war ich schon immer gut«, meint er und wendet den Blick ab.

»Da geb ich dir recht, und dieses Talent kannst du bestimmt prima bei Lagerfeuerabenden einsetzen.«

Mit leuchtenden Augen gesteht Thomas mir, dass er genau das auch vorhat, wenn er später mal den Hof seiner Eltern übernimmt. Er plant ein richtiges Ferienresort mit Reiterhofidylle, Indianerzeltstadt und Reitplatz. »Die paar Rösslein sind ein guter Anfang. Mein Traum ist es, eine richtige Ranch aufzubauen. Im Westernstil.«

»Das hört sich super an. Es ist schön, wenn man einen Plan hat. Ich habe keinen. Erst einmal die Schule schaffen und dann weitersehen. Meine Eltern wollen mich zwar immer dazu überreden, ins Bank- oder Immobiliengeschäft einzusteigen, aber ich hab kein gutes Gefühl dabei.«

»Lass dich nicht stressen. Du hast doch noch Zeit«, sagt Thomas. Er kaut auf einem Grashalm herum.

Ein paar Wildenten landen auf dem See. Vergnügt planschen sie mit den Flügeln im Wasser.

»Du … du … hast bestimmt einen Freund, oder?«, stottert Thomas plötzlich.

Ich verschlucke mich an meiner Erdbeere und huste wie verrückt. Die Enten flattern hektisch davon. Vor lauter Husten schießen mir die Tränen in die Augen. Thomas schlägt mir zwischen die Schulterblätter, und endlich bekomme ich wieder Luft.

»Sorry, ich hab wohl echt ein besonderes Talent, was Frauen betrifft. Da lerne ich endlich ein so nettes und traumhaft schönes Mädchen wie dich kennen, und dann bringe ich dich gleich zum Weinen!«

»Ach was, das lag am Husten«, sage ich schnell, bevor sich Thomas vor lauter Schuldgefühlen noch ins Moorwasser stürzt. Er ist ja irgendwie niedlich. Und unter anderen Umständen könnte er mir auch gefallen, aber momentan hab ich nur André im Kopf. Obwohl ich so viel Spaß habe, muss ich schon wieder an ihn denken. So ist das eben mit der Liebe.

»Weißt du, ich hab dich ein wenig beobachtet, und ich finde dich einfach toll. Ich weiß, du fliegst in ein paar Tagen zurück nach Paris. Aber vielleicht, wenn du es dir vorstellen kannst, dann kann ich auch mal nach Frankreich kommen, oder du …«

»Stopp«, sage ich und nehme seine Hand. »Du bist echt süß. So süß war noch nie ein Junge zu mir. Aber ich kann nicht.«

»Du hast einen festen Freund, stimmt's?« Thomas' Enttäuschung tut mir im Herzen weh. »Eh klar. Wie konnte ich nur glauben, dass so ein tolles Mädchen wie du noch Single ist!«

»So ist es aber. Ich bin nur in jemanden verliebt. Einen

Kerl, der es nicht verdient hat«, gestehe ich heiser, und dann erzähle ich Thomas einfach alles. Das ganze Desaster mit André, Helene, meinen fiesen Ratschlägen und meiner dummen Eifersucht. Er hört zu, ohne mich einmal zu unterbrechen. Mit jedem Wort fällt es mir leichter, und ich spüre, wie ein ganzer Steinhaufen von meinem Herzen purzelt. »Ich bin eine dumme Gans, nicht wahr?«, frage ich schließlich.

Thomas schüttelt den Kopf. »Nein, bist du nicht. Dämlich ist dieser André, wenn er nicht sieht, wie toll du bist. Er sollte eigentlich der glücklichste Junge der Welt sein. Der hat dich wirklich nicht verdient!«

Ich lache verlegen.

Thomas lächelt mich an. »Du bist viel zu schade für einen Kerl wie André. Ehrlich.«

»Danke.« Ich seufze. »Es hat gutgetan, sich alles einmal von der Seele zu reden. Glaubst du, dass Helene sehr sauer auf mich ist wegen dem Bowlen und dem Hard Rock Cafe?«

Thomas schüttelt den Kopf. »Wie ich sie kenne, gar nicht. Erzähl ihr einfach die ganze Story. Du wirst sehen, dass sie es locker nimmt. Sie hat ein gutes Herz, und in Sachen dämlich vor Liebe kennt sie sich bestens aus.«

»Okay. Dann werde ich ihr meine Eifersucht gestehen, sobald das Netz wieder funktioniert«, sage ich und bin plötzlich sehr erleichtert. In Thomas' Nähe fühle ich mich richtig wohl. Ich schätze, wir könnten echte Freunde werden, wenn ich länger hierbleiben würde. Schade, dass ich die Zeit hier nicht besser genutzt habe.

»Und traust du dir beim Heimritt einen leichten Trab zu, oder hast du Angst herunterzufallen?«

»Ich doch nicht. Mein zweiter Name ist Mut – Wagemut.«

»Dachte ich mir schon, dass du ein Mädchen bist, mit dem man Pferde stehlen kann.«

Wir sind viel zu schnell zurück in Fucking. Ich übergebe die Zügel wieder an Thomas und tätschle Fallabella noch mal den Hals.

»Danke für heute. Der Ausritt war wunderschön.«

»Mir hat es auch total gut gefallen. Versprichst du mir, wieder einmal nach Fucking zu kommen? Auch wenn dein Herz an Paris und diesem André hängt?« Thomas schaut mich erwartungsvoll an.

»Klar, ich muss doch meine Reitkünste verbessern. Außerdem sind wir doch Freunde.«

Thomas' Gesicht wird auf einmal ernst. »Ja, das sind wir«, sagt er dann überzeugt.

ZURÜCK AUF DEM HOF begrüßen mich eine quietschvergnügte Susi und ein frustrierter Florian. Ohne Internetverbindung ist er nur ein halber Mensch. Gelangweilt sitzt er auf der Ofenbank und krault das Ferkel.

»So ein Mist«, mault er. »Wie soll ich den Rest des Wochenendes nur überstehen? Der Mast soll erst am Montagnachmittag wieder in Betrieb gehen.«

Ich zucke mit den Schultern. »Du könntest die Zeit nutzen und an der Werbekampagne fürs Fuckinger Bier feilen. Um Fotos zu knipsen und zu texten, brauchst du kein Netz. Und wir haben auch noch genügend Material von unserem gemeinsamen Brauen. Das gehört ordentlich bearbeitet. Außerdem musst du noch deinen Vater überzeugen, endlich ein Gewerbe anzumelden. Das Bier, das sogar Handymasten in Maibäume verwandelt, muss einfach auf den Markt!«

Florian grinst. »Genau. So fucking crazy ist kein anderes Bier der Welt.«

Am nächsten Tag helfe ich Florian dabei, werbetaugliche Fotos zu schießen. Diesmal bleiben die Fuckinger Schürzen im Schrank. Stattdessen schlüpfen meine Gasteltern in ihre Trachten, die sie zuletzt beim Maifest trugen. Ich frisiere Erika noch die Haare, und auch beim Make-up lässt sie mir freie Hand. Als ich sie schminke, fühle ich mich wie eine richtige Masken- und Kostümbildnerin. Der Aufwand lohnt sich, denn am Ende sehen die beiden aus, als wären sie einer Almdudler-Werbung entsprungen.

»Fabienne, du solltest Stylistin werden«, meint Erika, als sie sich vor dem Spiegel dreht. »Oder Visagistin. Du bist ein echtes Naturtalent.«

Mir gefällt die Idee, und ich male mir aus, wie es wäre, in der Modebranche zu arbeiten.

»Mal sehen«, sage ich und schlage vor, auch gleich Erikas Unterwäsche neu in Szene zu setzen. Der Onlineshop ist zwar ganz nett, aber es fehlt der richtige Pfiff.

Meine Gastmutter holt eine alte Schaufensterpuppe aus dem Keller. Es macht Riesenspaß, die Slips und Hemdchen zu präsentieren.

»Ich hab die Idee«, ruft Florian grinsend. »Wir setzen Susi eine Unterhose auf den Kopf und schreiben als Slogan: Fuckinger Höschen, versauter geht's nicht!« Ohne eine Antwort abzuwarten, stürmt mein Gastbruder los und holt das kleine Schwein.

Erika meldet zwar Bedenken an, dass Susi mitmacht, aber ihre Sorgen sind unbegründet.

»Susi, sei lieb und lass den Schlüpfer auf. Dann gibt es nach der Knipserei auch ein Leckerli«, verspricht Florian. Anscheinend hat Susi jedes Wort verstanden, denn sie hält ganz still, während wir ihr einen mintgrünen Slip mit schweinchenrosa Stickerei aufsetzen. Die ungewöhnliche Kopfbedeckung scheint das Hausferkel nicht im Geringsten zu stören. Brav macht sie das Shooting mit und wird im Anschluss mit einer extragroßen Portion Speisereste belohnt.

Der Tag vergeht wahnsinnig schnell. Ich fühle mich richtig wohl inmitten meiner skurril-lieben Gastfamilie, und mir ist schon jetzt klar, dass mir alle schrecklich fehlen werden. Aber vielleicht schaffe ich es, dass meine Eltern auch etwas lockerer werden? Ein kleines bisschen mehr Familienleben wäre schon schön …

Abends im Bett fällt mir auf, dass ich in den letzten Stunden gar nicht mehr an André gedacht habe. Die Fuckinger haben mich glatt auf andere Gedanken gebracht. Schade, dass ich nur noch drei Tage hier bin. Jetzt, wo ich mich bei meiner Gastfamilie schon richtig zu Hause fühle und auch das kleine Schweinchen lieb gewonnen habe.

SEIT ICH IN DER SCHULE neben Marc sitze, kann ich mich nicht mehr auf den Unterricht konzentrieren. Es hat nicht lange gedauert, bis Marie-Claire und André gecheckt haben, dass wir zusammen sind. Kein Wunder, denn Marc und ich kleben aneinander, als hätte man uns Magnete eingebaut. Hin und wieder stichelt André zwar, aber ansonsten gibt er sich nach wie vor als charmanter Draufgänger.

»Er ist gekränkt, dass sich ein hübsches Mädchen wie du nicht für ihn, sondern für Marc interessiert«, erklärt mir Marie-Claire in der Pause. »Aber ich glaube, er freut sich auch für euch. Es ist halt schwer für ihn, nicht im Rampenlicht zu stehen.«

»Kann sein. Doch genau deswegen wäre André nicht der Richtige für mich gewesen. Ich und Rampenlicht, das passt nicht zusammen.«

Marie-Claire nickt nachdenklich. »Du hast wahrscheinlich recht. Du und Marc, ihr seid ein schönes Pärchen.«

Marc kommt in die Cafeteria. Er hat nur Augen für mich. Ich kann gar nicht wegsehen, so verzaubert er mich. Mein

Magen schlägt Purzelbäume. So ist das also, wenn man über beide Ohren verliebt ist. Man sieht nichts anderes mehr, leidet nach zehn Minuten ohne den anderen an Entzugserscheinungen und wartet nur darauf, dass er endlich wieder neben einem sitzt. Ich, Helene, bin fucking verliebt … und ich wage zu behaupten, Marc ist es auch.

Nach Schulschluss verabreden wir uns gleich für den Abend, zu einem Mondschein-Spaziergang. Quelle belle vie à Paris!

… dringend mit dir reden.

Mann, ich hab seit dem Zoobesuch nicht mehr in den Chat geguckt. Fabiennes Punkt leuchtet grün. Sie ist on. Ich überlege krampfhaft, was ich schreiben soll.

Hi, Fabienne. Ich glaube, ich weiß, was du mir sagen willst. Du hast mich absichtlich ins Hard Rock Cafe geschickt, stimmt's?

Helene! Mon Dieu, bin ich froh, dass du on bist. Du hast recht. Also, zuerst, es tut mir soooo unendlich leid. Ich war so eifersüchtig auf dich, weil du so viel mit André unterwegs warst. Meinem André, in den ich schon ewig verliebt bin. Leider. Aber wenn ihr beide inzwischen ein Paar seid, dann muss ich damit auch klarkommen. Viel wichtiger ist mir unsere Freundschaft. Verzeihst du mir?

Ich bin in Marc verliebt, nicht in André. Okay, André ist echt ein toller Typ, und ja, ich hab mich
anfangs auch ein wenig in ihn verguckt, aber wir
würden überhaupt nicht zusammenpassen. Weißt du,
ich hatte mal einen Freund, der war so ähnlich wie
André. Die Enttäuschung mit Levin hat mich gelehrt, vorsichtig zu sein. Aber erzähl, was ist mit
dem Dirndl und warum warst du so lange nicht on?

Fabiennes Geschichte mit dem umgesägten Mast und der
Trachten-Verwechslung ist so komisch, dass ich mit meinem Lachen Bastet verschrecke. Hocherhobenen Hauptes
stolziert die königliche Katze aus dem Zimmer. Dann stelle
ich die Frage, die mir auf der Seele brennt.

Was ist denn mit dir und André?

Ach, ich bin schon seit über einem Jahr in ihn verliebt, aber irgendwie ist alles schrecklich kompliziert. Als wir uns im Lycée kennengelernt haben,
war er erst total charmant zu mir, und es hat eindeutig geknistert zwischen uns. Doch ich war irgendwie zu schüchtern. Und dann hat er angefan-
gen, Musik zu machen, und hatte plötzlich lauter
Fans und Verehrerinnen. Tja, und ich war nur noch
sein Kumpel, bis zu dem Tag vor meinem Abflug.
Am Abend davor war ich noch bei einem seiner
Konzerte gewesen, und am Tag darauf hat er mich
geküsst. So richtig, mit Zunge. Ich würde ihm feh-

len, er würde an mich denken, er wünschte sich,
ich würde nicht fliegen … all das hat er gesagt.
Und ich dumme Kuh hab ihm geglaubt.

**Mann, du Arme. Du bist nicht dumm. Nur verliebt.
Ich kann dich so gut verstehen. Mir ging es damals
mit Levin genauso. Ich hab ihm alles geglaubt. Jedes Wort.**

Marc ist anders. Du wirst sehen. Er hat ein gutes
Herz. Marc ist deine Liebe wert. Ganz bestimmt.

**Glaub ich auch. Er ist so toll. Ich weiß gar nicht,
wie ich es ohne ihn in Fucking aushalten soll. Heul!
Wann komme ich denn wieder nach Paris?**

Na, in den Sommerferien, wenn du magst. Ich lad
dich ein, mein Gast zu sein.

Ehrlich?

Unbedingt. Meine Eltern haben bestimmt nichts
dagegen, und ich will Susis Mama endlich per-
sönlich kennenlernen.

**Oh, Fabienne. DANKE! Ich ruf gleich Marc an und
erzähl es ihm. Du bist die allerbeste Austausch-
freundin der Welt. Ich drück dir die Daumen, dass
du doch noch mit André zusammenkommst.**

Ich auch, glaub mir. Darum will ich ihm auch noch eine Chance geben. Es kann doch nicht alles gelogen sein, was er gesagt hat, oder?

Glaube nicht. Er macht einen auf großer Rockstar, aber das ist bestimmt nur Fassade.

MARC HOLT MICH UM SIEBEN UHR AB.

Es ist unser letzter gemeinsamer Abend. Mir schnürt es schon jetzt das Herz zusammen, wenn ich nur daran denke, dass ich Marc wochenlang nicht sehen werde.

Die Sonne versinkt orangerot am Himmel. Mehrere verliebte Paare schlendern durch den Park. Der Duft blühender Bäume hängt in der Luft. Es ist wie im Film. Fast zu schön, um wahr zu sein. Ich drücke Marcs Hand. Wieso hab ich nur so lange gebraucht, um zu erkennen, dass er der Richtige für mich ist?

Marc lächelt mich an. »Du bist so still«, sagt er.

»Ich bin nur etwas traurig. Wir hätten mehr Zeit gemeinsam verbringen können. Aber, tja …«

»Wahrscheinlich hätte ich mutiger sein sollen«, gesteht Marc. »Aber ich bin leider manchmal etwas feige. Außerdem hab ich mir gedacht, du stehst bestimmt auch nur auf …«

Ich wende mich ihm zu und nehme seine Hände.

»Du kannst immer noch mutig sein. Oder willst du den ganzen Abend nur reden?« Aufmunternd lächle ich ihn an.

Marc schluckt schwer, dann endlich küsst er mich. Alles ist genau so, wie es sein sollte. Paris im Frühling. Der aufgehende Mond über uns. Ein Straßenmusiker, der einen schwermütigen Chanson singt. Und ein Kuss unter dem Sternenhimmel. Für einen Moment steht die Zeit still. Dann dehnt sie sich zur Ewigkeit aus, und ich fühle, dass alles richtig ist. Marc und ich. Ich und Marc. So soll es sein ...

Dieser Abend gehört nur uns beiden. Mir wird leichter ums Herz. Unsere Liebe fühlt sich so stark an, da können uns auch keine Ländergrenzen trennen.

»Willst du ein Eis?«, fragt Marc und deutet auf einen kleinen Stand.

Der ergraute Verkäufer sieht uns fragend an.

»Schoko und Haselnuss«, sagen Marc und ich wie aus einem Mund. Verdutzt blicke ich Marc an, dann müssen wir beide lachen.

»L'amour. Die Liebe.« Der Verkäufer grinst wissend. »Wie es scheint, habt ihr beide den gleichen Geschmack.« Er reicht uns zwei Tüten mit Schoko- und Haselnusseis.

Marc lädt mich ein, und wir setzen uns auf eine Parkbank.

»Du bevorzugst wohl auch die Schokoladenseite des Lebens?«, sage ich lächelnd.

»Genau, und darum hab ich mir auch eine zuckersüße Freundin gesucht.«

»Zuckersüß wie Schokolade?«, frage ich und lecke frech über sein Eis.

»He! Du hast dein eigenes!«

»Deins schmeckt aber besser«, erwidere ich lachend.

»Warte, das hol ich mir zurück!«

Schnell verstecke ich meine Tüte hinterm Rücken. Doch Marc macht gar keine Anstalten, mein Eis zu stibitzen. Stattdessen zieht er mich an sich und küsst mich wie noch nie zuvor. Mir wird so heiß, dass die Eiscreme in meiner Hand schmilzt.

»Wow«, keuche ich.

»Mutig genug?«, fragt Marc und leckt jetzt doch über mein geschmolzenes Eis. Er grinst übers ganze Gesicht.

Ich nicke und kichere. »Wir haben übrigens auch ganz köstliches Eis in Österreich. Meine Mama stellt selbst welches her, Erdbeer- und Waldbeereis. Das schmeckt sogar mir, obwohl ich eigentlich ein Schokotiger bin.«

»Das würde ich gern mal probieren«, flüstert Marc.

»Vielleicht kannst du uns ja im Sommer besuchen kommen?«, frage ich hoffnungsvoll.

Marc nickt und lächelt. »Eigentlich wollte ich es dir erst morgen am Flughafen verraten. Aber dann eben schon jetzt ...«

»Was?«, will ich nervös wissen. »Sag schon!«

»Ich hab meine Eltern gefragt, ob wir nicht mal Urlaub in Österreich machen könnten. Meine Mutter fand die Idee super, weil sie schon immer mal nach Salzburg wollte, und zwei Tage später hatten wir auch meinen Vater überredet. Also fahren wir dieses Jahr ausnahmsweise nicht nach Korsika, sondern nach Österreich.«

»Ehrlich?« Ich falle Marc um den Hals. Das Eis tropft auf meine Hand, aber das ist mir egal.

»Ganz ehrlich! Drei Wochen Österreich. Und so, wie ich es verstanden hab, möchten meine Eltern auch gern den einen oder anderen Tag allein sein. Vielleicht kann ich ja ein paar Nächte bei euch – ?«

»Bestimmt sogar«, unterbreche ich ihn, »du kannst ganz sicher bei uns übernachten. Wir haben genug Platz. Ich werde mal mit Mama und Papa reden.«

»Super. Jetzt sollten wir aber endlich die kläglichen Reste von unserem Eis essen, bevor es ganz geschmolzen ist.«

Eng aneinandergeschmiegt beobachten wir das Treiben im Park.

Paris hat mein Herz erobert. Ich werde meine Zeit hier nie vergessen. Glücklich atme ich Marcs Duft ein. Er riecht so gut, genau so, wie Jungs riechen müssen.

Marc zieht sein Handy aus der Hosentasche und wirft einen Blick darauf. »Wir müssen los«, sagt er plötzlich. »Ich bin dir ja noch etwas schuldig, erinnerst du dich?«

Ich schüttle ahnungslos den Kopf.

»Leider muss ich dir den Großteil auch schuldig bleiben. Aber wenn du willst, dann kann ich dir zumindest einen kleinen Blick ermöglichen.«

Ich weiß nicht, was Marc vorhat. Er steht auf und hilft mir ebenfalls hoch. Wir spazieren zur Seine hinab. An einer unscheinbaren Anlegestelle liegt ein Boot. Es ist viel kleiner als der Touridampfer, mit dem wir letztes Mal gefahren sind. Neben dem Kapitän sind nur zehn Pärchen und eine Kartenverkäuferin an Bord. Marc wechselt ein paar Worte mit der Frau und drückt ihr einen Geldschein in die Hand. Nachdem wir unsere Tickets bekommen haben, gehen wir an Deck. Dort setzen wir uns auf eine Bank und kuscheln uns dicht aneinander.

Es gluckert laut, als der Kapitän den Motor startet und wir ablegen. Die Kartenverkäuferin meldet sich über den Lautsprecher zu Wort. »Willkommen an Bord der Petit coeur. Mein Name ist Veronique, und am Steuer sitzt heute Kapitän Pierre. Wir wünschen all unseren Gästen einen romantischen Abend. Gleich teile ich noch Decken und eine Liebesbowle aus. Lehnen Sie sich zurück und genießen Sie Paris bei Nacht. Unsere Endstation Notre-Dame erreichen wir in circa 40 Minuten. Viel Vergnügen!«, wünscht Veronique.

»Wir können die Kirche zwar nicht mehr besichtigen, aber ich dachte, die Aussicht vom Wasser aus ist auch ganz schön. Außerdem können wir dann noch um die große Dame herumschlendern, wenn du magst.«

Ich nicke und seufze. Genau so hab ich mir meinen ersten Freund immer erträumt. Was Marc verspricht, das hält er auch. Ich spüre, dass ich ihm wichtig bin. Zufrieden lehne ich mich an seine Schulter.

Veronique bringt uns eine warme Decke. Leise Musik klingt aus den Lautsprechern, und keine einzige Touriinformation stört das Ambiente. An Bord sind nur Verliebte, die Zeit mit ihren Liebsten verbringen wollen.

Jeder bekommt ein Glas mit Erdbeerbowle. Das süße Getränk prickelt fast genauso wie Marcs zärtliche Küsse. Mein neuer Freund legt den Arm um mich, und ich schmiege mich eng an ihn, während das glitzernde Lichtermeer von Paris an uns vorbeizieht.

Die Fahrt ist viel zu kurz. Schon taucht Notre-Dame vor uns auf. Es ist schon seltsam mit der Zeit. In der Schule, wenn ich Mathe hab, zieht sie sich wie klebriges Baumharz, und in Momenten wie diesen rast sie dahin wie eine Gnuherde, die von einem Löwen verfolgt wird.

»Meine Damen und Herren, in wenigen Augenblicken erreichen wir unsere Endstation. Wir hoffen, Sie hatten einen schönen Abend, und würden uns freuen, Sie bald wieder an Bord der Petit coeur begrüßen zu dürfen«, verabschiedet uns Veronique und sammelt die Gläser und Decken ein.

»Diese Fahrt hat mir viel besser gefallen als unsere erste«, sage ich und küsse Marc. »Tausend Dank.«

Er zuckt mit den Schultern, und ich möchte wetten, dass seine Wangen rot sind. »Gern geschehen. Komm, wir laufen einmal um Notre-Dame herum. Dann hab ich zumindest einen kleinen Teil meines Versprechens gehalten.«

»Du hast viel mehr als das«, sage ich.

Durch die nächtliche Beleuchtung wirkt Notre-Dame noch eindrucksvoller als am Tag.

»Schön«, ist alles, was ich herausbringe.

»Wie du«, sagt Marc und blickt mich an, als wäre ich ein ebenso imposantes Kunstwerk wie die Kathedrale.

Mir ist es in seiner Gegenwart nicht einmal mehr peinlich, dass ich rot werde. Ich nehme seine Hand und ziehe ihn mit mir. Langsam umrunden wir die große Kirche.

Marcs Griff wird immer fester. Die Glocken läuten.

»Oje, heute bring ich dich nicht rechtzeitig nach Hause. Ich hoffe, du verschwindest jetzt nicht einfach wie Aschenputtel, weil es schon nach Mitternacht ist. Ich hatte nämlich keine Zeit, die Stufen mit Pech zu bestreichen«, sagt Marc grinsend.

»Brigitte hat die Nach-Hause-komm-Regel für meinen letzten Abend ausgesetzt. Außerdem würdest du mich hoffentlich finden, wenn ich jetzt weglaufen würde. Schließlich weißt du, wo ich wohne.«

»Stimmt. Und wie viele Orte mag es schon mit dem Namen Fucking geben?«, meint Marc.

Ich boxe ihn in die Seite. Wir blicken hoch zu dem großen runden Kirchenfenster, das angeblich einen Durchmesser von zwölf Metern hat. Notre-Dame blickt auf uns herab, und ihre Glocken läuten nur für uns.

Marc zieht eine kleine Schachtel aus der Hosentasche und überreicht sie mir feierlich. »Damit du mich nicht vergisst.«

Mit zitternden Fingern öffne ich sie. Ein Herzanhänger liegt darin. Vorsichtig nehme ich ihn heraus. »Man kann ihn aufklappen«, sagt Marc und zeigt mir, wie es geht.

In dem Anhänger ist Marcs Bild eingraviert. Es ist das Foto, das wir auf dem Eiffelturm gemacht haben, als ich im wahrsten Sinne des Wortes zwischen Marc und André stand.

»Ich bin Hals über Kopf in dich verliebt, und ich hoffe, du wirst mich im Herzen tragen«, flüstert er.

»Ja«, murmele ich gerührt und umarme ihn. Heiße Tränen kullern mir über die Wangen. »Mir geht's genauso, aber ich komme mir so doof vor, dass ich jetzt gar kein Geschenk für dich hab.«

»Du bist mein größtes Geschenk.«

Zärtlich drückt er mich und nimmt mir meine Halskette ab.

»Darf ich?«, fragt er schüchtern. Als ich nicke, hängt er das Herz an meine Kette.

»Nicht weinen«, sagt er und legt mir meine Kette wieder um.

»Ich liebe dich«, sage ich heiser.

Seine Lippen trösten mein trauriges Herz. Marc und ich. Wir beide. Für immer. Diese Nacht könnte ewig dauern, aber das tut sie natürlich nicht. Als ich weit nach Mitternacht ins Bett falle, spüre ich Marcs Küsse noch immer auf meinem Hals. Alles ist gut.

DER MOMENT, vor dem ich so große Angst hatte, ist da. Ich kann die Tränen kaum zurückhalten. Alle sind am Flughafen, Marc, Marie-Claire und André, und sogar Brigitte und Richard haben sich extra freigenommen.

»Und einmal wöchentlich wird zu Hause gekocht, versprochen?«, sage ich zu Brigitte.

»Abgemacht«, ergibt sich Brigitte. »Ich weiß ja, dass du Fabienne danach fragen wirst.«

»Genau. Wenn ich wiederkomme, will ich deutliche Gebrauchsspuren am Herd sehen«, erwidere ich lachend.

Zum Abschied drücken und küssen mich noch mal alle. Dass es mir so schwerfallen würde, Paris zu verlassen, hätte ich nicht für möglich gehalten. Aber wie hätte ich auch ahnen können, was ich alles in Paris finden würde? Eine gehörige Portion Mut, einen großen Löffel Selbstbewusstsein und als Sahnehäubchen die Liebe. Als hätte Brigitte meine Gedanken gelesen, pfeift sie alle zurück. Meine Gastfamilie, André und Marie-Claire winken mir noch, bis sie außer Sichtweite sind. Nun bin ich mit Marc allein. Endlich.

Seine Arme umschließen mich und halten mich fest, als

wolle er mich nie wieder gehen lassen. »Bleib hier«, flüstert er.

»Ich komme wieder. Im August.«

Marc küsst mir meine Tränen von den Wangen. »Versprich es mir«, sagt er und schaut mich mit diesem süßen Dackelblick an, dem ich einfach nicht widerstehen kann.

»Ich schwöre es bei Susis Ringelschwänzchen«, sage ich und hebe die Hand.

»Das ist ein starker Schwur. Ich werde dich so vermissen«, haucht er mir ins Ohr.

Mein Flug wird aufgerufen. Ich muss los. Nach Hause. Weg von Paris. Weg von Marc.

Als ich im Flugzeug sitze, krampft sich alles in mir zusammen. Diesmal ist es nicht die Angst, die mir zu schaffen macht, sondern der Herzschmerz.

Paris, ich komme wieder. Bald. Ganz bald.

DA STEHE ICH, Fabienne Henry, und bin abfahrbereit. Neben mir wartet mein Riesen-Monster-Koffer mit dem kaputten Ausziehgriff. Inzwischen ist mir der Koffer egal. Die Zeit hier hat mich gelehrt, dass es Wichtigeres gibt als das perfekte Outfit. Ich werde meine Gastfamilie vermissen.

Auch Erika hat feuchte Augen. »Ich freu mich zwar so, meine Helene wieder in die Arme zu schließen. Aber du wirst mir schlimm fehlen, Fabienne. Durch dich hatten wir ein Stück große weite Welt in Fucking.«

»Ich werde euch auch alle vermissen. Es war wirklich schön hier. *Fucking good.*«

»Hab ich's dir nicht gleich gesagt?«, sagt Peter. Er hat zwar keine Tränen in den Augen, aber man sieht ihm an, wie schwer ihm der Abschied fällt.

Florian drückt kurz meine Hand. »Du denkst dran, daheim gleich die Fucking-Homepage zu checken? Ich lade deine Bilder sofort hoch. Du solltest sowieso unser Bier-Model werden. Papa eignet sich nicht so gut für unser Etikett, nicht mal mit lila Schürze.«

Ich nicke. Das ist wohl seine Art, mir zu sagen, dass er mich mag.

»Wir müssen, Fabienne. Sonst verpasst du noch deinen Flieger«, mahnt Peter zum Aufbruch.

In dem Moment kommt Susi wie ein Pfeil um die Ecke geschossen. Ihre Schweinsohren wackeln im Galopp.

»Tschüss, meine süße Susi«, verabschiede ich mich von dem Schweinchen und tätschle seinen Kopf. Seltsam, wie schnell ich mich mit der kleinen Sau angefreundet habe. Hier in Fucking habe ich tatsächlich ganz neue Seiten an mir entdeckt.

»Hast du die Unterwäsche eingepackt? Auch die für deine Eltern?«, fragt Erika aufgeregt.

Sie hat extra noch zwei Garnituren Fuckinger Unterhöschen gestickt. Ich nicke. Meine Mutter wird aus allen Wolken fallen, wenn ich sie ihr gebe. Da bin ich mir sicher. Peter lädt meinen Koffer ein und drängt zum Aufbruch.

Endlich steige ich ein. Der alte Wagen knattert, als Peter den Motor anlässt, aber selbst daran habe ich mich gewöhnt.

Ich winke meiner Gastfamilie und schlucke den Kloß hinunter, der sich in meiner Kehle gebildet hat. Jetzt drückt mein Herz. Mon Dieu, ich bin schon sehr sentimental.

Als wir das Ortsschild erreichen, fallen mir fast die Augen aus dem Kopf. Da stehen Thomas, seine Schwestern und die halbe Landjugend, sogar die kleine Blaskapelle ist gekommen. »Überraschung! Ein kleiner Abschiedsgruß, damit du uns Fuckinger in guter Erinnerung behältst«, erklärt Peter schmunzelnd.

Wir lassen die Fensterscheiben hinunter und fahren ganz langsam durch die Menge. Ich knipse ein paar Bilder mit dem Handy. So unglaublich nette Leute gibt es nur hier, und das muss ich einfach festhalten. Die Blaskapelle spielt ziemlich schräg die französische Nationalhymne, und dann grölen alle: »Fabienne is fucking good!«

Ich lache, und mir schießen vor lauter Rührung die Tränen in die Augen. Ich lehne mich weit aus dem Fenster.

»Danke! Ihr seid alle verrückt, total lieb verrückt. Danke!«, rufe ich.

Thomas kommt ans Fenster und drückt mir einen Kuss auf die feuchte Wange.

»Bis bald und grüß mir Paris,« sagt er und wischt mir die Tränen weg. Ich ringe mir ein Lächeln ab.

Dass mir der Abschied so wehtun würde, hätte ich niemals für möglich gehalten. Aber die Fuckinger haben mein Herz erobert. Nicht im Sturm, aber von Tag zu Tag mehr.

Wir fahren weiter. Ich winke den anderen, bis ich sie wirklich nicht mehr sehen kann. Madame Nain wird mir bestimmt nicht glauben, was ich hier alles erlebt habe, und meine Eltern werden die Köpfe schütteln.

Doch es stimmt wirklich: Ich kann jetzt Traktor fahren und reiten, hab mit einem Schwein in einem Zimmer geschlafen, Unterhöschen ins rechte Licht gerückt und Bier gebraut. Vor allem aber habe ich so viele liebe Menschen kennengelernt, dort, wo ich sie nie vermutet hätte: in Fucking.

Die Verabschiedung am Flughafen fällt zum Glück kurz aus. Peter schleppt meinen Koffer bis zum Schalter, dann umarmt er mich und wünscht mir eine gute Reise. Ich bin erleichtert, dass ich nicht noch mal weinen muss. Noch mehr Tränen hätte ich nicht verkraftet. Außerdem will ich nicht total verheult in Paris ankommen.

Nachdem die Maschine gestartet ist, lehne ich mich zurück und lasse die letzten drei Wochen Revue passieren. Ich bin glücklich. Fucking hat mich verändert, und zwar zum Guten. Zu Beginn meiner Reise konnte ich mir gar nicht vorstellen, wie lustig es hier werden würde. Doch rückblickend hatte ich wirklich eine tolle Zeit.

Jetzt gilt es nur noch, die Geschichte mit André zu klären. Ich atme tief durch und setze mir die Kopfhörer auf. Leise Musik rauscht in meinen Ohren, und ich spüre, dass alles gut werden wird. Paris, ich komme. André, ich komme!

ZWEI WOCHEN SPÄTER.

Und Susi geht es gut?

Die kleine Sau vermisst dich, Fabienne. Ich hab ihr die Socken, die du bei uns vergessen hast, ins Körbchen gelegt. Sie will nur noch darauf schlafen. Florian vermisst dich übrigens auch, oder besser gesagt, dein Talent, Fotos zu inszenieren. Paps hat ja die Brauerei angemeldet, und Florian bastelt gerade an einer Homepage dafür. Er ärgert sich immer tierisch, wenn Mama und Papa in ihren Alltagsklamotten zum Shooting kommen. Dann nennt er sie unprofessionell. Langsam glaube ich, Flo hat echt eine Meise. Er sieht sich selbst schon als großen Werbefachmann.

GG. Kann ich mir vorstellen. So wie André. Seitdem ihn diese Miniplattenfirma angesprochen hat, ist er völlig daneben. Er träumt schon davon, ein

ganz großer Star zu werden. Wenn er nicht auf-
passt, dann dreht er noch völlig durch, bevor er
überhaupt bei den Probeaufnahmen war. Ich muss
ihn immer wieder auf den Boden der Tatsachen
zurückholen.

**Kann ich mir vorstellen. Marc hat sich gestern am
Telefon auch schon gehörig beschwert. Mann, ich
kann es kaum erwarten, dass endlich Ferien sind.
Ich vermisse ihn so uneeeeeendlich. Aber zum Glück
werden wir uns bald sehen. Erst kommt er mit seiner Familie nach Salzburg, und dann fliege ich zu
euch nach Paris! Tausend Dank, dass ich noch mal
bei euch wohnen darf.**

Aber gerne doch. Ich freu mich schon sehr.

**Entschuldige, aber ich bin schrecklich neugierig
und muss dich einfach fragen: Was ist jetzt eigentlich mit dir und André? Marc konnte mir auch nichts
Genaueres sagen.**

Ach, ich verkauf mich nicht unter Wert. André hat
zwar geschworen, dass es nur noch mich in seinem Leben geben soll, aber Menschen ändern sich
nicht von heute auf morgen. Ich lass es langsam
angehen. Küssen ja, mehr nein. Auf jeden Fall haben wir am Samstag ein Date. Wir wollen ins Kino
gehen, danach vielleicht was essen und roman-

tisch durch den Park spazieren. Ich will etwas
Ernstes, nicht ein x-beliebiges Groupie sein.

Das klingt doch gut! Ich drück dir die Daumen. André soll endlich erkennen, was er an dir hat. Du bist so eine tolle Freundin.

Hm. Ich freu mich, wenn du kommst. Chatten ist
nicht das Gleiche. Wir werden bestimmt eine tolle
Zeit haben.

Ich kann es auch kaum erwarten. Jetzt muss ich leider Schluss machen für heute. Die letzten Prüfungen stehen an, und ich darf nur nach Paris, wenn die Noten stimmen. Da sind meine Eltern streng. Aber ich bin zuversichtlich, dass ich es schaffe. Meine Französischnote ist jedenfalls schon gerettet.
Bis ganz bald.
Küsschen von mir und Susi
Deine Helene

Alles Gute von mir. Du schaffst das!
Bises & à bientôt

Pink